FRUIT
OF THE
POISON
TREE

Jessica:

Hope you enjoy
the book!

Rosi Comp

3/23/2020

LISA COMPTON

FRUIT
OF THE
POISON
TREE

A NOVEL

PERPETUITY
·PUBLISHING·

Published by Perpetuity Publishing, LLC

Stafford, Virginia, USA

www.PerpetuityBooks.com

Printed in the United States of America

Paperback: 978-0-9981326-6-2

eBook: 978-0-9981326-7-9

Cover design by Damonza Design

Author photo by Carie Compton

To my Mom – the woman who taught me to love books.

PROLOGUE

His Excellency
The Most Reverend Nicefero Saldaña Mendoza
Archbishop of San Antonio

I hope this correspondence finds you well, Your Grace. I, unfortunately, am writing to impart troubling news. Events have recently transpired that I felt compelled to share with the Church. I do not know if you have followed the media coverage of the brutal murders, attributed to the man the press calls the Good Samaritan Killer. Jamie Smythe is accused of killing four people in one week. The women were eviscerated, the men defiled—some details were reported in the papers, but some were not. Police Sergeant Mark Austin was skinned alive—an act I'm convinced was a tribute to the killing of Saint Bartholomew.

I was in the home of Dr. Olivia Osborne, at her request, the night Smythe was arrested. Olivia and I have been colleagues and friends for many years. She is a woman of God, but she has certain gifts that draw darkness to her. This woman killer came for her, but he was merely a vessel. He did not come alone.

The Church teaches that demons are as real as our God. I truly believe that now. I have to confess, even during my service to the Church I was not fully convinced. It was a failing on my part. Olivia Osborne showed me the truth. Demons do exist. They are here, with us.

I was a witness to the possession of Jamie Smythe. He demonstrated the power of communication, initiating contact with Dr. Osborne. I heard his demonic voice, the impossible blackness of his eyes. He taunted her with knowledge of events both past and present. The demon declared himself by name and told her she owed him a debt.

Now is not the time for fear, but for action. Evil is here. There is no place to hide – especially not for her. The Church needs her to stay on the side of the light. Evil is a dark seductress and the cost of a crossover could be her very soul.

I am offering the Church my services to return this evil from whence it came, but most of all to protect Olivia Osborne.

I am humbly asking Your Excellency's blessing to serve the Church, to serve my God, to protect Olivia Osborne, and rid this world of this evil presence.

I am, Yours respectfully in Christ.

Father Dominic Acosta

Archbishop Nicefero Saldaña Mendoza's hands pushed the letter aside along with the tea he'd been drinking. He got up and poured himself wine instead. He had feared this day would come.

It had been almost thirty-five years since he first met Olivia Esme Osborne. He had been a priest at the time and she a mere child. She had been a pious, quiet little girl with fair blonde hair and the most luminous green eyes he'd ever seen—not the eyes of a child, even then. The priest writing the letter was correct, Dr. Osborne possessed gifts; ancient ones believed to be all but gone.

Her grandmother, Genevieve Larsin had come to him before the birth worried about the choices her own child had made, but her granddaughter restored Genevieve's hope for the future. She believed the babe could bring light to a family lineage full of shadows and break their alliance with the dark arts. She took great pains to protect Olivia from the past and taught her the ways of the Son as a shield against the storm.

Archbishop Mendoza, however, never believed that for all her good intentions Genevieve was completely honest with Olivia. The child had been conceived in darkness. Now he feared an unholy force had emerged to stake its claim. The time had come for Olivia Osborne to choose a side.

CHAPTER ONE

THEY WERE WAITING for him, and there were two of them this time. One of the men, Special Agent Miers, he knew; the other, he didn't. The older, unfamiliar agent in the less contemporary suit had identified himself as Brad Dillon—short for Bradford according to his proffered credentials.

"Thanks for indulging us, Agent Branch." Agent Miers said.

Silas nodded. What was he supposed to say? He didn't really have a choice. The Bureau's Office of Professional Responsibility took their own time. With nothing else to do but sit, Silas slid into the chair next to Miers across from Dillon.

"Did you believe your life to be in danger when you entered Dr. Osborne's residence?" Miers asked.

"My life?" Silas reiterated. "No. Not *my* life."

"Yet you entered the residence with your weapon drawn, is that correct?"

"I did. SAPD passed along information that led me to believe the suspect, Jamie Smythe, had commandeered a SAPD vehicle and was headed for Dr. Osborne's house."

"And was said vehicle at her house when you arrived?" Miers asked.

"As previously stated, yes."

"Do you think Dr. Osborne believed her life to be in danger?"

"I can't speak to what Dr. Osborne believed," Silas answered carefully.

Finally, Dillon turned in his chair, appraising Silas with flat blue eyes. "I think you can. And you should."

Silas met him head on. So this was about Olivia. He should have known.

"Smythe was identified as the number one suspect in a string of brutal murders. Three in five days."

At the time no one knew Smythe had just left Mark Austin to die on a dining room table. Mark Austin was probably still breathing when Smythe arrived at Olivia's. Silas had no doubt Jamie had some equally horrific end planned for her.

"Smythe entered her residence and immediately subdued Dominic Acosta, knocking him unconscious. Then he came for Dr. Osborne. The only thing that stopped him was the Glock in her hand. She wouldn't have drawn her weapon if she didn't believe her life was in danger."

"But he didn't have a weapon on him, did he?" Dillon asked.

"Dr. Osborne didn't know that. I doubt any of the women who stopped to help him knew that either." Jamie Smythe earned the name *Good Samaritan Killer* for a reason. Otherwise they wouldn't have stopped." Smythe liked to use a type of knife famously wielded by Jim Bowie of Alamo lore—similar to a common carving knife, but with a cross guard to protect the user's hand and characteristically sharp on both sides for several inches up the blade and with a curved tip. Were Mark Austin still alive, he could attest to it. Instead, the M.E. had relied on the distinctive wound pattern to tell the story.

"Just curious, why did she have a priest with her?" It was Miers.

Dillon didn't seem to care that Miers didn't get his answer. He had other things on his mind. "You've known Dr. Osborne for a long time, haven't you?"

Silas stared him down. Miers looked like he wanted to say something else, but after a side-eye from Silas he choked it back. "We've worked together for six years." He'd advanced in the BAU working with Olivia. He no longer hunted low hanging fruit. Just like her, no one called him for normal.

"She's consulted on several cases, is that right?" Dillon asked.

"Yes."

"Good results?"

"Impeccable."

"Guess they better be with the hefty amount we're paying her, huh?" Miers commented.

"She's a doctor of what, exactly?" Dillon redirected.

Silas stifled the response he wanted to give. The two OPR agents already knew the answer, regardless of which one was asking the questions. "Forensic Psychology."

"The crazies, huh?" It was Miers again. Silas wondered if he was there just to get on his nerves. "I guess you're used to that at the BAU."

"It does stand for Behavioral Analysis," Silas said tritely. He was tired of the questions because he could see where they were headed and he didn't like the destination. "You want to tell me what this is really about?" Silas asked looking at the older one. "Or do you just want me to keep reciting the case file for you?"

Miers cleared his throat trying to recapture Silas's attention. "Just trying to cross our *t*'s and dot our *i*'s so to speak, Agent Branch. In case you hadn't heard, the FBI is under a lot of scrutiny for agent involved shootings. Seems some people think we go too easy on our own," Miers explained.

Silas ignored Miers. He wasn't making the decisions here. Silas wondered if Dillon was waiting to see who would stand down first. Well, it wouldn't be him. Silas Branch was supremely confident in his skills both as an agent and a profiler. Besides, it was a good shoot. Body mass center. By the book. Just like they taught at the academy. Silas didn't give two shits about the complications Smythe had suffered following the shooting.

They reached a stalemate. "Do you trust her?" Dillon finally asked.

"With my life." Silas answered, his jaw tight. "Dr. Osborne's skills were invaluable to this investigation. She's why Smythe is in custody and not out there butchering more women. No one else could have done that," Silas told him, his voice firm. "She is the best behavioral analyst out there."

It would have been easier for everyone if Smythe was dead. This case wasn't over by a long shot. "I heard that as well. But it wasn't her skills as a psychologist that got her pushed out of the Bureau, was it? It was the lack of *verifiable* evidence."

Technically the agent was correct. It was Dr. Osborne's *gift*. Although, she'd argue communing with the dead wasn't a gift at all. It came with its own set of shackles. The Bureau was big on procedure and order. They wanted all the dots to connect. Thirty years ago, the idea of behavioral sciences itself was frowned upon and the first BAU agents were the heretics kept locked away in the basement. Now there was Olivia Osborne and her innate talents. She didn't fit any mold. The things Olivia knew came without facts, without patterns and without training. She was an evolution of more than just the five senses and that shook the foundation of those steeped in logic and order. Maybe the OPR investigator sitting across from him was one of 'those.'

"Someone with a paygrade bigger than both of ours thought enough of those skills to ask her back." Silas knew he was pushing the envelope with this man but at the moment he didn't care. "I guess they thought they would rather work with her than against her."

After an abrupt end to her short career with the Bureau, Olivia changed sides, but she was selective. She only took cases where outside influences were at play. *Other worldly* things Silas would call them. Olivia Osborne was a hunter of evil, a protector of those touched by it. She was something the man sitting across from him could never understand.

"I heard that too. Seems before we lured her back to consult, she was the golden ticket for high-priced defense attorneys."

"She's good at what she does," Silas snapped.

"She's good at playing both sides," the senior agent was pushing his buttons this time. "Your admiration for her is quite clear, Agent Branch. But that's not going to get us a conviction is it?" Dillon leaned forward. "We're right back to what got her booted in the first place. SAPD is short on evidence."

"Smythe confessed to killing Sergeant Austin," Silas reminded him, not liking the older agent's tone or his implication.

"A confession only Dr. Osborne can corroborate."

"Father Dominic was there."

"I interviewed the former priest myself. The suspect beat him unconscious. He can't tell me what he heard."

"Smythe threatened Dr. Osborne and the priest. They had retreated to the bathroom when I arrived. They both feared for their lives."

"That's not the question here. The question is how to hang six murders on him. She led the FBI and SAPD to Smythe. Did you have anything other than her word to prove it was him?"

Silas's gaze fell to the carpet. The answers the other agent was seeking weren't there. "We were getting there. SAPD was already stalled on the first two murders. With the death of victim number three, SAPD sought Dr.

Osborne's help. While in the neighborhood, the morning of Wendy Florren's murder, Dr. Osborne identified a person of interest. She spotted him two doors down from the victim's house. The bastard was walking her dog for God's sake." Wendy Florren's body was discovered later that afternoon. Olivia somehow ended up with the dog.

"Need I remind you the sketch artist's rendering of the description Dr. Osborne provided was not exactly an accurate representation of Mr. Smythe?"

Silas recalled the incident vividly. "A wig was found with the clothes Dr. Osborne described the suspect wearing. It makes sense why her description was not completely accurate."

"Forensics can't link the *someone* who wore the wig and those clothes to Smythe."

"The bicycle shoeprint found at the first four scenes matches the kind of bike owned by Smythe," Silas suggested.

"Yet we don't have the shoes Dr. Osborne described the dogwalker wearing. Nor do we have the bike shoes that link the print to Smythe. He was caught on the news outside Wendy Florren's house with the rest of the neighborhood. In the video he's wearing what looks like Nikes. He was wearing boots when he arrived at the hospital. We found Nikes at his house, but no bike shoes."

"What about the bloody clothes found down the street from Smythe's former coworker, Tyler Ames?"

"Lack of evidence traceable to Smythe, not to mention the victim, Mr. Ames, wasn't a choirboy. With the right defense attorney, the case could be made that *he* victimized Smythe."

"What about the knife?"

"Forensics can confirm it was the same in all murders, except Wendy Florren. Seems whoever did her, used one from her own set. But like the bike shoes, the knife used to kill the other five victims hasn't been found. Believe me SAPD has been up and down Highway 281 between Wendy Florren's house where they found Sergeant Austin and Dr. Osborne's place in Alamo Heights. That's roughly fourteen miles. Smythe didn't have the knife on him when he came to see her. A knife that big? Hard to miss it on a grid search."

"But he drove Sergeant Austin's car to get there," Silas pointed out. The interaction reminded him why he never became a lawyer.

"A seizure sufferer who doesn't drive? Agent Branch, you know that argument would fall apart in front of a jury," Dillon continued. "What I'm telling you is we have no smoking gun. What does it look like when the Bureau can't bring home the guy who killed one of SAPD's own? Especially when they're the ones who asked for Dr. Osborne to begin with."

Silas didn't want to hear it. "Doesn't mean Smythe didn't do it."

"It doesn't, but it's a reminder that we have a problem and some might say the problem is Dr. Osborne."

* * *

Silas was seething. He wanted to punch something. He wanted to pace, but he didn't do either of those things. He was still sitting across from the empty desk when his cell phone rang.

"OPR gave you the all clear," his boss said by way of a greeting. "You can pick up your weapon at SAPD."

"The OPR doesn't work that fast. You want to tell me what the hell today was really about?" Silas wanted to know.

Patrick Monahan, Director of the FBI's Behavior Analysis Unit was silent, but only for a moment. "An informal inquiry."

"A quick one," Silas added. "And from a level much higher than the OPR, I assume."

"I shouldn't have to tell you, Silas. Olivia Osborne makes people nervous."

* * *

They pulled up to the house in silence. Olivia took a moment to admire her home. She'd spent most of her life there, all but a decade or so in Virginia chasing something she could never catch. Before she knew it, Agent Branch was opening her car door.

"Home sweet home," he said, making it sound like a question.

"Stop hovering. I'm fine, Silas," Olivia assured him. She'd been saying the same thing to him, the FBI, SAPD and anyone else who cared enough to ask over the last eight days since the Smythe shooting.

"Just so you know, I had two separate electrical companies check out the lights – they both said everything was good." There had been an electronic chaos inside her house the night he pulled up and ran inside to confront a killer. He'd neglected to mention that in his OPR interview this morning. "I also got a recommendation from some of the crime scene techs on a good cleaning company, so you wouldn't have to come home to the mess."

Olivia nodded, grateful for his thoughtfulness. By mess he meant where an accused murderer had almost bled out in her downstairs bathroom. Since the shooting they'd been sequestered in a hotel. During that time Silas had taken his role of caretaker very seriously. The ease at which Silas adapted to his new role made her wonder what kind of role model he'd had. Whoever it was had instilled in him a calming sense of order and uncommon gentleness. Despite her tendency toward independence Olivia found his recent actions comforting. It was nice to be taken care of.

They'd worked together for years, but uninterrupted time together had broadened not only her perspective on him, but her appreciation. She'd always been particularly fond of his blue eyes yet she hadn't known until recently the color was due to contacts. Without them his eyes were muted, a soft greyish blue that she found even more attractive. She just didn't tell Silas.

Olivia sensed him even before he spoke. It was something else he was doing more often, straying into her personal space. "And then there's that," Silas said as he crossed the threshold to find her staring at the mark on the floor. Anyone else might not even know it was there, but she would never forget it. It was the spot where Dominic drove his cross into Jamie Smythe's foot, giving them time to flee and probably saving their lives as much as the Glock did.

"Martin sent some floor guys over." Martin Mendoza, the contractor who'd been redoing her house for the past year had been invaluable in helping him get her home back in order. "He said it was the best they could do without replacing the wood."

"It's okay," Olivia told him. "It's an old house." It had been in her family for over a century. "It's just a scar. A part of history now." But they both knew it was more than that. It was where a priest had stopped a demon.

* * *

The last week had been a series of interrogations. OPR, SAPD, FBI. The acronyms were as endless as their questions. Now that it was over, at least for the time being, Olivia and Silas spent the remainder of their day attempting normalcy. They could have stayed at the hotel another night, but Silas knew Olivia was eager to get home. He just wasn't so eager to let her do it alone. Surprisingly, she hadn't balked when he suggested he stay.

They got groceries. They walked her dogs. Her fur babies as she liked to call them seemed as pleased as their mistress at the return to familiar surroundings. Both were adoptees, Daisy from the rigors of greyhound racing and Alvin from Wendy Florren, Smythe's fourth victim. After dinner they sat on the couch and indulged in their newfound passion of spectator cooking via the *Food Network*. Silas found it amusing that while Olivia liked to watch other people cook, she didn't do it for herself. He surprised her by cooking dinner, making sure to include jalapeños since they seemed to be on almost everything she ate. He enjoyed the look of surprise on her face, not knowing if it was his offer or the fact he could actually cook that made her smile. Either way, he was glad to see it.

Being around her was easy and comfortable. She would eat almost anything and her beverage selections were simple. Water, wine, when she was feeling indulgent, the occasional Dr. Pepper, but most especially dark roast coffee in the morning. She wasn't fussy, but he did learn quickly she required a full cup before speaking in complete sentences. He wondered if she was even aware of the soft sound she uttered as she savored the first sip or how distracting it was. He couldn't help but think how much he would rather hear it in the dark than across the breakfast table.

She was the only woman he knew who could be ready to go in the same amount of time it took him. The estimation included shower, make-up, and hair. She came out looking effortlessly put together. Minimal make-up, and a no fuss appearance. Her consultant fees afforded her designer labels, but her style was understated. He wanted to tell her she was the most beautiful woman in the room but was afraid of how the compliment would sound. She saw him for the flat surface he was. He saw her in layers. It reminded him of opening a present.

They ended the day sipping a nightcap in her backyard. Olivia preferred the front porch, but her return home had produced a spark of neighborly curiosity and Silas thought it best if they tuck themselves away in the back. Olivia had an expansive yard, perfect for the retired greyhound he'd been playing fetch with until his arm gave out.

They sat in the dark, with only the lights of the house behind them. As the night loomed, Silas found himself thinking about these things and many more, but there was only one he dared discuss with her tonight. Work was still a safer topic.

"You lured him to you, didn't you?" Silas didn't even have to call him by name. Olivia knew he was talking about the *Good Samaritan Killer*.

"Lure is a pretty strong word," she hedged, surprised Silas hadn't brought it up before now. He had been gentle with her feelings; maybe he couldn't hold back anymore.

"You knew he would come for you."

"We both knew he would come for me, Silas. Isn't that why you wanted me hidden away? I found him for you, but you didn't want him to find me."

"You know what I mean, Livie." His words were soft as he called her by the pet name. He'd been doing that more and more as they grew more comfortable together. The lines between professional and personal were fading between them.

She looked over at him. Despite the darkness he could still see the green of her eyes. "I can do many things," she told him, "but foretelling the future is not one of them."

Silas wasn't sure he believed her, but she was doing what she always did – downplaying her role. She didn't like being the center of attention, but she almost always was.

Inside the house they parted ways at the staircase. Silas was relegated to the downstairs bedroom that had once been hers, while Olivia retreated upstairs to her new one. Silas caught her hand before she could get away. "What you did with Smythe was a ballsy move. And reckless."

"I know you think I was being reckless, but we have a dangerous job," Olivia reminded him quietly.

Silas nodded and moved in closer, his hand slipping from hers to rest on her hip. Olivia felt the tug. She wasn't sure if he was pulling her in or she was moving toward him, but she found herself in the circle of his arms. His emotions lapped on the edge of her consciousness. She was just getting a handle on sifting through his thoughts, shuttering away the most personal. Right now, they were still cluttered, full of infatuation with her. Over time she could master the skill of organization with a familial. The person didn't have to be blood, just someone close. The more accustomed she became to another's thoughts the easier it was to shut them out or let them in. Olivia disciplined herself not to take liberties no matter how easy the access.

Olivia suppressed the sigh that wanted to escape her lips. She put her hands on his chest and smoothed away invisible wrinkles of his shirt so she could keep herself in check. He felt firm and warm beneath her touch. His thoughts, on the realm of hers, were threatening to come ashore. She dipped her head. A curtain of blonde waves fell between them. She was hiding from him in so many ways.

Silas reached out and tucked the hair back behind one ear. His eyes studied hers. "I need you to know I'm going to miss saying good-night to you." He bent down and pressed his lips to hers. They were soft and full of warmth. "I am coming back."

Even though she hadn't asked for one, it was a promise.

CHAPTER TWO

OLIVIA ROLLED OVER and saw the soft glow of the bathroom light. She knew she hadn't turned it on. It was a sign from Alice – a ghostly reminder of the past. Alice had been Gran's childhood friend. Olivia thought she would cross over when Gran did, but Alice remained, even through the renovations. Once Olivia inherited the house, she'd transformed it into something she and Gran had always dreamed about, adding rooms Olivia didn't know if she would ever use. What did one woman need with four bedrooms anyway? Always make room for the future Gran said.

Olivia took a moment, enjoying the comfort of waking up in her own home. This place held the roots of her family. They offered protection and solace. It remained her safe haven no matter what breached these walls. She let her mind wander. There was something watching where Silas lay sleeping. It wasn't Alice, yet it was familiar. Olivia knew it had been there her whole life. It was no threat. Maybe the appearance of the demon had coaxed it from hiding and now it stood watch as a sentry would. Her Gran kept reams of family lore tucked away in the storage house outside. Gran had said she might need them one day. The answers to what was loitering downstairs and more were waiting.

Downstairs she surprised Silas and cooked breakfast. At the airport he kissed her goodbye. Sleep had not come easily for him. She sensed his restlessness. He was conflicted. About the case, about leaving, about her. *So was she.* She just didn't want to confuse his feelings with hers.

* * *

Wilted flowers covered the place where the last brother had come to rest, but he wasn't the one she'd come for. Olivia clutched the little silver cross that hung around her neck and whispered a prayer for the dead. *"Nunc quis mortuus, et vivit: ut non magnificasti laetitiam laetabuntur in regnum tuum: quo omnes lacrimae nostrae abstergantur.* Who died and now lives, may they rejoice in Your kingdom, where all our tears are wiped away. *Rursus in unum iterum.* Unite us together again. "

With the sign of the cross she placed a bouquet of lilies on the headstone that showed a life just beginning. *Jason Gabriel Austin. November 23, 1975 - August 8, 2007.*

Olivia took her place on the bench beneath the shade of the tree, enjoying the silence. Graveyards were peaceful – the quietest place she could find. This place wasn't a monument to the dead but a haven for the living. The dead were free, no longer bound by the lives or loves left behind.

* * *

A black stripe cut across Anthony Zavalla's badge. As captain of the San Antonio Police Department's homicide division, Sergeant Austin had been one of his. "Agent Branch assured me you were going to stay on the Atascosa County case. That's good news." Zavalla meant it. Working with Dr. Osborne had been invaluable and Zavalla didn't want to see her go. Initially he'd been unaware Mark Austin had reached out to her for help on their stalled investigation of the murders of two young women. The appearance of a third victim, Patricia Griffin, however, had upped the ante. The sergeant feared they may have a serial killer on their hands and, knowing her personally, Mark had felt compelled to call her. He knew if anyone could connect the murders and hunt the monster responsible she could. Mark's request for Olivia's help had saved lives, but it had cost him his own.

"I'm merely consulting," Olivia said. It was a reminder to herself if nothing else. It was what she was supposed to do on the last case, but somehow she'd ended up back in the field just like the old days when she was an FBI agent.

The murder of Atascosa County resident Ferdinand Roche intersected with her pursuit of the *Good Samaritan* killer. Silas had known about it when he arrived but they'd never dug any deeper because Smythe's killings kept getting in the way. Then someone stole Ferdinand Roche's body from the morgue. The incident pulled Silas out of the search for Smythe and left Mark Austin alone in the field to cross paths with a killer.

Olivia finally took a seat across from the captain's desk. She had an agenda but had disguised it as work. "I had some time on my hands and thought I would check on any news from our neighboring county." Currently Atascosa County was a jurisdictional hotbed. Not only was the FBI sniffing around, but the Texas Rangers were in play as well. Olivia had been called in because the murder of Ferdinand Roche had undertones of witchcraft and the occult. Roche had been impaled with a pitchfork and had a pentagram carved into his shoulder. Forensics also found red pepper and salt sprinkled on his skin. These findings all suggested his killer believed him to be a witch.

"The Atascosa DA has some pull with the Rangers because his dad and our friend Ranger Gaines go way back," Zavalla explained the dance around typical protocol. "The Rangers tossed Roche's place but they didn't find any of the drugs Sheriff Tennent alluded to," Zavalla explained.

"Sounds like the DA doesn't trust his own sheriff any more than we did." Olivia remembered Tennent, the shifty eyed sheriff with the cowboy hat who wouldn't make eye contact with her.

"Seems like it," Zavalla smiled. "The Ranger also put in a word for you. Told the DA if there was anything remotely *spooky* about Roche's death, you were the one to call." It was another reason Zavalla was glad he'd crossed paths with Dr. Osborne. Now he had someone who could explain the unexplainable.

"Great." In her interview with the sheriff, Olivia had wondered what was powerful enough to turn him or keep him quiet. Fear was always a good choice. Drug dealers could do that, but if there were no drugs, were they back to the occult? Is that what Ranger Gaines thought?

"Oh, it gets better," Zavalla assured her. "The DA is still on the warpath. The Rangers might not have found anything, but he's convinced the sheriff is involved with something. He requested the state fire marshal's office look into the burning of the body. I think it's his backdoor into getting a peek into the murder as well since the case is still active." Zavalla and Olivia both knew in a county with limited resources, a compromised sheriff's department and a murder investigation well over two weeks old, the chances of closure were slim to none.

"The state investigator in turn bounced it back to the Bexar County Fire Marshal." Atascosa County has a smaller staff of investigators, and with a neighboring county of over four million people just down the highway, the state fire marshal's office knew Bexar had the resources to share the load. "Because our medical examiner autopsied Roche *before* the burning, I want to be kept in the loop. I'm not convinced this is over so I'm sending Sergeant Will Ibarra out to the ranch where the body was found." Zavalla didn't want to have to play catch up later and it gave Ibarra something to do until Zavalla could decide what to do with him.

"I think that's pretty forward thinking of you, Captain." Olivia agreed. "Who's Ibarra?"

"Sergeant Ibarra is the new transfer to the homicide unit by way of the Jones sub-station. Before that he was an instructor at the Academy. I'm hoping his experience means he'll know how to liaise with the Bexar County fire boys." It was also the best way he could break it to Dr. Osborne that Sergeant Ibarra was the one he'd pegged to take Sergeant Austin's spot. Mark had requested a transfer to the Atascosa County case before he died. He'd wanted to cut ties with his lieutenant.

Olivia nodded at the explanation.

Not wanting to dwell on the changes, Zavalla shifted gears from his neighboring county to something closer to home. "Any news yet on who might take the Smythe case?" Smythe was currently represented by a court appointed attorney but given the attention the serial case had garnered, no one expected that to remain so for long. Even without funds, San Antonio's most prolific serial killer was acquiring some high-powered foot traffic in and out of his hospital room at the Bexar Country infirmary. Smythe's defense team would more than make their legal fees in TV time, book deals, and whatever else came with the coverage.

Olivia knew the players, having worked with some of them before returning to consult exclusively for the FBI. She also had the inside track on the name currently at the top of the list. "Brennon Kaine is flying in later today." She and Kaine had not worked together, at least not on the same team. Their relationship had been personal, not professional. "Brennon's set to interview Jamie tomorrow." It felt strange no longer referring to him as the UNSUB. Killing six people, one of them a police officer, ensured Smythe would never be the unknown subject again.

Zavalla had heard of Brennon Kaine. He was based in New York but traveled the country to sit next to some high-profile murderers. Dr. Osborne's use of the attorney's first name caught the captain's attention but he didn't want to ask about it directly so he went the indirect route. "So, he's dealt with *these types* of cases before?" Zavalla asked.

"He and I have crossed paths before," Olivia said and left it at that. Zavalla knew her history. She and Silas were responsible for the capture of Kaine's previous defendant, James Dean Ewing. Currently Seattle's *Hilltop Lover* was waiting for the state of Washington to put a needle in his arm and call it a day, but was dismayed to learn that the state of Washington had recently abolished the death penalty, which meant he would linger on death row, potentially for decades, without the benefit of an execution date.

Olivia knew that Ewing's current predicament had nothing to do with Kaine's skills as a litigator. Ewing had simply been relinquished by what had driven him to kill. Instead of proceeding with the insanity plea as Kaine advocated, Ewing proclaimed he should be punished for what he'd done and fired Kaine as soon as he was deemed competent to stand trial. Olivia had seen it happen before. Evil might have vacated the vessel but the damage inflicted could not be undone. Some of those she had saved ultimately took their own lives because they couldn't live with the atrocities they had committed while under the influence of evil.

Their conversation stalled and Olivia fidgeted with her purse. She wanted to say something but wasn't sure how to even start. Luckily, the captain saved her.

"Have you seen Lieutenant Bartholomew?" Zavalla asked carefully.

Olivia shook her head. The last time she saw Barry was at Mark's funeral. Olivia was struggling with her own loss, but she could only imagine what Barry was going through. Mark had not only been his partner, but also his best friend.

"Have you heard from him?" Olivia asked, relieved the captain breached the topic that brought her to his office in the first place. Atascosa County had just been a convenient excuse. She'd reached out to Barry, but he wasn't returning her phone calls. She'd tried not to take his silence personally, but it was growing more difficult with each passing day.

Zavalla nodded. "He's asked for administrative leave. Says he's taking another couple of weeks." He was surprised she didn't know. He didn't think he'd misread what was happening between the doctor and his lieutenant during the case. Neither had Mark Austin. It's what had prompted him to ask for reassignment to Atascosa County. Mark had been struggling with his own feelings for Olivia.

"Have you seen him?" Olivia asked. She had been the wedge between the two friends only days before Mark's death. *Mark is easy*, Barry had said. *"He'll come around. We'll work it out. The three of us. Together."* But that's not what happened. A day after their conversation, Mark was dead. She couldn't help but wonder if Barry felt guilty about how things ended. Not between them, but with Mark.

"No. Everything has been through email."

She wasn't sure if Zavalla's answer made her feel better or worse, but she knew what she had to do. It wasn't about her and Barry anymore. It was just about Barry.

* * *

"Thank you for seeing me, Your Excellency. The Catholic community is enriched by your service. I'm very grateful for your kindness and leadership, and your acceptance of my request."

They were sitting in the archbishop's private office with no desk in between them. They might be sitting as equals, but the bishop's robes set them apart. Dominic Acosta no longer wore the collar, but he still sounded like a priest. While teaching at the seminary in Virginia, Father Dominic received his own request for assistance against the forces of evil. Exorcisms were explicitly forbidden without permission from the Archdiocese, but the Father had been so compelled by a forensic psychologist that he circumvented the normal chain of command and performed the exorcism anyway. At the most severe he could have been excommunicated, or at the very least he could have been dispatched back to his home in the Dominican Republic to tend a flock. Rather than embarrass the seminary or the Church, Father Dominic elected to abdicate instead.

"Saint Paul teaches, we are merely 'the servants of Christ and the stewards of the mysteries of God.' I believe it is a mystery of God you've brought me today. Tell me, what made you believe Dr. Osborne the first time you met her?" The two men had never met, but the archbishop had done his research. When Father Dominic left the Church, he took with him the secrets of who led him to the young boy in the first place. The archbishop now knew that person was Olivia. The priest's loyalty to the doctor ran deep, rooted in faith.

"I listened to her story. I examined the boy myself. I sought counsel from a very old priest. He told me the story of being at the bedside of an accused murderer. She was dying. As she did, she repeated a name over and over. It was the first case Olivia ever worked. She was a student then. She lost someone she loved. He was killed by the girl. Yet Olivia saved her. I knew she had encountered evil before. And I knew that she knew what evil was."

"I read your letter, but I think there is more to the story. You mentioned the police sergeant. Why was he skinned?" the archbishop wanted to know. Demons were crafty. It had to be personal.

"He was the brother of the man she loved. The one murdered by the girl in the hospital. But it was also supposed to be a police lieutenant. Bartholomew."

The archbishop thought he was beginning to understand. According to ancient history, Saint Bartholomew was skinned alive. It was his punishment for the crime of converting the King of Armenia to Christianity. "You said communication was initiated."

"Messages were left at the crime scenes for her, written in the blood of the victims. I was present when the demon spoke through an elderly resident referencing the doctor's grandmother and the murder Dr. Osborne witnessed a decade before. The demon told her of the death of Sergeant Austin."

The archbishop absorbed the information, weighing the implications. The demon had an agenda. Referencing events only Dr. Osborne knew ensured *It* had her complete attention. Nicefero had often wondered of the validity of Genevieve Larsin's claims her granddaughter could commune with the dead. It seemed there was more to it than that.

Dominic passed him a scrap of paper. Speaking the demon's name aloud was forbidden.

The archbishop read it but didn't pass it back. "This is not a name I know." There was a hierarchy even among demons.

"Nor I," Dominic agreed. "I had to search some rather obscure text to find it. But it wasn't the first time I heard the name. It wasn't Olivia's either. I referred to the meeting as an introduction, but it was more than that. It was a reacquaintance. This was the same demon the dying girl in the hospital spoke of. The same one the old priest imparted to me. The same one who killed a man Olivia loved."

The archbishop gripped his own hands so the priest wouldn't see them shaking. All of it was important, but not as important as his next question. It would determine the path of the Church in this matter. "Did she answer him?"

"No. She refused."

The archbishop nodded, relieved. "I see." He let go of his hands and reached for his tea. It was too early in the day for wine. "So, would you say Dr. Osborne has been targeted specifically?"

"Yes, Your Grace." It was the reason Dominic requested the meeting. It was the same reason the archbishop had accepted.

"Is she a demon dealer?"

"No." The priest's response was swift and without hesitation.

"Then what is she?"

* * *

Olivia pulled into the parking lot and looked up at the building looming ahead of her. When it was built it was one of San Antonio's first high-rise apartment buildings located not far from her neighborhood, on the edge of Highway 281, just across from Incarnate Word University. Before she could talk herself out of it, Olivia gathered the packages she brought with her and went inside.

Once inside she was stopped by a doorman. She didn't know there were any buildings in San Antonio that employed one. When he asked her if the man on the thirteenth floor was expecting her, Olivia was honest and said no. There was an uncomfortable wait for a response from the other end. All the while Olivia shifted from one foot to the other and rearranged packages that were perfectly fine. It was going be awkward if he was forced to deny her passage.

"I see. Yes. I understand." The doorman hung up the phone and avoided looking at her for what seemed like an eternity. "He says to come on up."

The door was slightly ajar when she got there. Olivia nudged it open with her knee. Once inside, sliding glass doors across the living room greeted her with a stunning view of San Antonio. It was beautiful thirteen stories above the city. Barry was on the balcony, his back to her. Olivia bumped the door closed with her hip and moved inside without him ever turning around.

The room was spacious with expansive hardwood floors. A hallway jutted off to her left undoubtedly leading to bedrooms. The far wall of the great room was a long built-in bookcase, generously filled with books. In the middle was a mounted large screen TV. To her right was a large wooden dinner table and a full swinging door leading to the kitchen. The place didn't even look lived in. It was a stark contrast to the disorganization of his cluttered office. This was his quiet place.

Olivia set her packages on the table and moved out to the balcony to join him. He looked like he might have just come back from a run. He was holding a bottle of water. She wondered if he'd needed a shot of something in order to see her. She still had a bottle of Crown for him at her house. She recalled the subtle taste of whiskey on his lips the night they spent together.

"I wasn't sure you would let me in," she greeted him.

Barry was wearing long athletic shorts and a form fitting t-shirt. He had the legs of a runner and the upper body of someone who maintained it. She'd only ever seen him in work attire. She'd known he was solid underneath from the way he felt the few times he'd held her close. She just didn't realize how much time he spent conditioning his body. He was older than Silas. He had to work harder to look that way, but his drive wasn't born of vanity. It was to exorcise some demons of his own.

When at last he turned to look at her, Olivia noted the dust of stubble on his face. The angles of his face weren't pristine and carefully sculpted like Silas's. Barry didn't take center stage. He was the quiet presence in the room. But once discovered, he couldn't be unseen. At least not in her eyes.

"You shouldn't have come."

His words were flat and emotionless, triggering within her old feelings of self-doubt. Maybe she had misread his feelings. It happened sometimes, if she was too close or there were too many. Olivia retreated inside herself attempting to soothe the chord of vulnerability he struck inside of her. Peering into his gray eyes she saw storm clouds gathering. She'd seen them before, the day they met in a blood-soaked field. He had no idea who or what she was. He'd thought she was a psychic. Things had only gotten worse when he learned she had once been in the FBI. Two nights later he showed up at her door with a bottle of wine.

Olivia felt the need to justify her presence. "I brought you something to eat. I thought you might be hungry." The words came out in a rush, but they just hung there as silence enveloped them. One night, not so long ago, they'd talked about sitting together, maybe even on this very balcony enjoying the skyline together. "Captain Zavalla told me you're taking some time off," she stammered, shattering the picture they'd once shared.

Unsaid words hung between them, but neither of them knew where or how to begin. For Barry, it was easier to just not start. He did what he always did with his emotions. He shut them down and retreated. "I didn't want you to see me. Not like this."

Olivia swallowed her feelings. His were impenetrable. The wall he'd erected between them towered over her. She would have broken her own code and breached them if she could, but he had shut her out. Instead, Olivia lifted her chin and reached for the familiar. *Abandonment.* She spoke the only words she could find. "Then you shouldn't have let me in."

CHAPTER THREE

OLIVIA MET BRENNON Kaine at *La Mansion* for dinner. The restaurant selections were as excellent as the accommodations. Dining outside along the banks of the Riverwalk enjoying the sounds of soft Spanish guitar music strumming in the background would give Brennon a taste of her city.

He was on the phone when she spotted him. He'd already secured them a table for two away from everyone else. Athletically trim with thick gray hair and sparkling blue eyes, he was appreciatively noticeable. He saw her in time to end the call and stood up to welcome her with open arms. Olivia willingly returned his kiss to the cheek. Their time together had been short-lived, but the memories were pleasant. For him it was too soon after the loss of his wife of more than twenty years and, Olivia suspected, some additional pressure from his children over their fifteen-year age gap. For her, it was what it always was – a delicate balancing act between career and personal life. Their parting had been amicable and Olivia was genuinely glad to see him again.

A glass of wine soon arrived for her and a margarita for him. The drink was the only specific request he'd made regarding a dinner location. "My second," he told her as they toasted. "They are just as good as you promised."

They chatted easily through dinner, maneuvering around the real reason for Brennon's visit. Halfway through, he decided he wouldn't bring it up. Seeing her was enough. Her relationship with the Bureau was precarious at best, and being seen with him could rock the boat between her and the FBI. They only called her for what they couldn't understand. Other times they liked to pretend she didn't exist, much like the monsters in the dark. The waiter had just dropped off Olivia's request for a cappuccino in lieu of the fancy piece of cheesecake Brennon had ordered when she opened the door he wouldn't.

"He's asked to see me," Olivia suddenly said.

She didn't even have to say who *he* was. Jamie Lynne Smythe was the real reason they were having dinner, at least in her mind. "I haven't gone." She had checked up on him every day, at least in the beginning, but she didn't feel like telling Brennon that part. She still had a nurse friend or two in the system. No personal health information was exchanged, nothing more than if he was awake or not, or if he was going to live or die.

Brennon put his fork down. It had been suspended in mid-air with the bite he'd never taken.

"All I need you to do is listen."

"Look, Livie, you don't have to do this." The personal and professional parts of him were in conflict. She was one of Smythe's victims. The only one who survived.

"Yes, I do. I have no other choice." Brennon opened his mouth to protest, but she pressed on, reaching over to squeeze his arm. "I did what I had to do, *Bren*." She used the pet name ensuring she had his complete attention. "You need to do what *you* do best. That is why you're here, isn't it?"

Truth be told he wasn't sure why he was here, but he nodded nonetheless and slowly released the breath he'd been holding. He'd run through dozens of scenarios, prepared a multitude of questions, knowing he'd never get to ask her any of them. She did her best to keep out of the fray, but this monster had come for her. She couldn't outrun him.

Olivia pushed aside her full cup of coffee. "I think I'd like that second glass of wine you suggested instead."

"I admit I never expected you to get out." Brennon said after the drinks had been exchanged.

"You can't blame a girl for trying." Olivia was glad that he remembered. After their relationship ended, she left Virginia behind. She'd done what she'd gone there to do. She had obtained her PhD at Marymount and been accepted into the FBI. Her return to San Antonio was an excuse to make some changes in her life, but the homecoming hadn't worked out as planned. Gran was already sick and in six months Olivia was left with an empty house and no family. And the monsters were still there. *There was no running. She knew that now.*

"It wasn't about the FBI this time. I was helping a friend."

Brennon paused, mentally accessing what he'd read about the case. "Sergeant Austin." The name sounded familiar. It wasn't just this case. "The officer killed in the line of duty?"

The tears began to swim. Maybe because she hadn't talked about it, not even to Silas – he had his own cross to bear where Mark was concerned. His death lay quietly unopened between them. Olivia couldn't talk about it but not for the reasons he thought. She knew Silas blamed himself, no matter what he'd told anyone who asked. And she knew they had. Silas had been the last friendly face Mark ever saw.

Brennon reached over and took her hand. "I'm so sorry, Livie."

Olivia shook her head. "I'm fine," she assured him.

"You don't sound fine." His memory finally caught up with the name. "Mark Austin. You knew his brother, didn't you?" Brennon shook his head at the revelation. It was something personal.

Not answering him was an answer. All Olivia could think about was the remaining sibling. Madeline. She wasn't just Mark's sister, but his twin. Olivia wondered if because they entered the world together, she felt something when he left her behind. Olivia would never forget the way Madeline looked at her during the rosary service. The look she'd seen on Madeline's face said she did.

Brennon squeezed Olivia's hand, bringing her back. "Hey, what about you? How are you getting through this?" It was typical Olivia, thinking of others before herself. She would deny she was empathic, but even Brennon could see her for what she was.

"Silas." Thoughts of him chased back the tears.

Brennon gazed across the table at her. When they met, Silas was Agent Branch. What else had changed? "Silas, hmm. How is he?"

"He's good. Very well actually," Olivia said and felt a sting in her cheeks.

The look on her face prompted Brennon to let go of her hand. He'd been holding it longer than he should have. *Silas as rescuer. Olivia as the prize.* The scenario wasn't a total surprise. He'd seen the makings of it. "It appears he is." Brennon smiled. He propped his elbow on the table and rested his chin in his hand. "Is it all work?"

The question prompted the tingle in her cheeks to return. It sounded like he expected a confession.

"You're blushing," Brennon noted.

"Am not."

"I can see it. You can't."

Olivia waved him off.

"Silas always seemed…. *fond* of you. Protective," Brennon told her.

"Really?"

Olivia sounded like she didn't believe him – or didn't want to. "Imagine it from my perspective," Brennon encouraged her.

"You were jealous of Silas?" Olivia fidgeted and stared into her wine glass.

"I don't think there's a man who's interested in you that wouldn't be wary of Agent Branch. Not if they're paying attention. Silas is an impressive guy. Football star, lawyer, FBI agent. Tall. Good looking. He has it all. Or does he?" Brennon couldn't help but ask, even with the smile on her face.

"He's a good guy. I just sometimes wish he'd let more people see it," Olivia finally admitted. It felt strange talking about Silas this way. Especially with Brennon. Since she didn't have a circle of girlfriends, she guessed Brennon was the next best thing. In some ways he probably knew her better than she knew herself. He didn't look at her through the same lens.

"Protective goes both ways I see." Brennon was smiling at the revelation.

Olivia shook her head again. "Don't try and profile me. You're way out of your comfort zone, Counselor."

"Well, it seems to me there's some potential there," Brennon hedged.

"I plead the fifth," Olivia insisted. But in the back of her mind she wondered how someone else could see it so clearly. Brennon wasn't the first. Dominic had mentioned the same thing. Where had her head been before? Maybe in a place where men like Silas didn't pay attention to women like her.

Uncomfortable with where this was going, Olivia reached for her wine glass again, but found it was empty. Her eyes wandered across to the other side of the Riverwalk. Even in the dim evening light she saw her. Jessica Tate the *News You Need to Know* girl.

They'd first crossed paths during the Smythe case. The feisty reporter's inability to keep her mouth shut had alerted Smythe to Olivia's involvement in the case, causing a showdown with Silas. In the end, however, Jessica used the power of the press for good with an op-ed piece. Smythe was a harmless looking man-boy who didn't choose his victims. They chose him. He rode a bicycle to his murders, faking injury to entice his victims and then killing those who stopped to help him. Their desire to do good was what ultimately ended their lives, but Jessica Tate's article didn't focus on the killer. She wanted the people of San Antonio to know about Smythe's victims, with special emphasis on number three.

It was a simple yet touching story. Patricia Griffin, a nurse and woman who was living her life in the service of others when she stopped for the wrong person on her way home from work. In Patricia's case Jamie had been on his way to hunt, but this time he had truly been hurt, taking a turnabout too fast. She stopped to save him, but that didn't stop him from killing her. She died in an open grassy field in the middle of a suburban neighborhood.

The backstory no one would ever hear was that spilling the blood of three could be considered an offering. Blood represented both life and death. It was binding. The number three was historically significant. Earth, wind and fire. The Holy Trinity. Did Patricia's blood summon something from below, opening a door to the shadow world, allowing a demon inside this one? Or was it Olivia's presence that did that? Patricia Griffin's death was the third -- the catalyst that pulled Olivia and the FBI into the investigation. These were only some of the things that haunted Olivia about the case.

"You still with me?" Brennon asked, reaching for her hand again. He knew physical touch would bring her back from wherever she had wandered.

* * *

The reporter was waiting outside. "Was that Brennon Kaine I saw you having dinner with?" Jessica Tate asked, rushing to keep up with Olivia's clipped pace.

Olivia had already spotted the reporter which was why she'd insisted Brennon not walk her to her car. "No comment."

"I'm not working, Dr. Osborne."

Olivia smiled. Regardless of how irritating Jessica Tate could be, she reminded Olivia a little bit of herself. The girl was tenacious. "You're always working, Ms. Tate."

"Then do you want to tell me if Mr. Kaine's in town to see Jamie Smythe, or is he here for personal reasons?" The gleam in the reporter's eye told Olivia she had probably already done some homework on the last part of her question.

Olivia reached her vehicle. The brake lights blinked signaling Brennon her impending attempt at a getaway. She hoped he snuck back inside. "No comment."

"Found anything interesting in Atascosa County?" The question came out of nowhere.

Olivia's hand was clutching the SUV's door handle as she turned to face her shadow.

"You promised to talk to me," Jessica reminded her. It had been a quid pro quo. The FBI needed a look at Jessica's news footage to hopefully spot the killer outside Wendy Florren's house. In exchange, Jessica had angled for an interview with Olivia, hinting at a discussion of the paranormal. For the sake of the case Olivia had been willing to promise anything at the time, but an interview about that particular subject wasn't something she liked to encourage.

Jessica stepped closer so she could see Olivia better. The parking lot lights weren't the best. "You still don't know, do you?"

The reporter was studying her, profiling her while Olivia accessed her own recall of their previous discussion. It hadn't been just the paranormal Jessica wanted to talk about, but Atascosa County as well. She'd known about the murder. But what did she know? "I know Ferdinand Roche is dead," Olivia hedged for an observation of her own. None of the details of his death had been publicly released. Without them, his death wasn't newsworthy enough for the likes of Jessica Tate. Unless Jessica had some information connecting the dead man to the paranormal or something else equally interesting.

"That's what they'll tell you about the missing girls too. If you let them." The reporter's voice might be bitter but not her eyes. This was personal.

* * *

Jessica Tate had a story to tell. This one involving four missing girls. All of them from Atascosa County. "What time frame are we looking at?" Olivia asked when Jessica was done. To her credit it didn't take long.

"The first abduction happened a little over two years ago."

"So, tell me what makes you think I can help you with this?" Olivia asked getting to the point. It was a short story. There was a specific reason Jessica had chosen her. They just hadn't gotten there yet.

"No one's looking."

Jessica was right. No one was – for many different reasons, but Olivia wasn't prepared to go into them right now. "You used the word abduction. What makes you think these girls didn't go off on their own?"

"Ok, maybe they were lured. That's probably a better word. Even if they went on their own there could be something preventing them from coming back."

Olivia looked across the table at the reporter. Jessica hadn't touched her coffee. She didn't need the caffeine. The intensity she had for this story was all her, but she was still holding something back. Maybe rejection would do the trick. "I'm just not seeing it. There's nothing personal connecting these girls. There are way too many unknowns," Olivia told her.

"That's why I started with what I do know."

To find a killer, Olivia started with a study of the known - the victims. It sounded like the same strategy Jessica was using. "What is it that you know?"

"Two things. First, something we both know. There are believers in the paranormal in Atascosa County. Practitioners even. Whoever killed Ferdinand Roche for example. There are rumors of witches and ritual."

Olivia gave her a blank stare. "Roche was a transient worker someone found dead in a field."

"He was more than that, or you wouldn't know about him," Jessica said. "I know about the pitchfork and the pentagram."

That information about Roche wasn't public knowledge so Jessica had done some digging. She also had a piece of information Olivia did not. "That's why you came to me." It wasn't a question, just a statement of fact. Now they could move forward. "So, what's the paranormal connection to the girls?"

"It connects to one girl. The one girl I do know. Tell me, have you ever met others like you?" Jessica answered the doctor's question with one of her own.

"Not really." Olivia shifted in her seat, putting Atascosa County on the backburner for now, but she was going to want to come back to the rituals and witches. She filed it away for later. Maybe Jessica did have something interesting to tell.

Jessica Tate's own profiling skills told her that was all she was going to get out of the doctor. She would have to show her hand or she was going to lose her. "Kimberly Burleson has always been a little different." Jessica regretted her use of the word as soon as she heard it with her own ears.

"It's okay," Olivia stopped her before the reporter tried to apologize. "I'm not unfamiliar with the term." Olivia grew up in a small school and kids had long memories. Being the outcast was as familiar to her as abandonment. "Different how?"

"Sensitive, especially to places, old houses in particular. She *feels* events, if that makes sense."

"The energy left behind by events," Olivia clarified. "How did it make *her* feel?"

Jessica considered the question. "For the most part, not good."

"Every event produces energy. Bad things produce more, making it easier for someone who's sensitive to pick up on it." It wasn't the whole truth, but it would do for now. "Over time the residual builds, depending on the location. The energy can be good or bad."

"What kind of places?" Jessica seemed curious.

"Theaters produce an abundance of energy, for example. If there's enough residual it can be mistaken for something supernatural." For Olivia, until the actors took the stage, being in a theater made her feel like she had a hive of bees loose inside her heard. Once the live energy merged with the old, she could put the past to rest.

"Do you mean like a haunting?" Jessica asked.

"It can be a haunting or merely an echo. It's an abundance of energy. It depends on the amount of emotion and its origin.

"Did Kimberly have any other symptoms?" Olivia asked, slipping easily into her original profession. Nurses were investigators too.

"Such as?" Jessica needed direction.

"Did she ever see things, or hear things no one else could?"

"She didn't talk about seeing things. She sometimes heard things no one else could hear. Apparently, the sound of children laughing is a bad sign." Jessica paused, as though waiting for input.

Olivia took the cue. An alarm went off inside her head as thoughts of Alice sprang to mind. "Because laughter isn't supposed to be scary, is it?"

Jessica began to stir on her side of the booth. She wrapped both hands around the warmth of her coffee cup as though there were a chill in the air. "I read some people believe that children's spirits are actually demons in disguise." She looked at Olivia, who remained, impassive, so Jessica kept talking to fill the void. "Some of Kimmy's experiences were emotional, like, she would just start crying. She'd have to leave the room to make it stop."

Olivia nodded, swapping her aloofness for sympathy. "Did she ever wake up in the middle of the night and feel like she couldn't move? That someone or something was watching her or holding her down?"

"The feeling of helplessness, a loss of control," Jessica described. "You're talking about sleep paralysis?"

"Yes, that's the term of art."

"I've heard of it. Yes, Kimmy talked about feeling things like that," Jessica looked across the table at the woman she'd pinned her hopes on helping her. "Do you have it?"

Olivia shook her head. "No. That kind of thing doesn't work on me."

"Why? How are you different?" It was an unscripted question.

Olivia shook her head. *Instinct.* "I can see the other side of the dark." *Like a hunter.*

It grew quiet between them. Jessica wondering what all there was to know about the doctor. Was what she had a gift or a curse?

"She's the second thing, isn't she?" Olivia asked.

"The second? I don't understand."

Jessica Tate had gotten so caught up in reeling her in, she'd forgotten her own story. "You told me you knew two things. The first was there are believers of the paranormal in Atascosa County. The second is this girl, Kimberly. Who is she to you? Your sister?"

"Is it that obvious?" Jessica had hoped to keep the true nature of her connection to Kimberly under wraps long enough to secure her help.

"Only someone very close to Kimberly would know those things about her."

"She's my niece. I still call her Kimmy. She hates it." Jessica attempted a smile. The intensity in her had crumbled to desperation. "So, how do we find out if the other girls are like Kimmy?"

Olivia pondered her own family dynamic. "We don't. They won't talk about it." She and Gran talked openly about her gifts, but they didn't speak about them outside the family. Once Olivia left puberty behind, she seemed to have passed some kind of test with Gran and they spoke about them even less. By then Olivia's idiosyncrasies were hardwired into her personality. Gran had learned to accept them. When it came to her studies and her career Olivia was purposely vague about her work. Whether Gran had known the truth or not, she never said. Over time, Olivia grew to believe Gran was very good at keeping secrets.

"How long as it been, since Kimmy left?"

"Eight months."

Olivia wondered how many times Jessica had run the numbers. Statistically, chances were she would never see her niece again. No wonder she was desperate. "Tell me, is Kimmy the only one in your family who has these kinds of experiences?" Olivia guessed she probably was. Jessica wanted her help, but she also wanted answers. Answers she apparently couldn't get anywhere else.

"Yes. My grandmother used to talk about Kimmy and her *spells,* until my mother told her to stop calling them that. They made Kimmy feel different and not in a good way. She was as isolated inside the family as outside of it. I think that's why she had few friends."

Isolation was a good description. "Feeling the energy of others is emotionally exhausting," Olivia agreed. Always having to be on guard against the onslaught of other people's emotions, living or dead, was one of the reasons Olivia rarely went out. She wasn't antisocial. For her isolationism was an act of self-preservation. "It could be why there's no obvious connection between these girls. It's not like a club. They don't sit around and share."

"Reading people, knowing what they're feeling, that's paranormal isn't it?"

"Some say it is," Olivia agreed, her thoughts starting to shift down a dark path. "Some might see it as a very powerful gift."

Isolated. Gifted. A profile was starting to form.

"Do you think having those kinds of abilities could make Kimmy some kind of a target?" Jessica asked.

If she met the wrong person.

* * *

Olivia's return home to an empty house didn't bring her the solace she'd found earlier in the day. All that awaited her was emptiness. Her fur babies were there to greet her, but even they seemed out of sorts. On one of her many prowls through the house she found Daisy lying outside the downstairs bedroom where Silas had stayed. The greyhound had been pacing since Olivia's return as if looking for Silas to join them. Olivia opened the door and Daisy stood up wanting to cross the threshold that bound her to the hallway. The dog didn't like the room, even when Olivia slept there before the addition of the second floor. She refused to sleep on her bed next to Olivia's, preferring the hallway with her nose barely breaching the barrier. Daisy wanted to go inside. Olivia could see the tautness of her muscles, poised, ready to go.

"Miss him?" Olivia reached down and scratched behind the dog's ears. The greyhound had taken to Silas immediately. Daisy didn't typically like males, but somehow Silas had broken through her defenses. He had that effect on both of them. Telling herself not to linger, Olivia closed the door, stirring the faintest whiff of his cologne. Something masculine and woodsy invaded her senses, conjuring thoughts of wild abandonment that only added to her restlessness.

Daisy followed her to the kitchen where Olivia chose sparkling water over the wine she really wanted. The greyhound opted for her bed while Alvin joined Olivia on the couch. She tried watching television but the channel was set to the *Food Network* where she and Silas had last left it. Damn him for getting her hooked. She didn't feel like watching alone so she aimlessly channel surfed until she gave up the fight. She had just tucked herself in bed when Silas surprised her with a call to say goodnight. It was even later for him. Olivia wondered if he was restless too.

"Told you I was going to miss saying good night to you." The sound of his voice brought a smile to her face.

"I think I might miss you too," she confessed.

CHAPTER FOUR

"Do I need to tell you how much of a shit show it will be? Or can I assume you're fully aware of what you're asking for?" Supervisory Special Agent Patrick Monahan, chief of the FBI's Behavioral Analysis Unit, said as he studied Silas from across his desk.. He was hoping for some banter. Silas hadn't been himself at dinner last night. His mood seemed to have carried over into the morning. The trip to Texas had been costly and had changed the agent in more ways than one. Patrick knew it for sure with today's request. Maybe all of Silas's brooding last night hadn't been about the case.

Monahan had looked forward to having the agent back, but if Silas got his way he wouldn't be staying long. "The DA is trying to make this capital." *If he can find the knife.* Patrick didn't want to say it because he wanted Silas in a talkative mood. Besides this was about something else.

"As he should," Silas agreed.

"The line to make sure that doesn't happen is already forming," Patrick assured him.

"And yet Smythe still has a public defender," Silas countered.

"He has, but maybe not after today," Patrick told him, watching for a reaction. Silas's shift in posture told him what he suspected - the agent didn't know. He would have said so already if he did. "She didn't tell you?" Patrick didn't have to say her name. She was the reason they were even having this discussion, of that, Patrick was sure. "Brennon Kaine. My sources tell me they're meeting today."

"Smythe's turned down two offers already," Silas countered.

"Maybe Kaine knows something we don't."

"Kaine's a hustler," Silas told him. "He likes seeing himself on TV." It certainly had nothing to do with money. Kaine didn't need it and Smythe didn't have it.

"Are you sure he wasn't invited?" Patrick continued fully aware he was intentionally poking the bear.

"You're not suggesting Livie called him?" The response sounded vaguely like a growl.

Patrick shrugged. "She and Kaine have history."

Silas didn't want to think about it. He had worked the case that caused Olivia to cross paths with the attorney. Silas hadn't liked her involvement with Kaine then and he liked it even less now. He had a growing jealous streak where Olivia was concerned. It was taking some getting used to.

"Kaine is really good at tangling up juries. More than one of his clients has walked out of a courtroom and gone to some padded room and not a jail cell."

"It's what he's good at." Silas couldn't help but think back on the holes in the case the older OPR agent had pointed out. An internal investigation would be fodder for a defendant's advocate like Kaine. "Livie has nothing to do with his involvement."

Patrick put his hands up in surrender. "I'm only repeating whispers in the hall."

Silas shook his head. "She didn't and she wouldn't. When is this going to stop with her?"

Patrick could sympathize. He'd worked with Olivia; before any of them moved to the BAU. "It's been my experience that people don't trust what they don't understand."

"What's there to understand? She took down Smythe for Christ's sake. Hell, she's got bigger balls than half of this building."

"That include you?" Patrick asked.

Silas shifted again. "If you have something to say, say it now." His tone was vaguely insubordinate. He and Patrick had history. Patrick might be Silas's superior now, but they had been friends first and worked together as equals before Patrick's promotion to SSA and then chief of the BAU. He had a few years on Silas since he hadn't stopped first to go to law school.

"Let me be frank about your *suggestion*." Monahan used the term loosely because he felt it was more than that. Remaining in San Antonio as a full-time liaison for the Smythe case had been Silas's suggestion. Beyond this room, the idea was getting a lot of traction in light of the state of affairs of the San Antonio field office, but Silas had no way of knowing that at the time he floated the idea. "The move is doable. The Bureau is agreeable, given the circumstances. However, I feel compelled to add, it's my opinion that the move may have unforeseen consequences for you career-wise," Patrick advised.

"Is that your opinion as my boss or otherwise?" Silas asked, still on the argumentative side. He was might be back in Virginia, but being back home didn't bring its usual comfort. He was restless, distracted. Not being with Livie was harder than he expected. He'd turned down numerous requests to go out on the town last night and satiate that restlessness any number of ways. Instead, after dinner with Patrick and his wife Melinda, Silas had gone home to prowl the empty rooms of his bachelor pad, looking for what could only be found fifteen hundred miles away.

"Since you brought it up, is this request even intended to bolster your career? Or is this more about your personal life?" Patrick watched as Silas shifted in his chair again, a clear sign of discomfort. Not a normal state of affairs for Silas Branch. Patrick leaned forward and lowered his voice even though they were the only ones in the room, a ploy designed to inspire confession. "What's going on? Tell me the real reason you're asking to leave. It's an abrupt change in your career plans. It looks to me this request has more to do with Olivia Osborne than it does with your attempt to take my slot at the BAU." The immediate change in Silas's expression at the mention of her name signaled Patrick he was on point. This was serious and Silas Branch never got serious when it came to women. "Talk to me as your friend, not your boss," Patrick pushed.

Silas put the implications of the job aside and finally saw the man across the desk as his friend and drinking buddy before he met Melinda. It seemed like everyone he knew had paired up and settled down. "It's not about the case. Or the job. Spending time with Livie made me realize I've been missing out. Maybe I need to put down some roots. For the first time in my life I actually want to."

Patrick leaned back and absorbed the words. What had the lovely doctor done to him? Patrick was pretty sure it had started with a case Silas and Olivia worked in Florida. After that Silas had been angling for a way to get to San Antonio. Six weeks later came the call for assistance from SAPD. The request might have come through the usual channels, but the invitation had Olivia written all over it. All the pieces fell into place whether it was a coordinated effort or not. Maybe they had both been trying to get to each other. Patrick, on the other hand, had just never seen it coming.

"I hear you," Patrick conceded. "And I'm glad. It's about time, don't you think?"

Silas grinned but didn't comment. "So, when?"

"You're absolutely sure you don't want to think about it?" The question got him no response. Patrick wasn't sure corralling Silas Branch was possible, but this was the closest thing he'd seen. "Ok, since you're so eager, there's someone else you need to talk to first."

Silas didn't understand. "Like an interview?" He seemed put off by the suggestion. He was asking for a transfer not a promotion. He was thinking special assignment, lateral move, whatever they wanted to call it.

"Not exactly. Call it a condition. This is about Atascosa County."

*　*　*

Will Ibarra had always been an overachiever. His youthful appearance and a Master's degree in education paired with his criminal justice degree had served him well during his stint as an instructor at the police Academy. As he hit his early thirties though, he no longer felt so young and he feared his career was slipping away. He was lucky to escape the classroom and land at a substation in northeast San Antonio. After only a few months, his procedure for cruising McAllister Park looking for a missing victim's car got him noticed. It helped that the case was the one involving the *Good Samaritan Killer*. The only downside was he was winging it. The one responsible for his sudden rise, his new lieutenant, Barry Bartholomew, was nowhere to be found, and his new captain had tagged him to liaise with the fire marshal all on his own. Will appreciated the support, he just didn't want to screw it up.

The charred spot in the field marking the final resting place of Ferdinand Roche was still visible. It probably would be for some time. At least until it started raining again and the green began to spread. It was lucky the winds hadn't carried the fire to the nearby fields.

"Have you ever seen anything like this?" Will asked.

"Burned bodies? Yes. Car accident, house fires are the most common. But there's nothing normal about this one. At least we know he didn't do it to himself and the perp didn't do it to cover up a crime," Ruben Cruz told him. He was the fire investigator sent over from the Bexar County Fire Marshal's office. He was giving the SAPD officer a tour of the scene as a courtesy between his boss and Ibarra's.

"Any reason you know of why someone would pick this particular spot?" Will wanted to know, trying to get a feel for the place.

"Convenience," Cruz grinned.

Will looked around. For a city boy this looked like the middle of nowhere to him. He'd passed a house on his way in and there was a barn a couple of hundred yards to their right. Other than that, he and Cruz could have been the last two people on earth.

"Maybe I should have said opportunity. The owner of this place is a crabby old widower named Abram Sampson. He was unaware of the fire because he likes spending his time at the VFW more than anywhere else and he isn't always sober when he rolls back to the house once the VFW kicks him out."

Will got what Cruz was trying to say. "So, whoever did this was a planner and didn't mind the locale. Probably made things easier," Will said, thinking out loud. He squinted up the road but couldn't see a house he knew was there. "The closest neighbor is miles away. The spot's remote and the owner has a predictable schedule with a sizable drinking habit. A squatter's paradise," Will surmised.

Will turned back to the reason he was out here – the charred spot on the ground. Exsanguination was the official cause of death listed on Ferdinand Roche's death certificate. It came as a result of an ear to ear cut severing the carotid and jugular. "You'd think slitting the guy's throat would have been enough."

"Can't say I haven't thought the same thing," Ruben Cruz agreed as he watched the SAPD sergeant circle the burnt ground for the third time. Typically, the most difficult part of Cruz's investigation was establishing cause of death *prior* to burning. In this case he already had the M.E.'s report. "I don't think I've ever investigated a body that's already been to the morgue. Probably why the state fire marshal's office wasn't in a hurry to investigate. Desecration of a corpse doesn't really rise to the same level as murder. Still pretty fucked up though." *Whatever.* Cruz just did what he was told. Today, apparently it involved ushering around one of SAPD's finest.

"Curious, huh?" Will asked, surveying the ground. "How long would it take to burn a body?"

"In conditions like this - hours. It takes a sustained heat of at least twelve hundred degrees to dehydrate the skin and muscle. Bones burn last. And teeth – that's how the medical examiner made the ID. The marrow shrinks and eventually the bone shatters. The skull wasn't intact either. Which means the brain turned to liquid, began to boil, and the skull broke apart. Basically, all that happened to this guy."

"So, considering what you told me earlier, if burning this body took hours, this was as good a place as any to do it."

"Yep."

"Do you know what kind of accelerant was used?" Will asked, always looking to learn something new, but really trying to think of something other than exploding brains.

"Fires burn from a point of origin upward and outward. If a liquid accelerant is used it flows downward due to gravity. The fire doesn't consume all of the accelerant, which enables forensics to trace the fire to its point or points of origin. Just follow the trail, dig down and collect samples. In a case like this, body fat is the best source of accelerant, all the grease," Cruz explained, "but this guy was in pretty good shape so there wasn't much of that. He was missing most of his major organs from the post mortem, so that probably helped, but there was a chemical residue found in the soil as well. Mineral spirts. It's probably what they doused him with to the get the party started. Rags soaked in mineral spirits, acetone even, are highly combustible when they come in contact with a heat source. I'd say whoever did this was comfortable with these chemicals."

"Interesting. You would think out here on the land it would be gasoline or some other handy fuel," Will theorized.

"You've done some homework," Cruz said.

"I taught at the police academy for a few years. I know a little about a lot," Will smiled and made another pass around the body.

"I heard it was some ritualistic thing. How'd you manage to pull this duty?" Cruz ventured. SAPD was kind of hush-hush about the whole investigation.

"New guy," Sergeant Ibarra said quickly and tried to ignore the inquiry. "Ritualistic how?" Will had read the report about the murder and the subsequent body snatching from the morgue, but hadn't talked to anyone actually involved except the captain. Roche's murder occurred while he was still working the substation. Listening to the locals or the other professional on scene might give him a different perspective.

Cruz shrugged. "Hey, I'm as green as you are on this one. It's not even my office's jurisdiction. The pissed off County DA called a Texas Ranger and somehow the Bexar County Fire Marshal's office got involved, and here I am."

This wasn't SAPD's jurisdiction either. All Will knew was SAPD's only contribution to the case, if you could even call it that, was Sergeant Mark Austin. Unfortunately, he ended up being one of Smythe's victims even before the body was burned. Maybe the Feds were the driving force behind the investigation? All he knew is he was a novice at interjurisdictional politics. "You must know some locals," Will prompted him. Even if this wasn't Cruz's jurisdiction, he cut his teeth out in the field while Will spent his time in a classroom or behind a desk. He felt like a rookie despite his years on the force. "What have you heard?"

"You mean *unofficially?*" Cruz grinned. "Well, the Rangers got everyone stirred up looking for drugs, but apparently some people around here thought this guy Roche was a witch. The initial murder scene was something involving a pitchfork. Then someone attempted to steal the corpse from the morgue. When that didn't work, they faked some paperwork and left with him in broad daylight. Word on the street is this guy was into some voodoo-hoodoo stuff," Cruz told him. "Maybe something sacrificial, ritualistic, who the fuck the knows?" Cruz made an attempt at whistling what Will thought was the theme to *The X-files*.

"Really?" Will asked.

Cruz held his hands up in surrender. "Hey, I'm just repeating what I heard," Cruz confessed. "You aren't the only one to wonder why someone went to all the trouble to dispose of the body. It was the Atascosa District Attorney that asked for help sorting all this out, not the sheriff. Apparently, the DA thinks the sheriff has something to hide or he can't do job. Maybe both. Maybe neither. Maybe the two of them are in some sort of pissing contest."

Will shook his head. "Sounds like a jurisdictional circle jerk to me."

"Could be the Feds," Cruz suggested. "I heard the FBI brought in their *special doctor.* I don't know who suggested it, but they want her to come out here and take a look around. If I was her, I'd start over there." Cruz wondered if he was going to have to escort her too.

Will followed the fire investigator's gaze back to the barn two hundred yards to the east. "What's in there?"

"Not a lot according to forensics, but someone was in there was doing some freaky shit. The Rangers went there looking for drugs. We were in there looking for mineral spirits."

"And?"

"We all came up with nothing but the heebie jeebies."

Will wanted to scoff but didn't. He liked the investigator. He'd heard about the doctor. It tracked with what Cruz said about her coming out here. He'd heard plenty more too, but he steered clear of that loop. He'd grown up with three sisters and if he'd learned anything, men were worse gossips than girls any day.

Will looked back at the scorched mark on the ground and tried to stay on track. "You know, when I first got here, I thought it was luck the rest of the field didn't burn, but it looks like there's almost a perfect circle where the fire was. Is that strange?"

The question earned him another grin. "Good eyes. We think whoever set the fire also used something to contain it."

"Wouldn't that be kind of weird for a fire bug? I thought they liked to watch things burn."

"Whoever did this isn't a fire bug," Cruz corrected him. "If that was the case it would make my job a whole lot easier. I know how to track those suckers. You're right, one of *them* would have just as soon watched the whole place go up." Cruz shook his head. "No, whoever did this had a purpose in mind. As previously established, it had nothing to do with covering up a murder. This Roche guy had already been to the morgue. This little bonfire only involved the body. From what we could determine, what you're looking at is a result of rock salt. It would contain the fire and leave behind the distinctive pattern. If it was poured in a circle."

"I still don't get it," Will wasn't ashamed to admit.

"According to lore," Cruz smiled, making air quotes around the words, "salt is used to create a protective circle," Cruz smiled.

Will drug a hand over his face. He was very familiar with lore. He had a *tia*, his mother's older sister, who was big on it. *Ojo*, the evil eye, the *Chupacabra* who sucked the blood of its victims and the *Cucy*, the old lady who came at night to snatch little kids who misbehaved. As the youngest and the only boy, he was well acquainted with tales of naughty children.

"I thought the whole point of a protection circle was to provide safety to whatever was *inside*. If the guy inside the circle was dead, what were they protecting?" Will asked.

"Maybe it's all in your perspective," Cruz theorized. "Maybe whoever drew the circle didn't want whatever was *inside* of it to get out."

The words hit Will like a cold slap in the face, but Cruz wiped it away with a grin. "If you believe in all that. If you still have questions, the FBI doc would be the one to ask. She's supposed to be some kind of expert on things that go bump in the night. She also happens to be the one who took down the *Good Samaritan Killer*." He gave Will a tip of his hat as he headed in an easterly direction.

Will decided he definitely needed to meet the FBI doc. She might be a profiler, but Cruz was right, she also had some knowledge of the occult. Word was she'd shaken up the local sheriff. SAPD was being as closed mouthed about her as they were everything else associated with this case. Until then Will decided he should probably do some research on witchcraft and ritualism. Captain Zavalla had instructed him to read the report, come out here, take a look around, and come back to him with questions. None of it involved an empty barn.

CHAPTER FIVE

DOMINIC WAS SITTING on her porch front steps waiting for her when Olivia pulled into the driveway. They had agreed on a late breakfast. Since her culinary skills were lacking, it gave her time to make a quick trip down the street to the bakery for sweet breads, a treat she'd developed a fondness for when staying at the hotel. Long ago she'd learned eating for one was easier when someone else did the cooking. Olivia had all but abandoned the cooking lessons Gran taught her. The only thing she kept from those days was Gran's herb garden in the back yard. Martin Mendoza, the contractor she'd hired to renovate her house, also had land-scaping skills. He'd cordoned off Gran's garden from the dogs, added a birdbath and transformed the little patch of land into a focal point of the yard.

"Let me look at you," Olivia said, inspecting Dominic's face carefully as she approached the porch. His encounter with Jamie Smythe had left him with a broken nose. "The swelling looks better," she commented gesturing for him to turn his face from side to side. His dark skin hid the bruising, but he still looked like he'd encountered a horde of angry bees and his voice was more nasal sounding than usual.

"Better, but not gone. You see why I preferred not to have you seen in public with me," Dominic said with a grin.

Olivia was glad he was back in her life. She'd gone months without seeing her friend but then they faced Jamie and the demon inside of him together. Dominic's quick thinking, driving his silver cross into Jamie's foot had given them the time they needed to retreat. Olivia believed he'd saved their lives. She was sorry they had ever let their friendship lapse.

Dominic followed her inside, his eyes straying to the mark on the floor as he passed. His cross had made that one as well. "I don't want to get rid of it," Olivia told him because she knew he wouldn't ask. For one clear moment she caught a glimpse of Dominic's thoughts. "It's a good reminder," she said, hoping to soothe the fear inside him.

"Of what?" Dom was curious.

"That this is *my* house." There was a hard edge to her tone. It sounded a lot like the conviction he heard in her voice the night they faced Smythe and the demon he brought with him. Dom allowed the FBI agent who interviewed him to believe he didn't remember. But Dom would never forget.

"Did you cleanse the house?" Dom asked. The fragrance was strong in the living room, a blend of both sweet and pungent.

"At least your nose still works," Olivia smiled. "I have a sage plant on the window sill from the garden. It was Gran's, passed from her grandmother and hers before her. I added frankincense."

A good frankincense smelled like honey mixed with the woods. It explained the combination of aromas. "Frankincense is said to carry prayers to heaven," Dom commented. "And still the mind."

"It helps," Olivia agreed. "There was a lot of playback left in here from that night. I needed to stop the loop." It was the mixture of energies she'd talked about with Jessica Tate, all of which added to the constant background noise in her head. It was exhausting deploying active measures to block it all out.

Dom recalled Olivia had once told him she wasn't sure she wanted to know where her gifts came from. He wondered if the appearance of the demon had piqued her interest. "There's an abundance of history within these walls." Dom wasn't a sensitive like she was, but he was starting to learn her history from the bishop. "Are you exploring it?"

"I pulled out some of my Gran's things," Olivia confessed.

It wasn't just her breakfast plans with Dom that had her up early. It was barely daylight when she trekked out to the shed in the back where Gran had done laundry since the 1960's. Before all the renovations she too had done the same, lugging her dirty clothes outside and across the yard. An inside laundry room had been as important to her as a new master bed and bath. The building had also been used as storage since the closets were so small, one of the pitfalls of a turn of the century house. The little building her grandfather built had now been largely repurposed to serve as an extremely large doghouse for Alvin and Daisy. Inside there was a whole section reserved for Gran's things. Olivia sat on the dusty floor and rifled through the plastic bins until she found a starting point. Each seal she broke greeted her with the scent of lavender, bringing back memories of Gran and filling her with wonder about the stories Gran didn't share.

"I found my mother's old yearbook. I thought it was a good place to start," Olivia confessed. "It's strange what I don't know about her." She almost felt like she was intruding, mainly because she felt like she was reading about a stranger. All the personal messages written in those pages were addressed to Lila. The name must have been her mother's preference. Olivia had long wondered if there was some meaning behind Gran's choice of Sarah for the name of her own daughter. Sarah Osborne figured prominently in the Salem Witch Trials. Considering their famous ancestor's demise, was the name choice a gift or a curse? Family names were important to Gran. The day she adopted Olivia she added a middle name, something her own mother had failed to do. *Esme.* Gran said it was her aunt's name and explained that Esme had left the family for a new life.

After breakfast she and Dom retreated to the back where she and Silas had shared their nightcap. Under the sway of the trees, Olivia watched a cardinal dip into the birdbath Martin had added to the herb garden. The cardinal symbolized a visit from a dead loved one. Olivia believed the visits were her ancestors, not all of them Gran, watching over her..

"I want you to know I'm going away for a little while." Dom had waited to tell her.

"Where?" Olivia asked. She hoped his departure wouldn't be permanent.

"I've been offered reinstatement," Dom announced, watching her carefully for a reaction.

The decision to leave the Church had been his. There were things priests did not do without explicit permission from the local diocese. Dominic broke one of those sacred rules and he'd dismissed himself and surrendered his flock. He would always be a priest, as ordination was a lifetime sacrament which, once done, could not be undone. Dominic chose abdication willingly, but Olivia knew his departure left him feeling hollow inside.

The Church didn't typically change its mind, but had been known to bend the rules now and then, especially if it was in the Church's own interest. While she knew Dom missed his priestly life, she was concerned. Church politics being what they were, Olivia knew his reinstatement undoubtedly came with terms and conditions. "I'm sure this is a special circumstance," Olivia said, her voice laced with caution.

"It is. I'll be in Rome for a few months."

Olivia didn't comment. Dom knew she was reserving her judgment. He'd have time to tell her the rest later.

* * *

Mason Deveroux was a New Orleans native who spent four years in the Coast Guard before joining the Bureau. Silas first encountered Deveroux when he spent some time in New Orleans during clean-up efforts post Katrina. They met in an office Silas assumed belonged to Deveroux. There was no mention of what precipitated the move from his hometown or what he was doing now. The two agents sat across from one another at a small conference table, one that didn't designate who was in charge. Silas suspected it was because the man across from him wanted something.

Deveroux flashed Silas a grin that was supposed to put him at ease, but didn't. "Ferdinand and Andre Roche. Those are names I haven't heard in a while." Deveroux had a thin folder in front of him, but Silas doubted he needed it. The other agent had an agenda in mind and the folder was just a prop.

"All this time I had hoped they were swept away with everything else Katrina took with her. About all I can say now is that it's too bad Ferdinand was the one to bite it. Has there been an arrest?"

Silas shook his head. "Not that I know of, but we got kind of busy down in San Antonio."

Deveroux nodded. "I heard. Hell of a case." The agent gave a respectful pause, but kept moving. "Ferdinand's brother should be your number one suspect. Andre was always the problem child. Ferdinand did the best he could, but some people are just bad seeds."

When Patrick had said there was a San Antonio connection Silas had naturally assumed it had to do with Smythe. Now it looked like it was the Roches. If that was the case Silas needed some background. "What were those guys into?" Silas asked.

"Ferdinand liked marijuana. Small-time charges only. Claimed it was for his mom's cancer, which was probably true. He never had enough on him to be considered a dealer. Andre, on the other hand, followed in mom's footsteps."

"Which were what exactly?" As Silas recalled, the mother was no longer in the picture.

"The occult. The darker the better. She had quite a reputation. She'd channel dead relatives, or put a hex on your enemy for the right price. She cast spells, mixed herbs, concocted potions."

Potions was an interesting word. It conjured visions of a spooky little shop on some narrow back alley street in New Orleans selling black caldrons and mysterious substances. "So, what caught the attention of the FBI exactly?" Whatever it was, it wasn't someone playing witch. The Atascosa County sheriff had alluded to drugs and now so had Deveroux. "If this is about drugs, the Texas Rangers are already looking into that," Silas explained. "The guy's name's Herschel Gaines. I can put you two in touch."

Deveroux shook his head no. "Not drugs. I think Andre probably dabbled. Wouldn't surprise me if he added some ecstasy to some of Mom's old recipes - for a hallucinogenic effect."

Silas waited for Deveroux to continue. Whatever the other agent wanted, he wasn't in a hurry to get there. "So, what do you need me for exactly?"

"I was curious how you ended up with the Roche thing."

Silas's eyes narrowed. He should have known when they were talking about potions and ritualism. Agents, if they stuck around long enough, earned a reputation over time. Working with Olivia, he knew he had his share. "The way Roche was killed suggested he might be a witch." Silas didn't mind being the go-to guy for the strange and unusual. That meant any request for Dr. Osborne's expertise would go through him first.

"Your connection with Dr. Osborne, I assume?"

Maybe they were finally getting somewhere. "You could say that."

"What did she have to say about the dead Mr. Roche? Did she think he was a witch?" Deveroux wanted to know.

Maybe that's what was in the blue folder. Silas had no doubt Deveroux already knew how Roche was killed so he didn't feel the need to discuss pitchforks and pentagrams. They still hadn't gotten to what Deveroux was after. Silas was starting to think he should have accepted his dad's offer to go golfing this morning instead of sitting here doing this.

"She thinks whoever did it knew their stuff." Silas told him. Andre was Deveroux's target, but Silas still didn't know why. "The murder wasn't enough. Someone stole the body from the morgue and set it on fire." Silas decided sharing recent events might get him somewhere. News of what happened to the body might not have made it in the blue folder yet.

Deveroux nodded, thinking obviously about something else.

"I was told you wanted to talk, but I feel like you already know everything I've told you. Why don't you tell me why I'm here? Or what your deal is with the Roches."

Deveroux pushed away the folder and leaned forward in his chair. "You ever have one of those cases you can't get out of your head? The one that got away?"

Silas was the one that nodded this time. All agents or cops had *the one*. The case they couldn't let go. The one they'd take to the grave with them. Silas was no different. Only for him, the killer didn't get away. He'd confessed and was currently sitting in a jail cell in Florida awaiting sentencing. It still kept Silas up at night because he knew it wasn't the end of the story.

"Back when I was in the New Orleans office, we were looking at Andre Roche in a string of missing girl cases." Now they were getting somewhere. "It was slow going because most of them were runaways. Eventually most were accounted for, but there were still a few unresolved. Andre Roche was at the top of our list, but the case basically went by the wayside when Katrina hit."

"Did you find any of the girls?" Silas wanted to know.

"Yeah. One was dead. Forensics thought she was probably held somewhere for months prior. There were signs of sexual abuse. She became pregnant sometime after she went missing, before she ended up dead."

Silas pondered what he'd just heard. He was glad Deveroux was sharing, but the timeline was twelve years old. What did it have to do with now? Before Silas could think of how to ask, Deveroux interrupted him.

"I thought Andre Roche got away. Now you show up and tell me he's alive. But more than that, you gave me something else. You gave me Ana Lutz."

The name stopped Silas cold. It came out of nowhere. This wasn't about the Roches. At least not all of it.

"How did Ana Lutz get on your radar?" Deveroux wanted to know.

Silas thought a better question was how did Ana Lutz get on Deveroux's radar? Was she really the reason they were having this conversation? "She's a Wiccan priestess in San Antonio. Due to the particulars of Ferdinand Roche's murder and implications of the occult, I thought she might be helpful."

Deveroux's eyes narrowed. Silas had seen the look. It usually meant the person was assessing the truthfulness of the information. "Did you put this together, or did Dr. Osborne?"

"I picked up a thing or two working with Dr. Osborne," Silas hedged. It was the second time Deveroux had brought up Olivia.

Deveroux nodded, still in appraisal mode. "So, what did you find?"

Silas shook his head. "Nothing. Never got the chance. All hell broke loose with Smythe."

"But you have a line on her? A way to get to her?"

Silas didn't answer. He waited him out instead.

Deveroux ran a hand through the greying buzz cut he'd kept since his Coast Guard days. "Ana Lutz is a hard woman to find. Pretty much off the grid these days. What made you think she would talk to you?"

"I think you know," Silas stonewalled. If this guy wanted to get to Olivia, Silas wasn't going to make it easy for him because he didn't like Deveroux's questions anymore more than the ones from OPR.

Deveroux appraised the BAU agent. He had been warned Agent Branch could be obstinate. Deveroux hadn't noticed before, but their encounter came early in Silas's career. Before the BAU, before Dr. Osborne. "What I need to know is if Ana Lutz is an associate of Dr. Osborne's?"

"An associate? I wouldn't call her that."

"Then what's their connection?"

"People who dabble in the occult, like Ms. Lutz, make it a point to know people like Dr. Osborne," Silas explained, his gaze on the other agent. "Maybe you could tell me why you want to talk to Ms. Lutz."

Deveroux considered the question, but not for long. "I'm currently working a task force for human trafficking. Sex workers. During the course of that investigation I stumbled across a girl I'd once attributed to Roche."

Not an answer, but Silas knew Deveroux would get there. "Alive or dead?"

"Alive. Working in Vegas at a place called *Delilah's Den*. It's just the type of place runaways might end up. High-end strip club, probably some prostitution. I think it caters to clients with special tastes, if you know what I mean. This place has been under surveillance for sex and human trafficking for a while now, but we've come up empty so far. The owner is savvy and she apparently inspires loyalty not just with her patrons but her employees as well."

Silas pinched the bridge of his nose. It was a disturbing story. He didn't want to hear any more of it. "I need you to tell me what this has to with Dr. Osborne."

Deveroux knew he'd strung Silas Branch along as far as he could. The 1980's satanic scare might have been debunked, but there still a healthy interest in the occult. Enter Dr. Osborne. Some said she was gifted, but she was also educated. She gave the paranormal world legitimacy. She had a unique skill set valuable to the FBI, but she and the Bureau had a dysfunctional relationship. There were trust issues on both sides. What Deveroux wanted to know is if that included Agent Branch. "The place where we found the girl is owned by a woman Ana Lutz used to work for. Her name is Sarah Larsin, Olivia Osborne's mother."

* * *

First impressions were important. The detainee occupying the bed in room number seven of the Bexar County Jail Infirmary looked more like an adolescent boy than a monster who had allegedly murdered six people. According to Jamie Lynne Smythe's file, he was twenty-five years old but he could easily pass for a teenager. Brennon Kaine wasn't sure if it was Smythe's small stature or his shaved head that gave him the adolescent appearance, but the seasoned attorney knew if he was taken off guard by Smythe's persona, a jury would feel the same way. The wholesome, wide-eyed boyish look was definitely a plus.

"Mr. Smythe, do you mind if I call you Jamie?" He shook his head, giving Brennon the green light. "Jamie, do you know why I'm here?"

"You came to talk to me about those women and Travis." Smythe said. Travis Ames had been the accused killer's alleged fourth victim. Travis and Jamie had worked together. After an afternoon with Smythe, Travis was found dead in his shower with his penis shoved in his mouth.

Brennon waited for Smythe to add Mark Austin's name to the list, but he didn't. "That's right. I'm here to help you."

"I don't have any money," Jamie told him. "My aunts died and it's just me now."

Brennon knew from the available background Smythe had no living relatives. Not much in the way of friends either. The only one Brennon had been able to confirm was the unfortunate Travis Ames. There was no one to speak for this kid. "I'm not going to ask you for any money, Jamie. I'm willing to take your case *pro bono*. Do you know what that means?"

"Yeah. It means free. The other two guys told me the same thing when they came."

Brennon nodded. "That's right."

Jamie mimicked Brennon's nod. "I think I'd like that. Free sounds good."

Brennon reached for his briefcase wondering, not for the first time why he was here. He didn't understand why Smythe had turned down two previous offers. Caught in the sound of the briefcase zipper Brennon thought he heard the murmur of a whisper. He reached inside for the paperwork he'd filled out before ever leaving Long Island. Papers in hand he looked across at the boy. Dull, almost lifeless eyes locked on Brennon. A wave of vertigo washed over him as he stared back at bottomless eyes.

"Did I drift again?" It was Jamie's voice, calling him back. "Sometimes I do that. The nurses said maybe it's my medication."

Brennon wanted to shake his head, but he was waiting for the room to right itself. He forced a smile instead and heard himself speak. "They're probably right." He didn't feel as reassured as he sounded. Before entering the boy's room, he'd specifically asked when Smythe had been medicated last, but couldn't remember the answer.

"Do I need to sign something?"

Brennon hesitated and rubbed his jaw. He still looked 'classically handsome' according to a few journalists who had interviewed him over the course of his twenty-five-year career in criminal defense. Kane's first decade out of law school he spent in the district attorney's office of Suffolk County on Long Island before flipping sides. That's when his real career began. Maybe he didn't need this case. He still had a good five years before the retirement he'd promised his kids he'd start once he turned sixty. He'd become a father late in life. He'd been absent for most of their formative years, too busy making a name for himself. Then his wife passed away suddenly, never to see fifty. He couldn't blame them for wanting him to slow down. He could afford to retire now, but where was the fun in that? He just wanted one last good case. This could be the one. It could be book worthy. A good career ender.

Brennon watched as he lay the stack of papers next to Jamie. "I'll just leave these here. You should read over them." Brennon rose to go, but wasn't moving as fast as he wanted. His back was stiff from sitting in the chair too long. Turning away from the boy he felt better already.

"I only did three of them," Jamie said. He sounded meek, almost apologetic.

The confession slowed Brennon's trek to the door. "I don't need to know any of that," Brennon said quickly, hoping to shut him down.

"When you didn't come, I had to call. It was my one and only."

Brennon had been out of the country when the story broke. He was taking more and more vacations these days. He thought he'd missed his chance, but here he was. The attorney in him was already thinking of Jamie Lynn Smythe as *his* defendant.

"I know why I did what I did. I was waiting for you. It's why I said no to the other two." The confession was the answer to the question the attorney had never asked.

Brennon's hand wavered as he reached for the door handle. It was the boy's voice, but not the boy? Something was different. It didn't make sense. The nuance of the words had changed.

"I am sorry this has all been about me. What about you? Did you really come here to see the me or was it for someone else?"

Brennon stopped. His hand fell back to his side.

"You know her, don't you?"

Brennon remained rooted in place, still facing the door.

"I've asked to see her, but she won't come. Perhaps you can persuade her to accept my invitation." The pretense parted with those final words. Meekness gave way to something that hovered on ominous. Malevolent even.

"She? Who?" This time it was Brennon's voice that didn't sound like his own. Fear flowed through his veins.

"Dr. Osborne, of course."

Olivia had mentioned Jamie asked to see her, but how did he make the connection? How did the boy know of their past? The Internet was forbidden, so he didn't have access to Google in his current residence.

"Forgive me. Dr. Osborne is so formal. I bet you called her Liv, or Livie, am I right?"

The hair on Brennon's neck rose. The voice no longer sounded like the boy. It took on a deeper, older tone. "She was so much more than you expected, was she not? So different in private. You enjoyed her. In your house, on your boat, even in your car. She especially liked the boat. The water calms her, you know. It makes her feel peaceful. Ironic really since so many of her ancestors were drowned. Trial by ordeal it was called - *Judicium Dei*. Judgement of God. Such rituals must seem archaic by your standards."

Brennon concentrated on slow shallow breaths. He wanted to swallow, but couldn't. He reached for the door handle, clinging to it like an escape hatch.

"The age difference is particularly tantalizing, wouldn't you agree? There is something special about a younger woman. So firm and tight in all the right places. The ones you've had since her just can't compare. Can they?"

Brennon finally found his voice, the words coming on in a rush "Mr. Smythe, I believe our business is concluded for the day. You should probably get some rest now." Brennon felt a strange compulsion to look over his shoulder and back into those bottomless eyes. Brennon fixated on his hand instead, his knuckles blanched white from gripping the door handle.

"There is no rest for the wicked, Counselor. But no matter, you will be back. The boy will sign the precious papers. They are his 'get out of jail free' card. You can stay here, with him. With Livie. But if you want her for yourself, you had better hurry before the agent returns."

The guard waiting outside watched as the lawyer nearly stumbled out of the room but caught himself on the nearby wall. He also noticed he was sweating in his expensive suit, the one that probably cost more than his car. He'd heard the kid sometimes had that effect on people. Word on the ward was not to look him in the eyes for too long. The guard didn't know if he believed it or not, but he didn't like to take chances so he avoided eye contact altogether.

Brennon needed directions to find his way back to the nurse's station even though there was only one hall. The trek seemed to take longer than it should. He leaned against the counter once he finally got there waiting for his balance to return. "Has the boy in seven been evaluated by a psychiatrist yet?" He asked anyone who was listening.

A tall woman with dark red hair stepped forward. "I'm the nurse manager and you know I can't answer that question without paperwork identifying you as his legal representative. Do you have that paperwork?"

Brennon sighed. She was right, but he didn't care. "Is he on any antipsychotics?"

"Same answer, Mr. Kaine," the nurse told him.

Next to her the patient call bell system pinged. Brennon knew who was calling even if he couldn't see the monitor. The nurse manager picked up the handset to answer instead of using the intercom. She wanted to make sure the attorney couldn't hear what the patient had to say. She grabbed the receiver and listened. She hung up and looked back at him.

"Congratulations, Counselor. Looks like you've got yourself a client. Mr. Smythe says you forgot your paperwork."

CHAPTER SIX

CRUZ PULLED THE door open and Will half expected it to come off the hinges. The building had definitely seen better days. From the outside, the structure looked like it was on its knees. It wasn't one of those metal Quonset hut prefabricated jobs, but a non-descript wooden structure bleached by the sun. Will wondered if the place had ever been painted. The roof was slanted and from the inside he could see this would definitely not be the place to seek shelter during the rain. There was debris strewn around. Some rusty looking gardening tools, some long-forgotten fencing material, and a collection of what looked like old gas lanterns.

Straight ahead of them the roof sloped downward leading to another part of the building that might have once housed a couple of stalls for keeping animals. Will thought he caught a whiff of something grassy, like hay. Directly ahead of them was one of those sliding farm doors so popular on the home fixer-upper show his ex-girlfriend used to make him watch, only this one was an original. The door was partially open. Stepping through it set off a whole other vibe.

A wave of a different odor hit Will as he moved into the new space. It wiped out all thoughts of grass and replaced it with images of the silver bauble suspended by chains the priest waved during special ceremonies filling the church with a citrusy smell, but here it was something else. The aroma was woodsy with a hint of cinnamon or vanilla. Directly ahead was a platform, elevated a few feet off the ground.

Black candles burnt down to nubs were melted into the ground in a circle on the floor surrounding the platform. There were candle remnants on the platform itself, having been trampled by some kind of impromptu move out. Looking up Will saw what looked like old metal coat hangers straightened and hooked on either end. One end secured the wire from above. The other end curved around to hold a candle. It made him think of the dining hall at Hogwarts. He'd watched all those movies one too many times with his nephews. In the dark it probably gave the illusion the candles were floating. Probably looked creepy as hell in here when they were lit. Maybe that was the point. On the back wall beyond the platform was a symbol burned into the wood like a brand. ☥ It looked like it could have been made with a blow torch by someone with a steady hand.

"What do you make of that?" Cruz asked, watching Will study the symbol. The police sergeant walked closer to get a better look, but intentionally avoided stepping on the platform. "Looks like some kind of cross with a loop at the bottom to me," Cruz offered.

"Definitely not a cross." Will shook his head trying to clear himself of the vibe. "The loop should be at the top. It's called an *ankh*. I've just never seen one turned upside down before."

Cruz seemed surprised by the answer. "An ankh? How'd you know that?"

"Saw it in a movie once."

"Really?" The fire inspector seemed intrigued. "Which one?"

"*Logan's Run.*" Will spent many a Saturday afternoon of his youth gorging on sci-fi television.

"What does it mean, you think?"

In a movie where no one lived past thirty, it had something to do with the key to life. The ankh was the key to another world. This place, however, was about as far removed from some futuristic drama as one could get. "No idea," Will answered, his voice hushed. He wasn't sure why. Being here he felt the presence of something inanimate with an undercurrent of menace. It was not a world he would want to visit. He resisted the urge to dart back outside to the open field.

From behind them came the creak of the door. "Hey, who's in here?"

Will and Ruben Cruz stepped back through the sliding door leading back to the main part of the barn. It was obvious from the man's khaki and brown uniform he was with the sheriff's department. Atascosa County was stitched across the left breast pocket of his shirt, his eyes hidden by reflector shades. The shiny name tag pinned to his shirt said Eddie Calderon. He didn't offer a handshake.

"Mr. Sampson say y'all could be in here?"

Ruben Cruz smiled, but it wasn't like the ones he'd given Will Ibarra. "Warrant's right here in my pocket." In his defense there was a tri-folded piece of paper sticking out of it.

Calderon pushed his shades up. "It specifically covers the barn?"

"You a lawyer or a deputy?" Cruz asked.

Calderon looked like he wanted to spar some more, but Will put his hands on his hips highlighting the SAPD badge and gun he wore. Calderon's eyes flicked across the display and pushed his shades back down. "Sampson is kind of particular about who comes on his land."

"Seemed alright to me," Cruz challenged him.

"Well, he's also a trusting old man."

Will and Cruz watched the deputy go out the way he came. "I don't know about you, but I'm not so sure he was here about Sampson." Will turned back to look at the empty space the candles flanked. "How much land does he own anyway?"

Cruz shook his head. "No idea."

"That thing doesn't tell you?" Will asked inclining his head toward Cruz's pocket.

"Not likely. It's a menu to my favorite Chinese place. They deliver now. Best news I've had all day."

* * *

"Since you've never talked to Ms. Ana Lutz, let me introduce you," Deveroux offered. "Born Anabelle Swafford in San Diego, she was listed as a runaway at sixteen. Not much of a life before that. Her mother worked carnivals and Ana was always one step away from foster care. She made her way from San Diego to Las Vegas. Not long after that she earned herself a couple arrests for solicitation. Apparently, she didn't know anyone to bail her out so she sat out her time. The next time she gets popped someone named Bobby DuPree comes to the rescue."

Mentally, Silas was taking notes. Now that Deveroux had finally started talking he didn't want to interrupt him. So far, he had copied that Ana must have had a pretty shitty life. She fled hundreds of miles to get away and didn't call for help when she got in trouble. Maybe because she knew there was none. Two times in and she knew enough to get herself a pimp.

"DuPree's got a record. He had a small-time ring of girls for a while. He was known to get violent, didn't mind knocking his girls around. Fast forward six more months and Ana gets picked up again. This time Sarah Larsin is the one who pays. About the same time DuPree drops off the radar. A few months later, his body is found in the desert missing his head. No one ever found it. After that Ana spends several years in Vegas in the employment of Ms. Larsin."

"This is verifiable?" Silas asked.

"Ms. Larsin is legit. She's a business woman, trading in flesh. No more arrests for Ana. Years later Anabelle Swafford, now Ana Lutz shows up in New Orleans with a bachelor's degree in social work. Ends up in San Antonio circa late 2005, after Hurricane Katrina. Interestingly, the same time as the Roche brothers."

A lot of time and real estate in between Sarah Larsin, Ana Lutz, Andre Roche yet all roads led to San Antonio. Silas didn't believe in coincidences. He didn't know of anyone in his business who did. "So, what are you thinking?" He asked Deveroux.

"I'm thinking Ana traded one kind of a pimp for another. Ana had a bad life until she didn't and she owes the person who gave her a new one."

* * *

Steeped in Deveroux's Ana Lutz read-out, Silas was on his way back to his own office when Patrick beckoned him inside his, almost as if he had been watching for him.

"What did you think of what Agent Deveroux had to say?" Patrick asked, motioning for Silas to close the door behind him.

Silas shrugged and took a seat. He didn't know what to think. He hadn't had time to process.

"Look. Deveroux's drowning in a world full of sex and underaged girls. It was the Roche case that pushed him to the task force. Same kind of victims. The people he's chasing are ghosts and what do you do? You resurrect one of them and cross paths with a name that links up to his task force. It's too much for him to ignore."

Silas didn't look convinced. "What makes Deveroux think Ana's still in touch with Sarah Larsin?" Silas didn't know if he wasn't connecting the dots because he didn't want to or because they weren't there.

"People like Larsin don't give anything away for free. There's lots of access to wayward girls in social work, especially working for Health and Human Services in Bexar County," Patrick told him. He and Deveroux had obviously talked.

"It's thin," Silas said.

"That's what burn-out looks like. What did Deveroux say?"

"The devil is in the details."

"So, do you think you can do as Deveroux asks?" Patrick was back to business.

"Make contact with Ana Lutz. Leave Livie out of it? I don't like it. She does better when we give her the full scope of information we have available."

"It could be in Olivia's best interest."

"Olivia hasn't had contact with her mother since she dumped her off when she was four and drove away," Silas protested.

"Then don't dredge up the past. Sarah Larsin could be part of something larger or this whole thing could be a bust."

"I can't help Deveroux if I'm not in San Antonio," Silas reminded him. "By the way, Bexar is pronounced *Bear* like the animal," Silas corrected him. "The x is silent."

Patrick nodded, trying to conceal a smile. Where was his friend and what had Olivia Osborne done with him? Patrick met Olivia when she was with the FBI. She wasn't like other female agents. She didn't show up feeling like she had something to prove. She didn't portray herself as tough as nails or, worse yet, a ball buster. She carried herself with poise. Some attributed it to the credentials at the end of her name, but for those who took the time to get to know her, they learned the confidence came from within. Working with her, Patrick had learned to trust her instincts. Hocus pocus or not he was a believer of the claircognizant thing—the *gift of knowing*. He'd seen it in action. She must also have a gift of enchantment to cast this kind of spell over Silas Branch.

"Since it sounds like you miss it down there. I guess now is as good a time as any to tell you your request to go to San Antonio has officially been approved."

Silas sat up in the chair, feeling energized for the first time that morning. "Was it really dependent on Deveroux?"

"Deveroux was a bonus. But the move does come with conditions." Patrick reminded him. "You might want to hear those before you agree."

"What? Do you think I'm going to change my mind?" Silas asked.

"That might depend on Olivia." Patrick really hoped Silas knew what he was doing.

There was a soft knock at the door. Patrick looked irritated by the interruption. He was just getting to the good part.

"Excuse me, Agent Branch?" Patrick's admin clerk sheepishly interrupted. "You have an emergency call."

* * *

He'd been running every day. It helped him think. He needed it. Today Barry Bartholomew was vaguely aware he was taking another route. Across the highway and down busy Broadway until commercial storefronts gave way to picturesque houses under umbrellas of trees. It was only a little over two miles – one way. He would stop on his way back and grab lunch somewhere down the main thoroughfare.

Barry pulled his cap down and tried not to look up as he ran past her house. Just his luck there was activity. One man was leaving. Even though he wasn't wearing a collar, Barry pegged him for her priest friend, Father Dominic. Olivia was standing on the porch waiting for a handsome man in an expensive suit to join her. He was driving a high-end rental car and carrying a leather briefcase. If he wasn't mistaken the man was Brennon Kaine, high-profile attorney for dirtbags with a penchant for killing. If he was meeting with Olivia, then he must be the one taking the case. Their killer would have the best defense money could buy. Except it would be free. After the OJ trial some said the color of justice was green. For Jamie Lynn Smythe it would be red—the blood of his six victims. It didn't seem right after all the lives he'd destroyed. Although Barry didn't believe the life Brennon Kaine hoped to save would be worth living. The kid wouldn't do hard time, Barry was almost sure of it. Smythe would go to a place with padded rooms and lots of drugs. The only consolation was at least he wouldn't go free.

There was no sign of Agent Branch. Was it too much to hope that was a permanent thing? Barry could have the answer to that question and more if he would return phone calls or read emails. He knew his brothers in blue were worried about him, but he didn't want to discuss with them or anyone else that he was questioning every career decision he'd ever made. His introspection didn't stop there. He was questioning his life choices as well. Mainly why he'd let Olivia walk right out his door.

* * *

Brennon didn't ask if he could come over, he just said he was. Something was wrong. Olivia wasn't entirely surprised considering he was supposed to see Jamie today.

"Are you sure about this?" She asked, watching him log into his computer.

"I acknowledge that I am aware you are the person who shot my client. I am also aware that I am asking you to look at his medical records, but as his legal representative, it is my right." Brennon turned his laptop her way. "We both want the same thing. Right now, I have no one else to turn to. More than that, there is no one else I can trust. Not with this."

Olivia nodded. It was good enough for her. As Jamie's attorney, Brennon was right, it was his call. With his permission she focused her attention on the MAR, the medication administration record. It was a list of all medications prescribed to the patient, the dosage, and directions for usage. Lucky for Brennon she had a varied skill set. Her nursing degree and training still paid dividends.

"I don't see any antipsychotics prescribed," Olivia announced. Brennon was seeking an explanation she couldn't give him. He might not be a man of science, but he did ascribe to logic. "I warned you there were other influences at work," Olivia said gently. He was shaken by his visit with Jamie. She had known there would be a manifestation of some kind. She just hadn't known how it would show itself. Jamie was merely a vessel and while the man might be locked away, the monster was free to come and go.

"I had to see him for myself." Brennon was pacing her office in circles. "I was too full of chutzpah for my own good. I mistakenly thought because of the other case that I knew what I was dealing with."

Olivia had suspected as much, but never would have said it. Mainly because she knew Brennon Kaine. Once he set his sights on something, he was going for it. She had been one of those things. "What we saw in Washington was an energy your defendant got caught up in."

"He spoke in a different voice. He said things, that...." Brennon looked at her and stopped talking because he couldn't tell her what the thing inside Jamie had said.

"Was it true?" She asked, watching carefully for a reaction.

"Yes," Brennon admitted. He knew he couldn't lie to her. She could spot it, even if she didn't know him. Uncovering lies wrapped in truth was what they both did for a living.

"He'll twist it for his own pleasure," Olivia warned.

"It's like he could read my mind," Brennon confessed. "He said things that only you and I would know."

"Then it wasn't Jamie."

CHAPTER SEVEN

BARRY STEPPED OFF the elevator to find a woman sitting in the floor leaning against the door of his condo. She held up a finger signaling him to wait. "I'm going to have to call you back," she said and plucked the Bluetooth earbud out as she rose to greet him.

Barry ignored the gesture and slipped past her with indifference. He didn't know her. He would have remembered. She might have been his type not so long ago, classic beauty with olive skin and smoky eyes that danced with either excitement, annoyance, or crazy. It was hard to tell.

"Lieutenant Bartholomew, I'm Doctor Amanda Greene." Out of his peripheral vision he saw her stick her hand out, but he ignored it just like the greeting.

Barry turned around to close the door to his space when she snuck her foot inside the doorway. He gave an unpleasant grunt when he realized she had foiled his getaway.

"Do you know who I am?" Maybe she shouldn't have included her title with the introduction.

Barry had never seen her before, but her name corresponded to the multiple voicemails he'd deleted.

"I'm aware of who you are, Doctor," Barry tried pacifying her. He stopped directly in front of her, effectively blocking her entrance as well as invading her personal space. She would have to go through him to get inside.

Amanda Greene didn't back away. Instead, she appeared to be calculating the odds of how she could slip past him, but so was he. Barry guessed her to be all of five feet tall, maybe a hundred and ten pounds, but she looked pretty feisty. He'd have to give her an *A* for effort if she tried, but he really hoped she didn't. He was tired and really trying not to be irritable.

On the way back from Olivia's he'd rewarded himself with a stop off at the diner occupying the old filling station. He sat outside and watched the locals. It was strange to be among them in the middle of the week, with nothing to do. No bad guys to catch. He even pretended to enjoy the scenery. It lasted as long as it took him to finish his burger and fries.

"Then you know I've been retained by SAPD to see you for grief counseling."

"I already talked to the other guy. Thanks."

Steve Winn. Yep, that was the problem. "Listen, Lieutenant," Amanda said, angling her foot far enough across his threshold that he would have to take out her ankle if he decided to escape. "Please don't make this any harder than it has to be. You've got a sterling reputation among your fellow officers and a healthy, robust career. As for me, I've got a big enough case load as it is. Don't make me deal with anymore bullshit." Her brown eyes were pleading. If it was all an act, it was a pretty good one.

Barry leaned on the door frame and peered down at her. "Look, I did my part. It's not my fault the doctor assigned to me went off on his own crazy train. It must suck for you that you're the one who got sent out here to clean up the mess. But I'm good, thanks."

Amanda pulled off the biggest smile she could muster on an empty stomach. Her venti coffee and bagel had evaporated hours ago. She'd conned her way into the building only to find the lieutenant wasn't home. She set up camp outside his door and missed a lunch date because she didn't know if she'd get another chance. His captain had insisted on a visit and her boss had been accommodating. "Call it a welfare check so I can cross you off my list."

"No more phone calls?" Barry asked, giving her a hard stare.

"You don't answer them anyway."

He relented. Her fiery attitude won him over and the greasy burger he'd eaten for lunch had slowed his momentum. All the rest of the way home he'd contemplated a beer and a nap. And not necessarily in that order. Barry didn't say anything, just walked away and let her catch the door for herself. He'd speak to the doorman downstairs later.

Barry moved through the living room, opened the sliding glass door and escaped to his new favorite spot on the balcony. Dr. Greene trailed along behind him. Surprised, she'd won him over. Maybe not all the way, but at least they wouldn't be continuing their conversation in the hallway. "Nice place," Amanda said as she strolled through the living room.

The place was neat, decorated, and even clean. Not what she'd expected from a cop on leave due to his best friend's death. While he didn't have anything official in his file, he was also a cop who more than one person had said liked to drink. On initial inspection it didn't look like he was drowning himself in a bottle. At least not yet.

The lieutenant was dressed for a run. He might look a little scruffy, with a couple of day's hair growth on his chin, but all in all he looked good. Amanda had to check herself because she knew that was not a professional observation. She let her briefcase slide off her shoulder and land on one of the couches. She switched her phone to vibrate and tossed it on top. Relieved from the burden of the extra weight, she followed the lieutenant outside without being asked. He hadn't invited her, but he hadn't kicked her out either.

"Thinking of jumping?" Amanda asked as she joined him at the railing. The view straight ahead was full of trees. Directly below was the front parking lot of the building. A long way down.

"You don't have much of a bedside manner, do you?"

Amanda gave him a shrug. He had a preordained time limit for this conversation she was sure. "You prefer I beat around the bush?"

"No, actually, I don't." Barry took another look at her. He hadn't scared her off yet. She must be used to cops. "Maybe I just like the view." Not long ago he remembered saying how much he wanted to sit out here and enjoy it. This was not what he'd envisioned. There had been stars in the sky and Olivia.

Amanda nodded. Fair enough.

"For a cop," Barry said.

"What?" Amanda asked.

"You said, *nice place.* For a cop. I believe that's what you meant," Barry told her. Olivia would have said it too, if he'd given her a chance.

The lieutenant was pushing some buttons. Maybe she should go with it. "Ok, maybe not for a cop, but certainly for a man in your situation, yes," Amanda admitted.

"My situation? What does that mean?"

"For someone who's left his job and is basically checking out of his life—I expected messier."

* * *

Looking at his father was like looking into a future mirror of himself. Silas was his father's son, no doubt about it. Raymond Ellis Branch was an imposing figure, always had been. Gregarious was the word most often used to describe the retired Air Force colonel. At six foot four with a barrel chest, a head full of silver hair, and piercing blue eyes he commanded any room he walked into. But the man occupying the hospital bed before him was a stranger. Gone was the strong invincible character he had both feared and respected his whole life. Now, all Silas saw was man who couldn't breathe on his own.

"Your father suffered a major heart attack. We cleared the blockage but there is a very real possibility of some interruption of blood flow to the brain."

Interruption of blood flow? Silas repeated the doctor's words in his head, feeling like he was tangled in a dream. None of it seemed real.

"Right now, I want to get him through the next twenty-four hours."

The words stuck this time. They involved a timeline. Silas nodded, absorbing. "My brother is in England. He should come home for this." It wasn't a question. Silas knew medical personnel didn't like to give predictions, but plans needed to be made.

"I think that would be a good idea."

The doctor stepped outside the glass room, giving him a moment alone with his father. He didn't stay long. He couldn't. He was filled with regret that he'd had dinner with Patrick last night and not his parents. He hadn't played golf today because he'd gone to work instead. He'd put everything off until tonight. And now, what would the night bring? Silas found his way out of the maze of rooms and back to the waiting room where his mother sat.

Sally Branch was holding up remarkably well, but then again, Silas expected as much. She was a military wife who'd waited through two tours of war, raised four kids, and crossed two continents. She was calm when she told him the news. She'd been unable to reach him immediately even though she'd been calling his cell phone, the one he'd left in his office while he listened to Deveroux tell him about the case that haunted him. As a last resort Sally had called Patrick's office to track him down.

"Did the doctor explain it to you?" Sally asked Silas as he steered her to the coffee shop located within the hospital.

They found a corner and sipped on coffee neither one of them tasted. Silas hoped the jolt of caffeine would snap him out of it. It felt like the air had been knocked out of him. He was the eldest of four and he was suddenly in charge of the family. He felt the weight of responsibility on his shoulders already. There were calls to make, but so far his mother had only called him. He knew she didn't want to make a fuss. She never did. Maybe this time she should.

Silas looked across the table at her. She and his father met in college. They were the two pillars of strength and unity in his world, but even now Silas could see greyer hair than he remembered and a few more wrinkles.

Growing up, his parents had been the epitome of a loving couple. He couldn't recall cross words exchanged between them. Instead, he saw what every child should see. Loving parents. His memories included seeing his mother sitting on his father's lap or watching him steal a kiss in the kitchen. When they weren't busy driving him and his siblings to activities, his parents maintained their own circle of friends both social and spiritual. They played bridge regularly. They were active in the church. They traveled frequently. They had a good life and genuinely enjoyed each other's company. What was one going to do without the other?

"Where was he when it happened?" Silas asked.

"On the golf course, with Hugh."

Another punch in the gut. He should have been there.

Hugh and Nancy had been his parents' friends for decades. Both Raymond and Hugh ended their military careers at the Pentagon. They loved the hustle and bustle surrounding the nation's capital and decided to never leave. The families settled in Maryland. They were fruitful and multiplied with eight kids between them.

Hugh had been at the hospital when Silas arrived. He'd stayed until Silas could get there and didn't leave until Raymond was out of surgery. He'd only just left to go pick up Nancy. Today was her day with *Meals on Wheels*. When she wasn't doing that, she and Sally could be found volunteering at the St. Vincent DePaul thrift store. Retirement didn't mean they stopped doing. They just spent their time differently.

"Hugh said your father insisted on playing the back nine. They were halfway through when he reached down to pick up a ball and just fell over." Sally relayed the information as she stared off into the distance. "He was fine this morning." She shook her head. "Hugh was so upset. I thought he might have a coronary. I asked one of the nurses to take his blood pressure."

The gesture was so typical of his mother. She was a natural caretaker. Silas reached over and patted her hand. Over her head he saw Hugh and Nancy approaching. He was glad they were back as he needed to gather his siblings. Daniel first because he had the farthest to travel, next his only sister, Kate. She was the closest in New York and finally Kevin in Atlanta. He was always last. He was the oopsy baby.

He needed to bring his family together, but at the moment there was only one voice Silas wanted to hear.

* * *

Olivia was the one who suggested lunch. It was more for Brennon than her but when he opted for Thai, she was all in. Given Silas's proclivity as a carnivore and his new-found fondness for Mexican food, she could do with some noodles in her life. With food as a distraction maybe she could probe deeper into what exactly the thing inside of Jamie had said, before Brennon could bury it away. Except the attorney wasn't budging. He just kept saying it was something only she and he would know. Given the nature of what they were dealing with, it could only be something deeply personal and in all likelihood sexual. Maybe it was a good thing they weren't discussing it. They had been over for a long time.

Just as Olivia spied lunch heading their way, she felt the buzz of her phone. It was face down on the table so she could concentrate on Brennon. She turned it over for a sneak peak, not expecting to answer it until she saw the screen. *Silas.* Seeing his name on the screen was a lifeline to somewhere else. Olivia answered, excited at the unexpected opportunity to hear his voice. He began with three words that were as important to her as any other. *"I need you."*

* * *

Barry hadn't moved from his post at the railing. Amanda waited and watched, making herself at home in one of the two chairs around the high-top patio table.

"So, what do I need to say to convince you I'm fine," Barry asked, finally turning to face her.

The look on his face threatened a challenge. Lucky for her, he wasn't the first cop she'd ever met. He had no idea how persistent she could be. She'd survived four brothers. "Let's start with something easy." Amanda had perused his file before she came, but there wasn't much there. Just the basics. Both mom and dad were university professors. His father taught Philosophy at the University of the Incarnate Word, his mother English Literature at St. Mary's University. His brother had followed in their mom's footsteps, teaching English Lit at a small college in Oregon. Maybe he hadn't fulfilled their expectations. "What made you want to be a cop?"

"My uncle was a cop, my mother's brother." He paused for a moment, as if deciding what to reveal next. "I saw a lot of them growing up." Barry watched for a reaction. Maybe if he threw her a bone she'd leave.

Amanda's eyes narrowed. He was direct. When she could get him talking. She liked that. "Was it rough in your house?"

"My dad liked his female students as much as he liked his drinks."

"Did he put his hands on you?" Amanda asked.

"I didn't like the way he talked to my mother," Barry said instead. "She finally left when I was fourteen." Any older and he and his old man would have come to blows. Barry knew that's why she left. For her son. Not for her. "My brother was ten. Better late than never, I suppose. My father was never much of a giver in life, but hey, he left me the condo."

Amanda nodded. "You're trying very hard not to be your father." It wasn't a question.

Barry scoffed. This chick didn't hold back. "I've not been very successful with the whole marriage thing." At least he'd never been the one to cheat.

She knew about the two marriages, the last one ending three years ago. There were no complaints of domestic abuse. It didn't sound like the same could be said for his father. Legally the lieutenant was single although there was inconsistency on whether or not there was a woman currently in his life. She'd seen no outward signs of one on her pass through the living room. "Loving a cop is a tough gig." Amanda smiled. She knew from personal experience. She was surrounded by cops. Her family tree was full of them.

"Maybe we're just not very loveable," Barry said.

"Maybe."

"I didn't think doctors made house calls."

"You wouldn't call me back," she fired back.

She had him there. "Sorry you got the shit detail, cleaning up after your partner." It was the most he would concede.

"Colleague, *not* partner," Amanda corrected him.

"I didn't owe you a call."

Amanda dug in her briefcase for a pen before he could get started on Steve Winn. She'd sat through enough staff meetings discussing how the rest of the practice was going to handle his case load. "You're right. You have no further obligations, but losing a partner is a bad deal. It's understandable your captain wanted someone to check on you."

Barry stared off in the distance. He knew there were people out there who were worried about him, but opening up wasn't easy for him. He just wished he hadn't turned everyone away. His actions with Olivia had been a mistake.

"You know, he only wrote one word in your chart."

Barry was glad for the introspection. It was a desolate place, but Dr. Greene wasn't quick to share. Probably some psychobabble give and take. She just stared at him until he caved. "Are you going to make me guess which one?"

"Angry."

Barry nodded and offered no protest. It was a description he'd heard before.

Amanda forced her feet back where they belonged despite the protest from her toes. "I'll tell your captain you're alive. Required or not, maybe you should talk to someone." Amanda suggested on her way back into the condo. She was rummaging around in her briefcase looking for her keys and her phone when she noticed the lieutenant standing across from her behind the couch.

"My partner and I had a problem, a few days before he was killed. If it hadn't happened, he would never have been in the field alone."

"You feel responsible for your partner's death?"

"Nah," Barry shook his head. "I blame the FBI agent who left him there."

CHAPTER EIGHT

SILAS SAID HE needed her and Olivia acted on reflex. Going to him seemed like the most natural thing in the world. She would ponder the implications of her actions later, but right now, she just wanted to be there for him. Finding a place for the dogs was the most time-consuming hurdle to overcome. Before, when she needed to be out of the house, Mark had been always been there. It was surprising how his passing kept cropping up in the most unexpected ways. She would have to board them. At least Alvin and Daisy would share a room. She felt better knowing they had each other.

Olivia flew into Baltimore-Washington International. BWI was closer for Silas since his parents lived in Maryland. She insisted she could take a cab to the house, but Silas wouldn't have it. He was waiting for her just outside baggage claim. When she came up dragging the big bag behind her he pulled her into him and kissed her. "I'm so glad you came."

"I'm so glad you called," she whispered. Of all the things she'd been in her life, *needed* wasn't the usual. Not like this.

They held hands all the way to the car and inside. Now that she was with him Silas didn't want to break the connection. On the way to the Branch house, he filled her in on his father's condition. The colonel remained in the ICU and had not regained consciousness. The hospital staff had encouraged the family to go home, advising that they might have many more long days ahead of them and they needed to rest while they could.

Olivia remained quiet and wished she wasn't a nurse. She didn't say anything, but based on what Silas told her, the colonel's outlook didn't look promising. But she said nothing and let him talk. He needed a sympathetic ear, not a prognosis.

"I need to prepare you," Silas said as they neared the house. "My sister Kate is here. So is my little brother Kevin. Also, Nancy and Hugh Buchannan. They're my parents' best friends, and Hugh was with him when it happened."

Olivia nodded, starting to feel the first touch of anxiety. She and Silas were about to leave their bubble. "Tell me about Kate and Kevin again." She needed to focus to stave off the uncertainty.

"Kate's a labor attorney in New York, but don't let that fool you. She's feisty but really just a big softy on the inside."

Olivia couldn't help smile at the description. It made her think of Silas.

"Kev's into digital forensics. He looks for things no one is sure is missing. Nobody but dad seems to really understand what it is he does. All you need to know is he's the baby. We don't let him forget it," Silas smiled. He saw Olivia's nervousness, something he typically didn't see. He turned toward her and squeezed her hand. "They will adore you. I promise."

She tried to smile. "Don't you have another brother? Where is he?" Olivia felt like maybe she should be writing this all down for future reference.

"Daniel is in England. He and his wife, Rachel, and the little guy, Jakey, won't be here until tomorrow. Dan's a lieutenant in the Air Force, a pilot like dad. Rachel is an OB-GYN and Jake's four."

Olivia braved a smile. "Ok, good. A toddler. Maybe he and I will hit it off. Do you think maybe they could wear name tags?"

Silas reached across the console this time to stroke her face with his other hand. Now that she was staring him in the face, he couldn't stop touching her. He'd missed her, something he never would have expected of himself.

"You're joking. That's a good sign," Silas smiled. He didn't have the heart to tell her that he suspected the reason Nancy and Hugh were still there was so they could meet her. He didn't know if the family was more shocked, he'd called someone to come be with him or that she'd actually agreed to come. At least it kept them all from thinking about what really brought them together.

Sally Branch was waiting on the porch to greet them. She must have been watching from inside, because she had the door open before they could get out of the car. Silas took Olivia's hand in his and they crossed the lawn together. He stood behind her for support as his mother greeted Olivia literally with open arms. "Welcome to our home," Sally said. "Thank you so much for coming to be here for Silas," she whispered as they embraced. "He's not as tough as he thinks he is."

Olivia thought she detected a slight catch in the older woman's voice. Olivia nodded back with a smile. "He so seldom asks for help. I knew it was important when he called," she said and reached back for Silas's hand. She felt better already.

The rest of the group was gathered in the living room and introductions were made. Kevin hung back in the corner. The Buchannan's beamed as much as Sally. Kate brought up the rear, but took the lead by holding up her wine glass. "You look like you could use a drink."

Olivia liked her already. "Yes, please," Olivia gushed. She'd had a glass on the plane, but another one was definitely in order.

Kate beckoned for Olivia to follow her while the Buchannan's were saying good-night to Sally and making plans to meet the next day. "Red or white?"

"Red," Olivia said. A glance passed between her and Silas before severing their connection. His eyes encouraged her to go. He was pleased, Olivia could tell. She trailed along behind Kate while Silas remained behind with his mother and Kevin.

"Thank you," Olivia mouthed once they were alone in the kitchen.

"Welcome to our crazy family." Kate gave her a generous pour and passed her the glass. "I knew you would have to drink to put up with my brother." They both laughed and Kate clinked her glass against Olivia's.

* * *

Zavalla showed up uninvited, but with a bottle of Crown as a peace offering. He knew it was the lieutenant's favorite. Barry looked at him curiously but took it. "I brought soda too, just to be safe," the captain said and held up the cans. He'd just come from Atascosa County and it left him feeling like he needed a drink.

Barry cradled the liquor bottle and took the six pack in his other hand.

"Is that to lessen your conscience regarding my drinking habits?" Barry headed to the end of the bookcase nearest the door where he had a makeshift bar. He looked at Zavalla while he pulled out two glasses as if the captain was going to stop him. Barry poured some Crown and split a can of soda between them.

Zavalla followed him out through the patio doors with drink in hand. With the sun down the lights of the highway blinked with traffic for miles. "Nice view."

"It is," Barry agreed although he was leaning on his elbows facing inside and not out. Zavalla was the one enjoying the lights. Barry on the other hand had already been looking at them for the last hour. "You started making house calls now too? Is this another check on my welfare?" the lieutenant asked, referencing the feisty Dr. Greene.

"I got word you passed on talking to someone," Zavalla admitted.

"I did talk to someone," Barry reminded him. "It's not my fault he was crazy. According to my file he said I was angry."

Zavalla nodded, indulging in his first sip. He hadn't had a real soda in a long time, not with his wife watching everything that went into his mouth. He was enjoying the taste of real sugar as much as the liquor. The whiskey was for Bartholomew. The soda was for him. "Doesn't sound like to me he was crazy. He certainly had you pegged."

Barry sipped and stared, waiting for the captain to say what he had come to say but he seemed mesmerized by the ebb and flow of the city lights instead. They could be relaxing if you were watching from above. "Traffic's heavier than usual. Fiesta's starting," Barry commented. "But I'm really thinking you didn't come here for a traffic report."

"Can you believe my wife actually wants to go to NIOSA?" Zavalla was referring to the Night in Old San Antonio. It was an open party held in the market square. It went on for four nights, each busier and more drunken than the last. "I haven't been there in a decade. There's a reason for that."

"I don't think I've been there since my first wife dragged me there." Barry stared at his glass before taking a sip. "The place can't be falling apart without me. I am coming back, you know."

"The new guy is working out fine, in case you're wondering," Zavalla offered referring to Will Ibarra, not wanting to call him by his rank in case it conjured up thoughts of Mark Austin. "But he needs a mentor."

"He's a little older than some. I'm sure he can handle it." Barry knew Ibarra had done a long stint at the Academy. It was a curse he looked so young.

"I guess you're right. Anyway, I got him pinned down with plenty to do in Atascosa County. I might have to find him a temporary partner."

"Oh, yeah?" Barry scoffed. He was looking into his glass, debating on another. There'd been more soda than Crown in there anyway. Indecisive, he turned around and enjoyed the same view as his captain. "I hope not one of the local county boys."

"Oh, hell no. Someone with loads more experience. Someone he can actually learn from." Zavalla thought he saw a trace of jealousy scurry across the lieutenant's face. That was good. He was on the right track. "Dr. Osborne is back on the case." A clinch of the jaw and a stiffening of the posture told him Bartholomew was pretending it didn't bother him to hear her name.

Barry knocked back whatever was left. He should pace himself. With his glass as well as his questions, but couldn't stop himself. It was what Zavalla suspected. "There's another one?"

"Could be more to the Roche case," Zavalla hedged. He had yet to contact Dr. Osborne but Barry didn't have to know that.

"Why are you telling me this?"

There was the grumpy lieutenant Zavalla knew. "Thought you might be interested." Zavalla watched carefully for another reaction.

Barry raised the glass to his lips only to be reminded it was empty. He studied it for a minute as if expecting it to refill itself. "What does the FBI say about it? Where is Agent Branch?"

Barry spat the name, more than said it. Zavalla couldn't help but wonder if it had to do with Dr. Osborne or his former partner. Or the combination of the two. Either way Bartholomew had some issues to work through where Silas Branch was concerned. "Don't know. He's gone."

The response was swift. "He left her?"

"He left town," Zavalla clarified.

"Hmph." Barry's eyes had left his glass to stare back into the night and the lights of the city. Somewhere across the highway in the general direction of Dr. Osborne's house if Zavalla wasn't mistaken.

Zavalla had been there the night of the shooting. He'd followed Agent Branch in a police cruiser, lights blazing. He'd only been able to keep up because of the screaming siren. Zavalla arrived just in time to witness the agent exit his vehicle and draw his weapon before reaching the front porch at a full run. Impressive moves for such a big guy. No wonder he had been so formidable on the football field.

When the quiet had eaten up an uncomfortable amount of time Zavalla drained his glass and handed it off to Barry. "Take all the time you need. I'll see you when you're ready." The captain made his way back inside. His eyes trailing to the soda cans.

"Take them," Barry encouraged him. He didn't want them messing up his Crown anyway.

Zavalla looked at him. "Maybe just one. For the road. Estelle will have my ass if she knows I've gone off the reservation."

Barry smiled. The captain hadn't been called Big Tony for no reason back in the day. "She's just looking out for you, Cap."

"Yea." Zavalla waved him off but stopped again when he got to the door. "I just wanted to check on you. I was kind of worried when Dr. Osborne told me she hadn't seen you."

Barry's face clouded. "So, that's what she said."

For a moment Zavalla didn't know which way to go. He and Barry had never worked together until he became his commanding officer. Even with his advanced degree and stellar record Bartholomew had resisted the command track for as long as he could. He tended to be the loner type but he had just lost a friend. Maybe two. "Listen, I get that the shrink route might not be for you. I know how hard it is to let people into our world. If you need to talk about it, I'm here."

"That's why you should probably hand over the soda and not let Estelle catch you with it," Barry suggested.

Zavalla handed him the can. It was an offering. He just didn't know if the lieutenant would reciprocate.

"Olivia did see me. Yesterday," Barry confessed. "She came over just like you. Only I wasn't as hospitable. I didn't give her what she came for."

It wasn't the first time he'd been known for going radio silent during life's most inopportune times.

Both ex-wives had accused him of it.

Zavalla was unsure exactly what he meant, but it obviously still weighed heavy on Barry's mind. "So, that's it then. It's over?"

Barry stood in front of him, a man on the brink. In crisis about his career, his friends and whatever was in between. "I hope not."

CHAPTER NINE

IT WAS AFTER midnight and while traffic on I-95 in the Baltimore-
D.C. corridor never completely stopped it had lightened up enough to
allow them to drive the speed limit. Their destination was only three
miles from the Maryland border and seven miles from the hubbub of the
nation's capital. Their destination wasn't far from where Olivia had lived
before returning to San Antonio. Silas's place was in a gated community
full of townhomes offering clubhouse amenities, lawn service, and small
quaint yards. A perfect place for the upwardly mobile resident.

They talked little, but their hands remained intertwined throughout the
car ride. Olivia had to admit, she liked touching him. She knew there would
be more of it once they arrived at their destination. They each knew what
the other was thinking, no talking was required.

They pulled into the garage; Silas got her bag and they entered the
house from there. It was nice and neat, everything in its place, just like Silas.
They ascended the stairs together. Once they arrived at the top, he turned
to her. While he was pretty sure what she was thinking, he would never be
so presumptuous, not with her. Their next move was important. And it was
coming on like a head rush.

"Where would you like this?" Silas asked, referring to the luggage he
was dragging behind him.

Olivia stared him down, knowing exactly what he was asking. "Which
room is yours?"

Silas nodded to the room at the end of the hall.

"I think I'd like that one, please," Olivia told him.

"Excellent choice."

The room was clearly masculine, but not overly so. And there was no TV. She firmly believed the bedroom was no place for television. Olivia liked it already.

Silas showed her the closet. "Make yourself at home." His arm snaked its way around her waist as he pulled her into him. But he kept himself in check. Not yet. "I smell like a hospital," he said. "I won't be long."

While Silas showered Olivia put her things away and headed downstairs. She liked what she saw. His place was as orderly as her own. The condo community either came with maid service or Silas simply wasn't home enough to make much of a mess. He certainly hadn't been lately. More importantly, she felt comfortable in his space. He even had her favorite wine waiting. With everything going on today, he'd taken the time to shop for her.

Olivia smiled at his thoughtfulness, but she'd drink the wine later. Tonight, she reached for his bourbon instead. She knew it was what Silas liked at the end of a hard day. Today had definitely been one of those. She switched off most of the lights and turned on whatever he had listened to last. Soft jazz filled the room. Before she forgot, she dug her phone out of her purse and plugged it in next to the coffee maker in the kitchen. A perfect place for it to wait until morning. She didn't even bother to look at it. There wasn't anything more important than what she was doing right now.

She was reclining against the pillows, sipping the liquor, contemplating her life choices when Silas came down the stairs to join her on the couch. Her legs were stretched in front of her and he couldn't resist running his hand up one of them. It was smooth and taut and he knew from the feel of her the yoga pants she loved so much weren't just for show.

"The shirt looks much better on you than me." He liked her choice. It was one of his starched white Bureau shirts. She'd neglected to button it all the way and he saw just the hint of red lace underneath as she moved toward him.

Never taking her eyes off him, Olivia closed the gap between them and offered him the glass. He opened his arms to her and she came to him. She stretched one leg over him and slid into his lap. His breathing quickened at the feel of her.

Silas drained the glass, sat it next to them on the coffee table, and brushed aside the shirt with his hand. He would recall his first glimpse of her for as long as he could remember. The stark crimson lace against her pale skin. The rapid breaths she was taking, the rise and fall of her breasts as she leaned in closer. The glow of her green eyes as she bent down to kiss him.

Olivia dipped down to touch her lips to his. While he might be hungry, she was starving. She wanted to go slow, to savor every taste of him, but all her good intentions faded away by the touch of his hands on her as he stripped away the shirt in one swift movement and pulled her into him. One hand worked its way along her neck and into her hair bringing her lips back to his while his other hand freed her from the bra.

Olivia tugged at his shirt and Silas helped her peel it off. With it out of the way, she wrapped her arms around his neck and felt him slowly edge her back onto the couch. He was pushing her against the pillows with every intent on giving her exactly what she was telling him she wanted, but she shifted her hips and resisted. Looking to her for direction his arousal skyrocketed when he grasped what she wanted. Silas grabbed her by the wrists and eagerly pulled her toward him and back into his lap to finish what they had started.

Once they were finished Olivia didn't protest when they tumbled back on the couch. She let Silas cradle her next to him, their legs still tangled together. Their breaths kept pace with one another until finally they slowed and eased into a satisfied slumber. Only when Olivia cooled enough to stir did Silas wake. A few murmurs from her and he scooped her up and took her upstairs to his bed. This time she willingly let him take the lead.

* * *

Silas's phone woke them. He grabbed it on the second ring and listened. "I'll be right there."

"Your dad?" Olivia asked, her heart racing.

Silas bent down and kissed her nose. "No. Daniel and Rach are at the airport waiting for me. I forgot to set an alarm. Imagine that."

Olivia gave him a guilty smile. She sat up in bed pulling the sheet to her chest, enjoying watching him get dressed. He had been an athlete all his life and it showed.

"We're going to be modest now?" he asked and watched as her cheeks blazed. But there was truth in his words. She had not been at all what he expected. She was surprising and scary to him all at the same time, the kind of scary that could leave him in some deep emotional place. The one place in his whole life he had avoided going. Until now.

"I'll bring them back to the house to catch their breath. It's closer than Mom and Dad's. I can't even imagine being on a plane for six hours with a four-year-old." Dressed, Silas sat down on the bed next to her. "With any luck, I'll be back in about an hour."

She nodded. "Want me to make breakfast?"

"I didn't do that much shopping yesterday," he grinned. "But thank you. Your favorite bagel place is on the way. I'll pick something up and bring it back."

Olivia reached over and kissed him.

"So not the way I would have preferred to wake up this morning," he told her and peeked beneath the sheet she was still clutching.

"I'll let you make it up to me."

Downstairs Silas started coffee for her and noticed her phone. He took it to her along with a steaming cup. "This thing was going off and from the looks of the screen, it doesn't look like it was the first time."

* * *

Sharon Taylor was in early again. As the unit's nurse manager, she didn't have to be in for another couple of hours but given their celebrity patient she had decided she wanted to be present for shift report as long as he resided in their care. Even if it meant leaving the comforts of her bed sooner than she wanted. Maybe today would be the last day. Yesterday she had seen a glimmer of hope. The creepy kid had secured himself an attorney. A high end one that got things done.

After Mr. Kaine left, Sharon called the orthopedic surgeon and put a bug in his ear about moving the kid out of the infirmary and into solitary confinement. The kid had already been here longer than he should anyway, in her opinion. She thought it was more to do with the fact he was going to need solitary confinement downstairs than a medical need. But that wasn't her problem. She was running a small hospital here, not a babysitting service. For her part, she gave the doctor some bullshit about preparing for an upswing in their census due to the impending Fiesta. Drunken brawls were always up this time of year which translated into increased arrests with injuries. As a physician, he would be more sympathetic to her plight than those who carried the Billy clubs and the keys downstairs. He'd promised he'd write the order today when he made his rounds. It could turn out to be a good day. All that changed when she stepped off the elevator.

Frank, the night shift charge nurse, was waiting for her. "Thank god you're here. We have a situation."

"What kind of situation?" Sharon asked.

"It's Candy. I can't find her."

"Can't find her. What do you mean?" Sharon heard what Frank was saying but didn't understand. It was a small unit.

"She was having a difficult shift."

Sharon resisted the urge to roll her eyes. "What now?" She interrupted. Candy was a good nurse, but she had issues, none of them work-related. If she wasn't so desperate for help, she would have let Candy go by now. But finding a nurse who wanted to work the night shift in the Bexar County Jail infirmary was challenging to say the least. And the applicants she did receive were not the best and the brightest. It was easier to deal with the problems she had rather than gamble on new ones.

"The patient in seven." Frank didn't have to elaborate.

Sharon closed her eyes. *Of* course *it was room seven.*

"He kept complaining of pain. Demanding something other than the Norco he's been getting. Wanted to go back to the injectable."

Sharon shook her head. *No. No. No.* This could not be happening. New complaints of pain were sure to derail her plans for discharge.

"Dr. Fox ordered a shot of Dilaudid. About that time the Pyxis went down again. Someone from pharmacy is up here fixing it now," Frank rushed to explain before Sharon could go off. He could tell by the look on her face she wasn't far from an eruption. "In the meantime, our guest says he never got his shot. And that's when we couldn't find Candy."

"Well, shit." Sharon was already rethinking her decision to come in early. But quickly reminded herself in the end it really didn't matter. She would still be having this conversation. She just would be doing it from the comfort of her bed with the young correctional officer she left there instead of here.

"Uh, guys," the pharmacy tech was hovering beside Frank, trying to keep his distance from Sharon. "I got the Pyxis back on line." The state-of-the-art medication dispensing machine was nothing more than a finicky, high-dollar pain in the ass.

"Thank you," Frank said without turning around, but Roger didn't take the hint and leave.

Roger looked over Frank's shoulder and met Sharon's stare head on. "I heard y'all talking about the guy in seven. According to the machine Candy removed a Dilaudid injection for him forty-five minutes ago. And one for the guy down in five."

A perimeter alert went off in Sharon's head. "I'll talk to the patients. Frank, you keep looking for Candy. Don't forget to check the roof," she snapped. It was a favorite smoking spot of the employees. The entire facility was supposed to be smoke-free, but the roof was far enough away she knew some of the hardcore nicotine addicts still used it. Especially after hours when administration was gone.

"Get Josie to man the desk and Melva to sweep this end of the unit again." The day shift was starting to drift in so maybe they could keep this in their hands for now. She didn't want to have to call a deputy and report a missing employee. It was a situation Candy couldn't come back from and Sharon might have to explain why she hadn't disciplined the nurse sooner. Neither scenario was desirable.

"Make sure you check the closed rooms as well," she called after him. One of the other nurses had complained that Candy liked to sneak down there and use her cell phone. Another thing on the growing list of things she needed to talk to Candy about.

* * *

After a quick shower, Olivia went through her messages in triage fashion. With a second cup of coffee in hand she assessed each one, determining which was most important and then went to work. Captain Zavalla was pushed to the head of the line. Mainly because his text included a couple of interesting photos.

"Where were these taken?" Olivia asked. She had him on speaker so she could look at the pictures while they talked.

"In a barn. A few hundred yards from where we found Ferdinand Roche's body – the second time." Meaning the *burned* one.

The first scene to catch her attention was the one of the candles on the floor. "There appears to be something missing," she said, staring at the placement. "The platform is there for a reason, but," Olivia drug a nail over the vacant space wondering what could fill the spot, "it's conspicuously empty." For whatever reason she didn't want to ponder long. Zavalla moved on to the next picture. The one that had stopped her cold.

A symbol was burned into the wall adjacent to the platform but it was all kinds of wrong. Her unease escalated. "Is this picture upside down?" Olivia asked the question even though she already knew the answer. No one called her for normal.

"No." Even Zavalla knew something was wrong. "I drove out to see it myself."

There was a pause while she gathered her thoughts. The use of another inverted image forced her to consider the possibility they could be dealing with the same perpetrator who had carved an inverted pentagram into Ferdinand Roche's body just before killing him.

"My new sergeant says it's an ankh." Captain Zavalla's voice brought her back.

The ankh was an ancient symbol, borrowed by multiple practices. It had magical elements. Olivia's mind was racing. Her initial assessment of the Roche murder was that they were dealing with a dabbler of the arts. Dabblers were dangerous, mixing was a flirtation with darkness. Magic and evil together. Could they coexist? Which was stronger?

Olivia stopped the free flow of thoughts. She couldn't concentrate. Not now. Not here. She needed to walk the scene and feel the energy or *taste* it. "Your sergeant is correct."

"As you can imagine this kind of thing is a little out of our scope. I was hoping you could go take a look," Zavalla suggested.

Of course, it was. "I'm in DC at the moment, but I can when I get back."

"Everything okay?" Zavalla asked. Her response was not what he had expected.

"Yes. Thanks for asking," Olivia said. There was an awkward pause. The captain was obviously concerned about her well-being which is why he was still waiting for an answer. It was touching. "Agent Branch had a family emergency." The captain could take it from there. He was bound to find out sooner or later. She just wondered if he would share it with his lieutenant.

The first call out of the way, she moved on to Brennon. His was just a text, but she called anyway. She knew he was still upset from yesterday's visit with Jamie. Like Zavalla, Brennon expressed concern about her circumstances. Again, it was appreciated.

"I know now what you meant when you told me to do what I do," Brennon confessed. One meeting with his client was all it had taken. "I'm going to make sure he doesn't ever get out. I wanted you to hear it from me." He sounded tired. Like he'd spent the night considering it.

Olivia had no words. None were adequate. He was doing exactly what she wanted even though she couldn't ask.

"I've secured a corporate apartment downtown. The rest of my team will arrive over the weekend."

"And the psych eval?" Olivia pressed.

"Pending. I have a couple of leads. I'm talking to both of them again today. It's just going to be hard to get anyone in here until Monday at the earliest."

"Anyone I know?" she asked.

"Bob Thornton is at the top of my list," Brennon said. He was the psychiatrist they worked with on the Washington case. Olivia knew him before that. He was a man of science, but had been around long enough to know there were things beyond his realm of expertise. Things couldn't have been shaping up any better from her perspective.

Father Dominic had left a voicemail, his preferred method of communication, mentioning that the archbishop still wished to speak with her. She wondered if he went to the Archdiocese after he left her house. He'd undoubtedly been spending time there if he had accepted reinstatement. He also assured her he wasn't going to Rome any time soon. She wondered if this was really some kind of apology call for dropping the bomb on her yesterday.

Olivia reciprocated the gesture, her way of letting him know she had come to terms with it. It didn't mean they wouldn't revisit the subject again, but they were good. She got his voicemail and explained she was in DC and would keep him posted on her return.

Lastly, she discovered a text she almost missed. It was two days old. From Barry.

"I should have told you thank you. I'm sorry. I was hungry."

Olivia allowed herself to read it twice and then hit the delete button.

CHAPTER TEN

JESSICA JUMPED AT the buzz of an incoming call. It was one of her contacts inside the Bexar County jail. The infirmary to be exact. She'd quickly cultivated a network as soon as Jamie Smythe was moved there. It was paying off already. She'd been the first to know Brennon Kaine had taken the case. On a hunch she'd tracked him down at the same location where she'd seen him at dinner with Dr. Osborne. She caught him long enough for a hurried *"no comment at this time"* but despite his lack of cooperation, a sighting of the high-profile defender still made it on the air, especially after Jessica informed her boss, she had an unnamed source inside the infirmary.

Today's call was something else. Jessica grabbed a cameraman and headed down the street.

* * *

Barry saw the developing story on his morning Internet scroll. He couldn't remember the last time he'd turned on the TV, preferring the sound of quiet over the chatter of the idiot box. On the computer he could control what he saw and heard. The swarm of activity around the Bexar County jail piqued his interest. Especially when he learned the focus was concentrated on the infirmary.

It didn't take him long to decide he needed to hit the shower and maybe even shave for the first time in days. He should also take the car out. He'd neglected it almost as long as the TV. He hadn't needed it since Olivia saved him a trip to the grocery. At the thought of her he checked his phone.

Maybe he shouldn't have sent the text. Or he should have sent it earlier. Better yet, he shouldn't have done something he felt the need to apologize for in the first place.

* * *

Daniel Branch called his mother while he and Rachel waited for Silas. Initially he'd been concerned something had happened at the hospital because late was not a word used to describe his big brother. When Daniel learned all was as well as could be expected he decided he'd get out of Silas what was really going on. His mother had already spilled the beans and reported Silas had taken his "girlfriend" back to his place for the night. Sally Branch also happened to mention she was beautiful and smart. Daniel would expect nothing else from Silas.

Rachel cautioned her husband to go easy on his brother, but to no avail. She should have known after more than a decade in the family that wasn't going to happen. Silas was the golden child and any opportunity to give him grief and any three of the siblings would immediately pounce. The family definitely liked to have their fun and the opportunities to have it at Silas's expense were few and far between. Daniel insisted it was his duty as the second oldest to get his licks in while he could.

"So, spill it," Daniel said once they'd wrestled Jake's car seat into the back of Silas's SUV and Silas had safely navigated them out of the airport pick-up lane. "Mom said you picked up some beautiful woman from the airport, dropped by the house for introductions and then whisked her away. Let's hear it."

Silas looked at his sister-in-law through the rear-view mirror. She looked beat. "Rach, did this fool sleep on the plane?"

"He was probably the only one in a two-aisle radius," Rachel said with a tired smile. From the looks of it, all Jakey had needed was a different mode of transportation because his eyes were already closed and they had just hit the freeway. Silas wondered how far into her shift at the hospital Rachel had been when they made the decision to hop a plane and fly across the ocean. She looked like she wasn't too far from joining her son.

"Did you take her back to your place? Were blindfolds involved?"

"Be nice," Silas cautioned him.

Daniel knew then it was serious. Not that Silas ever kissed and told, but the look in his eye was different. "I'm just wondering if we have a hostage situation on our hands. I didn't think women were allowed to know where you lived."

Silas shot him a sideways glance and Daniel responded with a mischievous grin. He liked seeing his brother this way. Off his game. He was absent his standard FBI suit and tie. Maybe it left him vulnerable.

"Are you going to at least tell us how you met her? What she does for a living? Something so we don't have to conduct our own interrogation? My wife talks to women all day long. She's an expert at getting them to tell her all kinds of things," Daniel promised.

"Don't bring me into this," Rachel said, but she had to admit she was curious. For such a good looking, successful guy, Silas was closed mouth about his personal life and always absent a plus one at family functions. Why he was still single was a mystery to her.

"We worked together."

"Worked? Past? Present? Is she an agent? Does she carry a gun?" Daniel fired off a rapid succession of questions. This was fun already, a welcome distraction from the troubling events that brought the brothers together.

"She is no longer an agent. She moved to San Antonio a couple of years ago, but still lends her services to the Bureau from time to time. We just finished a case together. And yes, she carries a gun. She used it a couple of weeks ago, so don't piss her off," Silas warned.

"Services? What kind of services?" Daniel asked.

Rachel leaned forward as far as the seat belt would allow. "Oh my god. Was it the serial killer case in San Antonio?" she interrupted from the backseat. "The one where the cop was killed?" She had fully intended to follow Jake's lead and nap, but the conversation was too good to miss.

Silas concentrated on the road, looking for the bagel place. He was sure it was close.

"So, what kind of services?" Daniel was truly interested this time. He personally hadn't read about the San Antonio case but Rachel had kept him up to speed. Silas's lack of response told him Rachel was correct. Silas was involved.

"She's a forensic psychologist. A special kind of profiler," Silas said instead.

"Special? What do you mean, special?" Daniel asked.

"Hannibal Lector special I'll bet, if she's a forensic psychologist," Rachel guessed.

Silas confirmed her assumption with another glance in the rearview.

"Cunning, I like it," Daniel said seeing the exchange. "So, keeping you in line should be a snap." Beautiful and smart. Two things he was sure were high on his bachelor brother's priority list. Daniel caught sight of the bagel place Silas was making a U-turn in front of. If it had been up to Silas they would be heading to McDonalds. "Ah, I bet they don't have one of these in San Antonio."

"Livie likes it," Silas told him.

Daniel pulled down the visor and caught a glimpse of his wife as she settled back next to their son. "*Goner*," he mouthed into the mirror.

* * *

Will arrived at the infirmary in time to meet up with Bexar County Medical Examiner Walter Meeks. Will knew him from his occasional talks at the Academy. Meeks had been around the block a time or two having outlasted more than his fair share of others. He could be a little rough around the edges, but his talks were always entertaining. He delivered tales of death and mayhem in a straight, no nonsense style that came from years of time on the job. No one ever fell asleep during his visits. Will genuinely liked him and thought the M.E. felt the same. Even if he didn't, it felt good to see a familiar face.

"Moving up fast," Meeks said as he and Will almost collided outside what looked like a patient hospital room only this one was empty except for the dead girl. At the other end of the hall was a set of double doors that, according to his officer escort, housed the actual patients. These rooms were overflow. From the ones with open doors they looked to be storage space for discarded, mismatched office furniture and outdated medical equipment. It was like the junk drawer at your house, just on a larger scale. Despite the lack of people on this corridor Will had noticed the mounted cameras in the exit corners and at the double doors.

"Looks that way." Will's call from the captain about an incident at the jail had gone from missing person to a suspicious death during his trip downtown. "What can you tell me?" It didn't matter the doctor hadn't put knife to flesh yet. Will knew Meeks's wheels were turning.

"It's your missing nurse Candy Wilkerson, RN. She's still wearing her badge. Photo ID matches."

"Anything suspicious in this room?"

"You mean other than the needle still stuck in her arm?" Meeks asked. "I'm not the detective, but it looks like the staff comes down here for a little getaway. There's a table and a few chairs. Some empty soda cans in the trash can. That's about it."

"Any obvious track marks, other than the one she was using?"

Meeks shook his head. "Naw, but I'll take a good look once I get her on the table. As a nurse she'd know all the hiding spots."

"Idea on drug of choice?"

"Today's selection, according to staff scuttlebutt is Dilaudid. Heard something about some vials gone missing. Should be something easily accessible considering the accommodations."

Will nodded making notes in a flip notebook, old-school style. He caught Meeks looking over his shoulder as if expecting someone else. He'd done it at least twice already. "You expecting someone else?" Will smiled. Maybe the ME didn't think he should be here on his own.

"Just wondering if Dr. Osborne's going to join you."

"The FBI doc?" Will thought it was a strange question then again Will had heard she was a looker. Meeks could have a crush. It wouldn't be the first man Will had heard might have a thing for the doctor.

"Just wondering, considering who's beyond those doors at the end of the hall." Will must have looked confused. "Smythe," Meeks clarified.

Will wondered if that was one of the reasons Zavalla sent him. Potential interaction with Mark Austin's killer could be a volatile situation. He should be immune since he'd never met the sergeant.

"I'll let you know when I'm ready to do the post," Meeks told him with a clap on the shoulder. "Welcome to the big time."

A peek in the room confirmed Meeks's assessment. The body was still there. Will walked over to take a look. He'd only ever seen dead bodies during his trips to the morgue, never one this fresh or in the wild. She was young, maybe his age—mid-thirties. She didn't look like a typical druggie, but anymore what did that really look like? If drugs were her thing, she was certainly in a position to get the good stuff. But given security and protocol, the strict monitoring offered by the Pyxis system, how easy could that be?

Will stepped away when the guys with the gurney showed up. He rejoined the correctional officer in the hall who led him through the double doors, noting they required an access badge.

The whole unit was quiet. There were three staff members behind the desk who stopped and stared as they passed. One of them handed the officer a sheet of paper. He glanced at it before handing it over to Will. "Patient list and assignments for last night's shift." There were a total of eight patients with the corresponding staff name and titles. Two nurses besides the dead one and an aide who also doubled as the secretary. Will noted Candy Wilkerson's name didn't line up with any patient. The name Roger Donaldson was handwritten at the bottom.

Their trek ended at the end of the hall which was the designated conference room where a Bexar county jailor had sequestered the infirmary staff with instructions not to discuss any events connected to the nurse's death or anything else about their shift. Fortunately for Will, he was relieved of the duty of informing them of Candy's fate since it was one of these co-workers who found her.

The room was like a tomb. A tall, no nonsense looking woman immediately took the lead and introduced herself as the nurse manager Sharon Taylor. She helped Will put faces to the names in front of him

"Smythe had something to do with it, I know it." The comment came from Frank, the man Ms. Taylor had confirmed was the charge nurse on last night's shift. It was Will's first time hearing it, but it sounded like a mantra.

"Folks, unfortunately I'm going to need you to not make any further comments outside of my formal interview. I need to interview you'all separately. Officer Brighton here is going to stay with the group to ensure there's no chit-chat about what's going on. Feel free to take a quick nap, read a book, catch up on your social media, whatever. But please, no discussing with each other or anyone else, especially anyone on Facebook, what's happened here. I know it sucks, but just bear with me." Will caught the eye-rolls and tsk-tsking from adults who didn't appreciate being micro-managed, but independent human recall is so incredibly flawed that witness accounts blended together far too easily if not kept deliberately separate.

The remaining medical staff consisted of one other nurse, Josie, and a nurse's aide, Melva. Also joining them was Roger, a pharmacy tech. He had been called to the unit just after Nurse Wilkerson disappeared due to an issue with the Pyxis, a machine used to store patient medications. Since, according to Meeks, it appeared the dead nurse had died of an overdose Will figured he should start with Roger from pharmacy. As the non-team member, he was hovering in a corner alone clutching a clipboard and looking like he wanted to be anywhere but there. When he sat down with Will in the empty patient room across the hall, Roger explained he had been called to the floor because the Pyxis machine had malfunctioned. For whatever reason it had gone into lockdown, making it impossible for the nurses to withdraw medication.

Roger was obviously a tech guy and therefore had difficulty explaining things to mere mortals. After what was turning into a lengthy explanation regarding the inner workings of the Pyxis machine, Will had to stop him the only way he knew how. The subtle metal insignia stuck to the guy's pocket protector like a tie tac gave him away. Will always thought it looked like a double fingered victory sign where the middle and ring fingers parted ways. As a nine-year old he'd spent months perfecting the Vulcan greeting.

"Look, Roger, you're obviously really good at what you do, but I don't need to know how Scotty keeps the *Enterprise* flying, I just trust that he knows how," Will coaxed the fellow Trekkie.

Roger's eyes lit up.

"All I really need you to tell me is the who, the what, and the when."

According to Roger, Candy Wilkerson pulled two five-milligram doses of Dilaudid at 0545.

Frank Silva, the charge nurse, was next. He confirmed that he heard Candy on the phone obtaining a new order for Dilaudid for the patient in room seven. The remainder of his interview focused on his search for Candy and the discovery of her body. Despite being up all night, Will doubted the man was going to sleep much once he left this room.

Josie Cervantes, the other nurse, was the only one who claimed to be Candy's friend, but only at work. They didn't eat together last night, which was their usual, because Candy was in a fight with the boyfriend. Always making up or breaking up was how Josie described the relationship. Josie was also the first to notice Candy was missing. Mainly because her patient in room three had called to complain that he hadn't received his pain med that was scheduled for 0600. "He watches that clock like a hawk, but so does Candy. Or at least she did."

"So, according to the staff sheet, if I'm reading this right, it looks like Candy was assigned to giving meds? I don't see any patients by her name," Will clarified. He hadn't been able to ask Frank about it because he'd been too focused on how he found Candy and what he thought led to her demise.

"Yea, that's how we do it here. Old school. If one nurse is giving the meds, it helps us keep track of who might be trying to work the system. As you can imagine most of our patients have drug problems."

"Did you go look for her?" Will asked.

"Well, no. I decided to give the med myself. It was easier than listening to him complain. I figured I'd find Candy after. Probably down the hall on her phone." Josie's story of when and why she called the pharmacy matched Roger's.

Melva, the nurse's aide came next. She, like Candy, was the only one who had a reason to see all the patients on the unit since she took vital signs every four hours. She claimed it had been a quiet night when asked about the patients in five and seven, the ones Candy supposedly pulled meds for. According to Melva, the guy in five was asleep every time she saw him and the patient in room seven never slept. "Not really." She avoided eye contact as she said it.

"What does that mean?" Will asked.

"His eyes might be closed, but he's not sleeping." In her opinion he didn't appear to be in pain. He never did. She was upfront and said she made it a point to spend as little time in his room as her job would allow. She didn't speak to Candy and that wasn't unusual when she was in 'one of those moods,' confirming what Josie had said about problems with the boyfriend.

Will saved the nurse manager, Sharon Taylor, for last. She, unlike the rest of the staff, hadn't been there all night. "Any particular reason you were in early today?" Will asked.

"I've been in early every day since we received our celebrity guest," Sharon told him.

"Meaning?" Will said.

"The patient in seven."

"Any particular reason?"

"I've been monitoring his progress very carefully. I want him off my unit. He gives everyone the creeps. There's something not right about him. You can see it in his eyes. I'm running out of nurses that will take care of him at night."

"What happens at night?"

"He doesn't sleep, not really," she said, corroborating Melva's observation. "Sometimes his face doesn't look right."

"What do you mean by *not right*?"

"Everyone's description is different." Her looking at him was unnerving. "I've seen evil before. People think it's the person. Most of the time it is."

"What most people don't want to know, there's another kind of evil. It doesn't matter if they lock the kid away for life or kill him, the evil will just find somewhere else to go. That's the kind that's inside of him. It's a force all its own."

Will resisted the urge to rub the goosebumps away. He tapped his pen on the table instead and looked for redirection. They were off topic and he didn't like where this was going. "Did you talk to him today? Did you ask him about the Dilaudid?"

"Of course, I asked him about the Dilaudid. Even though I know he didn't ask for it."

"How did you know that?" Will asked, hoping for some enlightenment.

"Patients who are in pain don't normally shovel food in their mouth. It's what he was doing when I went in there. The way he eats is primal. Like it's something he hasn't done in a long time. His tongue darts in and out capturing every last morsel." She shivered at the memory. "There's a debate on the floor if his tongue's forked or not. Just no one wants to look at him long enough to find out."

CHAPTER ELEVEN

CAUGHT UP ON her phone calls, Olivia paced the kitchen. She filled the coffee pot with water and waited. To busy herself, she scrolled through the pictures Zavalla sent. The torch mark on the back of the wall still gave her pause. She should have asked Father Dominic about it as well. She pulled out her computer to start her own search but a swell of personal feelings nudged her unease back into the shadows when Silas texted her with a status update. They'd just left the bagel place and were on their way back. With more family on the way, she decided it would be prudent to shut off her computer and close herself off to the darkness waiting for her in San Antonio. Family, even if it wasn't her own, was what was important now. Sally Branch had gone a long way last night by simply opening her arms and giving her a hug. Olivia had a sense of belonging for the first time in a long time. Monsters would just have to wait.

* * *

Barry made the drive downtown to the precinct on autopilot. Muscle memory guiding him to the building where he's spent the last eighteen years of his life. He made his way to Captain Zavalla's office relatively unnoticed. He did what he always did at work; put his head down and moved forward. Besides the building was a flurry of activity. The latest news from the Bexar County Jail was that an employee had been found dead. Further details were pending. Jessica Tate of Channel Four News was the first to break the story. She'd done the same two weeks ago. Only then the lead story was how SAPD was tracking a serial killer. Life moved on.

* * *

Daniel and Rachel were as welcoming as the rest of the family. From the grins exchanged between them, Olivia got the impression Daniel must have given his big brother a hard time about something, but Silas was beaming so she took it as a good sign.

After half a bagel and juice, no coffee, Rachel trudged upstairs to join Jake. Olivia was surprised she made it through breakfast. She looked exhausted. Olivia wondered if there wasn't something else going on but didn't think about it because as soon as she and Silas were alone, he pulled her close. Touching him was the grounding she needed with all the emotions swirling around her.

Olivia smiled up at him. "They're teasing you, aren't they?"

"Subtle, aren't they?" Silas smiled back.

She giggled. "I think I kind of like it."

"It is all your fault," Silas admitted and dove in for another kiss.

Daniel came back down stairs and caught them. "Should I go out and come back in?"

Silas shook his head and looked back down at Olivia. "Danny and I are going to head to the hospital. I'm taking the suburban and leaving the SUV for you and Rachel. We'll end up at Mom and Dad's for dinner."

Olivia nodded. "Okay. I have a call with Captain Zavalla after lunch." She and Silas both looked to Daniel.

Daniel held up his hands. "Work talk; I get it." He smiled at Olivia. "Great to meet you. I'll see you later. I'll be just outside," he said to Silas. "You kids behave. Don't make me have to come back in here."

"Atascosa County, again." Olivia continued once they were alone.

"Can't wait to hear."

* * *

"Guillermo Ibarra, Barry Bartholomew," Captain Zavalla made the introductions.

"No one calls me Guillermo, Captain, except my grandmother." She was old school like that, preferring the Spanish version of William. The sergeant extended his hand to the man responsible for getting him out of the Jones substation faster than he ever anticipated. It was odd to finally meet him. "It's Will, Lieutenant."

Barry nodded and shook the sergeant's hand. Will Ibarra's organizational skills had been instrumental in leading them to the missing car of Smythe's third victim. Patricia Griffin's death had been a turning point in Jamie's evolution as a killer and the driving force that pushed Mark and Barry to seek outside help. He had been willing to do anything at that point to jumpstart his stalled investigation before the Feds or the Texas Rangers showed up to take it away from him. He'd known nothing of Olivia Osborne or her background. It had been Mark Austin who mentioned she might be able to help because of her *special skills*. Mark conveniently forgot to mention she once worked for the Bureau or that serial killers were her specialty. Little had Barry known that bringing Olivia into the mix would only hasten involvement from the Feds and completely turn his life upside down.

Barry knew he'd made a mistake letting her walk away. Since last night there'd been a gnawing feeling in the middle of his gut that told him it was going to be a costly one.

"Meeks called and said a nurse was found with a needle still in her arm. Please tell me, it's that cut and dry," Zavalla said.

Will wanted to say yes, and forget what the staff told him, but he couldn't. He'd have to let the lieutenant and captain decide. "There is computer evidence Candy Wilkerson's username and password were used to pull two five-milligram vials of Dilaudid out of a machine called a Pyxis."

"Was that her choice?" Barry wanted to know.

"There were doctor's orders on file for both patients to have the Dilaudid if that's what you mean. She was the medication nurse last night, so she was the only nurse giving meds. Everyone's intake is monitored and if drugs go missing, it's easy to pin the blame."

"Given the type of individuals they're dealing with," Zavalla mimicked the same methodology Josie had explained.

"Which patients?" Barry asked.

Will didn't have to look at his notes to know the answer. "Room five and room seven."

"What did the other nurses say?" It was Zavalla again.

Will hesitated. This was the tricky part. "Nurse Josie Cervantes was assigned to room five. Both she and the nurse's aide confirmed the patient slept all night."

"And the other one?"

"The charge nurse, Frank, said he never went into room seven. The nurse's aide said she only went in there when she had to."

"What about Nurse Wilkerson? Was she in there?" Will remained focused on the captain. It made him nervous the lieutenant had gone silent. "Frank said he heard her call the doctor and request a new order. He hadn't needed an injection for pain in two days so it was out of the ordinary."

"So, what changed?" Barry asked.

"Frank said she never told him. They're having IT open Wilkerson's charts from last night to see what she wrote. The nurse manager, Sharon Taylor, confirmed she'd expected the patient to transfer today."

"What does Nurse Taylor think about her staff's actions?"

"They followed protocol."

"What's her background?" Barry asked.

"She's been at the jailhouse infirmary for three years. Before that she spent seven years at San Antonio State Hospital in the psych ward," Will said slowly. He suspected the lieutenant could see where this was going, but he was going to have to ask the questions that would get him there.

"So, in the system long enough not to scare easily," Barry said.

His assessment matched Will's. "She said she'd seen enough crazy." Those weren't exactly the words she'd used, but they worked. He couldn't bring himself to repeat what she'd said about evil, maybe later when they got past the preliminaries, and after the lieutenant had digested the information and moved on to more pointed questions. Will was trying to make a good impression. He didn't want the lieutenant or captain to confuse Nurse Taylor's observations for his own.

"Did Taylor have any problems with the nurse in question?" Zavalla asked.

"Family issues. She has a file with something called TPAP. It stands for Texas Peer Assistance Program. It's a state program for Texas nurses who have had problems with substance abuse or psychiatric issues. I put in a call to HR. They're going to open the file so we can have a look while we wait for the subpoena to process." Will knew it was part of the investigation, but it seemed like a box that needed checking and nothing more.

Zavalla shook his head. Maybe this was going to be easy. "Sounds like to me Candy Wilkerson was the last person who should have been the med nurse on the night shift at the jailhouse infirmary."

"What did the patients have to say?" Barry asked, studying Will closely. The sergeant was holding back on them.

"They both told Nurse Taylor they never asked for anything for pain," Will answered still not looking at the lieutenant.

"What did they tell you?"

"Room five said he slept all night."

"Why do you keep referring to them by room number?" Zavalla asked.

"It's what the nurses do. It's easier to discuss them in public without using names. Patient confidentiality and all." Will knew the explanation wouldn't be enough for the lieutenant. "Eddie Zapata is the patient in room five."

"And room seven?" It was still the captain.

"He said he was going to have to call his lawyer." Will finally looked at his lieutenant. Barry's hands were on his hips. His fingers touching the handle of his gun. Will wondered if it was habit or intent. "He said he knew you were going to want to talk to him." He watched the color drain from Barry's face as the realization settled over him.

Barry was seething. "Smythe. Son of a bitch."

The captain drug a hand over his face.

"Sharon Taylor's calling the lawyer. Said she'd let us know when he arrived," Will explained.

"Who's he using?" Barry asked, hoping it didn't sound like he already knew the answer. At least he thought he did, considering the man he'd seen at Olivia's house.

"Word is Brennon Kaine," Captain Zavalla confirmed.

"I'd like to be there when you question him." Barry glanced past Will to Zavalla.

"If Kaine has no objections, I don't. Are you up to it?"

Barry nodded. "Yea." The additional time off he'd requested was starting to sound like a decision he wanted to change. "I shouldn't have to tell you we're going to need Dr. Osborne."

Will's cell phone buzzed and he stepped outside to take the call.

"She's not here." There was regret in Zavalla's voice.

"She's not here?" Barry repeated his voice loud enough that Will turned to look his way.

"Agent Branch had some kind of a family emergency. She's gone to be with him," Zavalla answered before Barry had to ask.

The shock didn't have time to sink in before Will poked his head back inside. "That was Ms. Taylor. Brennon Kaine is on his way. We're on."

* * *

Brennon Kaine was waiting for them in the same conference room where Will had interviewed the staff. Barry sized up the man he had spent time stalking on the Internet after the run by Olivia's. He knew she and Kaine had worked together on a serial case in Washington state. The defendant, who had fired Kaine after a stint in a psychiatric hospital, had asked for the death penalty. Something else Barry found during his search was a picture of Olivia and Brennon Kaine. They had arrived at the Alzheimer's charity event arm in arm. The photo was taken a few years ago before Olivia returned to San Antonio. From the looks of things, they had been more than colleagues. The smile on Olivia's face had been genuine. Looking at it made Barry sad that he'd seen her smile so little in the short amount of time they'd spent together. It also looked like her place on the attorney's arm that night appeared to be anything but work. The society column had said the same thing. Kaine's widower status made him one of Manhattan's most eligible bachelors.

Barry was vaguely aware his preoccupation with Olivia was teetering on the edge of obsession. He wondered what Dr. Greene would make of that. Olivia had wormed her way into his thoughts from the start. He had doubted her abilities at first, been defiant and more than a little impatient with her intuitions into his investigation. Looking back, his discomfort around her had been a defense mechanism. His response had been to erect a wall between them to save himself. He cursed himself for ever building it in the first place.

"Lieutenant Bartholomew, it was my understanding you are on administrative leave. Yet, here you are." It was Kaine's way of a greeting.

Kaine hadn't been here long, he had obviously done some homework. Or he had someone on the inside. *Olivia.* "Leave was at my request, not that of the SAPD. My captain is aware I'm here today, Counselor," Barry told him. "If you would like to speak to him, I'm sure he would be more than happy to take your call."

Brennon locked eyes with the lieutenant as if deciding the validity of his words. Neither blinked, but Brennon finally nodded. "A phone call won't be necessary. Dr. Osborne speaks very highly of you," Kaine told him. There had been a softness in her voice when she did it, elevating the attorney's curiosity level where the lieutenant was concerned. "I trust her judgement implicitly so don't do anything to make me regret allowing you time with my client. If whatever questions you have for him today deviate in the slightest from anything other than the events regarding this nurse's apparent accidental overdose, I will not hesitate to have you removed. Are we clear?"

"Crystal," Barry said.

They hadn't gone but two steps outside the door. The lieutenant's hands were still on his hips. They'd landed there while he and the attorney sized each other up—like they were trying to decide the pecking order.

"You good?" Will asked.

"I'm good. I just don't like him."

Will nodded. "Ok. I'm not keen on interviewing Smythe on my own, but I don't want us to get thrown out of here either. That guy looks like he doesn't fu—mess around."

Barry nodded. The new kid had a set of balls on him to go along with his good instincts. Barry was glad to see he'd made at least one right decision.

CHAPTER TWELVE

"I LIKE HER," Daniel said as they pulled out of the driveway.

Silas nodded. "Glad to hear it." He was careful to keep his eyes on the road and not on his brother. Otherwise he'd give himself away.

The doctor had already come and gone by the time they arrived at the hospital. Kate sent Silas a text informing him they were no longer in the ICU waiting room. "They've taken him back for an MRI," Kate filled them in once they were all together at the coffee bistro Silas and his mother had visited the day before. "The nurse said it's going to take a while since he's still hooked to the ventilator." Kate was talking quietly while their mother sat not far away with Hugh and Nancy. Kevin had walked up to the counter to get a muffin.

"Something else is going on, isn't it?" Silas prompted her.

Kate nodded. "The doctor was guarded, you know how they are," she said with a glance toward Daniel.

"Rach really wanted to come here right away, but she had to get some sleep," he explained. "She offered to have one of those doctor-to-doctor talks."

"Is Rachel okay?" Silas asked.

"Don't say anything, because we're supposed to announce this together, but Rachel's pregnant. We just found out. We haven't even told Jakey yet."

"Danny, that's great news," Kate said and gave him a quick squeeze.

"Congrats, little brother," Silas told him.

"I don't think the doctor thinks Dad is going to wake up," Kate blurted out. "He started talking about his neurological status." She shook her head, trying hard to fight back tears.

Silas opened his arms and she came to him while Daniel patted her shoulder.

"Uh, guys," Kevin said. "The doctor's back."

Gathered in the empty family room the Branch children flocked around their mother and listened to the stoic doctor tell them there would be no MRI. Silas didn't understand it all, but he did hear phrases likes too unstable, possibility of multiple cerebral infarcts as a result of the blockage in the heart and decreased urine output.

The doctor slipped out the door with Silas and Daniel on his heels.

"So, we're talking multiple events," Silas clarified, stopping the man in his tracks. "Give it to me straight. Is he...," Silas couldn't bring himself to say it.

"You're the FBI agent?"

Silas nodded.

"I didn't say anything else because your mother needs time to process." He was as good at reading people as any agent.

"Then say it to me," Silas told him.

"I'm concerned your father's brain is severely compromised. His kidneys also appear to be shutting down. Medication and dialysis may help, but if he is headed to multiple system organ failure." He shook his head. "There is no going back. Is the whole family here now?"

Daniel nodded. "Yes, sir."

"I'll get back to you as soon as I know something. The most important thing you can do right now is take care of your mother."

Silas appreciated the honesty.

* * *

Will asked the questions. They were simple.

"How are you feeling today, Mr. Smythe?"

"Fine. But I haven't been to physical therapy yet. I don't like going there."

"How did you feel last night?"

Jamie cocked his head to the side as if waiting for an answer to come. "Fine."

"Did you sleep through the night?" Will asked.

Jamie hesitated. "I don't know. It's hard to tell if it's night or day."

Barry noticed the window on the opposite side of the room. Jamie's eyes tracked the lieutenants.

"Did you see the nurse, Candy, last night?" Will asked.

"Yes."

"Did you request something for pain?"

"Why would I do that?" Jamie asked. "I don't have therapy at night."

"Were you in pain last night?" Will asked.

"No."

"Then how did you see Nurse Wilkerson?" Barry asked. If she was only assigned to giving meds, what other reason would she have to be in a patient's room?

Jamie's head slowly rotated toward Barry. The lips curled in what was supposed to be a smile, the curve of the lips didn't match the eyes.

The attorney shifted away from the bed his feet pointed toward the door. Barry wondered if Kaine even knew he'd done it. Or was it some ancient instinct? Spending so much time alongside predators, he had to have developed some sort of sixth sense in order to coexist with them.

"Good catch, Lieutenant. Too bad those skills did not save your partner. Tell me, do you regret not being there for poor Mark?"

"We're done here," Kaine snapped in motion toward the door.

"Oh, I do not think we are. We are just getting started," Jamie said and blinked. The lids lifted. *It* focused on Barry. Only it wasn't Jamie. Not really. Barry wondered if those were the same black bottomless eyes Olivia saw.

"Do you know why I took his tongue?"

Will froze. It was a part of the story he didn't know. Cops always held something back, from the public, from the family.

"As a keepsake. Because it was what he used to tell you about her. Think of how your life would be different if he had kept her to himself. You would not be here with me. You would not be wondering what she was doing or who she was doing it with. Mark told you she could help you. Tell me, has she?"

Barry wanted to close his eyes, turn off the sound of his voice, but he stood there and took it, forcing himself to listen.

"She has small delicate feet, does she not? They fit in your hands."

Brennon's hand slipped from the door knob at the comment, frozen in place.

Will concentrated on *not* looking at Smythe. He was watching the lieutenant instead.

She trailed her foot down his leg as they lay intertwined in her grandmother's bed. He reached down and caught it in his hand.

"The pink toe polish was a nice touch. I believe she called it Bubblegum."

Barry slid his hand underneath the hem of her flowy dress, but stopped himself at the knee. She was murmuring, her lips on his, something about taking things slow, doing it right.

Barry shook his head, scattering the memories. He took a step closer to the bed. A wave of vertigo rushed him. He reached for the bedrail, the cold metal snapping him free.

"It should have been you," Smythe hissed.

He might have lunged for Smythe. Barry wasn't sure, but those were the last words he heard before someone pulled him out of the room.

Back outside in the hall, his head was clear.

Barry turned when he heard Kaine shout. "What the hell was that?"

"He was talking about Olivia, and he was talking about Mark," Barry shot back.

Will intercepted from the side and pushed Barry against the wall. The lawyer had the good sense to walk away, but not far.

"Hey!" Will said, tapping Barry on the shoulder trying to redirect his focus from the attorney. "I thought we were supposed to be partners." Will was more scared than pissed.

Barry shook himself free and Will let him go. "You might want to rethink that. You heard what happened to my last one."

Will watched as Barry readjusted his coat. He hadn't bothered with a tie this morning. He looked like he was trying to shake it off. He stalked back to the conference room as Brennon Kaine fell in behind him. Will brought up the rear, his eyes scanning the hallway for reinforcements. He would need back up if the lieutenant decided to head back to Smythe's room. He might be younger by more than a decade, but he'd also had the element of surprise on his side. He wouldn't have it a second time and Will doubted he could best the lieutenant without it. Not in his current state.

They filed into the conference room. "You were out of line." Brennon muttered.

"So was he," Barry fired back, his voice just below a roar.

"Why don't you ask the counselor what that was," Barry turning back to Will, ignoring Kaine's protest. "It's his client."

"Obviously a disturbed individual," Brennon said.

"Is that you or his psych eval talking?" Barry wanted to know.

Brennon's eyes narrowed but he remained silent.

"Insanity plea?" Barry was clenching and unclenching his fists as he advanced on the attorney.

Brennon stood his ground. "Perhaps you should rethink the personal leave, Lieutenant."

Will put his hand on Barry's arm halting his advance before he could invade Kaine's personal space.

"What the hell is going on?" Sharon Taylor snapped, bursting through the door they'd never closed. The whole hall could hear them.

The stalemate between him and the lieutenant over, Brennon turned on the nurse manager. "These men are not allowed back in my client's room without me present."

"As the medication nurse, would there be any other reason Nurse Wilkerson would have gone into one of the patient rooms last night?" Barry asked, snapping Sharon and Will back to attention.

"No," Sharon shook her head. "Not unless another nurse asked her to."

"Did anyone actually see her go in or out of Smythe's room last night?"

"I'm sure they did. Frank said Candy called the doctor for another injection order," Sharon recalled.

"That doesn't answer the question," Barry said. He turned on Will next. "Did you ask that specific question of any of the staff?"

Will started to open his mouth, but nothing came out.

"Did anyone say they saw Nurse Wilkerson go in room seven? Yes, or no?" Barry asked, his voice returning to normal as he found the rhythm of interrogation.

Will pulled out his notebook and started flipping pages.

"Did you hear back from IT?" Barry whipped back to Sharon.

"I did." It sounded like a confession. "That's where I was when I should have been in the room with you." Sharon kept her voice level, hoping it signaled Barry needed to do the same. "Candy didn't document anything last night."

"So, from the looks of the system, all nurse Wilkerson did last night was pull two Dilaudid injections," Barry surmised.

"You're correct," Sharon agreed. She didn't want to believe it.

The flipping of pages finally stopped. "I never asked anyone if they saw Candy go into room seven," Will said. "But Smythe told us he saw her." He sounded triumphant.

"He also told us he wasn't sure of the time or the day," Barry snapped back. "His own attorney confirmed he is a disturbed individual." Barry shook his head at the same time he concentrated on breathing. How did she do this? How did Olivia fight monsters when there was no way to stop them?

"It doesn't matter." He was done. "Jamie Lynn Smythe didn't stick a needle in Candy Wilkerson's arm. She did it to herself. This is a waste of time." Barry started for the door, but Sharon stepped up to block his path.

"You can't just leave. You have to do something," she was pleading. "You know as well as I do that there's something not right with him."

"I'm well aware of that, Ms. Taylor. So is his attorney." Barry hurled a scowl in Kaine's direction. "You heard what he said about me and my partner. Brennon Kaine's calling the shots. It's why that poor excuse for a human being will be spending his time in a padded cell rather than in prison where he belongs." It was why Kaine was there. It was about getting this guy off the hook. If he was honest with himself, it was exactly what Olivia would want.

Sharon shook her head. She was caught in some eternal pissing contest and all she wanted was for it to end. She turned to the only person in the room who could help her. "Then you, Mr. Kaine. You need to get your client off my floor."

Brennon appreciated her candor. Fear did that. "Is he ready for discharge?"

"He can be," Sharon assured him.

"I'm sure there's a cell downstairs with his name on it," Barry told him.

"I'll need a physician's order," Brennon said, not taking his eyes off the lieutenant. "And a cell in the isolation unit with assurances of my client's safety."

"I don't work here. Talk to someone in jail administration," Barry said. He brushed past Kaine while Sharon cleared his path to the door. Will followed him out.

* * *

The house was quiet. Rachel and Jake were still sleeping. Olivia took the down time to call Dom again. Too much time on her hands and her thoughts had wandered back to the barn. This time he answered. "What do you know about the ankh?" She wanted a religious perspective and knew Dom's proclivity for symbols.

He ignored her absence of greeting knowing when she had something on her mind she didn't hold back. "The *crux ansata.*"

Olivia recognized the Latin. It was a simple description: *the cross with a handle.*

"It's Egyptian in origin. Known as the *Key of the Nile* since the river's floods brought life to the region. Probably why it's said to signify the union of heaven and earth. The horizontal part of the cross depicts the division between them while the vertical part represents communication between the two realms - heaven and earth."

"So, an inversion could mean..."

"Any number of things." Dom's tone was hesitant. "Please tell me why you're asking."

"It's a case. Maybe a case," Olivia fumbled. Atascosa County was still as much a mystery to her as it was the day Silas showed up asking her about the deceased Ferdinand Roche.

"Inversion negates its original purpose, doesn't it?" Olivia said what the priest couldn't. "Meaning it's Hell someone wants to communicate with."

Gran always warned against mixing the light with the dark. It turned everything to gray. Like twilight. *That magical time where the dark and the light swam together.*

Something was very wrong in Atascosa County.

* * *

Will waited until they were alone in the elevator. "Those things Smythe said. He was talking about Dr. Osborne, wasn't he?"

Barry didn't answer. His eyes were fixed in a corner, seeing things he wished he could *unsee*. Feeling things, he wished he didn't feel.

Will kept talking despite the voice in his own head screaming at him to shut up. "The staff thinks Smythe had something to do with Nurse Wilkerson's death. That can't be right, can it?" He was trying not to lose his shit, but he could feel cracks along the edges. "Smythe got inside your head. I watched him. If he can do that to you…"

"Would it make you feel better if I told you I have no illusions what Smythe is? Knowing things, you shouldn't know, describing events you didn't attend, those are signs of possession. Dr. Osborne taught me that."

"So, it's true. She's some kind of demon hunter?"

Barry shook his head. "She hunts them. They hunt her. I'm not sure anymore." *Neither was she.*

CHAPTER THIRTEEN

OLIVIA OPENED HER computer and trolled the internet for news from home. She noted an employee of Bexar County jail had been found dead. Before she could get very far Silas called. His first question was if Rachel and Jakey were still asleep.

"Yes, what's wrong?" His tone told her he didn't have good news.

"Dad is having seizures. They can't do an MRI because he's too unstable. And some kidney doctor is seeing him because the neurologist thinks he may be going into kidney failure."

"I'm sorry," Olivia told him wishing she was saying it in person.

There was a long pause on Silas's end. "After your call and when Rachel and Jake wake up, do you think the three of you could join us at the hospital?" He sounded hesitant. Asking for help wasn't something that came easy. She knew the feeling.

"I'll cancel the call. It's not important."

"You don't have to do that. I'm sure they need to sleep anyway."

"We'll leave as soon as they get up. I want to be there with you."

* * *

Barry and Will were in Zavalla's office detailing the events of their visit when Olivia called the captain to tell him she wasn't going to make their afternoon meeting. "Is everything alright?" Zavalla asked.

"It's touch and go which is why I can't guarantee I'll be available. I can review my findings with you now if you like or you can take questions and I can get back to you later."

Zavalla glanced at the men in front of him. "If you have time, then let's do it now. Have you seen the news from here? About what's happening at the jail?"

"Only that an employee was found dead."

"I've got you on speaker phone, if that's okay. I have Sergeant Will Ibarra and Lieutenant Bartholomew with me in my office."

Olivia was surprised to hear Barry was present. There could only be one reason. "It's Jamie, isn't it?"

All three men looked at each other. Barry nodded to his new partner. Will was still beating himself up about his questioning of the infirmary staff members. Barry wanted him to know this was still his show.

"You made a mistake. Learn from it. Move past it," Barry had told him on the way back. It was the closest thing the sergeant was going to get to a pep talk. Too bad he didn't follow his own advice.

A rookie mistake, said the little voice inside of Will's head. It was the difference between teaching and doing. With a nod from the lieutenant he leaned into the phone and as briefly as possible relayed the morning's events.

"What does the staff think?" Olivia wanted to know.

It wasn't a question Will would have expected if not for the conversation in the elevator. He looked at Barry who gave him another nod, but it wasn't necessary Olivia did it for him.

"They think Jamie is responsible for Ms. Wilkerson's death, don't they? You probably do too."

"I know it sounds crazy," Will conceded.

Barry could see Will was surprised Olivia had already caught up with him. Then again, he didn't know her.

"You mentioned Ms. Wilkerson had something on file with the Nurse Assistance Program. What was her drug of choice?" Olivia asked.

"It wasn't drugs." Will sounded dejected. He and Barry had stopped at HR on their way back to Zavalla's office.

"It was hospital treatment for depression," Barry decided he would relay the bit of news. He needed to get back in the game. He was going to have to play alongside her sooner or later.

There was a pause on Olivia's end. Barry wondered if she was as uncomfortable as he was. "It makes her vulnerable. Impressionable," she said.

"In other words, weak," Barry filled in the blanks.

"We all have our weaknesses, Lieutenant. Some of us are just better at building walls." She paused. Barry wondered if it was for her benefit or his.

"A perfect scenario for some sort of outside influence," Barry surmised.

"You could say that," Olivia agreed. "Tell me, how did Jamie react to questioning?"

"To be honest, I'm not sure we were talking to *him* the entire time." Unlike her, Barry couldn't call him by name. That made him a person and Barry knew that wasn't true.

It sounded like what Brennon had said. "This is likely an accurate assessment."

"What do we do about that, exactly?" Barry wanted to know.

"He needs a psych eval."

"Mr. Kaine wasn't so forthcoming."

"Brennon can't get anyone in there until Monday," Olivia revealed.

So, she had been talking to Kaine. "He seems leery of his client."

"He should be."

Her words hung in the air long enough to make everyone uncomfortable. Finally, Will broke the stalemate. "Are we going to discuss how crazy this sounds? Is any of this even possible?" Will asked. "Despite what the staff thinks, Smythe was confined to his room. He couldn't have been with Candy Wilkerson when she killed herself."

Olivia heard the frustration in his voice. "He didn't have to be." There was a note of finality to her voice. Will didn't feel like challenging her.

"So, what else?" It was Barry.

"Psych eval first," Olivia repeated. There was something else. "The nurse was accessible. If the demon remained with Jamie then he's a prisoner as well." *How long would it take him to get bored and move on?* "He needs to have as little contact with people as possible."

"Mr. Kaine was talking about an isolation cell," Will offered.

"That's a start."

"Not good enough," Barry said. "What about when that doesn't help?" Because he knew it wouldn't. "Why not Father Dominic?"

"If you're suggesting what I think you're suggesting he'll need permission from the bishop of the local Archdiocese," Olivia told him.

"Will he grant it?"

"If I speak to him." Olivia didn't want to be the one to tell him it wasn't the bishop who would need convincing. No matter what had happened today, Brennon Kaine was still in charge.

Captain Zavalla was done talking about things they couldn't control. "Atascosa County," he reminded them.

Olivia took a deep breath and redirected. "My initial impression from the photos I saw today is whoever is using the barn was involved in Ferdinand Roche's death. This person is trying very hard to convince others that there is some kind of dark force at work."

"Why? To what end?" Will was asking exactly what Olivia was trying to understand.

"Many reasons, fear being first among them." When paired with the overkill used on Roche before and *after* death, it fit with the profile she was building. "The second is desperation. This person is a seeker."

Her statement sounded ominous. "Of what?" Barry wanted to know.

Olivia's response was quick. "Unclear."

"And the symbol on the wall?" Will asked. "It's an ankh, isn't it?"

"You are correct."

There was hesitancy in her voice. A delay tactic maybe. "It shouldn't be inverted," Will said for her.

Zavalla's brow furrowed as he struggled to keep it all aligned. He needed to understand the normal before the *para*normal. "What does it mean? If it's *not* inverted," he emphasized. "Let's start there."

"The ankh is the symbol of life," Olivia told them.

"So, the inversion would mean what?"

Olivia didn't give Zavalla the opportunity to finish his sentence. "Let's don't get ahead of ourselves, Captain," Olivia said using Father Dominic's words. They were meant to be comforting. She knew that now, but doubted they would work on Zavalla any better than they had on her. "I can't give you anymore until I'm able to walk the site." A promise was all she could offer.

"When are you coming back?" It was Barry.

"I'm not certain. It depends on what happens here."

* * *

Olivia looked up to see Rachel standing in the hallway.

"I didn't mean to eavesdrop, I swear. It's just…,"

"No, I'm sorry. I should have closed the door," Olivia apologized. When she was submerged in work there was nothing else. Olivia couldn't help but wonder what she heard.

"Not at all." Rachel waved her off. "You didn't wake us up. But I have to ask. What is it you do exactly?" She thought Silas may have downplayed Olivia's position with the FBI.

"Hunt monsters," Olivia said. "Disguised as humans."

"I told you monsters were real, Mummy." From behind Rachel's legs the face of a little boy appeared. He gave Olivia a tentative smile she couldn't help but return.

"Jake, this is Miss Olivia," Rachel said taking his hand and pulling him from behind her. "She's Uncle Silas's friend."

Olivia stepped forward and bent down to Jake's level. "Nice to meet you, Jakey," she said. The boy had light red hair like his dad and blue eyes like his mom. A nice blend of both.

Jake turned a shade red darker than his hair and buried his face against his mother's leg.

"He likes blondes; probably why he's being so shy. It won't take him long to warm up to you," Rachel whispered, eliciting another smile from Olivia. "You have kids?" The question slipped out before Rachel could stop herself. She blamed it on the job. She saw women all day long either trying to have babies or trying not to have babies. Doing the calculations in her head, Rachel suspected Olivia was of the age the clock was starting to tick. How loud was it for Olivia? Or had she given it up for her career?

Olivia shook her head. It was something she tried not to think about. "No."

Rachel nodded, wishing she hadn't brought it up. "I'm assuming you heard from Silas." Daniel had left her a voicemail.

"Yes."

"Things don't sound good," Rachel said, her tone soft.

"Not when he started telling me about the decreased kidney function," Olivia agreed.

"Are you a PhD or an M.D.?" Rachel asked.

"I have a PhD in forensic psychology, but my first degree was in nursing."

"I'm sure that's an interesting story."

"One that would require adult beverages," Olivia cautioned her with a smile.

"I couldn't help but hear you mention an ankh," Rachel ventured.

"I did," Olivia agreed, quickly inventorying anything else the woman might have overheard.

"You were right. It is the symbol of life." Rachel pulled a little silver necklace out from beneath her t-shirt. It was much like the silver cross Olivia wore. "Also, immortality. Isis was an Egyptian goddess associated with fertility. When her husband Osiris died, she returned him to life. I see a lot of fertility patients in my business. Seeking it can make people desperate."

Olivia considered the new implications.

"What was your dissertation focus?" Rachel asked, preventing Olivia from wandering too far. Rachel was glad for some female companionship away from work, and she was curious to get to know the woman who had turned Silas Branch's head. Besides Daniel would want to know why she hadn't interrogated her when she had the chance.

"Similarities between the symptoms of Alzheimer's disease and demonic possession."

"Wow. Okay. No wonder you worked for the BAU."

* * *

Rachel was right. It didn't take Jake long. His little hand was wrapped securely inside Olivia's. Rachel wasn't sure who was enjoying it more Jakey or Olivia. They'd made fast friends. Inside the ICU meeting room, they found the family huddled together.

Silas was stoic, impossible to read. He kissed Olivia's forehead and bent down to see Jake, but his nephew held fast to Olivia.

"What's going on?" she whispered.

The EEG results showed little to no brain activity and the rest of Raymond Branch's body had systematically begun to let go. There was no going back. Sally Branch had already called for the priest. As soon as last rites were given, they would withdraw the colonel from the ventilator. Without outside help his body wouldn't have the capacity to breathe on its own. They wouldn't have to wait long for the end.

Olivia felt torn. She wanted to be there for Silas, but for the first time she felt out of place. This was definitely family time. Silas had his siblings and his mother. Rachel needed to be free to be with her husband. The most Olivia could offer was to shield the youngest member of the family, so she took Jake to the happiest place in the hospital: the nursery. It was the circle of life. With each death there was a new beginning. There was balance in the universe. There could be no dark without light. No evil without good.

Olivia was thankful the four-year-old was spared from what was happening around him. Memories were being made today with or without him. His grandfather's passing would be talked about for years to come and she hoped his memories of this day would consist of looking into the faces of new life. She only recalled memories from the time she was four because that's when she began to see *the others*. It was also the time in her life when her mother dropped her off with Gran and never came back.

* * *

News of Colonel Branch's passing spread quickly through the Branches' circle of friends. There was a steady stream of visitors at the house until close to midnight.

The ride back to Silas's was quiet. Both Jake and Rachel fell asleep on the way.

Silas and Daniel stayed awake for a while. Olivia left them to share bourbon and memories while she retreated upstairs to research fertility. The magic of creation made it a favorite following of many ancient cults. To some, the uterus was a powerful vessel, the center of a woman's power. Considering the use of the pentagram on Ferdinand Roche, Olivia explored the darker forms of fertility worship. There she found that certain cults considered the uterus to be "the lake of fire." Groups on the outer fringes went so far as to equate the image of Baphomet, considered by some to be a representation of Satan, to the image of a goddess in the shape of a uterus. Personally, she didn't see it. She believed something as beautiful as creation could not be evil.

Olivia could tell by the way Silas slipped into bed he believed she was asleep. Once he was settled in, she moved over. She heard the catch of his breath as bare skin moved against his. "I didn't expect you to still be awake," he whispered, burying his face in her hair.

"You'd rather I be asleep?" She kissed him, not waiting for an answer.

"No. Tell me about your day. Talk to me about anything but what's happened."

Silas knew then, just as his mother's life had changed that day, so had his.

CHAPTER FOURTEEN

OLIVIA TOOK AN early flight the morning after the funeral and headed to SAPD as soon as she landed. Captain Zavalla had scheduled a briefing immediately following her tour of the barn. Will Ibarra was playing chauffer. Their drive gave Olivia a chance to get to know him. He was personable but reserved, mentioning only briefly that he knew she'd been out of town for the past week but treading cautiously and not probing her for additional details. He was new to his role but the return of his lieutenant had helped his transition. Olivia had known Barry wouldn't stay away long. It wasn't in his nature. The job was his life and life moved forward ready or not. By choice or by some unforeseen force. The last week of her life reminded her of that. She didn't want to admit it, but it would be uncomfortable seeing Barry. Her circumstances had changed. Did he know? Did he even care? His actions at the condo said he didn't.

As Will turned off the main road and onto Sampson's land he noted the old man's car in the driveway. It was mid-day, too early for him to make his daily pilgrimage to the VFW. Will filled Olivia in on what he knew. "He's a widower. Lives alone. No family. Inherited the land from his father but hasn't worked it in years. He won some kind of wrongful death suit against the hospital where his wife died. Apparently, he likes to spend his days staring at the bottom of a beer glass."

"Did he know the Roches?"

"From what I read he hired Ferdinand to install the flooring in his house a few years back. No one knows for sure if that's how they met, but it seems plausible. According to the file it was Mr. Sampson's land where the body was found. Sampson had hired him to clear some brush in an area not far from here. There are a couple of other structures on this tract of land."

It fit with what Olivia remembered about Ferdinand. He'd been a day laborer taking any odd jobs he could find. "Was the murder scene visible from the house?"

"No," Will shook his head.

Murder in a remote location all but eliminated the possibility of any witnesses. They didn't even have motive, not now that the Rangers had come up empty on any kind of drug connection. "Familiarizing yourself with the murder book, that's good." She sensed Will could use the encouragement and she knew she could use the education. This had been Silas's case from the start, but they had both been out of the loop.

"It was basically my only job for a while. That and finding my way around headquarters," Will said with a sheepish grin. Even though they'd just met he felt comfortable around her. Working with the lieutenant, he felt like he'd gotten to know her by osmosis. He'd also learned that present or not, she played some role in his partner's life.

"Who found Roche's body?"

"His brother, Andre. Said he went to look for him when he wasn't answering his phone."

"Were they close?" Having spent so much time around the Branch family thoughts of a brotherly dynamic sprang to mind.

"That I don't know."

"Anyone talk to Andre recently?"

"I think I read something about the Rangers wanting to talk to him about the fire, but he wasn't home. According to his neighbor he packed some things and said he was heading to New Orleans to give his brother a proper burial."

The story struck a note with her, but she wasn't sure what part. Something Silas had said back during the original investigation. The story was disjointed with multiple hands in the pot. Maybe they all needed to come together. Olivia pulled out her phone and sent Zavalla a text with a request for just such a meeting.

"How much land does Mr. Sampson own?" Olivia asked, curious if there were other places worth investigating.

"A section," Will replied off the top of his head. He'd looked it up for himself when the fire inspector had been unable to answer the same question last week.

Olivia gave him a look that signaled she needed more information. He was obviously using some frame of reference she was unfamiliar with.

"Six hundred and thirty-four acres, or one mile if you laid it out side by side," Will explained.

"I'm pretty sure that wasn't in the murder book."

"My grandfather owns farmland in West Texas," Will explained. "I know some of the lingo."

They had reached the barn. It looked pretty much like it did in the pictures. "This place should be condemned," Olivia said as they approached the dilapidated building. "What's the possibility of someone using this place without the owner's knowledge?" Olivia asked as Will held the door open for her. The place was remote with only Sampson's house for company. Even then it was at least a half a block away by city standards. It was hard to believe a city of over four million people sprawled within an easy drive of where they stood.

"Highly likely."

"Closest neighbor?"

"A mile or so the way we came in. Some doctor who works on the south side of San Antonio. As for Sampson, by late afternoon you can find him at the local VFW until it closes or they kick him out. He comes home, sleeps it off, hits repeat the next day."

Great.

"He leases out portions of the land for wheat and hay grazer to other local farmers. Sometimes for hunting. Other than that, there doesn't seem to be any traffic out here."

Olivia scanned the surroundings. Remote. Isolated. No neighbors. Nobody home. "Perfect if you wanted to hide something or you were seeking no interruptions." Instinctively she turned and faced the open field.

"The burned body of Ferdinand Roche was found about two hundred yards that way," Will told her.

Interesting. Certainly not a coincidence. There was a reason someone had staked this place out as their own. With or without the owner's permission.

Inside she followed Will through the barn to the circle of candles. Passing through the sliding panel door to the platform area she was hit with a wave of dizziness. A nest of latent energy rippled as she walked. It was heavy, not created over time through the passage of events, like the descriptions she'd shared with Jessica Tate. The energy in here was *conjured*. It hovered in the shadows and played across the back of her mind as heaviness settled in the pit of her stomach. It was foreign yet familiar.

Olivia was drawn to the platform encircled by candles. They looked just like they did in the photo, but now, in person, there was residual energy. It hung above like a mist, unseen by the naked eye. What she was experiencing now was visceral, second sight. The ripples became a wake at her feet as she breached the circle. A hum of energy, ancient yet timeless, flowed through her body.

Will felt a prickle along his hairline and stepped out of her way. It faded the farther he got from her.

Olivia sat down on the ground and lay back on the empty platform. Instinctively she reached for the tiny silver cross around her neck. Her breathing slowed. She gazed upward, greeted by patches of sunlight. Particles danced in the beams of light. What lay beyond the veil beckoned her. It was all around her. She reached for it—just a toe dip in the water. It bent at her touch.

A low hum filled her ears. *Chanting.* There had been more than one here. She strained to hear and got lost in the sky. The sunlight melted. Blue became gray, streaked with purple lightening. It was eerily familiar. Energies lingered here, different kinds. Human, inhuman, otherworldly. Olivia couldn't pin it down. They registered her presence. Unaware of her own movements she let go of the cross and her hands crossed over her abdomen.

"Dr. Osborne? Olivia?"

She heard him on the other side of the fog. Olivia's eyes snapped open and she clamped down on her thoughts. Will was in front of her on her level.

"Are you alright? You look pale."

Olivia took a cleansing breath inhaling deeply to slow the rapid firing in her chest. She thrust her hand out, forcing Will to take it. He grabbed it and pulled her up. She pushed against him, breaking free of the circle. Once on the other side she brushed her hands down her arms, cleansing herself the best she could, returning to her bearings. She'd gone somewhere she shouldn't have. "Offerings were made here. Sacrifices," she said with conviction. She'd awakened something on the other side. It knew she was there.

Olivia reached for the piece of silver around her neck. Her eyes closed as her lips began to move. "*Benedicta tu in mulieribus, et benedictus fructus ventris tui.*"

"Blessed art thou among women, and blessed is the fruit of thy womb." Will made the sign of the cross and echoed the verse, as she ended the prayer. "My grandmother was old school. Made us learn the Hail Mary in Latin," he said in response to the stare he'd just earned from her. Will swallowed. "Did you say offerings? Is that like sacrifices?" he asked, looking as distressed as she felt. *What had he just witnessed?*

"He was seeking something on the other side, luring it with promises." She moved past him making a beeline for the door.

"He who? Where are you going?" She moved fast for someone with legs shorter than his.

"Somewhere other than here. Take me to the burn site." Will moved quickly to keep up, but she passed him by, not needing his direction. "What have you learned about the burning of Roche's body?" Olivia pressed on once they arrived at the charred spot on the ground. Outside, away from that place she was feeling better.

"The accelerant used was mineral spirits." So far it was the most interesting clue they had. Basically, the only one.

Olivia stared at the blackened ground. She walked it just as Will had, her steps quick and purposeful. "Why is this burn spot so circular?"

"I noticed that too." Although it had taken him longer. "According to the fire investigator, there was a ring of salt around it. As if whoever set it didn't want it to spread."

"I don't think it was the fire they were concerned about," Olivia commented. There was a question in his gaze. "If there's something you want to ask me sergeant, now's as good a time as any."

After what he'd just seen in the barn, he guessed it didn't matter how the question sounded. "Do you think this could be a protection circle of some kind?"

"Is that what you heard from the fire investigator?"

"It might have come up in the conversation."

Mentally Olivia counted to five. She didn't want to snap at the nice new sergeant. "In this case, it was used as a show of dominance."

Her words had an edge to them. Will watched as she circled the spot, her movements shark-like, predatory.

Roche's murder had troubled her from the start. "The official cause of death was exsanguination due to a throat laceration, correct?"

"Yeah," Will confirmed. There had been a blow to the head as well, but that was more likely to subdue.

"A pitchfork was used to pin him to the ground and red pepper and salt was rubbed on his body. What does that suggest to you?" Olivia knew the sergeant didn't know the answer but she was making a point.

She was describing some ritual. Ruben Cruz had mentioned it. Probably something to do with witchcraft. Will kicked himself for not looking it up but he hadn't known there was going to be a pop quiz. "Unnecessary." It was the first word that popped in his head. It came out sounding like a question.

Olivia looked at him and Will wished he could take it back. Maybe he could have a do-over. "No idea."

"You were right the first time, Sergeant. Trust your instincts." A slit to the throat would have done the job, but it wasn't just about that. Whoever did this was into theatrics. Blood was spilled and a sacrifice offered. The pitchfork and the condiments were just extras, but the target audience small. Whoever did this wanted to be seen. The question was *why?*

* * *

"I'm due in front of a judge here in a little bit so I'm on the phone until I'm not," Herschel Gaines said by way of a greeting.

For Olivia, his soothing Texas drawl conjured visions of Sam Elliott. Herschel Gaines's slow steady delivery gave the false impression he was slow on the uptake —a dangerous miscalculation from what Olivia had learned about him when she looked him up on the Texas Ranger website. He was one of the longest serving Rangers. He'd tracked the enemy in the jungles of Vietnam and had brought home those skills to take down drug runners in cases reminiscent of the glory days of the Texas Rangers. Olivia found herself looking forward to meeting him. It was his presence Olivia had requested from Zavalla.

"The captain tells me you've been to the barn. Does that symbol mean anything to you?"

"The symbol is an ankh," Olivia explained. "In some religions it means life."

"Religion is one of the oldest ways to control and intimidate," the Ranger pointed out.

"You are correct," Olivia agreed. She knew she had wanted to talk to him for a reason. He recognized something. "Fear and intimidation have been used for eons of time to exert dominance and maintain control."

"The symbol was inverted," Zavalla interrupted. "Shouldn't we be talking about that?" She'd avoided his question the first time and he was pretty sure it wasn't because she didn't know.

"Inversion typically means the opposite." Olivia hadn't wanted to share the information until she'd seen it for herself. The occult was her world, not theirs.

"Death?" Zavalla said it for her.

"Death is not what I sensed," Olivia corrected him. "But evil, conjured by men. It inhabits the barn. The ankh is created by a straight line with a loop at the end. The line is a division between heaven and earth, the loop represents open communication."

"So, if you invert the loop that opens communication to Hell." It was Will. He'd meant the idea to stay inside his head, but somehow it slipped past his lips instead.

"You're correct. There was an inverted pentagram on Roche. At the time I thought it was to send a message. It could have been a declaration that he killed a witch."

"I'm going to stop you right there, Doc." It was Gaines again. "I checked out the Roches myself. From everybody's account, Ferdinand was a gentle giant type. As for drugs, he was more the 'personal use only' type."

Olivia quickly shifted gears. "Ok, then given what we now know about Ferdinand, that's not it. The other choice was a cry for attention. 'See me'." Olivia looked over at Will thinking about what they'd found in the field.

"That's why Roche's body was circled with salt and burned. It was a message to the Underworld." *Or an offering.*

"So, you think the same fella who killed Ferdinand Roche has been using the barn." Ranger Gaines had given Olivia quite the ribbing a few weeks earlier when they gathered around a telephone much like this listening to her explanation regarding the manner of death and the condition of Ferdinand Roche's body. "And now he's talking to Hell." It wasn't even a question, just a summary. If Olivia had done her checking into the Ranger, he'd undoubtedly done the same with her. It sounded like she must have passed the audition.

"I think whoever used the barn killed Ferdinand Roche," Olivia said what the Ranger didn't. He was following her lead. "We have a seeker. Someone who is dabbling in dark magic in search of something. This conjurer has a dark purpose and he's invested. Enough to kill. I'm betting Ferdinand wasn't the first."

Will Ibarra scribbled something in his trusty notebook at the comment.

"And he won't be the last," Olivia warned.

"I'll cast a net and do some trolling on my own. See what I can come up with," the Ranger offered. "I was just looking for drugs last time."

"What's he searching for?" Zavalla asked.

"It sounds like you're describing a sacrifice," Barry said before Olivia could answer Zavalla. He'd slipped in quietly during the time Olivia had them mesmerized with thoughts of Hell. Barry's eyes locked with hers.

"You used the words sacrifice and offering in the barn," Will reminded her, breaking their stalemate.

"Sacrifices are a means to an end, are they not?" Barry asked.

Olivia was thinking about what the word sacrifice meant. "Or an offering. Something one gives in exchange for something else. With divine beings it could be considered worship." Mix the ritualism with the meaning of the ankh and they could have a bad combination on their hands.

"What's the end game here?" Barry wanted to know.

"I'm still working on that," Olivia conceded. Mentally she was connecting the dots to Andre as the killer. There was the familial connection and Will had said he was the one to discover the body. It meant he could also have been the last one to see his brother alive. Just she wasn't ready to share yet. "Ferdinand Roche's murder was overkill. Whoever killed him knows their *other world* stuff. Enough to make me wary." There was a long pause in the room and on the other line.

The room fell silent. All they could hear was the sound of Gaines inhaling his cigarette and then his edict. "I think wary is a very healthy attitude."

Olivia shifted in her seat. It sounded like a Silas response. Maybe her own headspace hadn't been far off. Or Barry's. It sounded like they were coming to the same conclusion.

"The witchy stuff I leave to you, Doc, because that's your business. But the rest of us trade in bad guys and I think that's exactly what we have. You said he wanted to be seen. *See me*," the Ranger repeated her words. "I don't know about the Hell part of it, but over here on God's green Earth if someone wanted attention, I'd say he certainly got it."

Olivia felt the air evaporate from the room. She watched concern form on the faces of the men surrounding her.

"Roche's death brought Agent Branch all the way to San Antonio and he went running straight to you Dr. Osborne. You might ought to consider that."

Zavalla and Will looked to Olivia. Barry sat up straighter in his chair, poised ready for whatever was to come.

The Roche brother Ranger Gains had described was not in life what he'd been made to be in death. It was an intentional misdirection. "What did you learn about Andre Roche?" Olivia asked Gaines.

"Basically, he's a vagabond. Claims he's an artist of life. Does metal work, sketches, and paintings. Also, concocts ointments and salves and with some help sells them at craft and trade shows. Was a mama's boy. Marceline was her name. He likes telling people she was a voodoo priestess. He claims to be a practitioner himself. Sounds like a *seeker* of something to me," the Ranger suggested using her words again.

Olivia had stopped listening, her memory pinging on the name *Marceline*. "Was Andre investigated for his brother's death?"

"If he was, it was conducted by the same sheriff office the Atascosa DA doesn't trust." The Ranger sounded distracted already running down his own rabbit holes. "Maybe I ought to give the DA a call. The boy might have been on to something. Just looking in the wrong place."

They were all on the same page. "I think that's an excellent idea." Mention of the DA reminded Olivia of something else. "Since you're speaking to him, do you think you could do me a favor and look into something else for me?"

"The DA already thinks you're doing him one, so I'd say he owes you. I'm inclined to oblige."

She was developing a soft spot for the old Ranger. Her Gran would have liked him too. He was a breath of fresh air from the up-tight FBI agents she was used to working with. Too many alphas, overflowing with testosterone. Herschel Gaines still had an edge to him but he was tempered in his older age. For a brief second, she wondered if this is how Silas would end up.

"I heard a story about some missing girls in Atascosa County. Maybe the DA knows something about them."

"There was background noise on the Ranger's end. "Looks like I'm up, Doc. I'll get back to you. And by the way, I'd like to say that was some nice trigger work you put down. Glad to see you came out of it okay. You and that agent of yours."

Olivia smiled at the compliment. She doubted the Ranger handed them out very often.

"Keep an eye on your six, Doc."

"Roger that, Ranger."

The telephone disconnected and the room fell silent around them. The four of them looked at each other. *Where to go from here?*

"You wrote something in your notebook, Sergeant," Olivia said turning to Will. "What was it?" He was a quick learner. She wondered what had captured his attention.

"You mentioned that whoever killed Ferdinand Roche—it probably wasn't their first. I thought I might run down some similarities, see if I could get any matches."

"If you run the database for pitchforks and undertones of witchcraft you'll get buried. The murder was similarly staged to that of Charles Walton in 1945 in England." Olivia recalled schooling Silas on the same topic when he showed up in San Antonio asking about Roche to begin with. He'd also asked about someone else. "Check out Andre Roche instead. See what his background is. If there were flagrant ritual killings in this area over the last decade or so, I'd know about them. See who Roche knows instead," Olivia suggested.

"You picked up on something else Gaines said there at the end," Barry prodded Olivia. He saw it in her eyes.

"The name Marceline. I've heard it before. She was a resident at one of those long-term care facilities where we searched for Jamie. Father Dominic would know."

Zavalla looked down at his phone. "It's a request from the Atascosa DA. He wants to know where to send the files on the girls Dr. Osborne was asking about."

"I'll take them," Barry said before he could ask. He looked at Olivia.

"Let me know what you find," she said, thinking her voice sounded curt. "I've got to go pick up my dogs. I know they missed me."

*   *   *

Olivia got out of downtown just in time to pick up Daisy and Alvin before the kennel closed for the night. Fiesta had begun and traffic was bumper-to-bumper, even after rush hour. She was right about her fur babies. They were as glad to see her as she was them. She pulled into the drive and set them free. From the laps Daisy ran it was obvious she'd also missed her own backyard. Alvin's little legs were too short to keep up for long so he plopped on the grass and rolled. It was good to be home.

As soon as Olivia opened the door to her house though she knew she'd had a visitor.

CHAPTER FIFTEEN

OLIVIA'S HOUSE WAS built on open land, before the city sprang up around it. For almost a century, life had ebbed and flowed within its walls. Her Gran was born there. Olivia grew up there. She knew the property intimately. It's how she knew someone had trespassed into her private space.

Her ability to sense things didn't happen only at crime scenes. She was in tune with the energies around her. People and events all left an imprint on their surroundings. The majority of these imprints waned, worn away by the passage of time. Traumatic events lingered longer. The dent left behind was clearer when it was wrapped in emotion. Alice, Gran's childhood friend was killed in front of the house. She lingered there on the property still, coexisting with Olivia's permission.

A demon had breached her house, but even its dark residual energy was gone. Wiped clean by Father Dominic's cross and her own cleansing. What she felt now was something else. Something new. As soon as Olivia crossed the threshold, her skin prickled with this unfamiliar energy. It was fresh and raw with emotion, an intrusion shrouded in malice. It radiated life. It was a human intruder.

Because it would be some time before SAPD forensics finished processing her Glock, she was relying on a smaller caliber pistol she normally kept in her glovebox. The .22 was smaller than the Glock, but it was better than a flashlight or a baseball bat. With it in hand, Olivia deactivated the alarm console and crossed the living room to the hallway with the gun leading her way. To her right the kitchen light snapped on. *Thank you, Alice?* The poltergeist had been slow to return since the demon's visit. *He can't touch you, Alice. I won't let him.*

The first thing Olivia noticed as she stepped into the hall was the door to Silas's room was open. She'd followed Daisy there the night before she left, both of them realizing how much they both missed him. Olivia knew she had closed the door when she was done, because she wanted to savor the smell of him. *And now it was gone.*

Methodically Olivia moved through the house checking the nooks and crannies finally ending up outside to feed the dogs. She watched through the window as the light in the kitchen blinked at her once and then twice. Was it a signal? Back inside she searched the kitchen but found nothing. She walked the house repeatedly, retracing her steps. She had set the house alarm when she left for Virginia. It was still set when she got home and there had been no calls from her security company signaling an intruder. Somehow Alice knew to avoid interrupting those circuits when she desired to make her presence known. Whoever had been there let themselves in, meaning they had a key and knew the alarm codes. It was a short list of people with that kind of access to her life. Olivia longed to call Silas, but they had just talked on her way to pick up the dogs. She knew if she called him back again so soon, he would know something was wrong. He would worry and she absolutely did not want that. He had other things on his mind.

Olivia vowed not to tell him when they said their goodnights. She wanted more information. Silas was a man of action and with fifteen hundred miles between them there was little he could do. She sensed no danger but as a precaution she kept the pistol nearby.

* * *

With a new job and a recent break-up Will was still looking for his new normal. His former coworkers even had a beer waiting for him when he showed up at The Rathskeller, their watering hole of choice. They were all two beers in and contemplating a change of venue for dinner when he caught sight of Doctor Amanda Greene. He'd invited her to speak to some of his classes, always toward the end of the eight-month long academy. She was a reminder to new recruits that help was available. Her presentations were always a hit. Then again, she was personable and damn fine looking.

She was a local girl. Santos had been her maiden name and with four brothers, all of whom carried some kind of a badge and gun, she knew her way around law enforcement. Some of the guys said she knew it a bit too well, the implication being that she had a type and used her profession to enhance her dating pool and vice versa. She'd been married to a cop but he was killed in the line of duty in Dallas. She'd moved back home after his death. At least that's what Will had heard, and he had been paying close attention.

"Incoming," Ron said. He was the firearms and toolmarks instructor at the academy and was the last one standing at the table. The others had reconvened in the parking lot and were plotting their next destination. "I'm going to leave you to it, brother. Just watch yourself."

"You're not going to stay and be my wingman?"

"I'm going to take a leak and make sure we're all settled up at the bar. I'll swing back and rescue you. If that's what you want." Ron winked and headed the other way. "You know what they say, it's just like riding a bike."

The conversation was easy enough. She knew how to put someone at ease. Then again that was her job. "So, how are the boys downtown treating you?" Amanda asked.

"Can't complain," Will said and took a cursory glance up and down. After spending the afternoon with the conservative Dr. Osborne, Dr. Greene looked flashy in her form-fitting skirt suit and heels.

"And your new lieutenant? Are you adjusting? How's he for a mentor?"

"He's a little rough around the edges sometimes, but hey, I think it's situational stress, you know. Of course, you probably know more about that stuff than me," Will said with a wave of his hand. He hoped the guys outside hadn't settled on a place yet, but he was hoping they did sooner rather than later. He needed some food to soak up the alcohol.

Amanda interpreted his statement as a generalization. She didn't see how he could know she'd met his new lieutenant. Maybe later he would question himself on how she knew. Maybe he wouldn't. Dr. Greene felt confident the only person who knew of her meeting with the handsome Lieutenant Bartholomew was his boss. *Or maybe someone else by now.* Maybe the sergeant knew. With the beer in his hand he was pretty talkative.

"He's smart. He's focused. With everything that's happened in the last few weeks it's got to be hard on him coming in every day, passing Sergeant Austin's desk every time he goes into his office," Will stopped himself. The alcohol had his tongue flapping. He sat the bottle down without finishing it.

"So, no chinks in the armor?" Amanda asked.

Will's eyes narrowed at the question. "The lieutenant's a rock."

"I heard the FBI doctor is still around. Have you met her? What she's like?"

That was a change of direction. Will wasn't sure where this was going, but he'd play. "Why do you ask?" Amanda Greene didn't strike him as someone looking for new gal pals.

Amanda smiled back over her drink. "Call it professional curiosity."

"She's not a doctor like you," Will corrected her.

"I heard she speaks Latin," Ron said, sidling up beside Amanda. Will had already disclosed to the group an edited version of his meeting with Dr. Osborne.

"Sounds charming." Amanda didn't even look Ron's way.

"No, she's the real deal," Will assured her.

"Aside from speaking Latin what else can she do?" Amanda asked.

"She can read energy." *Like a disturbance in the Force.* Will refrained from making the comparison, remembering Ron's comment that the movie references were "fucking annoying."

"Enlighten us," Ron urged him.

"Apparently every event leaves an imprint or an echo. The more emotion, the bigger the echo."

"It sounds like something out of a ghost story," Amanda scoffed and waved down the first passing waiter. "Who told you that?"

"Bartholomew. He's a believer."

"And a big fan I hear," Ron said with a grin. "You have a nice night, Doc." He shepherded Will away from the table and headed towards the door.

"So, where we going?" Will asked as they stepped outside.

"Somewhere with a big juicy steak," Ron told him. He caught Will looking across the parking lot. It looked like something had changed Dr. Greene's mind about having another drink. She was walking toward the other side of the parking lot, key fob in hand. "Sorry, if I was telling tales out of school in there. My wife always tells me men are worse gossips than women."

"I think that's what she was counting on," Will said watching Amanda walk to her car.

"Hey, some chicks dig that strong silent type. Your lieutenant has a couple of ex-wives under his belt. I think he can handle the likes of Dr. Greene." Ron followed Will's line of sight. "She likes her toys, huh? That's a sweet ride." It was a gold Lexus convertible still sporting dealer tags.

* * *

Olivia poured herself a glass of wine and considered the problem logically. There were only two people with a key to her house. Silas, she could rule out as the intruder. The other? Well, she wasn't sure how she was going to get that key back. She picked at the salad she'd gotten from the drive thru on the way home. When she was finished, she let the dogs inside and headed upstairs to unpack. Alvin tried to jump on the bed to watch her, but his little legs were too short. She gave him a boost, and he promptly curled up at the foot of the bed and watched her. His nub of a tail wagging every time she walked by. Daisy must have worn herself down with her laps outside. She curled up on her bed and tucked her head down for the night.

Olivia treated herself to a long hot bath in her new master bathroom. She had selected the sleigh-shaped tub just for such indulgences. While soaking she called Silas to say good-night. She also might have let it slip where she was and what she was doing. Entertaining him distracted her enough not to tell him about her unwelcome visitor. When she left, Silas said it would be a week before he could join her. She didn't believe him and she was pretty sure Silas didn't even believe himself.

* * *

"Telling her good-night. That's nice," Sally Branch said as she joined her son on the patio. The family might have just spent four long days together, but she didn't feel like she'd had a moment alone with him. Silas had taken care of everything she had been unable to deal with and she didn't know what she or the rest of them would have done without him. But if life had taught her anything, it was that it moved on.

"Yes, Mom. We were saying good-night."

Sally smiled at his uncharacteristic confession. "You know, you told your father and I you had something you wanted to talk to us about." She was referring to the dinner they would never have. The one scheduled for the same night her husband found himself in the ICU. "Were you going to tell us about Livie?" It was the pet name she'd heard her son affectionately call the woman who had suddenly come into their lives.

Silas hesitated.

"I was going to mention her. I was also going to say that I've asked for reassignment."

The confession was a surprise. "Reassignment? You're leaving the BAU?"

Silas shook his head.

"Why? Where?"

Silas took a deep breath. His feelings and reasons for the move hadn't changed, but his circumstances had. "The San Antonio field office."

Olivia just happened to live in San Antonio. Her son was serious about this woman.

"We just finished a high-profile case. With our confessed murderer alive and well in police custody it's going to be a media circus there for a while."

Silas was good at using work as a cover. The seriousness factor of this new relationship had just edged up a notch. Sally tried to hide a smile. "You might be a trained FBI profiler, but you're still my son. That all sounds like some gobbledygook to me. The simple answer is you want to be in San Antonio because that's where Olivia is. That's all you had to say. What does Livie say?"

"I haven't told her yet," Silas confessed sheepishly. She'd seen right through him. Mothers really were mysterious creatures.

"Don't you think you should tell her?"

Silas shook his head clearing those thoughts. He should have been paying more attention. "Things have changed. I can't just pick up and leave. Not now."

"Did spending time with her change your mind in some way? Was it not what you thought it would be? Was *she* not who you thought she was?"

The more he was with Olivia, the more he didn't want to be without her. The house felt empty tonight. And it wasn't just the absence of his father. Silas felt himself breaking every rule he'd ever made. *Don't get dependent. Don't settle down. Don't commit.*

He took too long to answer. "Didn't think so," Sally answered for him. "Your father is gone, but that is absolutely no reason for you to stay here and look after me. I'm a big girl, Silas." Amongst the sadness there were promises of good things to come. Daniel had just received word he was being promoted to major with a tour at the Pentagon and he and Rachel were expecting another baby. Sally Branch was a woman of strong faith and despite the unexpected turn in her life she knew she lived a blessed one.

"Take it from me, your father and I had more than forty-five years together. And I can tell you it wasn't enough. I don't want you to miss out on something because you feel the need to take care of me. Besides, you can't leave all the procreation up to your brother." She smiled at the look on her son's face. He might be thinking about Olivia and a future, but she wasn't so sure he'd thought that far ahead. "Neither of you is getting any younger," she told him.

Silas opened his mouth to say something but she cut him off.

"Listen to me, Silas Armstrong Branch, my advice is you better go after that girl. If you want to keep telling her good-night. Your father would have said the same thing and since he can't, I'm going to. Now get back to San Antonio before someone else snatches her up." Sally handed her son the two empty wine glasses she'd been holding. "Now, please go open a bottle and pour me a glass."

CHAPTER SIXTEEN

BARRY TURNED HIS car off and enjoyed the sound of silence, if for only a moment. Not just because he needed the quiet, but because he wanted to get a look at the car that had come up behind him. He could have sworn he'd met it head on before he did a U-turn and turned in. If it was the same car that meant it had circled back and was now making a slow pass by the house. Olivia lived on a half-street that ran alongside the main thoroughfare, but to Barry it didn't look like a car lost in the dark or confused by the layout. In his professional opinion it looked like a drive-by. He slumped down, adjusted the rearview mirror and strained to get a better look.

The car was sporty, high-end and not out of place in this neighborhood. Maybe they were checking him out because his car was the one that didn't belong. The SAPD logo might not be etched on the side, but the unmarked Crown Vic with dark tint and black rims still screamed cop just the same.

When the car didn't come around for another pass, Barry let it go. He was being obsessive. Or was it protective? He was guilty of both. He concentrated on getting it together. He had more pressing matters at hand. Like what was he doing here? He could have let Will bring the case file. But he hadn't.

The scenario reminded him all too well of another time when he came to her house late at night to steal some alone time with her, a case file as his golden ticket to gain entry. That night she'd cleared the path for him, telling him there was nothing between her and Mark. He'd gone full steam ahead, not expecting the FBI to come in and take it all away.

Just like that night, he had no idea what he was doing. He'd pushed her to make some choices. He had also pushed her away. He needed to see for himself if the damage was repairable.

* * *

Olivia had just gotten out of the bath when she saw the splash of headlights across the wall in her master bath, signaling her someone was there. It must be Will. Maybe he'd found something on Roche already.

Olivia was too busy throwing on clothes to get to the door before the bell rang. She was winding her damp hair into a loose bun when something stopped her. Daisy was having some kind of a doggy bad dream. But when she looked closer, she saw it was more than that. Olivia left her and raced down the stairs to the door.

He wasn't who she expected, but right now she didn't care about any of that. "Please help me. Something is wrong with Daisy."

The urgency in her voice set Barry in action. He tossed the files on the dining table and followed her upstairs. Daisy was actively vomiting by the time they got to her. Alvin was pacing the end of the bed with quick little steps stopping occasionally to let out a sharp yelp of concern, the new bed too tall for him to jump down.

"This looks bad," Barry said as Olivia dashed into the bathroom for towels. He thought he could see streaks of blood in the last upheaval. By the time she returned the greyhound was on her side, breathing heavily.

"I know an animal hospital that's open all night," Olivia said and reached for her phone. "Can you help me load her into my car? My keys are hanging by the front door."

Since he'd turned in the drive, Barry had to exchange his car for hers. When he got back Barry found Olivia in the floor cradling Daisy's head in her lap like a baby. Olivia was wiping her face with a wet cloth and murmuring to her. It didn't look like Daisy had vomited anymore, but she was still on her side. From where he was standing it looked like her panting had become shallow. "She was running around playing when we got home. All I did was feed her."

"Let me," Barry said gently, reaching for Daisy, having to go through Olivia to do it. She looked up, her face just inches from his. There were tears brimming, threatening to spill over. He looked into her eyes. They were a blaze of green. "You go grab the food and I'll get her in the car," Barry said. He picked up the greyhound as Olivia swaddled her in a blanket.

Olivia scooped Alvin off the bed and carried him downstairs with her. While Barry loaded Daisy, Olivia grabbed both bags of dog food and exited the house through the back door. Why wasn't Alvin sick? Should she take him too? Outside she found the bowls and her answer. Only Daisy's was empty. "Sorry, you're staying home," she said and tucked Alvin safely away in the little house outside. "Just water for now, buddy," she told him and shut the door.

Barry had the back hatch to her Volvo SUV open and was waiting with Daisy. "You ride back here with her and I'll drive."

Olivia nodded. "I didn't lock the house."

"I got it," Barry said as she climbed in beside the greyhound.

"You'll need the key," Olivia reminded him with a nod toward the ignition. She'd locked herself out of her house once. During the renovation she'd replaced her front door with one that couldn't lock behind her on accident.

"Got one, remember?" Barry reminded her and held up his own.

* * *

The all-night veterinary hospital was deserted on a Tuesday night hedging towards Wednesday. An assistant was waiting for them outside when they arrived. He flicked his cigarette away as soon as they pulled up. Barry lifted Daisy out of the car. She had vomited again on the way. Barry was right. It looked bad.

Olivia filled out the booklet of paperwork and then concentrated on not reaching across the desk to make the girl go faster as she typed in all the information she'd just written down. She didn't want to stand here. All she wanted to do was see Daisy. Barry had carried her back out of sight beyond the sweeping doors into the treatment area.

"I see two bags of food. Which one is hers?"

"Since her name is Daisy, it would be the one with the daisy drawn on it." Olivia bit back another sarcastic remark. *Don't be mean to the girl who looks twelve.* "I fed her a couple of hours ago. She ate everything. I also have a little schnauzer at home. The other bag is his. I brought both of them just in case."

"Is he sick, too?" the girl asked, peering over the counter looking for another dog.

"He didn't eat anything once we got home. He wasn't sick so I didn't bring him."

The girl nodded. "Okay. Please have a seat. The doctor will be with you when he can."

Like that was going to happen. Olivia didn't sit as instructed. She was still pacing when Barry emerged from the back. She rushed him, her eyes blazing. He stopped short of catching her in his arms. "What did they say?" She demanded.

"They asked me to leave while they finished checking her out."

"And?"

"And to take you with me." He smiled back at the girl at the counter as he steered Olivia outside. "They said it looks like poisoning. They suggested we walk next door and have a coffee or something."

Olivia opened her mouth to protest, but Barry stopped her.

"They said it might take a while."

Olivia let out a heavy sigh, obviously not happy, but powerless to do anything about it. Barry kept his hand on her elbow until they reached the hole in the wall café next door. Like the veterinary clinic, it too was open all night and at least had all-day breakfast going for it.

The low counter in the front and red vinyl booths conjured visions of something out of the 1950's. They could have their pick of places to sit but wandered to a booth in the corner where Barry took the cop's position with his eyes on the door. They gave their orders to a bored waitress who looked to be the only one on duty. Coffee for him, Dr. Pepper for her. Olivia passed on Barry's suggestion of pie. It was coconut cream, her favorite. She wondered if he remembered.

Barry had hoped the pie would help calm her down. It was one of the things he knew she liked, but she wasn't having it. He studied her in silence. The first thing he'd noticed when she greeted him earlier was her attire. Gone was the long clingy thing she wore the last time he visited. Instead it was a t-shirt and jeans hiding her curves this time. Her blonde hair was pulled back, but not neat and tidy like she wore in the field. A few strands had managed to work themselves free. He wanted to reach over and free them all. The cascade of loose waves softened the hard edges she used to shield herself. Some of the tendrils were damp, probably from a bath. He wished he didn't know the bathtub in her master was big enough for two.

Olivia snuck quick glances his way, noting both of them were avoiding eye contact. She wished for their drinks. She needed something to do with her hands. She clutched them under the table for now. With someone looking after Daisy, she could process the current situation. Had Barry brought the case files the DA promised? Is that why he had told Zavalla to send them to him?

Before Olivia could contemplate longer, the waitress showed up with their drinks, but didn't stay long. She walked away looking defeated after their second refusal to eat. She sat down at the counter with her back to them. Olivia could see she was watching them in the mirror.

Olivia was staring straight ahead, pondering. Barry just wasn't sure what. He waited for her to take a sip of caffeine before speaking. The silence between them was deafening. "So, who would want to hurt your dog?"

Olivia shook her head. "I don't know. They've been at the kennel for almost a week. I just picked them up on my way home from downtown. I'd called ahead and told them I was coming. I asked them not to feed Daisy. She gets sick in the car. They said Alvin hadn't been eating much. Separation anxiety, I guess." Between losing his owner, being adopted, and shuffled around the last couple of weeks, it was no wonder. Olivia felt sorry for the little guy.

"Maybe someone at the kennel fed Daisy and she just over ate." Her words were dressed in denial. Olivia realized she sounded like the families of patients she used to care for. *The image of the empty dog bowl told her this was no accident. Daisy was hungry when they got home. The kennel had done just as she asked. Daisy hadn't eaten, not until she fed her.*

"I think you should consider it wasn't an accident," Barry said gently. Now was the best time to push her. She was talkative. More so than usual. Nervous was not a word he would have used to describe her, but that's the way she was acting. He knew it was the dog that had her on edge. "Think. Who would want to poison Daisy?"

Olivia closed her eyes. It's what she would have asked if she were conducting the interview. She took a deep breath to calm herself. She felt drained. She hadn't stopped in days. She was physically and mentally exhausted, full of emotion and Barry's presence was kicking up more of it. A tidal wave of sensations was bearing down on her. She was struggling to keep her footing.

"Okay. If you can't come up with the who then let's move to the why," Barry suggested.

"Motive?" Olivia shook her head. It was almost as useless in her opinion. "I cannot imagine. Nearly everyone I've done consulting for is either incarcerated or dead. Someone walking free? It can't be a long list."

Barry knew she had a particular set of followers—the incarcerated who wanted a private audience with her, family members of criminals she'd help capture or the desperate who hoped she could put them in touch with their dearly departed. But how many of them were local? "Love, money, jealousy are all contenders," he suggested.

"I don't know about motive. But there was definitely opportunity," Olivia said slowly.

"You said the dogs were at the kennel."

"Did you go into my house while I was away?" Olivia didn't mean it to sound the way it did, but it seemed her filter was slipping as well.

Barry gave her a full-on stare. She could feel the heat of it. "No, I did not. Why?"

"I'm sorry," Olivia apologized, her eyes making their way over to his.

Again, Barry was filled with an overwhelming urge to touch her, offer her some measure of comfort. He opted for a two-handed death grip on his coffee cup instead.

"Someone was in my house. I felt it as soon as I stepped inside. You seemed the first, most obvious choice."

Barry couldn't fault her logic. He wished he was the obvious choice, but if that been the case, she wouldn't have left in the first place. "Is anything missing? Anything look out of place?"

"Just a feeling," Olivia said, dipping her head to look away again.

"Not *just*," he corrected her.

The gentleness of his words drew her eyes back to his, reminding her that with him she could be herself. "A door was open I know I closed. A few things weren't as neat as I typically leave them. Like someone was browsing. As far as I know nothing is missing. It just didn't *feel* right."

Barry nodded. Understanding who and what she was. "I'm not the only one who has a key." Neither one of them spoke his name. Barry looked away and reminded himself who she spent her time with was none of his business. He had to put away the personal and look for the plausible. "What about Martin?" Mendoza and his crew had worked on her house remodel for months.

Olivia shook her head. "I was usually home to let them in. I used to work at home before all of this, whatever this is…" Olivia stopped herself to focus, weariness creeping back in when she thought of how much her life had changed since Jamie had crossed her threshold. Falling down that rabbit hole now wasn't going to help. She reached for her soda. "I eventually had to give him one."

"Did he give it back?"

"Of course."

"He could have made a copy." Barry had met the contractor and didn't believe that. It was more about keeping the conversation rolling so he didn't have to the get to the unavoidable topic of Silas Branch. "Or someone on his crew."

Olivia shook her head. "Martin couldn't get most of those guys to be at my house even when he was paying them, remember?" Martin had gone through more than one crew to finish the renovations to her century-old home. Alice and the paranormal activity that came with her scared the workers. "It's possible one of his workers might've seen an opportunity to burglarize my home, but it doesn't seem very likely. I don't think we should focus on Martin or his crew." Olivia savored another sip.

"Then who, besides me, has a key?"

"Silas."

"I'm assuming we can rule him out?" Barry asked directly, hoping he sounded like a cop and not a jilted would-be lover.

"Yes. He's not here," she confirmed, but her eyes never left him. She'd heard his words. He'd just suggested he knew Silas was gone.

"The captain said something about an emergency back in DC," Barry admitted, but waited for her to explain.

Olivia took a deep breath. Her world had changed. "His dad died. It was sudden. Unexpected."

Barry nodded as he watched her not look at him. "I'm sorry to hear that." He heard himself say the words. He hoped he sounded contrite, but all he was really trying to do was breathe. His gut had been talking to him for a reason. What had she once said? *Death gives you perspective.* Had Silas gained some? Had she?

"Let's talk about something else." The suggestion was the easiest, best defense Olivia could muster. It beat discussing anything personal. "I'm assuming you came to see me about the Atascosa County files I requested."

Barry saw her change in direction for what it was. She was giving him an out—maybe she was giving herself one as well. This wasn't the time or place for a personal discussion. He couldn't get caught up in the implications of her running to Silas's side in his time of need or the agent requesting she join him. He'd need something stronger than the coffee in his hand for that. Barry did exactly as she asked and moved on.

"I left them on your dining room table, but I can give you the highlights. There wasn't much. Four girls over the course of the last two years. All with physical addresses in Atascosa County. I noticed the last one just happened to be Jessica Tate's niece."

"She came to me for help. She gave the impression not a lot was being done. Any other similarities other than location?"

Barry knew Jessica Tate wouldn't have come to Olivia if there wasn't something more to it than that. The reporter probably had a phone full of law enforcement contacts. "Why you specifically?"

Olivia should have known she couldn't keep anything from him. Barry Bartholomew was a good detective. "Because maybe there's more to this than just missing girls. You show me yours and I'll show you mine, but you first. Start with the basics."

Just like that he was right back in the rookie seat with her. Personal or professional he always submitted to her. Except when he didn't. "Looks. All blond hair, green eyes, all over seventeen years old. Cheerleader looking types."

"Were they cheerleaders?"

Barry shook his head. "Not my impression, no. No mention of school activities of any kind. My guess would be they were loners or outcasts." Barry was theorizing. There was practically nothing in the file. Like he said it was surprisingly thin. No wonder the tenacious reporter was frustrated.

Outcasts. Olivia indulged in more caffeine while she turned the description over in her mind assessing it from all angles. It fit with what Jessica had said about her niece Kimmy. The same could have been said about her at that age. She had the looks, but no friends and she didn't participate in school activities. There weren't many party invitations for the girl that was different. *The one who knew too much.*

"All these girls had difficulties at home and for some, like Jessica's niece, they had a history of running away. Just the type of girls no one is in a hurry to go look for. There's the assumption they don't want to be found."

It was the same thing she'd said to Jessica Tate. "In other words, all perfect targets," Olivia surmised.

"Where are you going with this?" Barry asked.

"Jessica told me her niece is like me."

"Like you how?"

"She senses things, emotions, energies. If the other girls are like Kimmy that could be the link no one's found. Use the known to find the unknown. Find the motive. It's where I would start. I doubt anyone in Atascosa County is looking at the victimology of these girls."

"Clearly no one is looking for them," Barry conceded. "From the looks of the files they didn't do much of anything other than take statements. I've seen this kind of sloppy policework before. It's what happens when the person doing the intake has a preconceived notion of the outcome."

"The feeling of isolation is intense," Olivia confessed softly. "I could have been one of those girls."

Her statement sparked a volley of thoughts. "From the sound of it you were one of those girls. But you didn't run away." From all accounts she was always the good girl. "Tell me why. What made you different?"

"I had Gran."

Barry had to hand it to Jessica Tate. She had made the smart move going to Olivia. She was the perfect person to get inside the mind of her niece. If Jessica was right about everything Olivia was their best shot at finding those girls. "What about your mother?" It wasn't a question Barry wanted to ask, but it was important. Olivia didn't talk about her. He'd only heard the story from Mark. "She also had your Gran."

How many times had Olivia wondered the exact same thing? Support from Gran had been the easy answer, but Barry was right. Her mother also had Gran. *Look where that got her. Look where it got them both.*

"Maybe these girls ran away because they were different. And they didn't have the support you had," Barry suggested.

Olivia tried to focus on the bits and pieces that made up what she knew about her mother. One word came to mind. *Rebellious.* "Or they were being made to conform in a way they couldn't," Olivia theorized. "My mother and Gran weren't close." She had never been able to pair the Gran she knew and loved with the woman who abandon her. How had the woman who left her behind been Gran's daughter? *Had Gran's unwavering support been intentional? Was Gran trying to make up for something, trying to right some wrong?* "I never understood what all happened between them. Gran didn't talk about it."

The polite thing would be not to ask, but now that he'd started Barry couldn't stop. He wanted to know and it had nothing to do with missing girls. "And your father?"

Olivia shook her head. It was a natural reaction, one learned from Gran. "As far as I know, my mother never said who he was. Gran used to say it was because my mother didn't know him. Guess that should tell you something. She was only seventeen."

"I'm sorry." It was an automatic response, but Barry meant it. He'd had a poor excuse for a father, but he couldn't imagine not having one. For better or worse, the experience was what shaped his life.

"Don't be. You can't miss something you never had." It was a flippant response to a statement she'd heard hundreds of times, but for the first time Olivia realized it was a lie. The caffeine flowing through her veins allowed her to see with clarity for the first time since he arrived at her door. She looked in his eyes and all she saw was longing.

Barry looked away and broke the connection.

Olivia felt a jolt—as if the carousel had stopped too soon.

CHAPTER SEVENTEEN

SHE HEARD THE vibration but it took her a minute to realize it was coming from Barry's hip. Olivia saw the waitress give a disapproving glance in the mirror as he stepped away to take the call.

"We're going to need another cup of coffee over here," Barry told the waitress on his way back. Might as well bring a pot." He slid back in the booth. "You want to reconsider the pie? We got time. Your priest friend is on his way. According to him, he doesn't sleep much so I suggested he join us."

Olivia nodded, unsurprised Dom wasn't sleeping. Meeting a demon could do that to a person. "Why was he calling you?"

"You mentioned he knew Marceline Roche."

The waitress approached the table and placed an empty coffee cup in front of Olivia. "Just put on a fresh pot," she told Barry before turning her attention to Olivia. "How 'bout that pie, hon?"

Olivia shrugged her acceptance. The adrenaline rush she'd gotten with Daisy had burned through her meager salad.

Barry watched her eat while they waited. He'd opted for more coffee, fresh or not. In his opinion she should eat more. She looked thinner than when they'd met just a few short weeks ago. "So, what do I call him?" Barry wanted to know. He'd specifically avoided calling him anything.

"Father or Dom are both acceptable," she explained. "He'll answer to either."

"Can't tell you the last time I talked to a priest," Barry confessed.

"Well, I don't expect he'll show up in a collar, at least not yet."

"I didn't think he was a priest anymore."

"I think the Church made him an offer he couldn't refuse."

Father Dom arrived just in time for fresh coffee. Collar or not, he was dressed all in black, and Father was the title one would expect him to have. He looked young for a priest, but up close Barry guessed he and the Father to be close to the same age. Past forty-five, coming up on fifty. Barry believed him when he said he didn't sleep. The smooth dark skin could hide the years, but not the eyes. They had seen humanity at its worst and beyond.

Dom slid in beside Olivia, forcing her into the middle of the curved booth closer to Barry. Barry noted the priest's gaze linger on their interaction and wondered what the priest thought he saw.

The waitress seemed immediately interested in the new addition to their party and quickly came over to fill the coffee cup for him. He, like Barry rejected the offer of food. She left with Olivia's empty plate instead.

"So we need to talk about Marceline Roche," Olivia began. "It's come up in connection with a different case, Dom."

It was a story Olivia already knew most of. After Dominic turned in his collar, he worked as a social worker for a healthcare company providing coverage to the elderly. Marceline Roche was a resident at one of the facilities he frequented. Wisteria Place was a locked Alzheimer's facility and home to Ms. Roche for the final year of her life. Her story was similar to the majority of the other residents. Her dementia had become unmanageable for her family.

"In a facility full of similar clients, how is it you remember Ms. Roche, Father?" Barry probed. Olivia had been right to call him. He had a story, Barry was sure of it.

"She was a memorable resident," Dom told him. "Not long before her passing I was involved in a committee review of her care."

"What does that mean?"

"Her residence at the facility was under review. The staff had been compiling complaints about her almost since her arrival. I was there as a representative of the health plan covering the cost of her care."

Barry noted the look on Olivia's face. "You seem surprised."

"I worked with the elderly when I was a nurse. Alzheimer's units in particular." It was where she first equated the symptoms of dementia with demonic possession. Her comparisons were the basis behind the Seven Second Theory she used as the topic of her dissertation. It was Olivia's belief the patients' condition made them an easy conduit for evil. Demons were tricksters and dementia was a fertile playground, a virtual revolving door. "It's rare and difficult to remove a patient once they're housed. It's difficult to get administration on board mainly because the facility doesn't want to lose a paying customer."

"Exactly," Dom gave her a nod of agreement.

"There are known hazards of working with the geriatric psych population. Violence is one of them, but it's typically manageable. The only time I saw administration step in was when the patient became a threat to everyone—staff and other patients alike." Olivia would never forget Mr. Anthony. He had been a happy healthy fifty-five-year old with a new wife until the day he was hit by a car. He suffered multiple injuries, but it was the blow to the head that completely changed his life and his personality. It was a wound that didn't heal. He became so violent he had to be moved to a more secure facility.

"In Ms. Roche's case the only reason administration was willing to listen was because the bulk of the complaints came from families of other residents. But still, it was more of a formality than anything else. It was hard to hear and even more difficult to believe."

Barry saw Olivia's attention pique. "So, what did they do? Anything?"

Dom shook his. "Like I said it couldn't be substantiated. Mentally impaired patients were telling stories of events that were physically impossible for the accused. Ms. Roche was a wanderer. It was one of the main reasons for her placement. Once at the facility, precautions were taken. Bed alarms, gates, all the usual techniques used to contain a resident."

"So how was she a problem for the others?" Barry was asking what Olivia wasn't.

"Other residents claimed she frightened them. There were stories she visited them in the night, despite being unable to leave her room without alerting the staff. She also talked in her sleep, to the point she couldn't keep a roommate. I think that's where the staff was going. They were hoping by pointing out there was an empty bed because of her that the administration would be more willing to listen. Money talks."

"What language did she speak?" It was a reluctant question from someone who looked like they already knew the answer. Dominic came from a poor background but he was also a learned man who spoke several languages. The staff, if they truly wanted to know what she was saying, would have sought him as a translator.

"I heard her—once. It sounded like French but was more like Haitian Creole." Dom grew up in the Dominican Republic. Spanish was the primary language but a close second was Haitian Creole which was influenced by French, Spanish, and West African dialects. The same could be said of the religions. "And of course, Latin."

Olivia rested her head in her hands and stared straight ahead, not looking at either of them. "You knew they were telling the truth."

Dom watched Barry reach out to touch her but pull back. Dom did what Barry couldn't do and placed his hand in the crook of her elbow. "Remember that day you came to see me and I mentioned to you I thought there was another influence present?"

"I believe you called it an infestation," Olivia said.

"I was talking about Ms. Roche. The occurrences seemed to increase when she arrived and for the most part, left with her. All except the remaining one you met."

Barry didn't understand. "There's someone else?"

Olivia recalled her conversation with the other Wisteria Place resident. She'd been there hunting for Jamie Smythe when the elderly woman sought her out. "Ms. Opal Collins," Olivia spoke the name with disdain. "She talked about my dead grandmother and gave me a message from Sophie the dead girl who first spoke the name of the demon who showed up in my living room a few hours later. The Roches were definitely connected to some very dark magic."

Barry pushed his coffee cup away. He didn't know what to say. They'd strayed into Olivia's world. He retreated to his good old-fashioned police work. "Anything else you can tell me about Ms. Roche?" He was speaking to Father Dominic.

The priest shrugged. "What else do you want to know?"

"Did her sons visit? Did she have any other visitors?"

"Ferdinand more than Andre. I don't think she was much good to Andre. She was quite demented most of the time."

"Anyone else?"

"Only one other. Ana Lutz."

"Ana Lutz?" Olivia repeated the information. "I thought Ana worked with young girls." Ana might be a Wiccan priestess but her day job was social work just like Dom.

"She does," Dom confirmed but could tell by the look on her face that wasn't the answer Olivia was expecting. "I thought you knew that. She didn't work there. She was visiting Ms. Roche. I think the woman was like family to her."

"I thought you met Ana because the two of you worked together." Olivia felt a tickle along the back of her neck. Something wasn't right.

Dom shook his head, searching his memories like a card catalog. "Ana said she knew you. She brought you up. She knew of your work with the BAU. But more than that she knew about Gran. Said she was sorry to hear about her passing."

"When Ana called me, she said she knew you. I assumed that's how she got my number. It was my private cell." Olivia told him.

Barry was watching Dom. A field of furrows spread across the smooth plateau of the priest's brow. He looked genuinely upset, blaming himself no doubt.

"Ana said she'd changed phones and lost some of her contacts. I thought she knew you." Dom's voice faded with realization.

"And, I thought she knew you," Olivia echoed. The words chilled Olivia more than they should have. The statement was innocuous in nature, but the fact a total stranger knew enough about both of them to fool the other one into thinking they were acquaintances was disturbing. Olivia digested the information. Her thoughts shifting like a kaleidoscope. Random pieces moving together, seeking clarity.

Dom looked to Barry. The police lieutenant looked ready to strike. "What are you thinking?"

"I'm thinking Ana Lutz sure went to a whole lot trouble to convince the two of you that she knew you, and it's time I get to know this woman."

"She's not originally from here," Dom offered, but couldn't recall the location, trying to relay anything he could think of.

Barry looked over at Olivia.

She shrugged. "I've been back in San Antonio less than three years.

Before that I was in Virginia for more than a decade. First school and then the FBI. I never heard of Ana Lutz until I came back here."

"I've been here longer, but I didn't meet Ana until Ms. Roche came to the facility. More than a year ago," Dom offered.

All Barry got out of that was Ana Lutz didn't show up until Olivia returned to San Antonio. He wondered if that was intentional. He looked at the two of them. They were at an impasse. He wouldn't press them for anything else tonight. Barry pulled out his phone and fired off a quick text to Will. He was trying to be cognizant of the time. Barry still didn't know enough about Will to know what he did in his off time, but Barry thought he'd said something about meeting some academy buddies for dinner and drinks.

Olivia had excused herself to use the restroom and slid out of the booth past Barry, who had watched her until he couldn't see her anymore. He was pretty sure the man across from him had seen it too.

"You're worried about her," Dom commented once they were alone.

"Worrying about her can become a full-time job."

Barry wondered if the priest was warning him or inquiring. Maybe both.

"It can be. But I'm not the only one applying for the job." Barry decided to be frank. In his experience, a priest could spot a lie as quickly as any cop.

"She trusts you," Dom told him.

Barry nodded. *Good.* He trusted her and his trust wasn't easy to earn. "Tell me, have you ever met anyone like her before?"

The priest raised an eyebrow.

"Anyone with her," Barry momentarily searched for a word, "gifts?"

Dom reached for his cold coffee. Not that he wanted a sip, but it gave him a moment to gather his thoughts. "None so gifted as Olivia," he said without drinking. "There are many who are sensitive to the other side in one form or another but her gifts are costly. The dark path is much easier to follow than the one full of light. And there are many terrors along the way."

"Costly, how?" Barry didn't understand. And he wanted to.

"She's a conduit. The other side is just as sensitive to her. She hunts it as much as it hunts her."

"So, you would say she's a rarity."

"Indeed. And a very valuable asset."

It was an ominous warning. Olivia wasn't currently hunting a monster but that didn't mean one wasn't hunting her, or others like her.

Dom was gone by the time she got back.

"So, what now?" Olivia wanted to know.

"I texted Will and I've got him checking into background on Ana Lutz. In the meantime, Will and I will talk to the families. I'm sure Jessica did, but I'd like a real interview this time." It was obvious none of Atascosa County's finest did a thorough investigation. Was it incompetence or something else? Barry needed to double check but he thought all the cases were handled by the same deputy. Maybe he should start there. "Going back to Jessica's niece."

"Kimmy," Olivia told him.

"Kimmy," Barry repeated, framing questions already. "Where would she meet other girls like her? Girls like you?"

"There are no girls like me," Olivia said with a slight smile. Barry resisted the urge to tell her he knew that all too well. "I went to a place once. I was in high school. It was one of those rare times when I actually had a friend. Or so I thought. She was the new girl. She said the place was haunted. I think she just wanted to test me—see if what the other kids said about me was true."

"Was it?"

"Of course, it was. I knew right away. She avoided me after that."

"I meant was it was haunted?" Barry admitted with a smile of his own.

"Not that day. There was something else there. Gran was mad when she found out I went. She didn't like me putting myself out there like that. In the end I think she was a little scared."

"Scared?" Barry wondered if it was because of what Father Dom said. Olivia was special.

"I think it's when she realized what she was dealing with. Some sensitives feel emotions, some experience past events. That's why they're called readers."

"Like you?"

"Yes and no. Whenever someone has this ability," Olivia carefully avoided the word *gift* because she wasn't sure it was true. "They don't go unnoticed. Their presence sends a signal to the other side."

"The bigger the rock the greater the ripples," Barry suggested. "I'm thinking you caused more than ripples. Is that what scared Gran?"

A smiled played across Olivia's lips. For once she almost seemed proud of her abilities. It wasn't something Barry had seen before.

"I do tend to rock the boat. Gran would have preferred I float undetected." Olivia flexed her fingers and almost reached for his, but stopped herself. They were sharing something. No matter the walls between them, there were cracks. "It was more than that. What I encountered during was something dark and evil, conjured through black magic. It gravitated to me. It's said sensitives attract a reflection of their true self. Up until then, Gran believed I drew the light because of Alice. Gran thought she was my guardian angel."

"You mentioned Gran was protective of you. Was it because things on the other side are attracted to you? Could that be true on this side as well? Could someone with your abilities be a target?"

Olivia studied him. "You and Dom talked while I was gone." She wasn't mad. Dom was her friend. He wouldn't have given away anything she wanted to keep hidden.

"Maybe," Barry admitted.

"Thou shalt not covet."

"It is one of the top ten," Barry reminded her. Many crimes were committed in the name of desire. *Want. Need.*

It was Jessica's theory but it was solid. "I suppose. Depends on the ability and what someone's seeking." *A dabbler of the arts could use someone with her connection to the other side.* "From a psychological standpoint, girls like Kimmy—like me—are isolated. When you know things you shouldn't, things no one else knows, it's hard to make a connection with the living. Girls like Kimmy just want to belong. To be like everyone else."

Vulnerable was what Barry heard. He had to find these girls. For them. For Olivia.

Olivia was tired of the introspection and stepping away from it had helped her see something else. Her mind was like a computer browser with too many tabs open. When one became too much to deal with, she shuffled to another. "I set the house alarm when I left for Virginia. It was still set when I got home. Martin doesn't have the alarm codes," Olivia said drifting back to where they had started.

Barry's gut clinched. "You didn't mention the alarm before." He'd focused on the keys.

"No. I only mentioned I knew someone had been in my house," Olivia whispered.

"What else is there? What are we missing?" Barry tallied who had access to her life. It had come down to him and Silas. Ironically Olivia had given them their keys at the same time. Barry stopped. That was a piece of the equation he hadn't considered. He and Silas were new additions since the Smythe case. Who'd come before?

She'd given them keys because Jamie Smythe was hunting her and Silas wanted to whisk her away to safety. He took Olivia and left Barry with the dogs, forcing him to call in reinforcements. Living in the condo, he had no place to keep them. Barry had gone to the one person he knew who had a backyard. The person Olivia had trusted first.

"Mark," Barry finally said aloud. "He had a key and the codes."

Barry's cell phone began to chirp, causing them both to jump.

The doctor will see you now.

CHAPTER EIGHTEEN

DAISY WAS GOING to be okay, but she wasn't coming home anytime soon. Olivia was quiet on the ride home. She didn't even protest when Barry insisted on staying. He suspected it was because she had little fight left in her. He confirmed his own theory when the first time he snuck upstairs to check on her she was asleep. He was glad. On many levels.

Barry lingered at the threshold of her bedroom, watching the slow rhythmic rise and fall of her chest. Alvin, the little white schnauzer they rescued together, was curled up next to her. Olivia lay on her side facing the door. A bank of pillows surrounded her. Were they a bunker against loneliness or monsters? Barry watched her brows pinch together and then relax. He hoped she could find peace.

Barry detached himself and surveyed the surroundings. The last time he saw this room it was empty. Since then new furniture for her new room had arrived. He couldn't help notice the bed. It was beautiful, intricately carved—old-world yet still with flairs of the whimsical. She had good taste. He wondered what she had done with the one they shared. It had been her grandmother's.

Barry forced himself back downstairs and focused his attention on the alarm's control panel. It's what he should have been doing all along. Luckily, he'd logged her password in his phone last time. Some playing around under the menu button gave him several options. The activity log looked promising. He could scroll through it, but his search was taking too long. A few more strokes and he found an option to narrow his quest by date range. He keyed in dates spanning six days. He'd seen her last Thursday, the same day she left for Virginia, and she'd returned yesterday, Tuesday.

Barry noted her departure time on Thursday afternoon as thirteen minutes past two and her return at seven forty-six last night. There was one entry in between. The alarm was deactivated and then reactivated twelve minutes later on Saturday night just after nine. If someone were watching her house, which they undoubtedly were, enough time had passed that they were assured she was gone for the weekend.

Barry called the security system's twenty-four-hour customer service hotline. Olivia had written her account number inside the control panel. He had a moment of panic when asked for her six-digit verbal passcode, but he took a shot in the dark and used the same set of numbers as her system passcode. He got it right on the first guess. He requested a copy of the entry log he'd uncovered.

"Do you want us to send it to the email you have on file, Dr. Osborne, sir?" the customer attendant asked.

At this point Barry just went with it. "Sure."

"You know, if you're interested in additional security, I can upgrade you for free for the next six months."

"What does that include?" Barry asked. He wasn't going to sleep at this point anyway.

"For the six-month free option, we offer a text message and/or email alert anytime your alarm code is activated. Also, each time your code is entered, the camera captures an image of who is entering or leaving the residence. The image will available for viewing via text or email, your choice. If you decide to upgrade to our top tier, we can offer you a discounted rate for the first twelve months. This option includes the installation of mini-cams on as many as three entryways. You can have more than three, of course, but at an additional cost per month. There is a live feed monitor installed inside your home. Also, if an alarm sounds that was not initiated by a manual entry code, the digital camera will stream a live feed with a link sent directly to your email and can be viewed on your smart phone—all in real time. Do either of these packages interest you?"

"Both actually, but let's get started with the one that doesn't require the mini-camera installation," Barry said. It was free for six months. Plenty of time for Olivia to decide if she didn't want it.

"The one that snaps a picture when the code is activated? Is that the one you want, sir?"

"Yes," Barry confirmed, "That one will work for now."

"Of course. I'll just have to send you a confidentiality agreement via email to authorize us to activate the camera embedded in your keypad. We will need to have your signature on file to verify your permission. You can sign electronically and return to us via email."

"Ok. Got it." Barry was ready to get off the phone. "Can you send something detailing the options we just discussed? Just so I don't forget?" Barry asked. *That way Olivia will know what I signed her up for.*

"Use the same email address, sir?"

"Yes."

"Of course, sir. If you decide you want to upgrade further, just give us a call back at the same number you called this morning to set up an installation date and time. Did I answer all of your questions to your satisfaction today, Dr. Osborne?"

The customer service attendant sounded way too chipper for this time of morning, but then again, he had elected to work the night shift. "Absolutely. Thank you," Barry said. He mimicked the cheerfulness of the customer service reps voice. Fortunately, no one could see his face.

Barry ended the call and started to make another when he stopped himself. He should use Olivia's phone for this one. He knew beyond a doubt the receiver would answer regardless of the time. Quietly, he climbed the stairs again and tiptoed into her room.

She was still curled up inside the barricade of pillows. She didn't look like she had moved. Barry tried to avoid looking at her, but up close he thought he could see tear tracks down her cheeks. He looked away and concentrated instead on being quiet as he reached across the bedside table and unplugged her phone. Alvin lifted his head at the intrusion but didn't make a sound. His little nub of a tail wagged a greeting. The white mound of fur had always liked him. At least the dog didn't mind he was in her room. Barry felt quite sure the other male figure in her life wouldn't feel the same. He resisted the urge to linger and turned around before he could change his mind.

Barry took the phone downstairs and was immediately stopped by her security code. *Damn.* Of course, it was passcode protected. On a whim he used the same six digits she'd chosen for the alarm system. *11-23-75.* It worked. Must be a birthday. Someone really needed to have a talk with her about security.

Barry scrolled to the last number called and down one. *There was a long call history.* He hit send before he could stop himself. As expected, it was answered on the first ring.

"Hey, babe." The longing behind the words was palpable.

"It's not who you think." Barry couldn't say it fast enough. He didn't want to hear anything else. Those two words were enough.

"Lieutenant." The change in tone was immediate. "What's happened? Where's Livie?"

"She's upstairs. Asleep. Safe. Unharmed."

"Then why are you there?" It was more of a growl than a question. It didn't sound like it came from the same man who answered the phone.

"I needed to make sure you would take this call," Barry said smoothly. He briefly envisioned a worm caught at the end of a hook. So far it was the highlight of his night. "You need to be aware of something. It's been a bad night. Someone poisoned Daisy."

"What? Who?"

"Don't know. But they were pretty damn good at it. Daisy almost didn't make it. She's going to be in the doggy hospital for a few days."

"Jesus. Did Livie find her? How is she?"

"I stopped by to drop off a case file. When I got here Daisy was already sick. I drove them to the vet and stayed until they kicked us out."

"Thank you, Barry." It was the first time the agent had ever called him by his first name. "It means a lot to me that you were there for her. Livie didn't need to go through that alone. She's been through enough already."

She has. "You're welcome."

"It's been a long night for you too. Why don't you go and get some rest? Call Father Dominic to stay with her," Silas suggested.

That was fast. But Barry had to admit it was the politest way he'd ever been asked to leave before. "There's more."

"More what?"

"When Olivia got home last night, before Daisy got sick, Olivia said she *sensed* someone had been in the house. Yet the doors were locked and the alarm was set."

"She's not wrong about those things," Silas told him.

"I'm aware." They'd come a long way in a short amount of time. Barry no longer questioned anything about her. "It's why we're having this discussion."

"Was anything missing, disturbed?"

"She said things were *off.* She described it as browsing."

"Did you call the alarm company?"

Barry could hear the agent was on the move now. Clicking keys on a computer. Making plans for his return. It would be swift, mere hours, he was sure. "I reviewed the activity files. There was one breach while she was gone. Saturday night. In and out in twelve minutes."

Good. Not a lot of time. "Wait." Silas stopped. He needed to focus on just one thing at a time. "None of this makes sense. Who the hell has a key *and* the alarm code?"

"You. Me. I'm going to go out on a limb and guess it wasn't you and I know it wasn't me. Before you ask, I don't have an alibi. You're just going to have to trust me." Barry paused, giving Silas an opportunity to argue with him, but the agent stayed quiet. He knew Silas didn't like it, but it was more about how deep he'd waded into Olivia's life than anything, not that the agent didn't trust him. Trust was something they had to share. They were in this together. Olivia's safety was at stake.

Before Silas had to think about it too long, Barry threw him a bone. It was the least he could do. He was the one alone in the house with Olivia. "Other than the two of us, the only other person who had both keys and codes was Mark."

There was another pause on Silas's end. "That's impossible," he finally said.

"I know. So, somehow, something's been compromised. I called her security company. They're sending her an email confirming the activity between the days she was gone, giving you evidence. I also took the liberty of upgrading her alarm system for free for six months. She just has to sign electronically giving them permission to activate the camera embedded in the key pad. It will take a photo of anyone who enters the alarm code. A copy will be sent straight to her phone. There are other packages I could go into, but they didn't offer me a commission. My suggestion is the top tier one." *If I was the one calling her babe in the wee hours of the morning, that's what I would recommend.* "Review them with her, please."

"Nice work, Lieutenant. I can be on a plane out of here in three hours," Silas told him. There was no hesitation in his voice. Only conviction that he was going to come and make it better. And hunt down the person who had done this. But not if Barry got to them first.

"One more thing."

"Look, Lieutenant, I don't know how much more of this I can take." Feeling had crept back in the agent's voice.

Barry thought he actually heard him sigh. *So, he wasn't invincible after all.* Barry had to remind himself Silas was emotionally compromised. He had just lost his father.

"Please tell me this is the last thing you have to tell me."

"It is. But it's important. When I got here last night, just after she got off the phone with you," Barry had noted the time in her call log. "There was a car on my bumper. Like maybe they were checking me out. I wouldn't have thought anything about it, but it did a slow crawl past the house. New model, small, sporty, pricey. Light in color, gold, maybe silver. Maybe it means something, maybe it doesn't."

"Anything on the plates?"

Barry shook his head even though no one was there to see. He was pacing a small perimeter in the living room. The more he thought about it the more he believed it was something. His gut, like Olivia's feelings, wasn't wrong. "Paper dealer tags."

"Not helpful," Silas muttered. It was a statement. Not an accusation. "That fits the description of most cars in her neighborhood." Paper tags meant new purchase but it would take time to trace it back to a dealership with only a vague description. "Ok. So, we know someone cased the house while she was gone. That's why they knew they could go in. They could still be watching," Silas theorized. *But if they had already been inside and nothing was taken then what was the point?*

"If I had known then what I know now, I would have paid more attention."

"I'll call Father Dominic," Silas told him. He didn't want Barry scrolling through her phone in search of the number. There were text messages the lieutenant might be tempted to read, but in the end would wish he hadn't.

"At least wait until the sun comes up. She needs her sleep," Barry told him.

There was hesitation on the other end. Silas was waiting for some verbal agreement from him on his departure, but Barry wouldn't concede. He sank down on the couch ended the call without saying good-bye. No matter how he felt, he'd done the right thing. Barry heard the unmistakable emotion in Silas's voice when he answered, expecting Olivia to be on the other end. If that's what she wanted, who was he to interfere? It was for the best. He should go outside to his car and watch for unsuspecting drive byes. Her driveway was long. If he pulled far enough in, he was undetectable. Maybe watching over her was his place in her life.

Olivia appeared in the doorway stopping him before he could go anywhere. "I should have known you wouldn't leave." She plopped down just an arm's reach away. She hadn't slept enough, but she looked better than when they left the diner. She'd washed her face, removing any trace of her tears.

Barry watched her tuck her legs under her and reach into a seagrass basket beside the couch to produce a big fuzzy pink blanket. She kept one end for herself and leaned forward to offer him the other.

He took her hand through the blanket as she handed it to him and held it longer than he should have. "If I woke you, I'm sorry."

Olivia looked down to find her phone. He'd dropped it on the couch between them when he let go of the blanket. "What have you done?"

Barry watched the lightening flash in her green eyes. Her stare told him he would be answering the question. "I called Silas," he admitted despite silent protest.

Her eyes narrowed and he saw more than a flash of green this time. There was a whole storm brewing in them. She tugged on the blanket, but Barry pulled back. "You should thank me. You were going to have to tell him eventually. I saved you an argument later."

Olivia loosened her grip and glared at him. "You shouldn't have called him. The last thing Silas needs right now is to worry about me."

"With a relationship comes responsibility," Barry snapped. It was easier to say the words in anger. Fighting with her was all he could do.

"It wasn't your call to make," Olivia snapped back.

"You're the one who skipped town at a moment's notice to join him in D.C. It was a natural assumption you'd want him to know."

Olivia looked at him, hurt filling her eyes. "At least he needed me. That's more than I can say for you." With that she tossed him her end of the blanket, a puff of pink catching him in the face. When it fell away, she was gone.

Barry stayed there. Waiting. Stopping her wasn't the right move. Things were heated between them. It would be too easy to cross a line he knew he shouldn't. Not with her. Not like this. When he didn't hear her go up the stairs he went after her. He found her in the downstairs bedroom, curled up on her grandmother's bed, the place they'd shared, her face buried in the pillows. Barry wanted to go to her, but he couldn't. He didn't trust himself. "I'm not leaving," he said from the doorway.

Her words were soft, defeated. "Do what you have to do."

CHAPTER NINETEEN

SHE WAS ALONE. Olivia felt it as soon as she woke up. Her heart caught in her throat until she spied him outside in his car. She scrambled out the door to go to him. She was breathless as she approached. The window was down.

Barry wanted to get out of the car, but she was standing by the door.

"We have to figure out a way." Her voice was full of emotion. Her knuckles were white where she was clutching the door frame where the window would have separated them if Barry hadn't rolled it down so they could talk.

"I'm working on it," Barry told her. "In the meantime, I need you to know it wasn't you. It was me." Barry heard a sob catch in her throat. "Don't say anything that will cause me to get out of this car. Just listen." From the periphery he saw her shaking her head. "I do know what I want. I fucked up. I know that too. If I could take that day back I would." The words out, he cranked the engine and pulled away.

*　*　*

Dom had just returned from early morning prayers when Silas called, requesting he go to Olivia. He said she needed comfort and the agent obviously preferred a priest over the police lieutenant.

"I should be the one feeding you," Olivia said between mouthfuls. The salad and pie she'd had last night were a distant memory.

Dom was happy to see Olivia had an appetite. "I thought sustenance might be in order." They were sitting on her front porch enjoying the breakfast tacos he brought with him. "Do you want to talk about what happened?" She had already given him an update on Daisy but considering the man who had requested his presence wasn't the same one he'd left her with, Dom wondered if there was more.

Olivia shook her head. While in the shower she'd burned away the memory of Barry's departure, and allowed Silas to resume his protector role. He'd sent her a text saying Dom was on his way and so was he. The look Dom gave her said that wasn't the answer he wanted.

"Maybe that shouldn't have been a question," he corrected himself.

"I told you about Daisy."

"It's the lieutenant I'm curious about."

Olivia resisted the urge to roll her eyes. She felt like she was back in high school. "I just met him. We worked the Good Samaritan case together."

"I was unaware there's a time limit on getting to know someone."

Olivia shook her head, her eyes roving the tree lined street of her block, the snapdragon bush in her front yard, anywhere but across the table to Dom.

"He cares about you. It's obvious."

"I'm aware." Olivia reached across the table and squeezed his hand. "Thank you for looking out for me."

"You know, your Gran didn't want you to be alone." Dom had met Gran not long before she died. He was sorry he hadn't known her before she was dying. "She wanted you to fall in love, have a family. Carry on."

"I haven't forgotten. I'm just a little late getting started."

It took a moment, but understanding came, despite what he'd seen. Affairs of her heart were not his matter. Not until she brought them to him. He'd intruded enough.

Olivia retrieved her hand, seeing she'd satisfied whatever worry had occupied Dom. "Why don't we talk about you instead? When are you going to start wearing the collar again?"

"There will be a small ceremony in a week or so."

"Can I come?"

Dom smiled, maybe he was even blushing. "I'll let you know when."

"I think it's ironic that the church is now asking you to do exactly what caused you to leave in the first place." Did the demon in her living room have something to do with the Church's change of heart?

"The Church is in dire need. There is fear the darkness is closing in on the light." Dom felt it was his calling to fight the forces of evil.

Olivia was aware of the Church's plight. She'd sensed an upsurge in incidents. It's what kept the FBI calling. "You're uniquely qualified," Olivia said. Her words hung between them as both their thoughts went to the demon they'd faced together. Dom had brushed against evil before. He had a penchant for looking in dark corners and uncovering ancient secrets. It's the reason she'd sought him out for the case that set them down the path of their friendship and his estrangement from the Church.

"Do you know where the Archdiocese will assign you?"

"They've asked me to remain here," Dom said, carefully watching for her reaction.

"Because of me?" A slight incline of the priest's head told her she was correct. "So, I'm part of your assignment?" Olivia concluded. "Was that at your request?" Even though she doubted it even as the words left her mouth.

Dom shook his head solemnly. "No. It was the archbishop. They have an exorcist here, but he'll transfer once I'm fully trained. The Church believes you need protection. I think they thought you would be more willing to accept it if it came from me."

Olivia opened her mouth to protest, but Dom signaled he wasn't finished. He'd wanted to discuss it last time they had breakfast, but she hadn't been ready. Now, considering what they'd uncovered last night with the lieutenant, she needed to be. "The bishop would like to speak to you regarding your experiences with Jamie Smythe."

Olivia studied him. "There's more. Isn't there?"

"The Church is interested in your family history."

"Why? Because some great-grandmother of mine was at the Salem witch trials?" Olivia snapped at her friend, the sudden swell of anger coming out of nowhere.

"Sarah Osborne asserted the theological claim that the Devil could take the shape of another person without their compliance. She claimed if the Devil was harming others while assuming her appearance, she had no idea of it and therefore could not be held accountable," Dom recited the tale even though he knew she knew it well.

Her long-lost ancestor was the inspiration behind her dissertation. "It was her defense that brought the trials to an end." Some three hundred years later science had caught up with Sarah Osborne's assertion when MRI scans showed an open window of time in the human brain. Based largely in theology but influenced by scientific and psychological findings, the Seven Second Theory raised serious questions regarding the idea of free will. "Why do you think I hunt the monsters? The *real* ones. Those who are truly possessed didn't summon evil, they are possessed by it through no fault of their own."

She might not be helpless to evil, but others were. She was fighting for them. Dom wondered if she knew the truth or was she just willing to look the other way when it came to family? "So, in your opinion, was Sarah Osborne an innocent, or a very convincing liar?"

Olivia's eyes narrowed at the inquiry. "Is that your question, or the archbishop's?" She didn't wait for Dom to answer. She knew he'd been pressured to ask it for another. "She might have died in jail, but as an innocent."

"In the eyes of the law or the eyes of the Church?" Dom asked.

"Not as a witch," Olivia made the distinction. Keeping the details of history was important. Maybe not to him, but it had been to Gran. And Gran had passed it on to her.

"I think you should know this gift or curse of yours grows stronger with each generation. It could be the reason this demon has targeted you. He said you owed him a debt. Those were his exact words. He's only going to keep coming until it is paid," Dom assured her.

Or a compromise is made. Faith was what kept the demon at bay. "Gran used to say the old ways weaken the bonds of faith." She touched the silver cross that hung around her neck. "Are there others like me?"

Dom shook his head, her question reminding him very much of the lieutenant's. "None like you. But there are many different levels of sensitivity. Many different *gifts*."

Olivia immediately thought of her mother, whose visions of the dead drove her to drugs—at least that was Gran's version. That didn't sound like a gift.

"Your ancestor in Salem wasn't the first," Dom said gently. "Don't you think if you exhibited your abilities at any other time in history, you might have found yourself…"

"Tied to a rock? Or a stake with fire at my feet?" Olivia filled in the blanks. "So, my kind, we've been around for a long time?"

"Versions of your kind. Look to the Book of Judges. Samson had a divine calling from birth, a secret strength. Would you call him gifted?"

Olivia knew the story well. "Then there was Delilah. A mere woman, yet she was powerful enough to extract Sampson's gift. Delilah took him down through the power of seduction."

"Gran taught you that story, didn't she?" he asked.

"It was one of her favorites."

Dom nodded. Wondering how much she really knew. "In some form or another there have always been gifted ones. As with you, as with Samson and Delilah, not all gifts are the same."

"So, possessing gifts makes one a target." Olivia had gone back to the cross. Clutching it this time, her thoughts in many places at once.

"Yes. You use yours for good. But where there is good there is also evil." He knew from his discussions with the archbishop that Gran had taught her that as well.

"Does the Church believe I need protection?"

Dom shook his head. "The bishop believes I can help you."

Olivia caught the undercurrent of his words. "You don't feel the same."

"I'm not sure what I believe."

It was a strange answer. Olivia studied him, trying to find some meaning behind his words. He had more to say, but he was *afraid? Cautious?* She remained silent, waiting. Either the weight of her stare or the noise inside his head pushed Dom to speak.

"I keep thinking about that night. It plays over and over in my mind. Most of the memories are cloudy, disjointed." It was a common reaction to trauma. "But one memory is clear."

"Which one?"

"You faced down a demon. And you weren't afraid."

* * *

The buzzing on the bedside table finally got his attention. Barry reached over swatting in search of the sound. He made contact and knocked his phone off the table. It hit the wooden floor and slid under the bed. Barry turned on his side and reached under the bedframe and fumbled for the phone. He squinted at the clock perched on the bedside table. He was old school and still had one, mainly so in the middle of the night he could calculate how many hours of sleep he wasn't getting. His fingers finally found his phone, but by then the irritating noise had stopped. Barry was still trying to focus on the time when the phone started buzzing again. He answered it, not knowing who was on the other end.

"I completed my assignment. Want to hear about it over a late lunch? There's a little Chinese place on Broadway I like. Not too far from you." It was Will sounding like the student eager to impress the teacher.

Barry's stomach rumbled at the thought of food. He wasn't exactly sure when he ate last. The last time he'd seen food Olivia had been the one eating. "Sure."

Will managed to snag them a table in the back. A few hours of sleep and a shower had done wonders, but Barry knew it was time he got moving for no other reason than to avoid thinking about things he shouldn't.

"You look like hell. Late night?" Based on where the lieutenant was headed last night and the assignment he left him via voicemail in the wee hours of the morning, Will guessed Olivia Osborne was involved.

Barry looked across the table and saw the sergeant looking at him expectantly. He'd seen the look before. It meant he was supposed to share. He took another couple of bites instead and deflected the question. "You said you finished your assignment. What'd you find?"

"Addresses for all families involved. I mapped who we should see first. I'm ready to knock on some doors when you are. I got a call back from Ranger Gaines on the way over. He gave the DA the heads up that we're going to be making a few inquiries. He gave us the green light."

"What did you find on the Wiccan lady? Ana Lutz?" She was Barry's main focus at the moment.

"She worked for Health and Human Services—a family planning clinic to be exact, but she left that job about six months ago. No updated employment information since. Last known address was in San Antonio. She moved out of there about the same time she left her job. Does she have some connection to the missing girls? I didn't see her name in the file."

"Not sure. Olivia thought Ms. Lutz might be helpful. There's something odd in how they crossed paths. This angle is still taking shape at this point," Barry said.

Will nodded slowly digesting the information. If he'd learned anything in the last week it was not to question too much where Dr. Osborne was concerned. So far, he'd found no fault with the logic, but he knew that wasn't the general consensus.

"So, where's Ms. Lutz getting her mail?" Barry wanted to know, rousing Will back to the matter at hand.

"She's got a P.O. box registered to her in Poteet. Wiccan, huh? Aren't they some kind of witchy tree worshippers? Dr. Osborne seems more old school religion."

"She is," Barry told him. "Father Dominic may have a phone number for Lutz."

"He's the priest Dr. Osborne mentioned yesterday? I thought he knew Marceline Roche? What does that have to do with Ana Lutz?"

Barry could see by the look on Will's face he wasn't making a connection. It was time for full disclosure whether the sergeant was ready to hear it or not. If he was going to keep working this case he was going to have to get used to the unexpected. "I had an interesting conversation with Father Dominic and Olivia last night. It seems all roads lead to Atascosa County." As succinctly as he could, Barry ran through what he'd learned last night connecting Ana Lutz to Andre Roche. "With Ms. Lutz's purposeful insertion to into Olivia's life, she's risen to a level that deserves our attention. Couple that with Jessica Tate's suggestion that at least one of the missing girls has abilities similar to Dr. Osborne, it gives us a victim profile to work with. It's more than we had yesterday."

"Speaking of profiles, is Dr. Osborne going with us on the interviews?" Will asked.

Barry shook his head. "She needs to sit this one out. She got a little too close to the action with the last case."

"The DA wants a smoking gun," Will blurted out. "Last night my Academy buddies told me the DA's office has deployed cadets more than once looking for the knife Smythe allegedly used. They've combed the route from Wendy Florren's house all the way to Dr. Osborne's place. So far, not a damn thing."

"Doesn't mean Smythe didn't do it," Barry told him.

"You don't have to convince me. I was in the room with Smythe, remember?"

"You tell your buddies that?" Barry asked.

Will shook his head. "Uh, no. Taking that one to the grave. I did tell them about Dr. Osborne's visit at the barn, though. She's ... *something*."

Barry couldn't help but smile. "She is."

"So, how do you want to handle the interviews?"

"Dr. Osborne sent over some pointers." Barry found it in his office email before heading out to meet Will, pleased to know that at least he and Olivia were on good terms professionally. Although Barry had expected nothing less. They would get through this, one way or another. She wasn't going anywhere and neither was he. "Did you get anything on Andre Roche?" Barry asked.

Will shook his head. "Put out some feelers. Nothing yet. Now that we're onto Ms. Lutz, I'll reach out to her former employer and see who I can sweet talk into giving me anything on where she might have gone," Will suggested. He should have thought of it already.

"Worth a shot." Barry was impressed at the sergeant's tenacity and his ability to roll with the curve balls of this case. Barry went back to his food, intent on cleaning his plate but was interrupted by a text message. A quick read through and his appetite evaporated. "Gotta make a quick detour back to the station before we start those interviews."

"Sure thing, partner."

The use of the word got Barry's attention. He'd just asked Will to take a leap with him that he would never have taken before meeting Olivia. They could be chasing their tails on a case that wasn't even theirs, *if* it was even a case at all. Will had complied without question. Maybe it was time to share a little. It was what *partners* did. Barry downed the rest of his tea and came clean. "Thanks for noticing how I look this morning. Last night was hell."

Will paused, unsure what to say. Maybe he shouldn't say anything at all. He knew he and the lieutenant were just getting to know each other, but still Bartholomew didn't seem like a sharer.

"Someone tried to kill Dr. Osborne's dog.

"Oh, wow." Maybe the doc did need to sit this one out. "Pooch going to be okay?"

"Hope so."

"Any ideas who?"

Barry shook his head.

"Something personal like that, top contender for motive would be revenge. Dr. Osborne hasn't crossed the wrong female, has she?" Will realized too late how personal his words sounded. Kind of like questioning the lieutenant's nocturnal activities.

"You have a point," Barry said, an idea forming.

"Poison is a female thing," Will offered by way of an explanation.

"In Ana Lutz's background information, did you happen to notice what kind of car she drives? Is it something sporty, luxury model, like a Mercedes or a BMW?"

Will shook his head. "Definitely not. A nondescript Ford or something like that. Why?"

"Just something I saw last night." Maybe the drive by had nothing to do with the dog.

CHAPTER TWENTY

DAISY SNIFFED OLIVIA'S hand, but she raised her head and whined at the sight of Silas.

"Guess we know who's the favorite," the vet said with a smile. Olivia shook her head in response while Silas gave her a wink. He took her hand as they followed the vet into his office.

"We still need to keep her another day to monitor her kidney function. She underwent dialysis today and did well, but we will probably have to do it at least one more time before we discharge her."

"What did you find in her food?" Silas asked.

"Antifreeze. Simplest way to poison a dog. It tastes sweet so it's easy to get them to eat it."

Olivia's face told him she didn't have antifreeze at her house, but he kept talking. "Just to be prudent, we called the kennel where you boarded the dogs. They checked their food supply and found nothing. As a further precaution, we searched all available literature for recalls on the food you use. Same results."

Olivia was grateful for his thoroughness. But none of it made sense. "Did you find antifreeze in both of the dog's bags?" Silas wanted to know.

The vet shook his head. "That was the curious thing. We only found it in Daisy's."

Olivia and Silas looked at each other. Daisy was definitely the target. "Doesn't make sense," she said quietly. Silas gave her hand another squeeze.

"We're going to need those bags back," Silas said. It might be a long shot but since they didn't have any answers maybe forensics could find one for them. "Are your employees required to be fingerprinted?"

"Fingerprinting is required here due to the ketamine we keep on hand," the vet explained. "You can pick up the bags at the front desk on your way out."

"Thank you. Someone will be calling you about those prints once we have the bags tested."

"Of course." The vet wasn't exactly sure what was going on, except that Daisy's owner was somehow affiliated with the FBI. From the looks of the big guy, he was too. That was enough to tell him he didn't want to know anything else. "I'll have someone call you in the morning to give you an update on how Daisy does overnight. Feel free to come back tomorrow and see her anytime."

* * *

"I could have brought his things to you and saved you a trip," Barry said. He'd known it was coming but seeing Mark's father and sister at his old partner's desk made it all too real. Everything was boxed already, but Madeline sat at Mark's desk sweeping the drawers for any remnants left behind while the captain stood by. Everyone else had cleared the room.

"Didn't want to trouble you," Alan Austin said, offering his hand.

Barry gripped the man's hand firmly trying to convey some sort of comfort, not surprised by the answer. Alan and Belinda Austin were some of the nicest, most genuinely good people he knew. Mark had been too.

"I thought you were taking some time off," Alan said.

"Oh, well, you know, best laid plans and all." Alan looked like he had aged since the funeral. Barry couldn't imagine losing a child, much less two. With both sons gone, Madeline was all he had left.

Alan nodded. He'd worked until he was forced to retire, then got a part time job. "I know. It's hard to stay away," he muttered. "Idle hands make for long days."

Barry nodded, glancing over at Madeline. She'd avoided him at the funeral and was still doing it. She wouldn't even look his way. He wondered if Mark had mentioned the rift between the two of them during the last week of his life. Barry would forever be haunted by the dispute. He told himself not to speculate what impact it made on Mark's last day, but Barry couldn't help but believe that if things had been good between them, Mark never would have been alone in the field that night.

"I should leave this for you," Alan said, passing Barry the picture frame he'd taken off Mark's desk. It was a picture of the two of them taken at Barry's promotion to lieutenant.

"Thanks. I appreciate it, I really do," Barry said and clapped the older man on the shoulder. He thought he saw Alan wipe away a tear and pulled him in for the embrace he'd wanted to give him earlier.

Alan desperately looked for somewhere to redirect his attention. He focused his attention on the small stack of post-it's Madeline had uncovered. "I forgot how much he liked to doodle."

"Maybe if he'd become an artist, we wouldn't be here," Madeline remarked. She wasn't loud, but both Barry and her father heard it.

"Maddie, there's no need for that," Alan said with a side glance her way.

Barry knew Mark's original career had been art. Both Austin boys had a creative streak. Jason, Mark's older brother, had been a budding journalist. It was Jason's death during a police investigation that went wrong that prompted Mark to change careers. Alongside Jason that night had been a PhD student, Olivia Osborne.

"It's time to go," Madeline announced. She picked up a box and left the other for her father. She brushed past Barry and the others without a word.

"She's having a hard time," Alan said, as if trying to explain her behavior.

Barry nodded. "If you need anything. Anything at all."

"We'll be going through Mark's things at his house soon. I'm pretty sure he kept some old case files there in his office. I'd appreciate your help, if you can find the time."

Barry nodded. "Of course." As if the memories left behind weren't enough, Mark's house was another reminder of the life he wouldn't live. Difficult as it was, Barry could understand why Alan preferred to do it sooner rather than later. Keeping it around only reminded them Mark wasn't coming back.

There was an eerie silence in the squad room after the father and daughter left. Barry and Zavalla wandered to Barry's office and away from the all too empty desk. "Thanks for having someone else gather his things," Barry told him.

"I didn't want to leave you to do it." Zavalla shook his head. "We should get some kind of volunteer list together to help the family. Mowing the lawn. Moving out. Anything to help them until they decide what they're doing with his house."

"That's a good idea." All Barry could think was that no parent should have to think about that kind of stuff.

Zavalla gave a respectful pause before moving on. Despite the ghosts of the past, the present still loomed. "You want to tell me about what happened at Dr. Osborne's house?" His arms were crossed over his sizeable chest in a pose that warranted an explanation.

Barry tried to hide his surprise. Will was the only person he'd told—less than an hour ago over lunch. How did the captain know already? "Someone tried to kill her dog. The dog's lucky to be alive."

"Sounds personal."

"Someone was also in her house while she was gone."

"How's that possible?" Zavalla knew his wife was notorious for not setting their alarm. She'd only wanted it for the internal alarms that told her what door in the house was open.

"Whoever it was had a key and the alarm codes."

"Like I said, this is personal. Did she name anyone?" Zavalla wanted to know.

"No." Barry said.

"What's your gut telling you? Are the two incidents related?"

"Maybe, but the suspect list makes no sense." Barry didn't even want to try and explain.

"I'm guessing you occupy a spot on that list." If Zavalla remembered correctly Barry had looked after Olivia's house when the FBI didn't think it was safe for her to be there.

"I'll save you the trouble of asking. It wasn't me." He wouldn't feel obligated to say it to anyone else, but given what the captain knew about Olivia, Barry felt he owed him. "I called and upgraded her alarm system so she'll have a visual on anyone entering the house. I also saw a suspicious car drive by. I know she's not going to like it, but we should step up neighborhood patrols over there just to be safe," Barry suggested. "I was going to come to you with this, but obviously someone got to you first."

"I got a call from Agent Branch," Zavalla explained. "He's bringing in a bag of dog food he wants tested for prints. As for patrols, I agree. I even offered, but the agent turned me down. He's circling the Bureau wagons." Zavalla watched his lieutenant nod as he simmered. "You don't agree?"

"I agree someone needs to be watching her, but technically it's our jurisdiction."

It sounded like a challenge. Agent Branch was territorial with Dr. Osborne and Zavalla could see it wasn't sitting well. "Technically, Dr. Osborne didn't request any of this," Zavalla reminded him. "Agent Branch, on the other hand, has the full resources of the San Antonio field office at his disposal and you can bet he's going to use them. Something tells me we're about to be seeing a whole lot more of him."

* * * *

"The driver might simply have been slowing down because he or she was unfamiliar with the neighborhood. It might not mean anything," Olivia protested as soon as they were alone and away from the agents she'd met outside her house. They'd been there when they returned from visiting Daisy.

"No one knows what it means," Silas reminded her.

"Why didn't someone tell me?"

Silas didn't realize until they got back to the house that Barry hadn't told her. "You'd been through enough," Silas placated her. "I'm sure Bartholomew didn't want to bring it up."

"Yet *you* knew."

She had a point. *Bartholomew must have known how she would react and decided to let him take the fall. He was learning fast.* "He called me, remember? He told me about the car when he told me about Daisy," Silas explained. He and the lieutenant were going to have to work on their communication skills.

Olivia's eyes narrowed at the prospect of Silas and Barry having a conversation of any kind.

"You're a victim on this one, Livie. Let me think like the agent, okay?" Silas kept talking. It kept her at bay. "They're just going to be keeping tabs. Not camping." She still didn't look happy. "If they do their job right you won't even see them." He reached for her hand and pulled her in his arms, ensuring he had her complete attention.

Olivia knew what he was trying to do. Distract her. Being this close to him, it wouldn't be very hard, but they couldn't get lost in each other right now. They had somewhere to be. "Why not ask SAPD to sit outside instead? Why does it have to be the FBI?"

"Think about it. SAPD could be where the breach is. Mark Austin was the only other one besides the lieutenant and I who have a key. What if he lost his, or it's at the station or who knows where? Anyone could have taken it or made a copy."

"The last time Mark was at the house was Saturday night, the day before…" Olivia trailed off from the rest of the story. *The day before Mark was murdered.*

"That would mean the key went missing in a short amount of time. It also means someone knew you were away. Having these extra sets of eyes on you and the neighborhood is a good thing," Silas reminded her. "So, you want to make the trip with me downtown to drop off the dog food bag or do you want to stay here?"

"I'm going with you. I just need to feed Alvin before we leave, since it could be late before we get back."

"I know I wouldn't be opposed to that little cantina I like. The one not far from SAPD. A nice patio table under the lights." It was a proposal. Wheels were in motion. His time for keeping Olivia in the dark was coming to an end.

Olivia smiled. San Antonio just might be growing on him. She untangled herself from him and went to the kitchen. As she reached for Alvin's food her eyes lingered on the bags at her feet. One large. One small. Two dogs. Two different kinds of food.

"You know, I was thinking, since Daisy has to eat special food, maybe we should get separate containers. One pink and one blue so I don't feed the wrong dog the wrong food," Silas suggested, following her to the kitchen.

Olivia turned to look at him. His thoughts were mirroring hers. She noticed he was holding another bag, a small one. "Where did that come from?" she asked, a thought struggling to break free.

She sounded on edge. Maybe he was rushing her. She was used to having her own space. Suggesting pink and blue containers might have been too much. He was settling in and he hadn't even told her yet. "It's Alvin's. We brought it back from the vet. Daisy's is by the door so we don't forget to take it with us downtown."

Olivia was looking right through him. Calculating. There were four bags when there should only be two. When she and Silas had gone to the grocery her first night back to the house, they'd had to get dog food because there was none. The food went with the dogs when they left her house. *Mark had to come back to her house after he picked up the dogs. It was a simple mistake. Barry didn't know each dog required their own food.*

"What's wrong?" Silas asked. Her posture told him something was.

"I'm wondering why I have two open bags of food for each dog."

CHAPTER TWENTY-ONE

OLIVIA SAID SHE wanted to go to police headquarters but changed her mind on the way. Silas had flown back to town eager to resume his caregiver role so maybe she should let him. He could handle the investigation into Daisy's poisoning while she did something else.

Olivia asked him to drop her off down the street from police headquarters at the television station instead. She wanted to see Jessica Tate. After her talk with Barry last night she felt like sharing some news, and she was starting to feel a bond with the reporter. By cooperating with the police and withholding information on Olivia's involvement in the *Good Samaritan* case, the pesky reporter may have inadvertently saved her life. Maybe this was one small step toward repayment.

* * *

Frank Tobias, head of Forensics, was busy when Silas arrived so he handed the bag off to a tech for inclusion in the next batch of specimens headed to the Bexar County Crime Lab. Silas decided to make the most of his time so he went to see the captain while he waited.

"Are you sure we can't help out with surveillance on Dr. Osborne's house?" Zavalla asked after expressing his condolences over the loss of the agent's father. From the pained look that crossed the agent's face it was evident he was still grieving, whether he acknowledged it or not.

"I've asked the FBI to handle it," Silas told Zavalla. "But thank you." Silas paused before continuing, making sure he chose his words carefully. "Captain, I have to tell you, after a thorough review of the situation, the only unaccounted for person who had access to Dr. Osborne's house, as well as knowledge of the alarm codes, was Sergeant Austin." Silas waited while the words sank in.

"That doesn't make sense," Zavalla finally said.

"That is the consensus," Silas agreed. "However, having said that, I have to assume the key to Dr. Osborne's house and the information regarding the alarm codes have fallen into someone else's hands."

"And you think those hands could possibly belong to one of my officers?" Zavalla said it for him as the implications mounted.

"I have to consider it a possibility."

"You're sure it's not Bartholomew you're after?" Zavalla had to know up front.

"No," Silas said quietly. "He's been ruled out."

Zavalla nodded, relieved for the moment. He didn't like the other implications, but he couldn't argue with Agent Branch's logic.

"I would like your permission to search Sergeant Austin's desk," Silas suggested.

Captain Zavalla shook his head. "I'm sorry, Agent Branch, but Mark's family came by just a couple of hours ago and cleaned out his things. I'm the one who boxed them up. I didn't find any keys. He probably had them on him."

Silas knew where Zavalla was going with this. If Zavalla was right and Mark had the keys with him, then they are sealed in evidence.

"I can call evidence and get someone to check it out," Zavalla offered before the agent could ask.

"If they're not there, then the only alternative I see is to talk to Sergeant Austin's family. Maybe he kept his personal keys separate," Silas finally said. "I know it's an inconvenience and terrible timing, but I have to go there before going through the DA."

"I get it, but you have to understand the trauma the Austin family has endured."

"I do," Silas acknowledged. "Olivia was involved in both cases. It's her safety I have to think about. She is my number one priority."

"You're right," Zavalla relented. "If I can't get an answer straight away, I'll get you access to the family. My only condition is you take Lieutenant

Bartholomew with you. You know he and Mark were close. It'll make things easier on everyone."

* * *

The receptionist at the news station escorted Olivia to Jessica Tate's dressing room and then headed off to track down the reporter. Olivia passed the time by surveying the space. It was small, but it was all Jessica's. The reporter for the station's *News You Need to Know* segment was moving up in her world. The *Good Samaritan* case had gone a long way toward making that happen.

Olivia noted the stack of flyers showing Jessica's niece, Kim, on the dressing table. Jessica's position at the station certainly helped spread the word, but it hadn't been enough. Due to Kim's age and history as a runaway, her disappearance had garnered zero public attention like so many other cold missing persons cases and the investigation had simply stalled.

Olivia stepped closer to the small wall space beside the dressing table. A framed collage of pictures hung there. From looking at the images sealed in glass, the reporter and young girl had been close their whole lives. Olivia knew Jessica saw her as her last chance to find out what happened to Kimmy.

Jessica stood in the door and watched Olivia until she felt Jessica's presence behind her. Olivia saw the look of expectant hope on Jessica's face. "The two of you seem close."

"We always have been. My brother and I are twelve years apart. Kimmy and I grew up more like sisters," Jessica explained.

Olivia caught a flash of sadness. But the feeling was older than Kimmy's disappearance. "Why?"

Jessica smiled, but it was pained and tight. Things might have been looking up for her, but personally, the disappearance of her niece was taking a toll. Olivia could see it nesting in her eyes "My sister in law, Allison, left when Kimmy was young. She always had problems. My brother was always trying to save her."

"But he couldn't," Olivia said it for her.

"No. She got pregnant with Kimmy when she and Gerry were in high school. Allie had personal issues even before that. Drugs let her escape. One day she just faded away and never came back."

The story reminded Olivia of her own mother. She looked back at the pictures of Kimmy, wondering if she had inherited her mother's demons. Jessica had said there was no one else in her family like Kimmy. It came from her mother.

Jessica was fingering the pictures. Olivia instinctively reached for her cross. Kimmy wore a similar keepsake. "The necklace Kimmy wears was her mother's. Allie put it on her the last time she left."

"Where is she now?"

Jessica shook her head. "No one knows. Kimmy stopped asking. Or she just doesn't remember her anymore."

Olivia could tell her Kimmy would always remember her mother no matter how little time they had together, but she didn't.

Jessica straightened the picture frame and turned back to Olivia composed and back to herself. "Please tell me this isn't just a social visit."

"I did want to come and see how you were," Olivia said quickly, wishing to move on. "Lieutenant Bartholomew is going to talk to the families of the missing girls again. Now that some time has passed, another interview might shake something loose." She didn't dare tell Jessica the first investigation had been little more than checking some boxes and filing paperwork.

"Thank you. Thank you so much." Jessica said. She was grateful and she felt lucky. Not only for Dr. Osborne, but that Lieutenant Bartholomew would be the one handling it. He was one of the good guys.

"It's a start."

"Just finding someone who would listen was a huge help," Jessica said.

"He'll be talking to your family as well. Give some thought to new people who may have come into Kimmy's life. Especially given the fact she felt different than other girls," Olivia urged the reporter.

"An opportunist," Jessica said. "I was talking to Dr. Greene the other day. She said something similar."

"Who's Dr. Greene?"

"She's a local psychiatrist specializing in trauma. She typically works with cops, but she also does some volunteer work with abused women. She takes calls at some of the hospitals for rape victims. I just interviewed her. I thought you knew her."

Olivia's curiosity was piqued. She didn't often get to work with other women. The Smythe case was the first San Antonio case she'd ever worked. "Why would you think that?"

Jessica shrugged. "She talked like she knew you. And Lieutenant Bartholomew."

* * *

A text message alerted Silas the bag he'd dropped off earlier was ready for pick up. The same tech who'd processed the bag in led him to Frank Tobias's office. "We lifted several prints. I'm sure yours and Dr. Osborne's will be easy enough to identify, but there are a metric crapload of fingerprints on these bags. If you think about it, everyone who touched this bag at the processing plant and all the flunkies at PetSmart who handled it have left their prints. Anyone else you know of that has prints in the system? Maybe give us another direction to look to?"

Silas handed the forensics director a card for the veterinary clinic treating Daisy. "Dr. Schaner is the treating vet. He has a list of employees who handled the bag. They have prints on file as well. Elimination of those known folks should be pretty straightforward, but beyond that I'm not sure who else might have handled this. Sorry to give you a needle in a haystack."

"It's all good. Just makes our job more interesting," Frank smiled. "We also took the liberty of looking for any hair or fibers."

"I should have thought of that," Silas muttered.

"Hey, don't worry about it. It's why they pay us the big bucks, right? We've got your back, Agent Branch," Frank told him and meant it. He liked working with the agent. He was tough, but thorough. And he got the job done.

"I appreciate that," Silas said at the unexpected show of support.

"Sorry to hear about your father," Frank said, as he gave Silas a firm handshake before handing the bag back.

"Thank you," Silas said, taking the bag.

"Clever, drawing a daisy on the dog's food bag. I guess that way you won't get them mixed up."

* * *

The sidewalks were extra crowded thanks to Fiesta, but as long as she wasn't driving, Olivia didn't mind. She liked the feel of the city and she rarely ventured downtown. It was a beautiful spring night and dinner on the patio would be nice.

Olivia texted Silas. *Got a table.* She didn't even have to tell him where. He hadn't specifically asked, because she knew he would leave their dinner location up to her, but he had mentioned it. It was an easy choice, each of them acquiescing in their own way to each other. They'd developed an easy rhythm between them. *Mi Tierra* was the first place they'd eaten when he arrived in San Antonio. Silas had come back, but for how long? He had mentioned being here to prep for the trial, but Olivia knew if Brennon had his way Jamie would never see the inside of a courtroom. What then? She'd told Dom she was thinking about family. About a future. But was Silas?

Olivia quickly redirected her thoughts. Two people in two days had claimed to know her, and she knew neither of them. Maybe this was part of that "following" Silas was always talking about. Or maybe it was something else. Olivia opened a browser on her phone. She preferred the known over the unknown and asked Google to introduce her to the trove of data it held on Dr. Amanda Greene.

Originally Amanda Santos, she was a thirty-six-year-old psychiatrist from San Antonio. She married Eric Greene, a Dallas police officer who was killed just four years later. Looking at the dates, it looked like it was Eric's death that prompted Amanda to return to her hometown. She was currently employed by a group practice that got a healthy number of referrals from SAPD for trauma counseling. She had four brothers, all of them in some form of law enforcement. When she wasn't working her day job, Dr. Greene was volunteering for a number of hospitals in the region, just as Jessica Tate had described. She seemed to be, on paper at least, a regular victim's advocate. God bless LinkedIn.

"The margaritas are wonderful." The suggestion brought Olivia back to her surroundings. She looked up to find a waitress. With the drink menu open in front of her she could have been mistaken for someone who couldn't make a decision.

"Unfortunately, I know," Olivia answered with a smile.

"I know that look. The *Ramos Gin Fizz* is a nice alternative if you're avoiding tequila," she suggested.

Olivia felt the hand trailing along her shoulders moments before he spoke. "I think avoiding the tequila is an excellent idea," Silas said. He planted a kiss in her hair and took the seat next to her.

They gorged on chips and salsa, enchiladas, and guacamole with Olivia more than happy to share hers.

Silas pushed his plate away. He'd been randomly swirling chips in the remaining salsa. He needed to get it together and say what he'd come here to say. "You're not going to pass out on me again, are you?" he whispered against her cheek.

She'd had a second Gin Fizz with dinner and he had joined in her solidarity against tequila even though the restaurant served the best margaritas he'd ever had. "Not a chance," Olivia said and took a hefty sip of her water. "I have plans for you."

"Good." Silas gave her a wink and delighted at the rise of color in her cheeks. She was one of the few women he knew who blushed. He reached out and took her hand. "I need you to know something."

His words were rushed and her stomach tightened. Any other time in their lives his next statement would have been about work. They had yet to talk about his visit to SAPD. Instead they had tabled work in favor of the food in front of them and each other. This was about them.

"How do you feel about me being in San Antonio?"

"The trial?" Olivia bobbed her head and tried not to look at him. Was this a beginning or an end?

Silas reached for her other hand, threading his fingers through hers, forcing her to look at him. "It's more than that."

Olivia looked up at him. "What does that mean?"

"They offered me the option to transfer to San Antonio."

Olivia felt her gut cinch again. She didn't understand. Silas had been climbing the FBI career ladder as long as she'd know him. She shook her head in protest. "Your career."

"They offered me the field office, Livie. SAC, if I want it."

Olivia opened her mouth, but nothing came out. *What if home isn't a place?* Olivia realized she was standing on the brink of something she never saw coming. No matter what'd she said to Dom. "Sounds serious."

Silas brought her fingers to his lips. "I think we both know it is."

CHAPTER TWENTY-TWO

SILAS'S PHONE WOKE them. Olivia could tell by the look on his face it was work. "I thought you had more time," she said. She was referring to bereavement leave. Instead of being here with her, he was supposed to be in Virginia with his family.

"It's local," Silas told her. She snuggled up next to him and rested her head on his chest. Silas stroked her hair, enjoying the feel of her close. "Sorry, it woke you." He'd known she wasn't a morning person before they ever spent a night together.

"Guess I had better get used to it." She knew he was smiling without even looking. She also knew he hadn't put the phone down. "I'll get us some coffee."

Silas ditched his phone and caught her hand before she could slip out of bed. He propped himself up on one elbow to look at her. "We need to make time for just us—no work."

Us. There was that word again. They done a lot of talking about the two of them last night. Olivia smiled and stretched out beside him. "Deal."

"Want to do me a favor?" Silas asked.

"What did you have in mind, exactly?" she asked, rethinking the whole getting out of bed thing.

"What do you have on tap today?"

"Barry and Will were checking into some missing girls for me. I'm hoping they have something to share."

"Missing girls? You didn't tell me about this." Missing girls made him think of Roche.

Silas was right. She hadn't, not with everything else that was going on.

Olivia quickly told him about Jessica Tate's missing niece but was especially light on the specifics.

"Is that really a case for Bartholomew?" Silas hoped he sounded casual as much as he hoped the lieutenant wasn't going to be a problem.

"It's another inheritance from Atascosa County, but Ranger Gaines is tight with the DA over there, so he was able got access to the files." Olivia made sure to explain the rationale behind why an SAPD lieutenant was poking his nose in another county's business. The fewer questions from Silas the better. For now.

"Look at you, liaising with the locals." Silas made it sound like a compliment, but the wheels were turning. What was really going on? "When did you talk to Gaines?" With his appointment to head up the San Antonio field office, he and Gaines were sure to bump up against each other and Livie was one hell of an ambassador.

"After I took a look at the barn near where he found Ferdinand Roche's body it was kind of a *quid pro quo*."

"Another thing you didn't tell me about," Silas reminded her. The Roches, like the neighboring county, just wouldn't go away. He also decided he should talk to the Ranger sooner rather than later.

Olivia sighed. Silas was getting that distant look in his eye. The one that said he was honing in on a target. "May I make another suggestion?"

"Huh?" Silas wasn't paying attention. He was stitching together bits and pieces of what she'd given him. Was he making something out of nothing?

Olivia rolled closer and snaked her arms around his neck. "I don't think we should talk work in bed." Silas couldn't resist. Her eyes were shining. He could get used to the view. "Are you going to tell me about that favor you needed or not?" Her voice was soft, full of promise.

"The office was calling to tell me my car is ready. I was hoping for a ride."

She pulled him closer. "I'm sure we can work something out."

* * *

"You rang," Barry said. He'd headed down to Forensics as soon as he got the call. He'd already been on his way to the break room for his second cup of coffee. He'd been in early, despite the late night. Sleep had been an elusive commodity for weeks now. Considering he'd just invited Silas Branch back to town he didn't see that changing anytime soon. Barry needed a distraction from the agent and Olivia. Amanda Greene had left him a voicemail on his cell phone last night. She'd dropped her professional title, making it sound like a personal call. She was beautiful, smart, and from what he'd heard, single. He was considering how much of a distraction he wanted.

"We're waiting on the captain. This way I only have to deliver this somber news once."

As if on cue, Zavalla stepped into Frank's office, still carrying his travel mug. It looked like this was his first stop, before his office. The fact they were in the confines of four walls and not in the open lab only escalated Barry's suspicions. In fact, he was pretty sure he knew what this was about. He didn't have to be present to know who had been in the building the day before. Word traveled fast.

"The prints on the dog food bag from Dr. Osborne's house came back." Barry and Zavalla shared a glance. "Pretty much what you'd expect, Dr. Osborne, Agent Branch, Sergeant Austin, and a vet clinic employee. Two wild cards: Alan and Madeline Austin."

"Alan did a stint as a security guard after he retired and Madeline is a dental hygienist," Barry said aloud, explaining why their prints were in the system.

Zavalla knew he didn't need to wait for that call back from Evidence after all. Mark Austin's keys to Dr. Osborne's house hadn't been with him the night he was killed.

Frank clasped his hands together, glad to be relieved of his piece in the evidence trail. "I'm going to happily pass that off to the two you to figure out which one did the deed. The next question I have is how long do I sit on this?" Frank got the quizzical look from Barry. "I expect Agent Branch to be calling me anytime this morning, which is why I called you guys first. He's going to want answers."

"Of course, he is," Barry muttered.

"Not long," Zavalla said.

"I need to make some calls," Barry interrupted.

"I'm aware, but cooperation starts now." Zavalla turned back to Frank.

"If and when he calls, tell him. No stalling." Frank nodded his understanding and Zavalla turned back to his lieutenant. "Walk with me," Zavalla encouraged him.

Barry knew he'd been out of line, now his boss was about to tell him so.

Zavalla steered Barry out of Forensics and to the elevators. He waited until they had one to themselves. Once the doors closed, he decided full disclosure as soon as possible was his best play. "You might as well know. Silas Branch has been named Special Agent in Charge of the San Antonio Field Office."

The news came out of left field. Barry averted his eyes to the ceiling, counted to ten, measured his breaths and held onto the anger swirling inside of him. *Unfuckingbelievable.* At least now he could let himself off the hook. He'd been beating himself up for summoning Silas back, but he'd already been on his way. It was time he faced facts. Silas was here for Olivia and there was nothing he could do to stop it.

"If it came to this, I made a promise that he could see the Austins, but I didn't say you wouldn't go first."

* * *

Olivia dropped Silas off at his new office but elected not to go inside. He'd gotten another call on the way. "So much for not working."

Silas was still sitting in the car, reluctant to get out. "The DA wants to talk. This time it's just me." Silas was preparing her for what was to come, defending her already. The need for such ignited a slow burn inside of her. The DA was on a witch hunt and she was the target.

"What's his problem today? Brennon Kaine?"

"There is some speculation that you got Kaine the case."

"I'm sure the DA suspects as much, but maybe he should check Jamie's communication log. He got one phone call just like everyone else. He used it to call Brennon. It's not my fault he let two other lawyers pass him by before he did it." Silas hadn't asked, and he wouldn't, but that didn't mean she didn't want him to hear the words. "Jamie is still not himself. I can't change any of that."

"There's more," Silas warned. There was still much unsaid between them. Here was the place to say it. Away from the house. Away from the personal bubble they were creating for themselves. "SAPD wants the knife. The DA wants a slam dunk. Smythe might have committed six murders, but the one the DA wants to nail him on is Sergeant Austin's. They've been using cadets from the Academy, wandering up and down Highway 281, the straightest shot from Wendy Florren's house to yours. They need the knife to make this stick. SAPD has nothing on the other murders."

"They never did. Which is why they called me." Olivia sat back in the seat, realizing her voice was too loud for such a small space. The DA was pushing her and she didn't like it. If pushed too far she might feel the need to tell him finding the knife wasn't her problem. "Why don't you remind him I found the killer? Something SAPD couldn't have done without me. The rest is up to someone else." Right now, she was more concerned about missing girls than missing murder weapons. "Are you sure about taking this job?" Olivia suddenly wanted to know.

Silas reached across the console for her hand, but she was holding her own. He swept the hair from the side of her face and tucked it behind her ear instead. She was feeling vulnerable and he wanted to make it go away. "Don't confuse me with the DA. I'm sure about a lot of things. You above all."

"It's not the best career move you could make." If the DA couldn't make this case, he would want to blame someone and she would be an easy target. Olivia had no illusions. The FBI would not put themselves on the line for a consultant.

"I already told you the move isn't about my career. Me being here makes it easier for us to be together." Silas made the decision sound easy. As if thinking of them together was the most natural thing in the world.

* * *

Barry was MIA, at least that's what Norma, the woman strategically stationed outside the lieutenant's office told her, but didn't get any farther because the phone was ringing. She waved Olivia toward the conference room down the hall instead.

Olivia opened it to find Will. He was placing pictures on a white board. She had asked for a glimpse into the world these girls lived in. She scanned the information until the door clicked closed behind her, rousing Will from his mission. He looked up, first at her and then his watch. "Is it time?"

"I have no idea," Olivia said continuing to gather info. "I got a text last night saying you two made some contacts."

"We did. I'm still wading through the minutia," Will said gesturing to the white board, watching her scan his notes. "I thought this might make it easier." He watched her survey his work.

"You have pictures of the girls too, right?" So far, she was seeing what she had expected.

"Yes. I planned on putting them at the top of the columns when I'm done."

Olivia nodded her approval. It made it personal and reminded them all of the goal. These weren't just names on a piece of paper. Already invested she readjusted and focused on the columns of neat block lettering full of miscellaneous data that contained the answers that would lead them somewhere. "Do you know where Barry is? He's not answering me."

"No." If he'd had to guess he would have thought she would know before anyone. "He flew out of here in a hurry. Said it was something he had to take care of sooner rather than later."

Olivia nodded. Will looked uncomfortable under her scrutiny. "I can come back," she started for the door, but then turned back. "The address written in the corner; there are no pictures of that place." She pointed even though it was the only address listed.

"None of the girls lived there. Sampson owns it, but we think he might have rented it to Marceline Roche. I have no confirmation on that yet, though. Sampson wasn't available for questioning yesterday," Will said.

Olivia deduced that to mean he'd been drunk at the VFW. "Where did you get your information?"

"One of Ana's talkative former coworkers."

"Former?"

"She was working at Atascosa County Health and Human Services up until about six months ago," Will explained, surprised the lieutenant hadn't told her already.

"What's she doing now?"

"According to her co-worker she does local festivals selling salves, essential oils and herbs. Claims to be a witch of some kind."

Olivia didn't recall seeing any other structures other than the house and the barn. "If I drove back to Sampson's place, could I find this place?" She pointed to his notes on the board. The country road number looked familiar.

"It's probably the land Sampson leases to hunters so it shouldn't be too far away. GPS may or may not be able to get you there, but if you head east you—"

Olivia held up her hand, stopping him mid-sentence. "I'm directionally challenged even with GPS. All I need to know is, if I retrace our route to Sampson's place, can I get there?"

Will seemed to consider it. "Probably. Based on the aerial map, you just follow the road parallel to the barn. It should take you where you need to go. Not the straightest shot, but there's more than one way to get from here to there." Will smiled. It was his attempt to convey his confidence in her navigation skills. "There's always more than one way."

Olivia felt the buzz of an incoming text. She pulled out her phone hoping for Barry. From the look on Will's face he did too. But this was something else. She looked around the room and remembered the first time she'd been here. Her eyes settled back on Will, but she wasn't really looking at him. She was turning pieces of information over in her head. "Sometimes the answers are in the minutia."

Will turned back to the white board, wondering what dots she'd connected because he didn't see them.

"You were at the police academy, right? Do they really use cadets to find missing things?"

"Sure, when they need boots on the ground." Will thought about Sergeant Austin and the search for the murder weapon. But couldn't bring himself to ask.

"Can you do something for me?"

"Anything."

CHAPTER TWENTY-THREE

BARRY FOUND ALAN at Mark's place cleaning and preparing for what was to come, a daunting task he'd delayed until his wife was away with her sisters. They were sitting in the garage, the door open looking out at the front lawn Barry had helped Mark seed. They'd also stained the deck in the back. The grill that sat on it was Barry's housewarming gift when Mark bought the place.

Alan offered him a cup of coffee, which Barry accepted, but he passed on the chaser of whiskey to go with it.

"If you'd told me I would have come over and helped you with some of this," Barry said solemnly glancing around the garage.

"Some of this I needed to do by myself, while Belinda was away. Kind of like the pact Maddie and I made. She didn't want her mother to have to deal with it," Alan explained. He'd texted Barry back immediately, his gut telling him the unexpected meeting wasn't about Mark. "At least Maddie made the decision to get inpatient treatment for herself and we didn't have to do it for her. I should have called you when they told me." Alan's gaze grew distant again. Barry noted he did that when referring to his daughter. "She didn't want to go at first, but it was the right choice. At least for now. *Danger to self or others* kind of a thing, they said."

Barry watched and waited, letting the older man talk. He couldn't fathom the pain he was going through. Madeline, his only daughter. His only remaining child. At least she was getting the help she needed.

"She wanted to go with me yesterday to pick up Mark's things. I checked her in after. They're recommending thirty days to begin with," Alan explained. "Snowden Hills is the name of the place." As a father his only good news was at least she'd gone voluntarily. "I knew Maddie was upset. I just never would have believed she'd do something like this. I swear I didn't know about the dog."

"It's not your fault," Barry soothed him. "None of this is your fault."

Alan looked past him—out the open garage door—anywhere but at the man he associated with his son. "Is she going to be okay?"

"The vet said she'll be fine," Barry assured him.

"I meant Liv," Alan corrected him. "Jason called her Liv," Alan explained at the look on his face. The old man managed a small smile as a fond memory bubbled to the surface. Jason was his eldest son, the first one he had lost. "No one was more surprised than me and Belinda when Jason called to tell us he'd met someone. He never talked to us about his life. Jason never stuck with one girl long enough to want to bring one home. We were so happy he'd met someone. For the first time he was thinking about something beyond his career."

Barry listened with interest. Neither Olivia nor Mark had ever let on how close she and Jason had been. In fact, Mark had said virtually nothing about Olivia and his brother. Only that they knew each other. "What did Jason do?"

Alan smiled at the thought. "He liked hunting the unexplainable. Crimes. Legends. Once we got to know more about Liv it made sense. Jason said she was the real deal. His last case was right up her alley. Very coincidental. Looking back on it, I think Maddie always blamed Liv for what happened. But it was Jason who was chasing murderers then, not Liv."

"It was over so fast." Alan reached for his cup again. The pleasant memories scattered. By the time he and Belinda met Liv their son was dead. "I drove by her house today, but she wasn't home. Maybe I knew, but I didn't want to. Maybe I wanted to talk to her because of my boys. If I had called sooner, maybe this wouldn't have happened." Alan shook his head. "I was just too late."

"Don't beat yourself up about it. You couldn't have stopped it," Barry assured him. "Madeline left the dog food in Olivia's house. It must have been the bags Mark had for them. There was no way to predict when it would happen." Barry gave him a minute hoping he was listening. While Alan indulged in another sip from his cup, Barry's eyes wandered to the maroon sedan in the driveway. "What kind of car does Maddie drive?"

"Blue Toyota Land Cruiser. Why?" Alan looked pensive at the threat of more bad news.

Barry shook his head, not wanting to add to the burden, but knowing full disclosure was necessary. "I saw someone driving by Olivia's place the other night. I was just wondering."

Alan heaved a sigh. "Couldn't have been. I took Maddie's keys away from her after her mother left on Monday. At first I thought it might be herself she wanted to hurt." Alan shook his head again and looked in his coffee cup. "I guess I'm going to be hearing from the Feds?"

Barry shook his head. "No, I'll handle it." He wouldn't subject this man to questioning from Silas Branch no matter what the captain had promised. "Olivia wouldn't want that." After the story he'd just heard he knew it was the truth.

* * *

The keys to his new ride were in his pocket, but Silas had time so he decided to check out his office before heading downtown to see the DA. He sat behind the desk and fired up the computer, happy to see his username and password worked on the first try. He scrolled through email. There were as many condolences as there were congratulations. From the look of things Olivia was right. So much for *not* working. He clicked through until he found one from Agent Deveroux. There was an attachment. Pictures of Andre Roche's suspected victims. He was building a profile.

Silas looked away and mentally began an inventory of what he was going to bring from Virginia. Both here and to Livie's house. They had covered a lot of ground last night, but there were still more plans to be made. Now that he'd set things in motion, there was forward momentum both inside and outside the office. Juggling work and a personal life was a new skill he needed to master.

There was buzzing coming from his pocket. Silas reached for his phone, at the same time there was a soft knock at the door followed by Agent Jon Sharpe filling his doorway. Silas waved him in while he looked down at the caller ID. It was Bobby Marshall, one of the local FBI guys Silas had tagged with watching Olivia's place.

"You said to call if we saw anything," the agent said without preamble. "A car came by just after the two of you left. It slowed in front of the house like it was going to stop. That's when I got a good look at the plates."

"And," Silas rushed him, hoping he already knew the answer. Agent Sharpe looked like he had something on his mind. Silas was also vaguely aware that if it hadn't been for his sudden arrival, Agent Sharpe would very likely be the one sitting in this chair.

"The car came back registered to an Alan and Belinda Austin."

"Did you see who was driving?"

"Negative. You know the layout of the street. Her house is in the middle of the half street just after the curve. That's where the car slowed so I never saw the driver head on."

"Okay, good work," Silas told him. "I appreciate it. So, does Dr. Osborne. You guys can head back. I think that's all I need to know." Silas looked back up giving Agent Sharpe his full attention.

"There's a call for you. I just wanted to make sure you were going to pick up."

"For me? Already?"

"News travels fast around here." Sharpe told him. "And I kind of might have let it slip you were here." Sharpe flashed him a smile. Silas didn't know how sincere it was. "It's a Texas Ranger. I thought you might want to take it."

Herschel Gaines quickly got to the point. "I'm glad you're not letting this Roche thing go. I told the doc the witchy stuff she found in the barn was all hers, but she put it together the same as me. Whoever killed Ferdinand Roche was using the place. She called him a dabbler - someone who was into dark magic. Seeking fertility and communing with the underworld or some such nonsense."

"And what would you call him?" Silas was careful to measure his words and not careen down some dark highway to Hell. He should have known something was up when Olivia was sketchy on the details. He hadn't picked up on it because she'd distracted him. She was right. They shouldn't talk work in bed.

"Andre Roche. He was the last one to see his brother alive and the first one to find him dead. Andre is a bad boy with a penchant for barely legal girls. Prowls the local festival circuit calling himself an artist offering portraits and selling homespun concoctions with some woman who claims she's a witch. Might have been why Ferdinand was killed the way he was. It sure got your and Dr. Osborne's attention."

Maybe that's what he wanted all along.

There was silence on the other end, but the Ranger knew he'd made his point. "I told the doc to watch herself." Gaines flicked his lighter and sucked in air laced with nicotine. "I got the files she asked for. Considering they were of missing girls I figured she was looking at Roche—the living one." The Ranger paused and exhaled. "She didn't tell you, did she?"

Silas ignored the question and the implications. "Andre," Silas said, the name leaving behind a bad taste on his tongue. "You looked into him, right? Do you know where he is now?" The air in the room was stale. The wagons were circling and Livie was in the middle of it.

"Saw him packing up his truck myself. Said he was headed back to the Big Easy to give his brother a proper burial."

Silas was rubbing the back of his neck. It had stiffened with the news. "That doesn't sound right. I interviewed him when Ferdinand's body went missing there was clearly no love lost there. Send me his address. I want to check it out."

"I'll rustle it up. I'm finishing up something right now. I plan to make it over there today. You might ask that lieutenant, Bartholomew, he seemed motivated to get this thing settled. Since you seemed to be hittin' the ground running I reckon he'd be willing to help."

"I'm sure he would," Silas told him. "Thanks for the head's up."

"I'd say you've got your hands full," Ranger Gaines commented. "I think I'm looking forward to meeting this doc of yours. She's a fearless one, ain't she?"

* * *

"They found him seizing in his cell this morning."

Brennon had secured a private conference room near administration and far away from the Intensive Care Unit at University Hospital where Jamie was currently admitted.

He also had her favorite soda waiting for her when she arrived. Olivia suspected the Dr. Pepper was some kind of peace offering. She was grateful. She and Silas had a late night and it was starting to catch up with her. She'd noticed a nagging pain in her side. Maybe it was because she was using muscles, she'd forgotten she had.

"The drug therapy isn't working," Brennon said with a shake of his head.

Barely a week with his new client and already Olivia sensed a change in him. He looked as tired as she felt and he seemed off his game. Rattled. Unsure. Words she would never have used to describe him before.

"Did Jamie have some kind of a reaction? Is that why he's in ICU? Or did he do something to himself?" Olivia wanted to know.

The use of the name sounded foreign to Brennon's ears. It brought a false sense of normalcy to his client. "He's reacted to every medication Todd has ordered."

"Who is Todd? Why isn't Bob Thornton handling this for you?"

"Todd Thornton is Bob Thornton's son and medical partner. Bob was unavailable due to injuries he'd sustained in a car accident, nothing serious but I guess there is a femur fracture involved. Todd is treating Jamie."

The fact Brennon was calling the younger Thornton by his first name and not by his medical title told Olivia how he felt about the replacement.

"They're evaluating him now for something called neuroleptic malignant syndrome. His blood pressure was through the roof when they found him. Earlier in the week it was something called tardive dyskinesia."

"Both conditions you're describing are severe reactions to antipsychotic drugs," Olivia explained. She had a sinking feeling about where this was headed. "Neuroleptic syndrome is a potentially fatal condition that typically manifests as high blood pressure and an irregular heartbeat. The treating physician should be doing a thorough work-up to rule out any underlying medical condition that could be reacting with the medication. As for the tardive dyskinesia, it's usually only seen in patients who've been on long-term therapy with high doses of antipsychotics. TD causes involuntary muscle movements that sometimes mimic cerebral palsy or even Parkinson's.

Over time the muscle movements became irreversible. None of these are symptoms Jamie should be having."

"That's pretty much the consensus," he said.

"What is Todd Thornton's actual diagnosis?" Olivia wanted to know.

"Schizophrenia," Brennon said. Even he sounded skeptical. "What would be your diagnosis, Dr. Osborne?"

Olivia shook her head. "No, I'm not taking that bait, Counselor. I'm not a medical doctor and you know it." It was her standard answer to a loaded question when on the stand. It was a distinction she was familiar with making. She could provide expert testimony, but she had to tread lightly not to stray outside her training. She had not gone to medical school. She did not hold a medical degree. *An academic* was how prosecuting attorneys liked to describe her, as though it was a dirty word. Although she had received specialized training, she was not authorized to prescribe medication. She could recommend, but it had been her experience that most physicians didn't want to hear her opinion. Bob Thornton had been one of the rare ones who was willing to listen to an alternative approach, a philosophy his son apparently did not embrace.

"Let's cut the crap. You and I both know you know more about what's going on with my client than any one of the psychiatrists who have seen him. And you've been in his presence once." Brennon wished she was his side, legally speaking.

The fire had returned to his eyes and Olivia caught a glimpse of the familiar counselor she knew before. It's what mesmerized her, both inside and outside of the courtroom. She was glad to see it return. He was going to need it. "Look, Bren, I shouldn't even be talking to you about this. I was called in to consult for law enforcement on this case. The conflict is clear here."

"Come on, Olivia. This is about far more than prosecuting a case under the mortal system of justice."

She relented and set aside her conflict for the moment. "I would think the fact he's not responding to the medication should tell us something. Like perhaps he's not schizophrenic. It's not a medical condition that makes him act the way he does. Something else forced him to commit those murders."

"We're talking about the Seven Second Theory, now aren't we?"

Brennon had gone back and reread her dissertation. The first time had been for his client in Washington, but he'd needed a refresher. "That small window of time when a person doesn't have complete control over one's self and or their decisions," Brennon recapped.

"I am a subscriber to the theory, yes," Olivia said. It was the seven-second lag in time before making a decision that she and others believed allowed those from the other side to cross over. It was a vague description of what the Church would call possession.

"So, my client was no longer in control of his own actions?"

"There are observable changes in electrical patterns related to cognition. MRI scans performed just before a decision is made shows brain activity not initiated by the subject." She sounded like the academic now.

"Meaning we have no idea what we are doing? We have lost the ability of free will?" Brennon summarized.

"Seriously, Bren. Is this a pre-trial strategy session? You should be paying me a hefty consultant fee with questions like these, nevermind the huge conflict of interest you're pulling me into here." Brennon smirked at her, knowing she couldn't stop herself from speaking the truth. She was growing more uncomfortable with the meeting with each moment that passed, yet she couldn't escape the fact that her role was to highlight these very truths, uncomfortable though they may be.

"In a nutshell, yes. Once the door is open there is no way to say how long the influence remains." Olivia let the notion hang there. She watched his eyes narrow. Brennon wanted a slam-dunk case just liked the San Antonio DA. But those were never guaranteed. Not in law. Not in medicine. Not in life. "I've given you the science of it. That's all I can do."

"I'm not trying this case in a hospital. Where are the roots of your theory?" He was pretty sure he knew from what he'd read, but he wanted to hear it in her words. It was a story that meant something to her.

"There is legal precedent, albeit pretty thin. At the Salem Witch Trials, Sarah Osborne, in her defense, claimed if the devil was causing harm while assuming her appearance then she could not be held accountable. Her argument brought the trials to an end. It does lend credence to the possibility we might not always be in control."

Brennon took a moment and considered her argument. "Your profile of my client was dead on. You knew what he was before you met him."

"It's what I do. It's my job," Olivia told him.

"It's more than a job, Livie. You're gifted." He said it easily.

Olivia held his gaze. *You owe me a debt. Was it payment for services rendered?*

When she didn't respond Brennon continued with questions about his client. It was the only way keep her talking. She would tell him nothing of her abilities. "So, if my client isn't schizophrenic, then what is he?"

"This is not a compulsion or an infestation like you experienced with your other client," Olivia cautioned him. "Jamie has a demon inside of him. The symptoms of the neuroleptic syndrome have to be addressed, but the tardive dyskinesia symptoms could be demonic manipulation. I saw Jamie exhibit strange movements before he tried to attack me."

"The medical staff at Bexar County observed similar occurrences," Brennon told her.

"Either way, it is my belief that the demon is the cause of the side effects, all of them, because *it* doesn't want Jamie medicated."

"The medication inhibits the demon's ability somehow?" Brennon mused. "Good to know it has a weakness."

"Only when it is inside your client," she cautioned. Maybe it was time to go to the archbishop, but for him to even consider what she was suggesting, Jamie would need medical clearance. It was a requirement from the Church, but it didn't look like Jamie's current clinician was a believer.

From behind, the door to their meeting room opened. A man stuck his head inside. "Dr. Osborne, I presume," Todd Thornton said by way of introduction. He might have been looking for her, but he was obviously not happy to have found her. His attention quickly shifted to Brennon. "Your client is awake and he's asking for her. He said he knew she was in the building. His exact words were, 'he could smell her'."

CHAPTER TWENTY-FOUR

SILAS GOT THE text from Olivia while he was talking to Ranger Gaines on the phone just outside Barry's office.

The DA is looking in the wrong place. Talk to Will Ibarra about bus routes.

The harried woman sitting outside Lieutenant Bartholomew's office directed him across the bullpen where Will was expecting him. Will was sitting in front of his computer. A map with two bolded lines filled his screen. One red, one blue.

Will sized up the agent as he approached. He walked with a purpose and took command of the room regardless of the audience. Even though he was wearing chinos and a golf shirt, Will would have pegged Silas Branch as a Fed. Although his clothes were casual, his demeanor wasn't, and Will surmised the reason for the visit was personal.

"What have you got, Sergeant?" Silas dispensed with greetings and cut straight to the map on the screen.

The sergeant traced the blue route on his monitor with his finger while Silas leaned over him. After a couple of neck craning glances over his shoulder, Silas got the hint and parked himself in a chair at the edge of the desk. "This one goes from Blossom Point to Lafayette," Will explained the streets he'd highlighted.

"Blossom Pointe is Wendy Florren's. Lafayette street is Dr. Osborne's place."

"The route Smythe took after he killed Sergeant Austin," Will hated to point out the obvious.

"According to the DA," Silas emphasized. "Bearing that in mind it would have also been the same course SAPD followed when they searched for the missing murder weapon. The one they theorized Smythe ditched somewhere along the way."

"That they didn't find," Will added.

"Dr. Osborne led us to Smythe. She knows him better than anyone else." Silas reached over and tapped the blue line on the screen. "But this is the route a VIA bus would have taken between those same two points."

"Correct. But Smythe didn't take a city bus. He drove the sergeant's cruiser."

"He did but Smythe never had a license in his life. He's not an experienced driver. The only way he knows to get to Dr. Osborne's is by bus. We know because he went there a couple of nights before the murder to stake out her place." Silas tapped the blue line again. "So we can infer that Smythe would have taken the route he was familiar with to get to Dr. Osborne's. There's only a few blocks difference but somewhere in there could be what we've all been looking for."

"The DA should have been able to recover the car's last trip from the GPS tracking system on Sergeant Austin's car."

"He should. But did he?"

* * *

"He came back from his tests awake and asking for you, Dr. Osborne." Todd Thornton hovered in the conference room doorway and finally sat with Brennon and Olivia only after Brennon insisted.

"Dr. Osborne and I were just discussing our client."

"And your diagnosis, Dr. Osborne?" Todd asked. The tone in his voice told Brennon he was looking for a fight despite the fact they had just met.

"I'm not a medical doctor," she said.

"That's exactly what I have been trying to explain to Mr. Kaine," Todd agreed.

"It doesn't mean Dr. Osborne doesn't have an opinion," Brennon said, his voice tight. "An *expert* opinion." He was attempting to keep his temper at bay.

"So, what is your opinion, Dr. Osborne?" Todd asked. "Enlighten us."

"Perhaps the reason none of the meds are working on your patient is because he isn't schizophrenic," Olivia suggested.

"And maybe my patient knows how to work the system. It looks like learned behavior to me. He's a product of the world we live in. People of his age, twenty to twenty-five, have had access to the Internet their entire lives. We are arming your 'would-be monsters' with much more information these days than a generation ago. Their skill set is only going to grow. If he can learn to elude the police and not leave behind evidence, maybe he also knows what reactions to exhibit in order to avoid medication."

"Whose side are you on here, damnit? The prosecution's or mine?" Brennon asked.

Olivia didn't give Todd an opportunity to respond to Brennon's angry rhetorical question. "With the muscle movements yes, not with the elevated blood pressure."

"Well, we can't find anything medically wrong with him," Todd reported.

"It still doesn't mean he's schizophrenic," Olivia repeated. She could feel the anger seething in her midsection, next to the nagging pain in her side. "He would have to be highly functional, which, considering he has a high school education and has been plagued by seizures since the age of six, I don't believe he is."

"What would you suggest we do with the demon inside of my patient?" Todd asked. Olivia looked stunned and did not have a ready response. "Oh, don't look so surprised. I know who you are. I'm familiar with my father's cases and I have done my research."

"Exorcize it," she deadpanned. "There is no medical course of treatment for what's inside him, not without eventually destroying the host, your patient, *Doctor*."

Brennon looked from Todd to Olivia. "Where would this exorcism take place?"

"I can't believe you're even entertaining this," Todd said.

Olivia ignored the outburst. "In the church."

Brennon shook his head. "We'd never be able to convince the DA to sign off on transporting him. The need for security is enormous. The flight risk involved is too great."

"It works best when done on sacred ground," Olivia insisted. "For this case we have to do it by the book. No shortcuts. This demon is nasty, not to mention strong."

"And there's no killing it, I suppose," Brennon said. He wasn't knowledgeable about these kinds of things. For one thing he was Jewish and for another, he had Olivia.

Olivia was already shaking her head. "It can't be killed, but Jamie can."

"That is a possible side effect of exorcism?" Todd asked.

Olivia ignored him and continued. "Demons were once angels and, according to the Catholic Church, they are immortal."

"My human patient, Jamie Smythe, however is not," Todd asserted.

"Your patient is an unwilling host. Would you let him keep any other kind of parasite in his body?" Olivia felt her frustration with Todd's disbelief reaching a point of no return. She turned to Kaine and attempted to extricate herself from what had turned into a mock trial. "If you'll excuse me, I think it's better if I go speak to Jamie myself," she said as she stood up from the table and left the room.

"I think you should wait here," Brennon said to Todd.

"He's my patient. You have no right to keep me out of his room."

"Your behavior with Dr. Osborne was inappropriate and unprofessional. It'd be a shame if that information circulated through the medical community. God forbid your father should catch wind. Wait here, Todd."

The ICU had strict visitation times, but given the circumstances, Brennon was prepared to challenge those rules. Olivia was waiting a few steps away, not even pretending she couldn't hear their discussion.

"We won't be long." Brennon turned and hit the intercom that would allow them to enter.

Olivia followed in silence down the hallway lined with glass sliding doors providing a window into a place most people couldn't see and did not know existed. It was a halfway place, at least that's how Olivia would describe this section of the hospital, a way station of sorts. The patients here hovered between two worlds: the life they knew and the unknown that lie ahead of them. Some were ready to go, some weren't. Some saw light, some saw only darkness. Some would leave this place only to return another day.

Jamie's glass-walled room was at the end of the hall. The Bexar County deputy stationed outside the door sat up straighter when he saw Brennon and Olivia approaching. Olivia couldn't help but wonder what he had done to get this assignment. It had to be mind-numbing.

The nurse monitoring the desk in the center of the unit lifted her head up from her computer monitor to greet them.

"We need to see my client," Brennon said.

"If he's stable," Olivia added.

"He's remarkably better," the nurse told them, looking from Brennon to Olivia. She knew who he was, but the woman, she wasn't sure. "He's awake and eating ice chips. His blood pressure seems to have stabilized. If it stays that way, the doctor is thinking of transferring him to the step-down unit."

"That's good news," Brennon said, but he didn't sound like he was happy.

"I need to speak with him, briefly," Olivia said.

"Are you Dr. Osborne?" the nurse asked.

Olivia exchanged a quick glance with Brennon. "Yes."

The nurse smiled. "Oh, good. He's been asking for you."

* * *

Silas was careful not to knock anything off as he rounded the desk. The harried woman parked outside Bartholomew's office didn't try to stop him. She'd just mumbled something about rethinking his plan to go in there. Now Silas knew why. The room surprised him. It was chaos where the man was not. The contrast gave Silas a peek inside the person who occupied it. The lieutenant was a cop who preferred the field over paperwork. He knew the real work was done outside.

Silas stopped building his profile of Barry Bartholomew because he didn't like where it was taking him. He concentrated instead on carefully maneuvering himself around the edges of the chaotically cluttered desk to get to the lieutenant's chair. It was the only surface not covered in disorganized paper. He didn't want to disturb whatever filing system Bartholomew had going on, but he couldn't sit outside anymore. All he saw out there was an empty desk staring him in the face. The new sergeant, Ibarra, had been helpful making some calls, trying to wrangle information out of his contacts at the Academy, but after that he'd wandered off down the hall, leaving Silas on his own with the ghost of Mark Austin.

Surveying the chaos from Bartholomew's seat, Silas noticed the picture of Mark. He and the lieutenant had their arms thrown over each other's shoulders, smiling, toasting the photographer, each of them with a beer in their hands. Mark looked the way Silas remembered him on his last day. As for Barry, Silas couldn't recall ever seeing him smile. A push of his finger and the picture toppled face down on the desk. Silas ignored it and tried to call Livie, but she didn't pick up. Where was she? *Where was the lieutenant?*

Silas was startled when the man himself threw open his office door. The scowl on his face told Silas the office chair was off limits. Silas took the hint and hopped up without being asked. As Silas exited one side of the desk, Barry rounded the other. He had a box and laptop computer slung under his arm. They both belonged to Mark. Alan had insisted he take them.

Barry turned his back on Silas, as though he might make him disappear by ignoring him. He searched for a clear spot in the cluttered mess to set down the box and computer. The windowsill behind his desk had no room to spare so he opted for the floor. He'd debated on leaving items in the car, but wasn't sure he wanted to take them home. When Barry turned around Silas was waiting. "You're still here?"

"Where have you been?" Silas asked.

Barry bit back his initial response that his whereabouts were none of the agent's concern, but in the interest of the cooperation he'd promised Zavalla, he swallowed it.

"I thought you were supposed to meet with Livie," Silas said.

Barry looked up at him. He'd gotten her text, but had been in the middle of his discussion with Alan. He hadn't texted back because he had mistakenly thought she would be here. "Zavalla made you a promise I didn't keep."

Silas didn't like the way his gut seized at the statement or the places his mind wandered. It felt like jealousy.

"Among the dozens of fingerprint database hits from the dog food bag were two I recognized immediately, and it just all fell together. I went to see Alan Austin. He told me everything. It was Madeline, Jason and Mark's sister, who poisoned Daisy. This morning she sought voluntary admission at the Snowden Hills Center. It's a mental health treatment facility where she can get the help she needs. I assured him they wouldn't be hearing from SAPD or the FBI on this," Barry rushed to say before Silas could protest. "The family doesn't need any more trouble. It's the way Olivia will want it." Barry knew using Olivia as leverage was the only way.

"I don't understand. Madeline? The sister?" Silas shook his head, trying to catch up. The attack seemed too personal. He must be missing something. "Why would she want to hurt Livie? Mark's death was on *me*, not her."

The words *it wasn't about Mark* died on Barry's tongue, tamped down by the realization that *Silas didn't know about Jason.*

"I shouldn't have left him that night." Silas finally admitted it out loud.

Barry and Silas had never talked about Mark or anything else between them. They hadn't talked at all. Barry stayed silent. He knew Silas's admission didn't come easy. Questioning himself wasn't something Silas Branch did. It made him a good athlete and a formidable agent. He was a decisive man. For a woman such as Olivia, who lived in a shadow world, she had to find such resolve attractive.

Barry decided it was time for his own confession. There was one thing he had to let go. "Mark knew better. He should never have gone into that house alone."

CHAPTER TWENTY-FIVE

THE NURSE STEPPED away to check on her patient. The monitors told her his vital signs were stable, but she needed to lay eyes on him at least every half hour. The curtain surrounding Jamie's bed was closed. It was the only privacy provided in the glass box. Jamie couldn't see he had visitors, but the thing inside him knew she was there. She felt a tingle just below her scalp like ants marching to their queen.

"I should go in alone," she told Brennon.

Brennon looked worried at the suggestion, but there was relief there too. She could see it. "Is that wise?"

"If we want him to respond fully, it should be just me. It's why I'm here, isn't it? To make contact?" There was a demon in there waiting for her. Even Todd knew it.

Olivia sat her purse down on the desk and instinctively reached for the cross around her neck. She took a cleansing breath, shutting out the sights and sounds all around her.

Brennon loosened his tie and reached under the collar of his shirt. He removed the Star of David necklace he was wearing and pressed it into Olivia's hand. "A gift from my granddaughter. I know you're not Jewish, but faith is faith, isn't it?"

Olivia had all she needed, but this was for him, not her. "I believe it is," Olivia assured him. She wrapped the chain around her wrist and tucked the Star inside her hand out of sight. "Thank you."

"His vitals look good," the nurse said as she exited Jamie's room. "I'll call his doctor and report while you're inside. Just make it brief."

Olivia nodded and entered the glass box. The space was small, but with the curtain drawn, it bordered on claustrophobic. She never liked the ICU as a nurse. It was easy to lose the patient in here, especially when surrounded by machines. Fortunately, Jamie's were few. One monitor for heart rate and blood pressure, and he still had an IV. He wasn't cuffed to the bedrail, there was probably a rule against that in the ICU, but Olivia did notice he had a bed alarm that would emit a deafening sound, should he leave the bed. Currently he was facing away from the door, looking out the long narrow window to the outside world.

His head turned slowly towards her when she entered. "Olivia Esme Osborne," the demon, *Alleracsap,* greeted her. "I smelled you when you came in. *Eternity* is the perfume, is it not?" Olivia didn't respond. She didn't have to. "Apropos of our dichotomy." Jamie's head rose and stretched, elongating his neck. His nostrils flared as if smelling something else.

"I want to talk to Jamie," she said, interrupting whatever it was going to say next.

"He is not the one who asked for you, nor is he the one you came to see."

All six points of the star were digging into her hand. "He is. And I'm not talking to you without speaking to Jamie first," Olivia said, hoping her voice sounded calm.

The eyes blinked slowly as the face changed. She watched as the skin relaxed to reveal the humanity beneath. "Dr. Osborne. What are you doing here?" Jamie asked. He attempted a smile, but his muscles were slow to respond.

"I came to check on you. How are you feeling?"

Jamie looked around the room as if seeing it for the first time. "Did they move me to another cell? Where am I?"

"You're at the hospital. You were sick. Do you remember anything?"

Jamie looked at her and slowly shook his head. "No, but I don't feel so good." His head slumped back on his pillow before snapping upright. Blackness pooled in the eyes that watched her. The irises blazed green, the pupils parting to reveal the eyes of a serpent. "You have seen the pestilent little child. Now that unpleasant business is out of the way, let us begin," the voice that wasn't Jamie's hissed. "Interesting you chose the Star of David today. It can be a potent symbol for magic. Is that why you brought it?"

The demon was right. The Star of David could be confused with the pentagram. Olivia felt her grip loosen.

"Of course, in its current form it is the symbol of slaves. You do not need it. Your gifts are more powerful than any of those amulets you keep." Its eyes shown bright when it said the words. "They are merely symbols, talismans of something old and forgotten. I could teach you."

"I seem to be doing just fine on my own," Olivia heard herself say. There was a rushing sound in her ears. Like a waterfall.

"Not even close," it snapped, feigning disappointment.

Olivia stood her ground and breathed deeply.

Its demeanor seemed to change. Withdraw. "You have come here to ask for something, have you not?" Jamie's hands smoothed the bedsheet in front of him. The movement was jerky, almost alien.

"Jamie needs medication," she insisted.

"He is no good to me medicated."

"He shouldn't be any good to you at all now that he's locked up. He won't be any good to you dead."

"Dead, not so much. Especially since the possession was not his idea."

"Then how?" Olivia interrupted him. She knew Jamie had killed on his own, two murders prior to whatever changed the night Patricia Griffin stopped to help him. His victims chose him. Not the other way around. *If Jamie hadn't been the one, then that meant Alleracsap had come here all on his own.*

"You know the answer," *Alleracsap* snapped. "Nonetheless, a soul is a soul." He sounded bored with their conversation already. "I do collect them. We all do. There is a tally, you know."

No, she didn't know. She didn't want to know. Olivia tucked the information away and moved on to other things. There was something more. The demon wouldn't be here otherwise. She was reluctant to take that path, but she didn't have to. *Alleracsap* took her there instead.

"You were so intent on running away, burying your head in the sand. Perhaps I got tired of waiting on you. Decisions need to be made or your abilities will evaporate." The demon paused, waiting for a response from her, but got none. "When are you going to take charge and show us who you really are? Are you not curious? I know I am."

"I could have you exorcized," Olivia threatened.

"You could try." Jamie's eyes narrowed, even though she could see nothing of the boy inside them. "If you can convince the *causidicus*." Olivia noted the demon chose the Latin term for lawyer. "You do have certain powers of persuasion with him. He thinks of you often. If you give him another go, I'm sure he would give you anything you ask. It is risky. In your effort to send me away, you could kill the boy. It has happened before."

"It doesn't have to be that way," Olivia said.

"Clever girl. Now we are getting somewhere." The hand movements ceased. Its gaze slid back to hers. "No. It does not have to be that way." Each word was spoken with force. She had recaptured *Alleracsap's* full attention. "Jamie can spend the rest of his pathetic life in some padded room. I know that is what you want for him. Are you sure he wants the same?" *Alleracsap* paused, giving her the chance to argue but she didn't. "As for me, my needs are simple. Find me a replacement and I will set him free. All you have to do is give me another. I am positive you can find one. You already know where to look."

"I won't," Olivia snapped, feeling the stir of anger and something else. The ants on her scalp had picked up the pace. It was another surge of energy. Hospitals were full of it. Her fingertips tingled in response.

For a moment the demon closed Jamie's eyes, reveling in the atmosphere around him, feeding on the same energy she felt. "Awww.... there it is."

Olivia saw the flash of pink as the forked tongue darted through Jamie's lips, tasting the air. Like she had done in the barn. Olivia realized *Alleracsap* felt it too. *The stir.* She shut it down.

The demon snapped out of it. Eyes open, it said, "That was over much too quickly. It can become intoxicating." *It* pulled in a raspy breath. "Now, where were we?"

"I won't do it. I'm not a demon dealer."

Alleracsap smiled or at least tried, but the lips pulled too tight, exposing too many teeth. "I have heard those same words before from someone who looked very much like you. You owe me a debt which I have not collected and now you are asking for another. Be very careful before you tell me, or yourself, what you will and will not do."

Energy pulsed from just under her skull as electrons danced in a haze all around her.

"You have things in your life you hold dear now. You are learning a lot about that, are you not? What would you do to protect this new life you are building? I do not believe even you know."

The look in Olivia's eyes changed. *It* was baiting her and she was following along.

"In your house, you were fearless. But you are considering a future with another, and I have finally seen fear in you. Fear and vulnerability. Your grandmother tried to prepare you, but fear stopped her too. She was afraid of what was truly inside of you."

Olivia swallowed hard and tried to force out thoughts of Gran. Of Silas. Barry.

"I could ensure his safety," the thing promised. "And the others to come. It is the least I can do. Especially considering what happened the last time."

Jason. *Alleracsap* had been there then too. It was where she first heard the name. "And me? What about my safety?" Olivia wanted to know.

"Oh my, what a lost little girl you are. You do not need my protection. You are the one to be feared." The thing tried to smile again or maybe it was supposed to be a sneer. *It* stretched its neck again, an unnatural movement and one Jamie would not make.

"There is another smell, sweet and salty. Beneath the enticing perfume. The nagging pain you have in your side. You and I both know what it is." *Its* eyes roved over her stripping her naked. "Ovulation. Fertility is life. You are the last of your bloodline. Such a shame not to carry it on."

"Don't use her words," Olivia told him. She could feel the anger begin to bubble.

"Gran only wanted the best for you." The thing tried to smile again. "Who knows, the die could already be cast. It could have happened last night or this morning. Am I correct? So much fornicating. It is a sin, you know."

"Stop it," Olivia snapped.

"I would be remiss if I did not warn you. You should be very careful. But you already know this. You have thought about whether or not your FBI agent would make a good father. I sense doubt. You know you are the only thing he wants. But tick, tock, Olivia. Your future is waiting."

* * *

Will stopped just inside the doorway. The agent was peering at Barry from across the desk. Silas Branch looked intimidating even with his hands in his pockets. The lieutenant, however, appeared unaffected. Will got the impression the two were finding their way toward working together.

Will tapped on the door frame to get their attention. He extended a piece of paper to Silas. "You might want to take a look at this." It was the email they'd both been waiting for. "It's the grid the DA had the Academy recruits search."

"The supposed route Sergeant Austin's car took?" Silas asked.

"Correct," Will confirmed.

"To prove Dr. Osborne's theory, I need the data from Sergeant Austin's GPS tracking system for comparison," Silas told Barry.

"I've already requested a copy of the downloaded data from the server. It shouldn't take long," Will added.

Silas smiled for the first time since he'd arrived. "Good work, Sergeant. Let me guess. They hadn't done it already." The look on Will's face was his answer. Silas looked across the desk at Barry. "In that case I think SAPD owes the FBI one. Livie told me something about a barn, but she was pretty light on the specifics."

Will noted the clinch of his lieutenant's jaw at the use of the name and decided to speak up. "I went with her. The Ranger wanted her to take a look. It wasn't far from where Ferdinand Roche's body was found. Someone burned a symbol into the wall. She didn't like it."

"What was the symbol?" Silas asked.

"An ankh. It represents life," Will said.

"Or fertility." Barry offered. Silas noted the angry tone in his voice.

"But it was inverted," Will said. "She thought someone might have been using the barn for worship or sacrifice. Or both."

"Communing with the underworld, she said," Barry added.

"Trading a life for a life?" Silas felt sick to his stomach. "She was looking at Andre Roche, wasn't she?"

"If she didn't give specifics, how did you put that together?" Barry wanted to know.

"Based on the line of questioning, looks like she thought Andre killed Ferdinand," Will answered instead.

Will's version matched that of Ranger Gaines. "What did you learn from Ferdinand's body?" Silas was playing catch up and he didn't like the way it felt. Livie shouldn't have been doing this on her own.

"According to the fire investigator, the accelerant was mineral spirts. Something a painter would use," Will continued.

"Andre Roche is an artist," Silas told them.

"What else is he?" Barry wanted to know. His hands had gone to his hips.

"A predator. Had a penchant for young teenage girls back when he was in New Orleans. The FBI was looking at him, but stopped when he fell off the grid after Katrina."

Will heard his desk phone ringing just before Barry's office phone started to ring. Will headed to his desk, shaking his head at Norma as he passed, signaling her their boss wasn't going to answer his phone.

"And you didn't think to tell Olivia?" Barry's voice was on the rise along with his anger.

"She didn't tell me until this morning. Even then all she said was you and your new partner were looking into some missing girls for her," Silas snapped. "Things have been a little hectic. Has anyone talked to Ana Lutz?" Silas asked, hoping to deflect anything else Barry had to say.

Barry's eyes narrowed. The agent knew something. "No one here had ever heard of Ana Lutz until you brought her up," Barry reminded him. "When you first came to town, after Roche was murdered, you said you wanted an audience with her. What you never said was why. Does she have something to do with Roche?"

Silas didn't look at him. "You're not going to get that?" he asked instead, referring to the phone.

Barry folded his arms across his chest and stared him down, ignoring the question and the ringing.

"A local FBI matter," Silas finally admitted.

"Let me guess, you didn't share that with *Livie* either?" Barry spat the name. The look of disgust matched the tone of his voice. "You should really work on your communication skills. I've seen her less in the last week and I know more about what she's doing than you do." Barry knew it was a shitty thing to say but right now he didn't care.

Will stepped back in the room, his presence easing the tension in the room like air escaping a balloon. At least the phone had stopped ringing. He took a moment to appraise the two men across from him. So much for working together. "The download from the tracking system in Sergeant Austin's car is in, and those wizards even took the liberty of overlaying the data points on an aerial map," Will said, not caring if he interrupted. From the looks of things, he came back just in time. "Dr. Osborne was right. Smythe took the bus route."

Silas pulled the phone from his pocket and punched in a number. "Tell your boss I'm on my way to see the District Attorney, ready or not." He looked at Will. "Grab those maps and everything else you showed me. You'll do a much better job explaining this than me." Silas turned to Barry. "After I get back from tearing the DA a new asshole someone needs to tell me about the missing girls."

CHAPTER TWENTY-SIX

BRENNON WAS WAITING for her. "Livie, what happened?" Touching her jolted him. He resisted the urge to pull back.

Olivia shook herself free and kept walking. "Get me out of here," she said making a beeline for the door. Brennon quickened his pace to keep up with her.

Olivia saw Todd waiting, but bypassed him in her rush to the elevators. Todd tried to follow, but Brennon stopped him. "Not, now," Brennon said with a shake of his head and pushed the button before anyone else could catch up with them.

Brennon watched as Olivia sucked in shallow breaths of air. Her eyes roamed the small enclosed space, frantically searching for a way out, seeing things he could never see. When the doors opened, he reclaimed her arm and steered her along. He opted for somewhere beyond the shadow of the hospital, away from the people who carried the smell of that place with them. He didn't stop until they were far down the sidewalk by a bench under a canopy of purple blossoms.

Olivia sank down on the bench and focused on the cool cement beneath her, untangling herself from the demon's words, *Gran's words*. That's what demons did. They twisted and tormented. They tricked and they taunted. Olivia clutched the cross, seeking refuge and focus. Eyes closed, she lifted her face to the sun and basked in the warmth. She breathed deeply, slowing her heart rate, inhaling the sweet smell of lilac. After a few cleansing gulps, Olivia opened her eyes. "The fragrance was a nice choice," she told him. "It cleanses."

"It works, even if they're not real lilacs?" Brennon asked, referring to the crepe myrtle blossoms. San Antonio summers were too hot for real lilacs.

"How do you know?" Olivia offered him a small smile, easing some of his own anxiety.

"Since meeting my new client, I don't sleep much." Brennon confessed with a smile of his own. It was one thing to believe what Olivia could do, it was another to delve into the world she lived in. "I've spent a lot of time reading up on your little corner of the world."

Olivia reached over and gave him back his necklace. "Thank you," she said.

Brennon took it, carefully searching her face to get some kind of idea what was going on inside of her head. "Please tell me," he urged.

"It's not leaving," Olivia finally said.

"I'm assuming you're not talking about Jamie."

"Correct. Not Jamie," Olivia confirmed.

"What did he say?"

Olivia paused. They were supposed to talk about Jamie, but instead it had been about her.

"*It* has a name?" Brennon asked interrupting her thoughts. He was trying to understand. She wasn't telling him what he wanted to know.

"Yes, and I won't give it to you so don't ask," Olivia told him. "Speaking it aloud gives it power."

"How do you know it? Why is having the name significant?" Brennon needed to know.

"Demons don't typically give their name. During an exorcism the priest will eventually get it out of them, but not until the end—just before they're banished."

"Since it's not ever just given willingly, then he must want you to have it." Olivia was struggling to get back to her own thoughts, but Brennon kept pressing. "Quid pro quo."

"He says I owe him a debt. He says he'll leave Jamie only if I find him another."

Brennon studied her. "Think, Olivia. He gave you his name for a reason. What does it mean?" Her eyes were still searching. But they weren't frantic anymore. They were moving with purpose.

"By giving me his name, I have the power to expel him," Olivia paused, dissatisfied with the answer. That wasn't it. There must be something else.

What else could she do with a demon's name? "It also gives me the ability to summon him," Olivia said slowly, the implications leaking into her brain. It was a test. *When are you going to show us who you really are?*

* * *

Norma rarely came into Barry's office. The last time was to rescue the plant someone had given him for his third-year anniversary as lieutenant. She'd gotten tired of watching it die a slow death on his windowsill. Norma had taken the plant home and nursed it back to health. Norma had hoped the pretty blonde doctor could do the same for her boss. He might be one of the good guys, but he needed all the help he could get when it came to the personal stuff. He was easy on the eyes but rough around the edges.

Barry was standing behind his desk, his hands still on his hips even though the agent was gone. Norma ignored the head shake from the nice new sergeant on his way out. If she had to be up close and personal with the lieutenant to get his attention, then so be it. She barged to the end of his desk and thrust the little pink slip Barry's way. "You need to call Ranger Gaines. Don't put it in the pile to do later. Do it now. It's important." She put her hands on her hips, mimicking him.

Barry studied the address written at the bottom in Norma's neat handwriting. It looked just like he'd been taught in the third grade. "What's this?"

"It's an address. The Ranger will tell you all about who lives there and what he wants you to do, but not if you don't call him." The urgency in her voice came through. "He said he needs this done. Now." She finally stopped talking long enough to see how his cool grey eyes had settled on her. She probably had his attention for the first time in three years since he'd inherited her along with the new rank and the cramped little office. "Call him."

* * *

They sat under the trees until her energy stabilized. Brennon didn't wait for her agreement to lunch before steering her toward one of the food trucks parked nearby. The smoky fragrances had teased him long enough.

She and Silas hadn't taken time for breakfast, given they didn't get out of bed when he got his phone call. Then they'd shared the shower. While she and Brennon waited in line, Olivia scrolled through her phone. Silas had called earlier but she'd been too busy arguing with Todd to answer. For a brief moment she wondered where Todd had gone but then decided she really didn't care as long as he didn't join them for lunch. She sent a quick text asking Silas where he was instead.

"These are growing on me," Brennon said taking a hefty bite of his taco. He was sampling everything with generous helpings of guacamole and pico de gallo dabbed across his street tacos.

"Silas says the same thing."

The news caused him to put the taco down. "So, Silas is back? Is he staying for the case?" Brennon wasn't looking forward to dealing with him again. If they were on the same side of the issue it would be different. Silas Branch was very good at his job. He would have made a formidable lawyer. Brennon also pegged him for the jealous type. He wondered if Silas knew Olivia was with him right now.

Olivia looked up to give him her full attention, but kept her phone in her hand anticipating a prompt reply. "Longer. He's going to be heading up the San Antonio Field Office."

Brennon tried to hide his surprise. He would have never guessed Silas would leave Quantico. "Sounds serious." He reached over and patted her hand. "I'm happy for you."

Olivia felt the buzz in her hand and flashed him a smile. "Thank you." She put the phone to her ear without looking at the screen. "Sorry it took so long for me to get back to you."

"That was supposed to be my line." Her heart thudded. It wasn't Silas. "Where are you?"

"I need you come back to the office. You can get that briefing you were promised," Barry said.

His words were soft, but Olivia could hear the undercurrent of worry in his voice. He was trying to hide it from her. Whatever it was troubling him had to do with her. His concern tempered her blossoming irritation. "Why? What's wrong?"

"Ranger Gaines called. He left his card with some of Andre Roche's neighbors. He got a hit. I'm headed there now."

"A hit? What does that mean?"

"A smell. Coming from the apartment. You shouldn't be alone."

"I'm not. I'm with Brennon." Olivia had no idea why she told him. "You're worried."

"There's a bad smell and they're calling a Texas Rangers and not the gas company." It was the same line Gaines had used. "If someone is dead, I'm figuring Roche is the doer. Wouldn't be the first time, right? He did his own brother."

"You are correct," Olivia told him.

"Maybe more," Barry said. "He has a thing for teenage girls. Atascosa County's not the first time."

"He had to have a partner," Olivia said, her mind swirling.

"This leads back to those girls and you're the one stirring the pot." Barry had felt it in his gut, but Silas's confession about Roche's past sealed the deal. "If it's Roche who's dead, then there's someone else higher on the totem pole. They could be looking for you. Or coming for you next. So, yes, I'm worried."

Olivia digested the story. It made sense. Barry's instincts were on target. So were the Ranger's. "And what about you? Is Will with you?"

Barry hesitated, but only for a moment. It wouldn't do any good to lie to her. "No."

Olivia felt a catch in her throat. Worry went both ways. "If things are going sideways like you say, no one should be out there alone." She couldn't help but think about Mark.

"Will's with your boyfriend and the DA. You were right. They were looking in the wrong place all along."

She should be elated at the news, but there was no sense of relief being proven right when she had known it all along. *When are you going to show us who you really are? What you can really do?* Hadn't she been doing that for years? And for what? Only to have to keep proving herself? No one wanted to listen to her until they had no other choice.

Olivia had gone quiet. Barry wondered if she was thinking about her love/hate relationship with the FBI or if she was mad about the boyfriend comment. "Why didn't you tell me he was coming back to stay?" His voice was soft. It was a question. Not an accusation.

Olivia clamped down on her feelings. Whatever they were she couldn't feel them. Not now. She'd made a decision and there was no turning back. "He didn't tell me until he got here."

Silas was pushing. *Hard.* Was it because he was afraid if given the opportunity, she might make another choice? And why hadn't she told Silas about Jason? Barry's hands gripped the steering wheel as he barreled toward Atascosa County. He shouldn't think about it and he shouldn't lash out, but he did it anyway. "Maybe you should ask him why he also didn't tell you the FBI's been looking at Ana Lutz all along."

* * *

Olivia was so angry she was shaking. Anger would be her undoing—Gran had said it many times. Gran liked to tell stories about those who couldn't control their emotions. Parables that transcended the ages because the lessons were valuable. Her favorite story was the one of Lucifer. It was his anger that turned him away from the light. Gran always warned he wasn't the only one to fall.

We all fall. Olivia's only question had been how far?

Olivia left Brennon with barely a goodbye. She just started driving and not to the briefing like Barry wanted. She needed to do this. She was the only one. The only one who understood. She'd read the board full of Sergeant Ibarra's neat, block writing. All it did was confirm her suspicions. Kimmy wasn't the only one of the girls who was *gifted,* but she had been Olivia's starting point. If she hadn't been one of them, Olivia wouldn't have seen it. It's how she'd been able to tell Barry and Will what to ask the families and what to look for. They didn't think they'd found anything. Will called it minutia, but it was more than that to her. The signs were there. The girls might not know what they were, but there were those who did. The monsters were always waiting, whether it was on this side or the other.

Andre Roche was both the artist and the dabbler. He had a mother who taught him. The girls may have been seeking the same—a teacher. Who better than a witch? A perfect partner. The artist and the witch. Andre and Ana.

Olivia knew where to find at least one of them.

On the way she left a message for Silas. More relationship rules.

* * *

It took a minute for Barry to understand what he was seeing. Without the head there was no face to look at. Barry backed out of the room, careful to retrace his steps. The first step of crime scene management was to secure the area.

The sign on the door to the shop said *Closed for NIOSA*, but that hadn't stopped him from climbing the rickety wooden steps to the apartment over the storefront that Ranger Gaines told him was rented to Andre Roche. Every few steps Barry thought he caught a whiff of the "smell" the anonymous neighbor had complained about. As he climbed, Barry had noticed the overflowing trash bins below. Maybe part of what this body was missing was in there.

Barry called for backup first. Then he called the Texas Ranger.

"So, what have you got? Was the odor our friend Roche left out too long to spoil?"

Barry was outside, leaning over the rail of the small upstairs patio. Closing the door behind him had helped contain the smell and preserve the scene. "Hard to say. Beyond my level of expertise."

CHAPTER TWENTY-SEVEN

THE MEETING TOOK longer than it should have, but that didn't dampen Silas's excitement. Patrick was the first one he called. "You should have seen his face."

Patrick could hear the jubilation in Silas's voice despite the background noise. "Where are you?"

"Downtown." Luckily the district attorney's office was within walking distance of SAPD headquarters. There was heavy traffic and street closures. "This whole place is shutting down for something called the *Battle of Flowers*," Silas told him.

"The battle of flowers?" Patrick laughed. "I thought you were in Texas where everybody carried a gun."

"Have you told Olivia yet?" Patrick asked.

"No, not yet." She'd left him a voicemail while he was in with the DA, but he hadn't checked it. He would have preferred to tell her in person.

Will had gotten in line for one of the food trucks dotting the street corners. Another good call on the sergeant's part. After the adrenaline burn, hunger was setting in. "They're assembling a team to walk the area tomorrow. I plan on being there. I'll update you later with specifics."

Patrick didn't want to burst Silas's bubble and tell him they hadn't found the knife yet, but at least they had forward momentum. Maybe in more than one place. "When you talk to her see if she knows why Smythe has been moved to University Hospital." Olivia wasn't the only one who kept up with Smythe's every move.

It made sense. If something medical had happened to him, Kaine would have called Livie. While Will got their food, Silas listened to his message and hoped for an update. He was happy to hear her voice, but his mood didn't last long. She sounded pissed.

"You should have told me about Ana." Silas felt like he'd been punched in the gut. He didn't get to the end of the message before Will was nudging him.

The sergeant held up a paper bag signaling he'd gotten their food to go. "Got to get back. Something's happened." Will was already threading his way back to SAPD, hunger forgotten for the moment.

Silas dropped his phone back in his pocket, without listening to the rest. She was angry. The fact her anger was directed his way wasn't something he wanted to think about.

* * *

Barry waited outside. Not that he hadn't seen his share of crime scenes, but the body laid out on the dining table inside reminded him too much of Mark.

"Forty-eight hours," Meeks said, coming to join Barry at the railing. "That's my best guess anyway. It's hot up here, it's been hotter outside than normal. The environment will impact my ability to get a more specific time of death until I open him up."

"I'll take your best guess over anyone else's," Barry said as he and the medical examiner watched the flurry of activity below as a gaggle of forensic techs descended on the overflowing trash bins. Maybe part of the smell was coming from there. "I guess you'll be waiting around to see if they find the rest?"

"I will but they won't," Meeks told him in his matter of fact way.

Barry looked over at him. "Playing detective again, Doc?"

"No, I decided to go with blood spatter expert today. The real experts are still processing, but I saw no arterial spray inside. Doesn't match what you'd expect with injuries of this nature. Just hacking. Purposeful. All of it done post mortem, for dissection rather than death. That's why what they're looking for isn't down there. But I'll wait, just the same. Traffic back into the city will be a bitch anyway. Maybe they'll find his clothes."

Barry looked at the doctor. Meeks was on to something. The missing parts could be trophies, but why take the clothes?

* * *

Norma was still at her desk. Barry was gone. Zavalla was waiting for them instead. Will and Silas followed the captain into the lieutenant's empty office. "Lieutenant Bartholomew won't be back for a while. He went out to Atascosa County. They found a body."

"Please tell me it's not one of those girls," Will said.

Zavalla shook his head. "No. This one is male."

Silas waited a beat, but Zavalla had stopped talking. "That's all you've got?"

"For now." Zavalla turned his eyes on Will. "I need you to run the case down for me."

Will turned and pointed out the door, down the hall to the conference room. "Been trying to get there all day."

"Wait a minute. I need more information," Silas interrupted.

"And I'd like nothing more to give it to you, but there isn't much. Our Texas Ranger friend called and asked the lieutenant to go take a swing by Andre Roche's place."

Silas knew where this was going. "I talked to Gaines earlier today. I asked if he knew where to locate Roche. He gave me an address and said if I needed some help I should talk to Bartholomew because he was already investigating the girls. Something must have happened for him to call the lieutenant," Silas suggested, looking back to Zavalla for the rest of the story.

"Gaines left his card around when he was trying to pin down Roche. One of the neighbors kept it and called him to complain about the smell. Bartholomew made entry under exigent circumstances—those circumstances being the foul odor. A naked, decapitated body was stretched out on the dining room table. Been there a couple days, maybe more, according to Meeks. Hard to tell in an upstairs apartment with the windows closed and the air off. Couple that with the south Texas humidity and I guess you get the picture."

At that point Will decided two things. He wasn't hungry anymore and he was glad he'd been with the agent and not the lieutenant.

"Is it Roche?" Silas sounded hopeful.

"Hard to tell. Our male is a John Doe for now since he's missing his head and his hands. According to Barry, Dr. Meeks says it looks like the cutting was done post-mortem. As the profiler, any thoughts on that?"

"Slows down identification." Silas went with the obvious. He was also cataloging recent events. He came up with one, but wasn't inclined to share the particulars with Zavalla. He'd need Patrick for that.

*　*　*

"He's splayed out like a Christmas ham. Sorry I sent you straight into *that* horror show." Herschel Gaines sounded apologetic. He looked every bit the Texas Ranger in his starched white shirt, and cowboy hat complete with the star shaped badge pinned over his left shirt pocket. He and Barry moved off the patio and walked away from the building because the Ranger needed a smoke. It was his one vice.

Barry had never met Andre Roche but he knew the Ranger had interviewed him. "Does the dead guy look like Roche to you?"

"According to your M.E. the height sounds about right. He was shorter than me."

That wasn't saying a lot. Most everyone was shorter than the Ranger. Barry was six feet and he had to look up to meet the Ranger's eyes. He'd guess the Ranger topped off about Silas's height, six three, six four maybe. Meeks had already told Barry the man on the table was between five six and five eight with a slight build and a paunch in the middle.

"Other than that, I can't really say. I didn't talk to him more than ten minutes. He was in a hurry to leave." The Ranger plucked a cigarette from the pack but didn't move to light it. The look on the lieutenant's face said he wasn't happy with the lack of confirmation. That was probably the point of this whole thing. "You're not pleased."

"I don't like not knowing where he is."

"Does Dr. Osborne know?"

"Not yet," Barry told him. "I thought it best she go to SAPD."

"You're worried about her because you don't know if that's Roche or not."

"Aren't you the one that put that together?" Barry asked him, recalling their phone conference after her trip to the barn.

"I did. I've never met her, but she seems like someone who can take care of herself." Gaines finally managed to move the cigarette from his hand to his mouth. The look the lieutenant gave him said that wasn't the issue. Gaines flicked his lighter and got started on what he'd come out there to do. "After this, I'll call the DA and make sure he's talked to the sheriff about how things are gonna go over here. I'm surprised he hasn't caught wind of this already."

* * *

Ana Lutz. Olivia had been pinging on her for days. Going in circles. Ana was like background noise she couldn't get out of her head. Olivia might have it figured where she fit in this case, but that still didn't explain where she fit in her life. And what had Ana done to get on the FBI's radar?

When Silas showed up to take over the Smythe case, he'd also come with knowledge of Ferdinand Roche's murder. Silas wouldn't have waded into the paranormal without her. Barry made it sound like it was the FBI that was interested in Ana specifically, not Silas. So, why didn't she know about it? What were they keeping from her this time? As ridiculous as it sounded, Olivia wondered if this was personal.

She was so absorbed in her own questions Olivia missed the turn. She had to go down to Sampson's road instead. Just as Will had said, she followed the dirt path until she got to the barn and pulled along side it. Olivia stayed inside her car not wanting to go back inside that place. It was tainted with dark magic and it still lingered, waiting to be fed. She thought about the symbol burned into the wood and the sacrifices that were made there.

Communication with the Underworld. Fertility. Creation.

An offspring of one of her kind with a dabbler of the dark arts. It was a match made in Hell or an offering of the most innocent kind. The pain in her side stabbed at her. *Procreation.*

Creation should be borne of love, not something dark and evil.

Olivia drove back past Sampson's house. She saw his car in the driveway and thought about stopping to ask him about his neighbor who lived up the road. If she remembered correctly, Will said he was a retired doctor who had traded delivering babies for raising horses.

* * *

Before going in the conference room, Silas stopped to make two calls. The first was to Livie. Her phone's automatically generated safety message told him she was driving and not accepting calls at this time. He didn't feel like leaving a message. The second was to Patrick.

"Remember the story Deveroux told about Bobby Dupree, Ana Lutz's pimp? Deveroux said when they found Dupree, he was missing his head. How did they make an ID?" Silas knew Patrick would know because Deveroux would have briefed him first.

There was a long pause on the other end while Patrick caught up since Silas offered no preamble. "The old-fashioned way. Fingerprints. He had a record. Go figure. Why?"

That answered Silas's other question. Dupree got to keep his hands. "They ever find his head?"

"Not that I know of. I'm going need you to start filling in some blanks here."

Silas explained what Bartholomew had found at Roche's place. "I need to know, is there more? Did Deveroux leave anything out?" There was another pause on the other end.

"I'm not sure what all Mason Deveroux told you, but the prevailing theory is Sarah Larsin was responsible for Dupree's death. Her business dealings are hush-hush, but the one thing Deveroux's people do know about her is she's got a temper and she's very protective of *her girls*."

Silas felt the pressure building behind his eyes and it had nothing to do with hunger. Both he and Will had donated their lunches to Norma.

Patrick continued. "If you're connecting dots between Dupree and this John Doe, removing the head had nothing to do with IDing the body. Decapitation is a classic form of intimidation, but I'm sure Olivia's probably already told you that."

Silas wished she had. That would mean she was talking to him.

"It does make a statement."

* * *

They were waiting on him, but Silas had one more call to make. He didn't want to, but he had to. It was quicker that way. Bartholomew answered on the first ring.

"The missing hands are an obvious effort to delay identification. The doer needs time for something. Look for someone who would be easily identified with his prints. He'll be in the system." It sounded cryptic, but Silas knew the lieutenant was smart of enough to understand.

"This is bigger than these missing girls, isn't it? That's what taking the head was about."

"Probably."

It wasn't a definitive enough answer. "Is that what Olivia said?"

"She's driving," was all Silas said.

"She was with Kaine. She should be there already," Barry objected. He knew traffic was a bitch downtown today with the parade, but the jail wasn't far from where she should be going. It was less than a minute's walk if parking was a problem.

"Smythe's been moved from the jail back to the hospital across town. Some unknown medical issue."

Silas's explanation mollified Barry's worry for the moment. A cross-town drive in today's traffic would take some time. He could move back to making an ID. He didn't like waiting. He needed to know who the man on the table was. He wanted Andre Roche out of action. "You met Roche, right?"

"Yeah." It was why Silas left Mark alone that last day. Silas went to interview Roche about his brother Ferdinand's missing body. At the time it seemed like no big deal.

"How would you describe him, physically?"

"Much shorter than me. Five seven or so."

"Other than that?" Barry demanded. "On the small side? Slight of build?"

"I wouldn't say that. What he lacked in height, he made up in bulk. The guy looks like a gym rat."

Damn. Barry took a breath. "Unless he's made some dramatic lifestyle changes, I don't think the dead guy is Roche."

CHAPTER TWENTY-EIGHT

THE HOUSE LOOKED like it was built before the barn and it had weathered the years only slightly better. The drapes were drawn and it didn't look like anyone was home. She didn't care if they were or not. There was a mailbox outside the gate to the yard. Olivia opened the box and saw a plastic sleeve inside with a card that said *M. Roche*, but she knew the house was owned by Abram Sampson.

Olivia approached the house and went through the motions of knocking on the door. As expected, there was no answer. She walked around to the back and stepped onto a small covered porch. There were two doors—one to a portion of the house with a wooden exterior, the other to a section of the structure with a stone surface. The front part of the house must have been an add-on. Olivia sensed that the stone structure was older; left over from the original. Something had happened to the rest. Olivia laid her hand on the rocks and closed her eyes. *Fire.* She usually got no feelings from inanimate objects, but there was energy contained in the stones. Both old and new. *Someone had practiced magic here.* But that came after the fire.

The entrance to the original part of the house was a screen door with the mesh hanging loose. Olivia didn't bother to knock this time. The bottom hinge had rusted off and the door screeched across the concrete porch. She turned the knob to the door and pushed. It didn't budge. Olivia looked above her to the ledge. Standing on her tiptoes her fingers fumbled blindly until she found the nail. It's where her Gran used to hide the key to their back door.

With a turn of the key and a firm push with her knee, the door opened. There was a crescent shape carved into the floor from years of that motion.

The room was part of the original house. The exposed walls were made of something called shiplap. Olivia knew because when she and Silas got tired of watching other people cook, they switched over to HGTV and watched other people renovate houses. Across the room in the corner was a closed door with the same crescent marking on the floor from where the door opened. The original hardwood was at her feet. If she wasn't mistaken, she could see a trail of footprints from the entryway to the door. She couldn't immediately discern whether or not the footprints were made of dust or particles of remnant energy, invisible to anyone other than her. Olivia ignored what the sensory confusion might mean and followed beside them, the boards beneath creaking as she went.

She opened the door and saw it was a closet with a trapdoor in the floor, secured with a slide bolt. Olivia imagined the cellar below the trapdoor and recalled Gran telling her how her own grandmother had one before it was destroyed in a flood one spring. Gran called it a 'root cellar' because it was dug into the earth. It stayed warm and dark and was an excellent place to store the homemade canned vegetables her grandmother made for the family. She also kept her herbs there. The ones she didn't want in the light of day.

Wondering what was in this one, Olivia knelt down and opened the door. She was hit with an odd combination of smells. Wet dirt, stale air and something else. She cocked her head and tuned in to what emanated from below.

* * *

Sergeant Ibarra was detailed. Silas had to give him that. The columns of information were neat and tidy. Will was shuffling through more pictures to add to the board. Silas was drawn to the ones that were already on display.

"What am I looking at?" They were random pictures of the outside of what he assumed were the victim's homes. But he wasn't sure why he was looking at them. Captain Zavalla had wanted to ask the same thing but was trying not to rush the sergeant. Will knew he should have explained, but all he wanted was to get started. The agent was impatient. Will put down the pictures in his hand and concentrated on the ones Silas was asking about. "Dr.

Osborne wanted to see where the victims lived, since she couldn't be there. She said that would be easier than getting them to answer some questions."

Silas nodded slowly. He was looking at a visual profile through Livie's eyes. She assessed people and scenes differently. She called it her second sight. "And she told you specifically what to look for?" Silas asked the obvious. She had to have, but even with the photos he had no idea what any of them meant.

"All the houses had wind chimes. One had cinnamon sticks, another had shiny glass balls hanging in the trees, one had a wreath of rosemary on the door." Will tapped the pictures as he spoke. "The most interesting one was the house with the mirror on the porch beside the front door."

Zavalla had to agree. His wife had a mirror beside the front door but on the *inside* because she liked to check her appearance before answering the door. Having one on the outside kind of defeated the purpose.

"We didn't make it to Kimberly Burleson's house last night, but Dr. Osborne said it was okay if we didn't because Kimmy didn't live with her maternal family. Her mother left when she was young. She lives with her paternal grandmother since her dad works on an oil rig in the gulf and doesn't get home often."

"Kimberly Burleson?" Silas asked.

"She was the last girl to go missing. Eight months ago. Jessica Tate approached Dr. Osborne about her because she didn't think the locals in Atascosa County were doing enough."

"She's Jessica's niece. Tate's her professional name," Will explained.

Silas nodded recalling the few details Olivia had provided.

"Anyway, I called Jessica last night after we got back." Barry had dipped out somewhere and he'd passed the call to Will. "I went to see her. She told me things I think the doc would be interested in."

"Pretend she's here and tell me," Silas encouraged him. Livie was already way ahead of him. He needed to catch up before she got here.

"Kimmy became fascinated with dream catchers. Jessica thought it was because of her sleep paralysis. She started making them and gave them to some woman to sell at festivals. She also started covering her bedroom mirror at night."

"Why? What's the deal with mirrors?" Zavalla wanted to know.

"Spirts use them. Having one outside the door to your house deflects evil. The wind chimes, the baubles in the trees, the rosemary, the cinnamon sticks—same idea. The doc needed the visual because she said these beliefs weren't something the families would talk about openly."

"Why was Dr. Osborne focused on these things?" Silas asked. It was her world, but what started her down this path? Abduction of young girls was a man-made evil in his book. What was he missing?

"Jessica Tate went to Dr. Osborne because she knew she would understand. Jessica believed Kimmy was like the doc. She *felt* things. According to the lieutenant Dr. Osborne believed if these girls were special in some paranormal way then that's what made them a target."

"Did you find anything to refute her belief?"

"No. It's as plausible a theory as anything else. We found no other connection."

"So, she analyzed the victimology to get to the offender," Silas said. It was Behavioral Analysis 101. "These girls all have some kind of paranormal ability. That's why their families kept these talismans." Livie had often talked about evil stalking her, but yet she kept none of these objects.

"She said it was all in the minutia," Will told him.

"And she was the only one who could see it." Silas's eyes wandered over the pictures. Something was missing.

"That and the offender, obviously."

"They were running away from evil, but the offender was running toward it. Why?" Silas was speaking out loud, but talking to himself.

"He wants it for himself." It was Will.

Zavalla turned to Silas. "The dabbler in the barn."

* * *

Barry heard the rumble of a diesel engine. He stuck his head around the building to see the Ranger heading toward the vehicle before anyone else. Barry saw the Atascosa Country Sheriff Department's logo on the side of the truck and stopped. The Ranger threw down his cigarette, snubbed it out with his boot and then scooped it up and put it in his pocket. He waved to Barry that he'd handle the new arrival.

Barry went back to heading toward the trash bins. The throng of techs was thinning. "We found bloody towels so far. No weapon and no body parts," the lead tech told him before he had to ask.

Barry looked over at Meeks who had taken a seat in the shade out of the way. From behind he heard someone head up the stairs to the apartment. A stocky man in a brown polo and khaki pants was ascending the stairs. He was also wearing a cowboy hat but he couldn't pull it off like the Ranger.

Gaines stopped to confer with Barry while nodding to the man to wait for him. "Sheriff Tennent's going to take a look at the body. He's pretty sure he can ID it if it's Roche."

Barry nodded. He was hopeful.

"He also asked if one of his deputies had stopped by here already." Gaines looked at Barry. He already knew the answer, he just needed confirmation.

"No. Why?"

Gaines hitched his jeans up and looked around. "He said he's not heard from one of his deputies in a while. Guy named Calderon."

"I've heard of him," Barry said, sounding annoyed. "He's the one that investigated the missing girls, if you want to call it that."

"Well, yesterday was supposed to be his day off, but Tennent still expected him to be working. He'd agreed to overtime. It looks like another girl might have gone missing from the Poteet Strawberry Festival over the weekend."

"Another one? And we're just now hearing about this?" Barry was suddenly angry.

Gaines reached out and put a big hand on his shoulder. "Not your jurisdiction."

"That was days ago. What do they mean 'might' have gone missing?" Barry tried to curb his tone. It would do no good to lash out at Gaines. He should save it for the sheriff.

"You read up on those girls. Part of the problem is their circumstances and their family situations."

Barry shook his head, pissed, but knew there was nothing he could do about it. The Ranger was right.

"I got this," Gaines told him. "You stay down here with your people."

Barry was going to follow when the buzzing on his hip stopped him.

He grabbed his phone and put it to his ear. "Bartholomew," Barry said to whoever was on the other end. He didn't bother to check the caller ID. If it was Silas he didn't want to know until he had to.

"Mr. Bartholomew, this is Dr. Schaner."

Barry stopped, frozen in place.

"Daisy's veterinarian. We met yesterday," the voice on the other end said.

Barry's contact information was on the dog's paperwork because he was there the night she was admitted, but he had never met the veterinarian. Barry closed his eyes. "How can I help you?" he asked, keeping his patience in check. It wasn't this guy's fault he had called at the worst possible time.

"Your information is the alternate contact we have," the vet explained quickly. It sounded like he'd interrupted something. "We're closing early and I wanted you to know Daisy is ready for discharge."

Barry told himself to keep the sarcasm out of his voice. "Have you tried to call Dr. Osborne?" He hated asking the obvious.

"I have. Several times. She's not answering her phone. If she doesn't come soon, Daisy will be spending another night."

Barry looked at his watch, trying to calculate how much time had passed since he talked to Olivia. That was the thing about crime scenes. They swallowed you whole and suspended time. He looked up at the sky for a clue. The sun was dipping. He was still standing there, his phone in his hand when he saw Gaines and the sheriff emerge from the apartment upstairs. The sheriff looked like he was going to be sick. If he didn't move away from the edge of railing Barry would need to warn Meeks.

The sheriff's level of upset gave Barry the answer he'd been looking for. It wasn't Roche on that table.

*　*　*

One name stuck out. It was all over the board. Silas had no way of knowing but it was the same one Barry kept seeing when he reviewed the file.

"Who is Deputy Calderon?" Silas wanted to know.

"Sheriff Tennent's chief deputy. He conducted the initial missing person's interviews with the families," Will told him.

"You think he wasn't doing his job?" Silas prompted.

"That's what the lieutenant thought. From the looks of things, I have to agree."

"You think he was covering for someone?" Silas asked.

"I know he's shady as shit," Will told him. "The fire investigator, Cruz, and I ran into him when we were at Sampson's place. He seemed to have a real problem with us nosing around Sampson's barn."

"This thing in Atascosa County was never about drugs." It was Zavalla this time. "Sheriff Tennent only said that to get you and the Rangers off his back," he looked over at Silas. "It was about something else just as valuable. Girls."

Silas looked at him, knowing the captain was right.

"Roche's the one, isn't he?"

"What makes you say that?" Silas asked. He was stalling, assessing how much the captain knew.

"That thing with Ferdinand. All that witchy stuff. Roche's the dabbler of the dark arts Dr. Osborne talked about. If these girls are like her, then you'd think he'd want to get to know her." Zavalla saw the flash in the agent's eyes. That probably wasn't the best phrasing he could have used. "You and she haven't talked about the barn, have you?"

Silas looked at the captain. He was going to have to start trusting. He was on his own. When he came here a month ago, he hadn't been interested in building relationships or making friends. He was here to catch a monster, but all that had changed. His whole life was changing. "Livie and I hadn't exactly gotten to that. I came back early because of the break-in at her house and then the dog."

It was a rare personal confession from the agent. That's when Zavalla realized it. Agent Branch's transfer to San Antonio had nothing to do with Smythe, this case or any other one. He was moving here to be with Dr. Osborne. No wonder Bartholomew hadn't taken the news well.

"She said there were offerings in the barn. What if Roche is sacrificing these girls or," Will stopped talking as he thought about the symbol on the wall. *Life.* "Or something worse?"

Silas listened while the captain and Will told him about the barn. It made sense now why the Ranger had told her to watch herself. Silas knew then he should never have kept secrets from her. He'd never do it again.

"Every predator has a type," Silas said, looking at Will. "Your board is missing something. Where are the pictures of the victims?"

"Hadn't gotten that far." Will turned around and started pulling them from the file and tacking them above the corresponding column of notes.

While Will did his thing, Silas pulled out his phone in search of the email Deveroux sent him—the one he'd opened earlier but closed before he looked at it. He wanted to see Roche's original victims. Every serial had a type, whether they were killers or rapists.

All the girls looked like Olivia, if they had gotten to live long enough. Roche had a type and Olivia fit the bill.

His phone buzzed and Silas snapped the photos closed, praying it was Livie.

It was the lieutenant. "I need you at the crime scene. Have Will drive. The sheriff is here. He took one look at the dead guy and said he won't talk to anyone but you. That tells me the dead guy isn't Roche. And please tell me Olivia is with you."

* * *

"That smell is snake. One by itself and you wouldn't notice it, but get a group of them together and they stink."

Olivia went still at the unexpected intrusion, the trapdoor handle frozen in her hand. From the corner of her eye she saw the toe of a boot. She hadn't heard him come in because he'd stepped where he'd stepped before. In the prints. He'd known where the creaks were. Her visitor squatted down behind her, impinging on her space. She could feel his breath on the back of her neck, in her hair. She was hoping he didn't touch her.

"There is something else, though, isn't there? A sound. It's from the rattle on the ends of their tails. I'd say there's more than one down there."

She didn't like the intruder being that close to her. Olivia stood up, slowly. The one behind her mirrored her movements. She turned to face him. She had to look up at him, but not far. He was dressed in a uniform that wasn't his. The pants fit but the shirt was stretched too tight across his chest. He might be wearing an Atascosa County hat, but the name on the nametag wasn't his. She knew because of the pony tail that hung down his back. He was pretending to be someone he was not. Olivia knew it wasn't a new game for him. And he knew she knew.

"I got all dressed up and I didn't even have to."

His eyes were dark with flecks of amber. They were wild, openly crawling across her chest. "Older than I like, but I'll make an exception in your case." Finally, his gaze fixed on the silver cross that hung around her neck. He smiled. "Thanks for coming. Now I don't have to go and find you."

He reached out and she instinctively recoiled, but Olivia had nowhere to go. He was blocking her path. The edge of her shoes hung over the open pit. He reached for the necklace, breaking the chain as he pulled. "Abandon hope all ye who enter here," he said recanting the inscription carved at the entrance of Dante's Hell.

With one swift motion he pushed her into the darkness below.

CHAPTER TWENTY-NINE

OLIVIA HIT WITH a thud. Shards of bright light exploded behind her eyelids before they were washed away by the tears filling her eyes. It was an autonomic response from the blow to her back when she hit the ground. Olivia rolled to her side and curled into a fetal position. All the while her diaphragm convulsed, the spasms interrupting the natural order of things, unable to move air in or out of her lungs. Olivia quivered as she struggled. There was no air to breathe.

* * *

The parade was over, but the narrow one-way streets of downtown were still clogged and not moving fast enough for the agent. The emergency lights helped when there was room to pass, but they didn't start making headway until they hit the highway. Traffic was thick due to ongoing celebrations, but at least they were moving away from the epicenter, going the opposite direction. Will flipped the siren and starting making up for lost time.

While Will drove, Silas busied himself with phone calls. It was better than yelling at the sergeant about things neither one of them could control. The auto response text message about driving was gone from Livie's phone. Instead he was shuffled to voicemail. Silas bypassed the main number to the local field office and went straight to Agent Jon Sharpe asking him to locate Olivia's phone signal. Since she was still tagged as an FBI asset from the Smythe case, it shouldn't be too hard to locate her. Silas had contemplated outfitting her vehicle with a GPS tracking system now that he'd been promoted and they would be living under the same roof, but that would be a tough sell. Things were moving too fast.

At the moment all Sharpe could confirm was that her phone was still on, but he couldn't get a pinpoint on her location. "My guess would be she's somewhere with spotty coverage," Sharpe told him.

"Atascosa County?" Silas asked.

"That qualifies. I'll keep checking and let you know when I get something."

* * *

Her breaths were ragged and painful, but she was moving air. Her nostrils filled with the earthy smell of the snakes. The stench caused her to swallow a gag. She began breathing through her mouth to avoid the odor and bring some regularity to her breathing.

Now that she was regaining her bearings, Olivia pushed herself off the ground but only so far as her knees. She didn't try and stand. The hole had looked shallow and she didn't want to hit her head. She felt disoriented. Maybe it was the fall. She blinked, but was lost in a sea of darkness. Her other senses took over. To her left she heard a rattle. More than one. It was a warning she was too close. It sounded like the snakes were on the move, but they would be slow. Even though it was spring outside, down here the air was still cool and damp keeping them in hibernation mode, but they would be coming for her soon. Staying put was not an option.

She'd left her purse and keys inside the Volvo. All she had with her was her phone. Olivia patted the pocket on her right side, but came up empty. It must have fallen out when she fell. Olivia inched her fingers forward and heard a hiss. Another warning. She snatched her hand back and moved it to her neck, but it was bare. Her cross was gone. Before she knew it, she was panting.

Olivia bowed her head and closed her eyes. She couldn't find the words. Her mind was still and silent until she heard Gran's voice. "*You can walk in the twilight. You are their equal.*" The cool earth beneath her offered comfort, a haven to *somewhere else*. The fear retreated, reminding her there were other guides to follow.

Her second sight opened and the blackness gave way to gray. Another place, eerily familiar full of dry air and black lightening. The last time she felt the tug was when she sat in Patricia Griffin's car. Griffin was Jamie's third victim and the turning point in the case. Patricia's murder changed everything and brought Olivia into the mix. The raw energy left behind from her death had wrapped itself around Olivia and transported her to a shadow land. This time was different. There was no death. No murder. No barriers. The door between the light and dark was open.

* * *

Silas went back to the voicemail she'd left him. The one he didn't finish.

"I'm a consultant, not a Federal agent. You don't compartmentalize me. When they call me, it's because I have expertise they don't. Those services come with a price—a hefty one. You don't think I'd give up my expert testimony fee without ample compensation, do you?" Her voice was shrill, full of cynicism as she said the words. *"I'm telling you this only one time, Silas Branch. The next time the FBI wants my help, I insist on complete disclosure. I'm done working in the dark."*

* * *

Olivia had no idea how long she sat there, but the hissing had gone silent. So had the warning rattles. Her second sight retreated and she opened her eyes. Her night vision returned and she found her phone. She touched the screen, the light framing her face in a halo. She noticed she had no service. Olivia activated the flashlight and shined it above. She wasn't far from the trapdoor where she'd come in. She knew she wasn't getting out that way even without checking. What Olivia wanted to know now was what was worth locking inside.

* * *

Silas was out of the car before Will could stop. Too late, Will realized it was because the agent's sights were set on the lieutenant. Barry wheeled around just in time to see Silas coming. Hands on his hips, he stood his ground and waited.

Silas made note of the time of Olivia's voicemail. Replaying events, trying to nail down a timeline. "Dammit, you told her, didn't you?" he accused Barry as he advanced. He didn't stop until he'd breached the lieutenant's personal space.

Will was out of the car, but stopped short of approaching once the two men were face to face. Beyond them, on the other side, Will saw the Texas Ranger exit his own vehicle and slowly make his way towards them. He wasn't making any sudden moves. No one planned on interfering unless they had to. This was a confrontation that had been waiting to happen.

Barry didn't move. "Somebody needed to tell her." His cool gray eyes slid up to meet the agent's. "You asked me once if I knew what she was. *Who* she was. I think you're the one who doesn't know her. You don't have the first damn clue."

"I was following orders."

"Then you're a poor excuse for a partner." Silas blanched at the remark and Barry saw he'd hit a soft spot. "You don't deserve her. You know that, right?"

Silas broke eye contact.

Barry leaned in closer. He didn't have much longer to poke the bear. "You fuck this up—I'll pick up the pieces and there will be no place for you in her life. You and I both know I can. And I will."

* * *

Olivia scanned her surroundings. Stone walls. No exit. She should have known. She was facing the way she'd come in, toward the front of the house. She held the phone at eye level, sweeping the light across the walls until she had to rotate her body to continue. She couldn't stand upright and the crouched posture she needed to maintain hurt her neck. Even though she didn't hear the snakes anymore, she knew they were there. Her skin prickled with their ambient energy. It was foreign, yet somehow eerily familiar. She pushed past that connection and concentrated on getting out. Awkwardly she pivoted clockwise, putting the trap door behind her.

She scanned the walls, occasionally catching a glimpse of movement. The layers of darkness were playing havoc with her vision. The distance of her phone flashlight was limited and in her inky surroundings she had little concept of the width of the room. She knew she had to make a move. The exit wasn't going to come to her, but moving forward meant she was going to have to look at the floor. Where the snakes were.

Olivia lowered her phone and surveyed the ground beneath her. Her gaze from above had been brief, but she had noticed some parts of the room were darker than others. Now with the glow of the light she knew why. The darker parts were the snakes, twisted and knotted together in undulating bunches.

Olivia forced herself to step forward, focusing the light on her feet before raising the phone again.

* * *

Silas sized up the Texas Ranger approaching him, now that he and the lieutenant had parted ways. Herschel Gaines was an imposing man and would have been even without the silver badge and the gun strapped to his hip. He was taller than Silas. A height disadvantage wasn't something Silas was used to. His age was indeterminant, years of weather and the hot Texas sun had left their mark, but handsome features were still obvious. Olivia had said he sounded like Sam Elliott. He looked a little like him too with thick snowy white hair, a moustache to match and eyes as black as currants.

"You've got how many years with the FBI?" Gaines asked.

"Seventeen."

"Then I'm guessing you know to make a deal."

"The sheriff?" Silas asked.

"Sad but true, I'm afraid. I secured his weapon in the trunk of my car. He's been in the backseat ever since. We pulled his truck around back at his request to keep it away from the looky-loos over yonder."

Silas looked across the street to see a few neighborly types and a couple members of the media. He was glad someone had kept them that far away. At least Bartholomew knew how to secure a crime scene. There would have been more of them if there wasn't a party going on a few miles away or if the gory details had managed to make it out. Silas made a brief scan of the crowd and didn't see Roche.

Silas slid in the front seat while Gaines waited outside. Silas and the sheriff had met before so he dispensed with the pleasantries and simply stared at him in the rearview. "Make it short and snappy. I don't have a lot of time."

*   *   *

There was a door on the other side of the underground room. With her exit in sight Olivia had to decide the best way to get from here to there. She panned the floor with her light not wanting to step on anything that was already moving.

Snakes slithered on either side of her, but instead of coming for her, some of them had started to crawl the walls in search of their own escape. The remaining ones had parted like the Red Sea and cleared her a path.

A few short steps and she was at the door. She'd grown used to the soft glow of light and didn't want to let it go, but she couldn't open the door and hold her phone too. She slid it in her pocket, knowing without looking the path behind her was closing. She needed to get away from the snakes. There was buzzing in her head and she knew she needed to leave this place before she got sucked down again into where she'd been in the barn. The grey place. Maybe she should never have gone there. Something felt off with her, something was stirring and she wasn't sure if it was a good thing.

Olivia pulled on the door with all her might. Just when she didn't think she could pull anymore something dropped from the ceiling and landed on her head, entangling itself briefly in her hair before it fell to the ground. Olivia screamed and the door flung open.

*   *   *

"So, where's Dr. Osborne?" Barry asked.

Will hadn't moved from his spot after watching the confrontation. Will shook his head. "He doesn't know," he explained, referring to Silas. "The FBI is trying to track her phone, but they can't get a signal on her. I'm pretty sure she left him a message and he didn't like what he heard."

Barry glanced over his shoulder and saw Silas in the Ranger's car with the sheriff. "She didn't tell you anything?"

Will shook his head again. He felt useless.

"Think," Barry insisted, trying not to lash out at his partner. "Did you tell her anything about what we learned yesterday?"

Will paused, taking inventory. "I didn't get to say much. She came in while I was working and was reading my notes. I don't think she found anything she didn't already know, except," Will paused, replaying the exchange in his head. "I gave her directions to where we thought Ana Lutz might be."

*　*　*

Olivia bent down and peeled the slithering snake off of her ankle. Instead of fear she felt anger. "*Qui autem timet?*" She felt it coil in her hands. She squeezed and it stopped moving.

"*Derelinquas me. Ego autem solus ire formidas,*" she hissed and flung it. She heard it hit something hard and then nothing. No hissing. No buzzing. Olivia leaned back and forced the door shut. The snakes retreated. She could feel them slither away.

Olivia left thoughts of them behind and focused on what was in front of her. Dark still, but not as dark as where she'd been. She realized as her eyes adjusted that she was standing upright and the dirt beneath her feet was gone, replaced by concrete.

To her left she saw a flicker of light. A face appeared as a door opened. "You told it to leave you alone."

"*Leave me. I go alone,*" Olivia repeated. "That's what I said."

"I speak Latin sometimes too. Did you come to join us?"

CHAPTER THIRTY

THEY WERE IN what probably started as out as another cellar or a fall-out shelter built in the 1950's during the Cold War. Either way, someone else had taken it over as their own and given it a new purpose.

The face in the hallway wasn't one Olivia knew. She had yet to make it onto the white board Sergeant Ibarra had so painstakingly constructed. According to her story, the girl had been at the Poteet Strawberry Festival on Sunday and hadn't been home since.

"How did you get here?" Olivia asked.

"Andre. He said he saw my purpose."

"And what's that?"

"To be myself."

Behind the girl Olivia heard someone else. "Who's here? Who's with you?"

The girl opened the door to let her in. "This is Kim. Andre went to get the doctor. It's almost time."

* * *

Bartholomew was right. Roche wasn't the dead guy. It was an Atascosa County deputy named Eddie Calderon. The sheriff was certain Roche was responsible. Although the sheriff wasn't clear on the specifics other than to say Roche might have been angry about SAPD's involvement and blamed Calderon for it. The sheriff admitted to looking the other way when it was just Ana taking in underage girls and sending them to wherever they went. "She promised she was sending them to someone who would take care of them. Give them jobs."

Silas resisted the urge to comment. He needed the man to keep talking.

There was another player in this game, but who or what it involved, the sheriff wasn't saying until he had a deal in place. Deveroux could handle that part when he got here. Silas knew he'd be on a plane as soon as he called him, but he had other calls to make first.

"Anything?" Silas asked into the phone once he was out of the car.

"Nothing. She's still out of range," Agent Sharpe told him. "We tracked pings off the cell towers from her last calls. You were right. She was heading towards Atascosa County. A bird from the Tactical Helicopter Unit is on stand-by."

"Thank you," Silas said and meant it. He looked around for Will, but didn't see him. The SAPD crime scene unit was around back. The van from the M.E.'s office had come and gone while he questioned the sheriff.

"I'll get a location and get back to you," Silas told Sharpe and ended the call.

Will was at the back of the building with the SAPD forensics team centered around the dumpsters. He looked like he was doing what Bartholomew should have been doing.

"I need an address for the barn where you took Dr. Osborne," Silas said. "It looks like that might be where she was headed."

"She's gone to find Ana Lutz," Will told him.

* * *

It was Kimmy, but she wasn't the same innocent girl form the photos in Jessica Tate's office. That girl was gone now, having evolved into something new, a role she'd have for the rest of her life.

"Is it what I think it is?" Kim asked. She watched Olivia's face as she cradled her swollen belly. Kim could tell she was avoiding the question. Or the truth. "I've read about you. I know you're a nurse."

"Not that kind of nurse," Olivia told her. She'd dealt with the end of life. Not the beginning. "How far along are you?"

"More than eight months."

So, she had been this way before she went missing. Olivia read the green eyes that looked so much like her own. The pain was gone replaced by resolve. Roche had no idea what he was doing. *Or what he was creating.*

"This doctor that's coming, do you know him?" Olivia asked.

"He's nice to me. But he does what Andre says." Kim had lowered her voice prompting Olivia to look over her shoulder. The other girl was gone.

"And what about your friend?"

"She just got here. Her name's Rose. She has thorns. Andre really wants to keep her, but I heard Ana tell him she's sending her away. She said there was a lady waiting on the other end for her."

Olivia slid her phone out of her pocket and passed it to Kim.

* * *

Olivia found Rose bent over the dead snake. She couldn't make out the exact words, but it was a familiar chant. She'd heard it before. In her own home when she'd tip-toe to the bathroom in the middle of the night and see the flicker of candlelight beneath Gran's bedroom door.

"Stop that," Olivia snapped. "You can't bring it back."

"Andre says he can teach me."

"Necromancy is forbidden. Besides, it doesn't work on cold blood. And *I* killed it. There is no coming back. Even if it was warm."

"You can do it. If it's a familiar."

"No." Olivia's voice was sharp.

Rose left the snake and stood up. She turned to face Olivia her chin up, a hint of challenge on her face. "You asked it if it was afraid. Those were the words you said before you threw it."

"*Who's afraid now* is the literal translation," Olivia said, staring the younger girl down.

"It was afraid. I felt it."

"It should have been." Olivia took a step closer. "You should be too."

Rose bowed her head and accepted her position.

Olivia understood the true significance of the snake. Shedding its skin was an ancient symbol of transformation and Rose was right. The snake was a familiar. Andre Roche was going to wish he'd never pushed her into the dark.

* * *

Will had given him two possible locations. The first one, the house, appeared empty. There was also no sign of Olivia's vehicle so he didn't stop. Barry followed the road until he found the hunting trailers Sampson leased out every deer season. Andre Roche, with help from Ana Lutz, had probably found a different use for them. The only part Barry hadn't worked out was how and why Ana had quit her job. Maybe he would ask her.

He banged on the trailer door and shouted, "Police, open up." When the door opened, the look on Ana Lutz's face told Barry she was expecting him. It also told him she knew where Olivia was, but he'd work up to that. There were no pleasantries, only a rapid fire of questions. Ana told him nothing he hadn't heard before. Her speech was all about empowering women, about women learning who they really were, choosing how to use their bodies. Giving nothing away for free. She claimed that's what she gave the girls that came her way. She called herself their pathway to true freedom.

"Is that what you told Kimberly Burleson?" Barry asked, when he couldn't listen to her anymore. "She's a girl. Not a woman."

"You have no idea what she is. And neither did she. Until she met me." Her black eyes sparkled as she said it.

Just like that, it all fell into place. Until that utterance, there was nothing tying the Burleson girl to Ana except what Olivia had known all along. Barry started to feel queasy. When things felt too easy it meant he was missing something.

The smirk on Ana's face angered him. Barry crossed the cramped, dimly lit trailer living room to invade her personal space. She didn't flinch. She didn't retreat. What traumas had Ana suffered in her life that she wasn't afraid of him? "What about Andre Roche? What did he give Kimberly?"

Ana was looking toward the window before he heard it. A pickup had just pulled up outside; the Atascosa County's sheriff's logo on the side. Barry thought he had more time before Silas caught up with him.

Ana shrugged like she was bored.

Barry glared at her and turned to leave. Now that reinforcements had arrived, she suddenly didn't feel so conversational. Barry jerked open the door and saw the deputy standing beside the steps. He took two steps down before falling the rest of the way.

* * *

His head was spinning, an odyssey of smells filling his nose. His face and back hurt. His side was on fire. His stomach ached. He couldn't remember the last time he'd put anything in it. He'd had one too many drinks last night, of that he was sure. Was that why his shirt was wet? Then he remembered the cups of coffee followed by the day from hell. Silas Branch, a dead body.... needing Olivia safe.

Barry slowly opened his eyes. His chin was tucked to his chest and moving was too painful to consider, so he surveyed what he could. He was on the ground. His legs were stretched in front of him, his feet bound together. From behind someone pulled his hair, jerking his head up too fast, bringing on waves of nausea. He felt fingers in his mouth, forcing it open, cold liquid going down his throat. Choking, he gurgled up and spat out what he could.

"What? Too much lemon? I use it to help cover up the taste of the valerian root."

Barry blinked, trying to focus.

Anna Lutz peered at him. Too close. He tried to push back but realized he couldn't move. There were cords around his chest binding him to something behind him. He hadn't felt the bands around his wrists until now. They were behind him as well. His fingers were cramping with the lack of movement. At the thought of being restrained, Barry turned his head around to see what else he didn't know or had forgotten and was hit with another wave of nausea. Before he succumbed to the latest blast of vertigo, Barry saw enough to know they weren't in the trailer anymore.

* * *

Olivia was right. The cellar under the old part of the house led to the new part. In the extended version the walls were made of cinder blocks instead of dirt and there were three rooms instead of one. After the doctor saw to Kimberly, Olivia made her appearance. The man was scared of her, she could tell. She didn't even have to mention the FBI and he showed her the way out and made sure the cellar door was left unlocked. He even gave her his phone when she asked. She sent a text to Andre Roche. When she was done, she locked him in one of the rooms with Rose and kept his phone.

Olivia had somewhere to be. She took the stairs up to the top. She pushed the metal door open just like the good doctor told her. It landed with a clang, but luckily there was no one around to hear it. There was a piece of plywood lying nearby which was probably used to conceal the door. She left it. Kim would follow as soon as she was able, but their destinations were different.

Hearing what she thought sounded like an engine, Olivia quickly scurried to the doctor's pickup parked by the house. Conveniently he'd left the keys inside just as she had. The Volvo wasn't where she'd left it, but she didn't think it was far. Besides, for now, that was Kimmy's problem. Once hidden behind the tinted glass of the truck's interior, Olivia noticed twilight was quickly surrendering itself to night. It was later than she realized. When everything was dark it was easy to get lost.

Olivia drove the truck, headlights off, up the road to the trailers where she was told she could find Ana, but Ana wasn't home. The trailer might have been empty, but Olivia knew Ana had been there. It reeked of incense. Something pungent and spicy with a hint of sweet. Maybe ginger and lilac? Whatever it was, the aroma only boosted Olivia's connection with what she'd found in the cellar and automatically reached for her cross. When she was younger, Olivia believed the cross Gran gave her was a show of faith.

"Let it be your guide," Gran had said.

Only when Olivia was older did she learn the true meaning: a shield against the call of darkness. When Roche stripped it from her, he brought down the veil between her two worlds. That's why it had been so easy for her to get to the other side.

* * *

"He must be a sensitive." Ana sounded awe struck. "The incense in the trailer and the tea is really doing a number on him."

"Not to mention I tasered him twice," Andre pointed out.

"I think he's more than that." Ana was still studying the police lieutenant. He seemed to have lost consciousness again. "I think he's her watcher."

"Then the stories must be true," Roche surmised. He knew enough from Ana to know *watcher* was synonymous with protector.

"She has the power. Whether she uses it, I don't know."

"But you're sure she can cross the lines?"

"Yes," Ana assured him.

"She communes with the dead?"

"They commune with her. She doesn't have to go to them. They come to her. Which is why you should never have taken that," Ana said, referring to the sliver chain she could see dangling out of Roche's shirt pocket. "You also shouldn't have put her with the snakes. Snakes are dangerous. They help any witch concoct potent magic," Ana reminded Andre. "I shouldn't have to tell you that when a snake is used as a familiar it opens a conduit to the underworld."

"I thought you said she already had a conduit."

"She does. But with the addition of the snake…" Ana didn't finish her own sentence. Her warnings wouldn't do any good. Andre was reckless and growing more so. He thought taking Calderon's head would appease their mistress, but she knew the killing was only for him. As with the rapes. The drugs he concocted for self-recreation were clouding his already short-sighted vision. He was an abuser, nothing more. As much as he wanted, there was nothing special about him. It's why he used the girls. Killing his brother Ferdinand had only been one of many offerings to the other side. Tonight was the first night he planned to spill the blood of the innocent.

Andre snapped his fingers, bringing her back. "Maybe she's like her mother and has only one talent."

Ana scowled at him. He'd never met Lila. She was a master enchantress. It's why she traded in the pleasures of the flesh. It's why she'd sent Ana in search of more. Anyone could trade in pleasure, but Ana knew what particular talents Lila wanted. Not just any girl would do. It's just that Andre had started picking off the ones with a little something extra for himself. He was using them as tokens to get what he wanted. *Dark magic.* He would sell his soul or take someone else's to get it.

"It's not her mother's influence I'm worried about," Ana muttered.

"Her own mother doesn't even know who her father was," Andre scoffed. He'd heard the story before. Olivia Osborne was supposed to be something special, yet he'd locked her away in the dark without any trouble at all.

Lila once told Ana she didn't know if she could have survived her night with Olivia's father if her charms hadn't been so potent. Afterwards he told her he should have killed her. That way there would be no trace he was ever with her. Olivia's paternal influence remained a vast unknown. Lila often referred to her baby girl as the *fruit of the poison tree.*

"You should never have taken the cross off her," Ana spat.

"I thought you said she didn't practice."

"I know what I was told, but the information I have is at least thirty-five years old. She could be wild. Unmanageable even," Ana cautioned him.

"That's what he's for," Andre said with a nod toward the sleeping policeman.

CHAPTER THIRTY-ONE

"PLEASE TELL ME you have something?" Silas asked. He'd commandeered the radio because according to the sheriff the cell service was spotty. The sergeant was back behind the wheel.

Will knew he shouldn't have let Barry go off on his own, but he had been powerless to stop him. Silas had been more amenable. Like Barry, his main priority was finding Olivia, but Silas knew enough to know he had no idea where he was going. The sheriff was in the back seat, under protest, but Silas insisted he come along to give directions. Will could have gotten them there, but Silas told the sheriff it was a show of good faith and would help him secure the deal he was so desperate to make with the FBI. Ranger Gaines stayed behind at the crime scene.

"We're up." A load roar accompanied Agent Jon Sharpe's reply. He was in the THU helicopter, after deciding he needed to see for himself. "We're over Sampson's land now. No car at his place. No sign of Dr. Osborne's Volvo either. A marked Atascosa County vehicle is parked in front of the barn."

Talking to the sheriff, Silas had been able to conclude Roche had likely taken not only Calderon's uniform, but also his vehicle, his firearm, taser and handcuffs.

"The only movement I've seen is another pick-up. Plates came back to a Dr. Carlton Pace. He lives down the road. Retired OB/GYN."

"Where's he headed?"

"Truck stopped at a cluster of trailers not far from the house the sergeant told us about." Silas looked across at Will. "So, no sign of the SAPD Crown Vic?"

"There could be another vehicle behind the trailers, but the woodline is dense and there's no light out here." Jon Sharpe knew that wasn't what his new boss wanted to hear, but three passes over and that was the best he could do.

"Roger that." Silas noted Will's eyes had gone back to the road. "Can you guys find a place to land?" According to the sheriff they were still too far away for Silas' liking.

"Looking for one now. Can't do it anywhere near the houses or the barn due to power lines. Sampson's got some open fields. We'll get there on foot. It's not that far."

Silas ended the call and saw the sergeant looking at him. "Just because they don't see his car doesn't mean he's not there," Silas told Will. It was the same thing he was telling himself. They might not have found Olivia's Volvo, but she was there, he was sure of it.

* * *

The instructions for Olivia were uncomplicated. Assess the target, push her, strip away her barriers. As far as anyone knew Olivia kept her gifts under wraps. It was clever of her working as a forensic psychologist. She could hide in plain sight, but it was time to see what she could really do.

Ana felt her psychic connections awaken, heightened by the incense she was burning. She told herself the prickle she felt was from the dark magic Andre had been conjuring. Roche was nothing but a dreamer and an abuser. Whatever drugs he was mixing were eating holes in his brain. Marceline had been the real deal, a true practitioner of the arts, but she was dead. Andre thought because his mother could demon deal he could too, but he was wrong; that's why he'd gone in search of another way. It was one thing to operate in the shadows, trading those who wouldn't be missed, but Andre had crossed too many lines, first with the deputy and now the police lieutenant. As for Olivia? "She's not one you can keep," Ana had warned him more than once.

They needed to finish their business and cross the border into Mexico while they still could. They were only still here because the doctor had texted saying tonight was the night. Andre could collect the innocent and Olivia. *If* she was still with the snakes. Somehow Ana didn't think she was. She knew her awakening connections came as a warning. If she dared listen, she knew it would tell her to run.

* * *

Thirst woke him this time. The stabbing pain in his side was worse now and had joined a band that marched across his chest every time he took a breath. Roche must have used a taser to subdue him resulting in him falling down the wooden steps of the trailer, probably cracking a rib or two along the way. Up top, something was giving him one hell of a headache. Underneath it all was a heightened sense of awareness, a direct line to the old fight or flight response. Something was coming.

Except he was going nowhere. He was still bound. His hands were zip tied in front of him this time and his legs were secured, but not his feet. Barry guessed Ana and Roche would need him mobile in order to move him. He was on his back, staring up at the starlight through the opening in the barn's boarded roof. He was off the ground, a hard surface beneath him. He suspected it was something akin to an altar. He was tightly wrapped like a lamb to the slaughter, which probably wasn't too far from the truth. This was the place Olivia spoke of where innocence was lost or taken. Barry's imagination didn't have to wander far to know what Roche had been doing with the missing girls. The *special* ones. The ankh said it all. They were a valuable commodity on the other side and any fruit they bore a delectable offering.

These were not words Barry would have used, but they were the ones that popped in his head. He was pretty sure they piggybacked off his headache and snuck in through the buzzing inside his skull. He wondered if this was how it was for Olivia. How she *knew* things. If so, how did she stay sane?

Andre Roche wanted the gifts she had and the power that came with them. He called it demon dealing. Barry had only ever heard the term from Olivia and it meant exactly what it sounded like. Roche wanted a partnership, but he was unskilled. Ana Lutz knew that. Barry sensed the same foreboding from her. She was ready to flee. The only reason she hadn't yet was because she feared something more, beyond this place.

Roche was seeking a demon and Barry was pretty sure one was coming. The buzzing was getting louder in his head, erupting along his neck and down his spine. Barry's breaths came faster despite the pain. Something not of this world was on its way.

* * *

Olivia parked the doctor's truck far enough away so that they wouldn't hear her coming. She didn't have a plan. Not really. All she had was a burlap bag, and the usefulness of its contents were questionable at best. She couldn't let Ana and Roche escape. They were predators. They wouldn't stop, not unless someone stopped them and right now she was the only one who could.

Olivia sensed the dark energy before she entered. Between her visit to the cellar and the incense in Ana's trailer her psyche was all over the place, roaming free. Without her cross it was unbridled. Inside Roche was calling to whatever deities he worshiped, the ones he thought would grant his wish. Instinct drove Olivia to respond. She circled the perimeter of the barn. She didn't need the salt Roche had used. She was more powerful than that. It was ritual. She'd seen Gran do it in the backyard under the moonlight. Gran's ways of the old were hard to break. They were an imprint from her ancestors.

Olivia slipped inside, the door sliding silently behind her. If Roche was surprised to see her, he didn't show it. Ana wasn't as good at masking her emotions, but Olivia never saw the look on her face. Olivia's eyes were drawn to the altar. Roche was standing over it, a knife in his hands with a wide blade and a sharp pointed end. He held it in a two-fisted grip ready to plunge it at any time. Ready to make a sacrifice she could not allow.

Olivia stopped where she was, holding tight to the bag. Roche saw it. She concentrated on making him believe whatever he wanted. She had never expected this. She was supposed to be the one. Just her. She'd set Kimmy free. All Olivia had planned to do was buy some time until Kimmy could get far enough down the road to get a clear signal and call for help. But now time was something Olivia didn't have.

Roche moved the knife to Barry's neck. "A blood sacrifice is required."

Anger flared inside of her. Emotion swept through her like wildfire. A gust of hot wind swirled at her feet rising up to snuff out the candles hanging above them. Lanterns surrounded the altar. The flames inside them flared, one of the glass globes shattered, spilling kerosene, causing Ana to jump. Fleeing the glass, she moved beside Roche.

Olivia felt the tingle flow through her to her fingers. She could feel the static in her hair. She'd felt it earlier in Jamie's room. She hadn't known what it was at the time, but she did now. *Alleracsap* had shown her the way. *"When are you going to take charge and show us who you really are?"*

Gran had done her part. *"You are a reader. You have the most profound gift of all."* Being a reader meant she could tap the energy left behind. Olivia had never understood before. Gift or curse? It was both. Life was the key. Not death. No good without evil. No light without dark.

Olivia searched for grounding. Any other time she would have reached for her cross. In her hand the bag stirred. It offered guidance, strength even, but she didn't trust it. She found the torched symbol of the ankh on the wall behind Roche and hung her energy and psychic around it. Fertility was life and she would do whatever she had to do to preserve it. In the cellar she'd discovered new pieces of herself. She was still trying to put them together, but she refused to lose what was important to her.

Olivia slowed her breathing and drank in the room. She could feel *everything.* Dormant energy swam all around her, embryonic in nature and only she could give it life. She reached out. It bent at her touch. It was hers for the taking. Mixed with her anger, the altar in front of her was a powder keg. She had the power. It was all around her, growing inside her.

More glass shattered as Olivia focused all her attention on Roche. He had upset her balance and now he dared threaten her world. The command slipped off her tongue easily. *"Proximare."* She used a dead language and disguised it as a lover's plea. *Come closer.*

Roche had no way of knowing what she meant, but he was defenseless to her demands. *"Ma Cherie?"* He sounded drunk. He felt intoxicated. The room was spinning, alive with a power he'd never felt before. He gazed at her and was sucked into the green blaze of her eyes. He couldn't look away. He dropped the knife.

Barry's attention was drawn to the lanterns. The remaining ones had dimmed to an amber glow, yet the room was brighter. Maybe because there was the bright glow of a fire starting in the corners. Despite the flames an earthy smell stirred the air. Breathing was getting harder. The hair on his arms bent like blades of grass. His skin prickled and formed goosebumps. The whole room felt alive, possessed with a strange kind of wild energy.

"Release him," Olivia snarled at Ana. Ana used the knife Roche had dropped to free him and dropped it again before Olivia told her to.

Barry pushed himself up and hunched forward looking for a breath Olivia didn't have time for him to find. He stood up and bumped into Roche taking something from his pocket. Barry was unsteady but he managed to remain on his feet. He stepped off the platform and staggered away on his own.

"Get out of here," Olivia hissed as Barry came toward her. That's when he saw the burlap bag she was holding at her side. He didn't ask. He kept moving just like she told him.

Olivia moved to the altar. Ana's eyes followed her, mesmerized by the bag. "I know your mother. Can you imagine what you could become with her by your side?"

"You should worry about what I've become without her."

Roche's eyes were drawn to the movement of the bag. "You brought the baby?" It was a struggle for him to speak.

"No. It's with Kimmy. It's not yours. It never was." Olivia placed the bag on the altar. "I brought this instead." Free from her, the bag slithered open on its own. "*Proximare*" she whispered the command.

Too late Ana realized what was happening. She knew then she would never leave this place.

"You shouldn't have come looking for someone like me," Olivia told her. Her lips moved in another whisper. There was no command this time. Just a name. A summoning. *Alleracsap, Alleracsap, Alleracsap.*

Ana opened her mouth to protest, but a scream came out instead as the first set of fangs sank into her skin. She looked into the flames and she saw what was coming and the real screaming began.

Olivia slowly backed away. All four corners of the room were burning now. The symbol on the wall caught fire in a burst of flame. The debris on the ground around the lights sizzled. The energy lapped at her, like soft waves. Calming, powerful and fulfilling, almost orgasmic. She had no idea the strength of what she had amassed, but it didn't matter. She didn't care. It was hers.

* * *

She didn't follow him. Barry had to go back for her. She was mesmerized by the fire. Barry grabbed her hand and pulled her out of the barn. Only when they were far enough away did he collapse.

* * *

"We're on the ground." That was all Agent Jon Sharpe said. He couldn't tell Silas the rest. He headed for the barn as flames engulfed it.

Silas didn't know how much more of the car he could take. He was glaring at the sheriff in the rearview mirror about to ask again how much longer when his phone buzzed in his hand. He looked down at the screen and saw Livie's name.

"Agent Branch. This is Kimmy Burleson. I just left Mr. Sampson's place. Olivia wants you to know she's at the barn. You better hurry."

* * *

Olivia could see the light bobbing their way. Help was coming.

She'd gone down with him, pulling him up as far as she could using her body to keep Barry upright. It was the only way to keep him breathing. She held fast to the little silver cross he'd pressed into her hand. She counted each ragged breath he took, holding her own until the next one came.

Hurry, please hurry, she prayed.

EPILOGUE

OLIVIA DIDN'T LEAVE Barry until the EMTs made her.

Silas caught up with her in the E.R. She agreed to the infusion of fluids the doctor offered, but refused his request she stay the night. All she wanted was to go home and soak in her own tub. When they finally got there, Silas washed her hair and held her until the water turned cold.

Lying in the dark with Olivia's head on his chest, Silas started to tell her about Ana Lutz. *No more secrets* he declared. Olivia sat up and stopped him. "I already know. I don't care. None of that matters anymore."

"The lieutenant." Silas was aware of how he avoided using his name. Calling him Barry made it personal. He couldn't ignore it anymore.

"No work talk in bed, remember?" Olivia squeezed him but Silas remained tense beneath her touch. This wasn't about work.

"You saved his life."

The fall down the rickety stairs of the trailer had broken a rib, causing a pneumothorax. The rib also nicked the pleural cavity surrounding the lung. Luckily, it wasn't a major bleed, but it would have been enough to cause him to go into respiratory distress. If he had been alone or passed out when he hit the ground, he could have died by the time help arrived.

"I saw you with him. If there's something more—something you need to tell me..."

Olivia propped herself up on her elbow so she could look down at him. "Silas, I told you, nothing happened."

"I know what you said, but if things have changed, you can tell me." He was thinking about the night Barry was here with her. "We can work it out."

"Silas, there is nothing to work out. There is only us." Olivia smiled down at him. "This is good, isn't it?"

"Of course, it is. Better than."

"This is for real."

"As real as it gets."

Olivia laid her hand on his chest. Enjoying the feel of his heart, the strength, the goodness and the love he felt for her. "Tonight was about me being the person I had to be. I'm not cursed. If I can save another person's life, then it's a gift. I know that now. I need to be who and what I am. To do that, I have to have both of you in my life. But it's you that I want. Like this." Olivia bent down and kissed him.

"Just like this," she whispered. She let Silas roll her over and snaked her arms around his neck as she stared into his eyes. "And more."

Silas smiled. "More?"

Olivia gave him one of her shy smiles. "I came back home because I wanted more. I want a life. I've neglected a lot of things. Personal things that if I wait too long, I can't get back."

Silas's breathing turned shallow. His grip on her tightened. "Can I be a part of those things?"

"I'd like you to be."

Silas nodded and pressed his lips to her forehead. "There's no place I'd rather be. It's why I came here."

"Then no more secrets," Olivia whispered. She looked up at him and took a leap of faith. "I should have told you before, but I'm not on birth control."

Silas didn't miss a beat. "I should have asked." It was a true confession. What he didn't say is he hadn't asked because for the first time he wasn't worried about the consequences.

Olivia could feel his heart beating fast against her chest. "I listen to my body. I know my fertility cycle."

"Meaning?" Silas asked.

"Meaning I'm ovulating right now. So, if we didn't want to run the risk of getting pregnant…"

"What are you saying?" Silas's breath was coming in short bursts. He had to know for sure. He didn't want to mess this up. She was talking about the future. *Their future.*

"That I love you. And, I'm going to be forty this year. Maybe I don't consider it a risk so much as an opportunity."

Silas burst into a smile. "Is that your way of telling me you want to have a baby?"

Olivia smiled back the shyness gone. "Yeah, I guess it is."

"Then you're going to have to let me make an honest woman out of you."

* * *

Barry was supposed to be taking it easy, but he was restless. They met in Meeks's small windowless office. As chief medical examiner, Walter Meeks could have had better accommodations, but he preferred the same cell where he began his career. The locale cut down on the visitors and the ones who did come didn't stay long.

Meeks reached into the bottom drawer of his desk and pulled out the bottle of Woodford Reserve along with a couple of coffee mugs. He poured a generous gulp in each. "As a medical professional I feel obliged to warn you against mixing alcohol with any narcotics you may be taking for those busted ribs of yours."

"Duly noted," Barry said and took a sip. The bottle of pills he had stashed back at the apartment was almost full. His ribs hurt like hell, but the drugs only made his dreams worse.

"Have you seen her?" Meeks asked, waiting until Barry swallowed his first sip.

"That night. At the hospital." Not since. Will had told him she and Silas were taking a road trip to Virginia. Maybe it was for the best she was gone—for now, considering the day after the incident at the barn Jamie Lynne Smythe overpowered his psychiatrist and was now on the loose. It happened about the same time SAPD cadets found the murder weapon.

"I heard Roche was trying to create something," Meeks said.

Barry peered at him over the rim of last year's Fiesta commemorative mug. "He didn't," Barry told him. He'd also heard from Will that Kimmy had her baby. DNA tests confirmed what she had claimed. It wasn't Roche's. Will was taking the partner thing seriously. He'd been checking on him daily. According to Barry's other daily source of information, Will had also been spending time with Jessica Tate.

"So, are you here just to make sure those two are dead?" Meeks didn't mind telling the lieutenant he was glad Ana Lutz and Andre Roche were gone. Meeks had been doing this too long to get the willies, but occasionally a case came along that got under his skin. Maybe the fact he'd had to glue Roche's eyes shut three times had something to do with it.

"Something like that," Barry admitted and took another sip.

"Official cause of death was smoke inhalation," Meeks told him.

"Is there an *unofficial* version?" Barry wanted to know.

"For that you'll have ask the Feds," Meeks said. "I still have questions."

Barry wasn't surprised. It's why he'd come. Meeks would say what was on his mind.

"I'm having a hard time with my final report. I keep asking myself how you and Dr. Osborne were able to escape, yet the other two stayed on the altar. They never left it." Meeks paused, giving the lieutenant the opportunity to chime in.

Barry held the old man's eyes a fraction of a second too long before he shook his head. "There was some kind of strange incense burning in there. I don't remember much."

"Toxicology came back. They both had an interesting mixture of substances on board. Could have been hallucinogens. Then, of course, there was the snake venom."

"Maybe that's your answer. I'm sure that's all the FBI needs to hear," Barry assured him. It would make for an interesting story.

"They're waiting on my final report from the post. I just haven't sent it. I guess I needed someone else to hear it first," Meeks said with an eye on the lieutenant.

Barry shook his head again. "I'm sorry. I was out of it."

Meeks nodded. "It's a good thing Dr. Osborne got there when she did."

"She saved my life." Barry drained the last of his bourbon. He needed to go. He had plans. "So, what are you going to do about your report?"

"Something I haven't done my entire career."

"What's that?"

"Exactly as I was told."

* * *

Barry jumped as he slid back into consciousness. He'd been doing that lately. He had consulted a mental health professional and she told him it could be a side effect of trauma. What he didn't tell her is it always came with the same reoccurring dream. The one he could have shared with Meeks, but didn't. Barry just needed someone else to confirm what he'd known all along.

Someone else, something else had been with them in the barn.

* * *

"Do you remember how Gran used to say you slept the sleep of the dead?" It was Alleracsap, the sound of his voice inside her dreams. "Maybe she should have said you sleep with the dead."

Olivia considered his words, but not for long. "Did you get what you wanted?"

"Yes, but like you I always want more."

"You asked for one," Olivia reminded him. "I gave you two. That should settle my debt and the boy's."

"And now he is free. Are you?"

ACKNOWLEDGEMENTS

Writing the second book of this series was harder than the first. I created a world and characters I love—and thankfully some of you do too. I wanted to do right by them. I hope I've done that.

Writing can be a lonely journey, but some people manage to make their way into your life:

R. Edward Harris, thanks for your patience and your guidance.

Leiana, thanks for always being up for an adventure and always willing to promote Olivia.

A special thanks (I can never repay) to Shevawn. You read and re-read this book more times than anyone should have had to do. You never said no.

Everyone needs a cheerleader in life and I'm glad you're mine....

Thanks to Sheri and Sara for continuing to believe in Olivia and me.

And last but not least—Mom, I wish you were here to see this one too....

CPSIA information can be obtained
at www.ICGtesting.com
Printed in the USA
FSHW011013150320
68115FS